THE INN

"What kind of ghosts are at this place we're headed to?" Neville asked.

Priscilla riffled through the brochures on her lap. "The Blue Boy Inn," she read aloud. "Dates back to the American Civil War. Oh, wow, there could be a lot of ghosts here."

"What do you mean by a lot?"

"It says here that there have been several murders at the inn. And some mysterious disappearances."

"That's probably just hype."

"No, it's real," Priscilla said, reading the history of the place. "The first murder was a girl named Sally Brown. Nearly a hundred years ago. They never found her body, just her blood, splattered all over the walls. Then there was this guy Andrew McGurk, whose body was found, but not his head." She shivered. "And then—oh, this is terrible—a little baby, who disappeared. And there's more."

Priscilla glanced down at the description of the Blue Boy. "Quite a bit more." She looked over at Neville. "I think we've hit the jackpot with this place. If we're looking for ghosts, this is the place that will have them."

"I can hardly wait . . ."

Books by William Patterson

SLICE

THE INN

Published by Kensington Publishing Corp.

THE INN

WILLIAM PATTERSON

PINNACLE BOOKS
Kensington Publishing Corp.
www.kensingtonbooks.com

PINNACLE BOOKS are published by

Kensington Publishing Corp.
119 West 40th Street
New York, NY 10018

All Kensington titles, imprints, and distributed lines are available at special quantity discounts for bulk purchases for sales promotions, premiums, fund-raising, educational, or institutional use. Special book excerpts or customized printings can also be created to fit specific needs. For details, write or phone the office of the Kensington special sales manager: Kensington Publishing Corp., 119 West 40th Street, New York, NY 10018, attn: Special Sales Department; phone 1-800-221-2647.

ISBN-13: 978-0-7860-3323-2
ISBN-10: 0-7860-3323-1

First printing: January 2015

10 9 8 7 6 5 4 3 2 1

Printed in the United States of America

First electronic edition: January 2015

ISBN-13: 978-0-7860-3324-9
ISBN-10: 0-7860-3324-X

1

Annabel Wish had a fear of closed spaces. A year ago, she'd been stuck, alone, in an elevator for thirty-six hours, and that had simply been too much to bear. When workers had finally pried open the elevator doors on the morning of Annabel's second day of confinement, they'd found her stark raving mad.

That was why she kept rolling her car window down now, despite outdoor temperatures hovering around thirty-two degrees, and despite her husband, Jack, constantly admonishing her to roll it back up.

"Really, Annabel," Jack said. "You're freezing me to death."

"I just need the air," she told him.

He sighed. "We're almost there. We're not more than forty minutes away now."

Annabel took several deep gulps of air, and then rolled the window up again.

They'd been on the road for three hours. That was two and a half hours too long for Annabel. Even a subway ride from lower Manhattan to Washington Heights left her uneasy. It wasn't that their car was small: It was a good-sized SUV, some name and brand Annabel wasn't sure of. She never paid much attention to such things. But it was an enclosed space, which meant that she couldn't get up and move around, and that made her want to crawl out of her skin. Annabel kept looking out the window, trying to focus on the trees and houses going by and hoping that Jack was right, that this move would be good for her. Good for them. Good for their marriage.

All she knew was that she needed air.

"I remember these roads so well from when I was a boy," Jack was saying. "In the spring and summer there'd be farm stands all through here, selling beans and corn and tomatoes. Dad would stop and we'd load up the car and take it all back with us to the city."

Annabel could see only stark, frozen, bare trees.

She had never been this far out into the country before. In her twenty-six years, Annabel had been all over the world. London, Paris, Milan, Sydney, Tokyo. It came with the job of being a fashion editor. But it was always cities that she visited. Annabel had never had any interest in seeing life beyond urban boundaries. Even as a girl, she'd always spent her summers in the city. All the grass and trees she had needed she had found in Central Park, and when she grew tired of nature—which was often—there were shops and movies and restaurants and museums. Not for Annabel any regular trips into the pollen-and-ragweed-infested countryside of western Massachusetts of the kind Jack so fondly remembered, visiting his grandfather's rustic old bed-and-breakfast in the village of Woodfield. Annabel had been exquisitely content to remain in the city.

But they were far away from the city now. They were retracing the route of Jack's summer-vacation sojourns to Woodfield.

Except that it wasn't summer. It was the onset of a very cold but so far snowless winter. And the bed-and-breakfast they were heading to no longer belonged to Jack's grandfather.

It belonged to them.

Annabel looked out her window. They were passing a cemetery. A fat black crow was perched on a granite cross. As Annabel watched, the bird flapped its enormous wings.

She rolled down the window again and breathed in some more air.

When they'd put her in the hospital, the worst thing had been the terrible, confining air. She needed air that flowed freely, and if there was a bit of taxicab exhaust in it, so much the better. How Annabel had wanted to send a chair crashing through the hermetically sealed hospital window and just stand there, her face inches from the jagged glass, and gulp in buckets of air. The sounds of traffic rising from First Avenue would have been far more soothing to her than all that canned hospital Muzak.

"Annabel," Jack said, lifting an eyebrow over at the window and shivering. "Please?"

She rolled it shut.

They were crossing the Massachusetts line. "We'll be there in time for lunch," Jack said, beaming. "And Gran's making her famous rabbit stew."

"Jack, you know I've become a vegetarian."

He frowned. "You can't offend Gran."

Annabel turned away, resisting the urge for air.

"I'm sure you and Gran will get along just fine," Jack said. "She'll like that you have an eye for color and design. You know the place is going to need a great deal of fixing up, and I'm counting on you, sweetheart, to really give it your signature pizzazz."

"I'm not so sure I'm all that pizzazzy anymore," Annabel said, her eyes searching out the window for something. But all she saw were trees and more trees.

"Oh, come on, sure you are, sweetheart. You haven't lost your eye."

"That wasn't what Carmine thought."

Carmine had been her boss at *Orbit*. The magazine had just launched when Annabel had had her breakdown. She'd been the fashion editor for the premiere issue, but by the time she had come back, after all those months in the hospital, there had been three more editions that had hit the stands. Carmine had brought in what he'd assured Annabel was just a temporary replacement, but the new girl had proven so fresh and hip and original that no one had wanted to let her go. Annabel was offered a "contributing" editorship— which was a nice way of telling her that she was no longer needed.

"I just don't want you to overwork yourself again, baby cakes," Carmine had said, trying to sugarcoat his decision.

Annabel had told him what to do with his contributing editorship and stalked out of his office, breaking a heel on her Manolo Blahnik Sorrita shoe as she did so, much to her humiliation.

"Well," Jack said, "Carmine doesn't know what he lost by letting you go, sweetheart."

But he did. Carmine had known full well what he

was losing. A woman who drank too much, who snorted too much cocaine, who thought the world owed her fame and fortune. Annabel had worked herself to a very lofty place in New York society, but she had burned every bridge she'd crossed to get there. She might have been the city's new fashion darling, but she was tired and angry and frustrated and jealous and insecure. That was hardly the recipe for success in New York. Or success anywhere.

Annabel had thought that success would drive away all those feelings, which stretched all the way back to her childhood, but in fact success had only made them worse. And so when the day came when the elevator up to the *Orbit* penthouse got stuck between the forty-first and forty-second floors, Annabel had simply crumbled. The poised, articulate woman dressed in Givenchy and Karl Lagerfeld who had stepped into the elevator late one Friday night had been reduced to a sobbing, quivering mass of jelly on the floor by early Sunday morning, when a janitor discovered the malfunctioning lift. Annabel was once again a child terrified of being eaten alive by a little blue demon named Tommy Tricky.

"We haven't had any snow yet this winter," Jack was saying, drawing Annabel's thoughts back to the present, "but western Mass can really get sucker punched by nor'easters." He smiled over at Annabel. "So when we get all snowbound, sweetheart, and the power goes off, we're going to use the time to get creative. We can scrape old paint and wallpaper off the walls, and polish the antiques that Gran has down in the basement— there's a mother lode of treasures in that dark old space, Annabel, you'll see."

Air. Oh, how she needed air.

"And we'll go snowboarding and cross-country skiing and skating on the pond—"

Suddenly, Jack slammed on the brakes and yelled. There was something ahead of them in the road. Something big. Something with antlers.

Annabel shrieked.

"Jesus Christ!" Jack shouted. "That's a moose! A goddamn moose!"

The animal was standing perfectly still in the middle of the narrow, two-lane road. It was at least six feet tall and probably nine feet long, with an enormous head crowned with a rack of sharp antlers. Black eyes stared serenely through the windshield at Annabel and Jack.

"Holy shit," Jack said in a sort of awe. "I'd heard of moose out in Worcester County, but never out this way before."

He tooted the horn.

Annabel stared at the creature. Its black eyes unnerved her.

Finally, the moose began to move, plodding the rest of the way across the road and then disappearing into the woods.

Jack was grinning like an idiot. "Who'd ever have thought we'd see a goddam *moose*?" he asked as he began moving the car forward again.

Annabel couldn't speak.

"Wait'll I tell Morrison," Jack was saying. "He's gonna have a stroke when I tell him we saw a moose!"

"I . . ." Annabel tried again to speak.

"I wonder if the moose population is spreading west—"

"I can't do this," Annabel finally said, very softly.

"What'd you say, sweetheart?"

"I said I can't do this," she repeated, louder now, looking over at her husband. "I want to go back to New York."

"Now, Annabel, we've been over this—"

"I want go back to New York right now!"

Jack quickly pulled the car over to the side of the road and threw it into park. He turned to face Annabel. "Now, look, sweetheart. You know this is the only way we can move forward. You know there is nothing left for you in New York. . . ."

"Yes, there is! It's my home!"

Jack looked wearily into her eyes. "We've talked about this many times, Annabel. We made a decision! Dr. Adler helped us make the decision. Remember? And we all decided that the best way for you and I to start over was to leave the city and to accept Gran's offer to take over running the B&B. . . ."

"No, you decided. I just agreed. There's a difference."

Annabel turned to look out the car window. How she wanted to roll the window down and climb through it. How she wanted to get out of this car and just start to run. She didn't care where she ran. She'd just run any which way, simply because she *could*, because she was *free*. She hated being closed up in a car for so long. It was like being closed up in that hospital . . . which, of course, was like being put in that closet in her stepfather's apartment and told that if she made a sound, Tommy Tricky would hear her and chop her up with his little blue axe.

"Annabel," her mother had told her, "there's no such thing as Tommy Tricky. Your dad just tells you that so you'll be a good girl."

Except that he wasn't her dad. Her dad, Malcolm Wish, had been killed in the first Gulf War. Annabel's stepfather was a loathsome man she was forced to call Daddy Ron. And he didn't tell her about Tommy Tricky to induce her into being good. He told her about Tommy Tricky because he was a sadist—a terrible, evil man who got his jollies from scaring little children.

"Tommy Tricky is a little blue boy with a very sharp axe, and he's always hungry," Daddy Ron had told her, as he put her in the linen closet. "He sleeps in here, somewhere under that pile of sheets and tablecloths. So if you make a sound or move around, you'll wake him up. And if Tommy Tricky wakes up, he'll chop you up with his blue axe and eat you up, lickety-split, with his blue lips and blue tongue and big blue teeth."

"Annabel."

She jumped as Jack touched her arm.

"It was bad in New York," he said quietly. "Do you remember how bad it got?"

She nodded, slowly.

"So this is the only way," Jack told her.

Annabel said nothing more. Her husband put the car into drive and steered it back onto the road.

She was moving to Woodfield because it was the only way she could keep Jack. He'd leave her otherwise. Annabel knew that. And Jack was all she had left. She couldn't lose Jack, too, not after losing everything else.

She wanted this move to work. She *did* want to start over, to find happiness once again in her life and in her marriage. Jack was right that there was nothing left for her in New York. Her friends had all turned on her, put off by Annabel's excesses in those last frantic, hedonistic months before the breakdown. She didn't want that life any longer. She never really had; she'd just gotten caught up in the idea of success, intoxicated by glitz and access. What Annabel wanted was what she'd always wanted, deep down, ever since she was a little girl treated cruelly by her stepfather and ignored by her mother. She wanted a place where she mattered, where she fit in, where she was loved.

And where she could move around freely, without any constraints.

Maybe, then, this *would* be the place for her. True, she sometimes felt a creeping sense of claustrophobia knowing that theaters and museums and couturier shops were hours away—and reachable only by car, and Annabel hated to drive   and that western Massachusetts got very dark at night, and frequently lost power in storms, and was susceptible to being snowbound. But in good weather she could take long walks, or ride a bike into the village. It would be a very different way of life, to be sure, but it needn't be too restrictive. And there was more to recommend Woodfield, too: All of the temptations of Annabel's old life, which had dragged her down to the depths, were very far away.

Finally, there was Jack.

Annabel glanced over at her husband. How happy he looked. How excited for their new venture. Jack had stuck by her through the worst. He was the only one who had. She owed him this much. But she also had no choice. Jack had been wanting out of the city for the last several years. His own career had stalled as Annabel's had skyrocketed. He had thought he was going to be a big, important writer—but after his first book tanked, he couldn't get another advance. He was done with writing, he said; he hadn't opened his laptop in nearly two years. Annabel knew that Jack would have left New York whether she had agreed to go with him or not. He saw it as the only way forward, for him and for them.

If Annabel had refused to go with Jack on this new venture, he would have gone without her, and she would have been alone. And by herself, Annabel felt certain she would have slid right back to the depths, and never come back up for air.

"There it is!" Jack shouted suddenly, pointing ahead through the windshield. "You see that roof poking out through the trees?"

Annabel tried, but all she saw was a mass of gnarled trunks and limbs, like thousands of skeletal arms reaching up through the soil.

"We're home, sweetheart, we're home!"

Jack turned up a side road. The SUV rattled over a surface gutted with holes and bumps.

"Gotta get this road repaved," Jack said, more to himself than to Annabel.

As they rounded a bend, the house came into view. Jack had told her that it was an exceptional survivor of Second Empire French Victorian architecture, and Annabel could see it had once been a very grand house indeed. But now it was quite run-down, with faded, peeling paint that might once have been yellow, but was now a dull gray. Its mansard roof was cut by eight protruding gabled windows and topped by a cupola. A portico supported by two columns ornamented the front door. Around the house, ancient oak trees stood like sentinels, hunched over the structure as if to shield it from decades of wind and rain.

"I can smell Gran's rabbit stew from here!" Jack exclaimed, as he turned into the driveway of the house.

Annabel saw the weather-eaten sign that swung in the slight breeze from an old post. She read it once, and then read it again, as cold fingers played her spine like a xylophone.

THE BLUE BOY INN

Below the name was an old engraving of a smiling little boy that looked just like Tommy Tricky.

2

"You're going to have to tell him, you know," the wizened caretaker told the old woman as they spotted the SUV pull into the driveway.

"Of course, I know I have to tell him," she replied. "That's the whole reason I offered the house to him. I wasn't about to just put it on the market."

"No, that wouldn't have been a good idea."

The caretaker had a long memory. He'd lived in this house for sixty of his seventy-nine years. He had seen a great deal in that time. He'd become inured to most of it. Nothing much shocked him. But still some images remained seared on his mind. The little pink arm, for instance, resting among the cinders. The caretaker had thought, at first glance, that it had been a doll's arm.

He had been wrong.

"He's going to have to tend to the place," the caretaker told the old woman. "Your grandson. He's going to have to do it all eventually. I'm not strong enough anymore."

"I'll explain everything to him," the old woman said.

Her eyes narrowed as she watched the automobile come to a stop in front of the house. Its doors opened.

"But what if he . . . if he's not willing?" the caretaker asked her.

A queer smile crusted the old woman's lips. "I know my grandson. He'll be willing." She peered through the window. A pretty girl was stepping out of the passenger's side of the car. The old woman frowned. "I just wish he wasn't bringing a wife with him."

3

Getting out of the car—how good that felt!—Annabel walked slowly over to the sign.

"You never told me the place was called the Blue Boy Inn," she called to Jack.

He was busy hauling out their luggage from the back of the SUV. "Yup. It's had the same name for over a hundred years."

Annabel studied the engraving on the sign. The boy was smiling. It wasn't a nice smile. It was the kind of smile that a little demon might make before polishing off a trapped little girl as a tasty snack. In his hand, he carried a gun, but for Annabel it might as well have been Tommy Tricky's axe.

"Why the gun?" she asked Jack over her shoulder.

Her husband had sauntered over to stare up at the sign with her. "It's a musket. The place dates to just after the Civil War. He's supposed to be a Union soldier."

Annabel noticed the gold buttons and epaulets the boy was wearing, faded like the rest of the image.

"Maybe we should change the name," she suggested. "Put up a new sign."

Jack put his arm around her. "Hey, babe, we can't start messing with tradition."

He led her up to the front steps of the house.

"We'll get our bags later," he told her. "Let's go in and see Gran."

The front door was weathered and flaking with old paint. Jack rapped hard with the old rusted knocker.

"As a kid, coming to this house was always so much fun for me," he said. "I can't believe it's mine now . . . ours, I mean." He grinned down at Annabel.

The door was opened by a small old man, his face creased in a thousand wrinkles. His eyes were bright and very blue, practically popping out of his gray face.

"Hello, Mr. Jack," the old man said, looking up at them.

"Zeke!" Jack exclaimed.

He shook the old man's hand heartily.

"This is my wife, Annabel," Jack said.

"How do you do?" Annabel asked, doing her best to smile down at the old man, though she found it difficult for some reason.

"Pleased to make your acquaintance," Zeke replied, nodding slightly.

"Zeke taught me how to fish," Jack was saying as they entered the house. "Taught me how to fire a gun, too."

Annabel kept her eyes on the little man. He didn't seem the outdoorsy type. He was frail and slight, hunched over and unsteady on his feet. His skin was a pale yellow, as if he hadn't left the house in decades.

The place felt damp. The pungent smell of whatever was cooking on the stove—Jack had said it was rabbit stew—permeated the small, low-ceilinged rooms, filling Annabel's nostrils with an unfamiliar aroma she couldn't call either pleasant or unpleasant. Just strong. The house was very dark. Its small windows were nearly obscured by the bushes outside. Ancient, uneven floorboards creaked under foot. Annabel was sure the house was infested with mice. She repressed a shudder.

They found Gran in the kitchen. She didn't rise to greet them. She remained seated at the old wooden table, a tiny figure dressed in black with a face as pale as her caretaker's. Her shockingly white hair was pulled back from her face and knotted in an untidy bun at the back of her head. Hands like talons rubbed each other as she watched them enter.

"Gran!" Jack exclaimed, rushing over to embrace the old woman.

"Welcome home," she said to him, in a low, yet surprisingly girlish voice.

"This is Annabel," he told her, gesturing to his wife to join him.

Annabel extended her hand. "I'm very happy to meet you, Mrs. Devlin."

"You must call me Cordelia," the old woman told her, taking Annabel's hand and squeezing it tight.

Annabel smiled. "All right, Cordelia. Thank you."

"I had Zeke air out your room," the old woman said. "I hope it will be all right."

"I'm sure it's fine," Jack replied.

Cordelia sighed. "It's an old house. There are a lot of cobwebs. We don't quite have the strength to keep up with it the way we used to. During the season, we've been hiring some college students to come in and give us some help. But now that you're here . . ."

Jack was beaming. "We'll get the place in tip-top shape!"

"In fact," Annabel said, "I'm a designer. I'd love to maybe look at opening up the space a little bit. The rooms are so small. If we open things up a little bit—"

"I wouldn't go around opening things up willy-nilly," Cordelia said, cutting her off. Her old blue eyes shone in Annabel's direction. "The architecture of the house is fragile. You wouldn't want to open something up and find the whole place falling down on you."

Annabel smiled. "Of course not. We'll definitely work with the blueprints."

"Don't worry, Gran," Jack said. "We're not coming in with a wrecking ball. We'll respect tradition. That's what you said in your letter to me. That there was a tradition here and that you'd give us the house if we respected it. And we intend to."

The old woman smiled.

Annabel looked away. She had the sudden sensation of claustrophobia. The rooms were so small here, so dark. The ceilings were so low. But it was worse than that. She had the sudden fear that she had been lured into this place with false promises. They would make it their own, Jack had promised. They could start over, build something that was theirs. But if Cordelia was always going to be there, overseeing things, nixing ideas and squelching their creativity, then what sort of life would this be? Once again, Annabel wanted to run. She wanted to throw open the back door and run out through the woods until she found the road, and then hitchhike her way back to New York.

But there was nothing in New York for her anymore. All her bridges back into the city had been burned, all her tunnels filled in with cement. She was on her own.

At the Blue Boy Inn.

This is where Tommy Tricky lives, she heard Daddy Ron tell her.

How badly Annabel wanted to run.

4

Priscilla Morton thought of herself as a ghost hunter. Ever since she'd been a kid, she'd searched out every supposedly haunted house or mysterious grave-yard she could find, traipsing all over the south of England, where there were plenty such places. When she and her boyfriend, Neville, decided to take a two-week holiday to the United States, Priscilla had insisted that their first week be spent visiting different haunted inns. She'd discovered that there were as many of them in New England as there were in Old England. Neville, who thought Priscilla's ideas about ghosts were non-sense, had agreed, only if their second week could be spent in Florida, at Disney World.

Priscilla had told him they had a deal.

That didn't mean Neville was suffering that first week gladly.

"Really, Priscilla," he was saying, driving north on Interstate 91 through Hartford, "it's freezing cold out there. What kind of holiday is this? If we'd wanted cold and gray skies, we could have stayed in England."

"You have to admit that inn last night was worth it,"

Priscilla replied. "I heard the wailing, just as the inn-keeper promised."

Her boyfriend scoffed. "That was just the wind. Really, you believe anything."

The place in Connecticut had dated from 1799. Two centuries ago a woman had been killed in the room they'd stayed in, and legend had it that her screams still sounded through the house, waking guests and sending them running for the manager. Priscilla had heard the poor woman's wails and had sat straight up in bed. She'd woken Neville, snoring like a bear beside her, but he'd only grunted and gone back to sleep.

"I'd say we got our money's worth on that one," she said, looking down her list of haunted guesthouses. And it was a good thing, too. The first two places, one in Rhode Island and the other near New Haven, had been busts. No screams, no apparitions. Neville couldn't wait to get to Florida.

"The temperature this morning is eighty-five de-grees Fahrenheit in Orlando," he told her. "We could be sitting by a pool right now, sipping margaritas."

Priscilla stuck her tongue out at him. She wasn't sure what she saw in him. He wasn't very handsome, with kind of a pimply face and stringy hair and a gut that hung over his belt. And he could be such a stick in the mud. Neville didn't like most of the things that Priscilla liked, be they ghost hunting or bird watching or kayaking. All Neville liked was to watch football and drink beer. But he was good to her, Priscilla sup-posed. He put up with her. Her mother had always said it would take a rare man to put up with Priscilla's ec-centricities. She was only twenty-four, but she knew that sometimes she acted older. Like how she'd preferred quilting bees to rock concerts growing up. Priscilla had never been into television or fashion or rap music or any of the sorts of things other young girls liked. Even now she would rather go on an architectural tour of old churches than go out to a pub. She and Neville had been dating for three years. Priscilla doubted they'd ever get married. But that was okay by her. She didn't think she was the marrying type.

Neville was older than she was, by almost ten years, and Priscilla supposed he stayed with her because, all of her quirks aside, he figured he couldn't do much better. In fact, he'd done very well. For all her peculiarities, Priscilla was quite pretty, with long, silky blond hair, full breasts, and a tiny waist. If not for the thick, black, oversized eyeglasses she wore, she might have been mistaken for a blond bombshell. She figured if she put her mind to it, she could get a much hotter guy than Neville. But she didn't have time to put her mind to such things. She'd much rather concentrate on ghost hunting or gravestone rubbing.

"Where is this next place we're heading for?" Neville asked, steering the car past the glittering skyline of Hartford. "It's in Massachusetts?"

"Yes," Priscilla replied. "Just keep north on this road. When you get to the Massachusetts Turnpike, you'll go west."

"How many miles?"

"I don't know. I can't read American maps all that well. But I'll keep navigating."

Neville grunted. "We'd better see a real ghost this time, covered in chains. If not, we're heading out early to Florida."

"It's not my fault that you wouldn't wake up last

night to listen to the wailing of that poor dead spirit."
Priscilla shuddered. "It was absolutely spine-tingling."

"You're crazy. I heard the wind. That's all it was."

Priscilla just snorted. Neville was such a skeptic.
Really, what was she doing with him?

"So what kind of ghosts are at this place we're
headed to?" he asked her.

She riffled through the brochures on her lap. She
found the one that described their destination.

"The Blue Boy Inn," she read out loud. "Dates back
to the American Civil War." She read a little further
along. "Oh, wow, there could be a lot of ghosts here."

"What do you mean by a lot?"

"It says here that there have been several murders at
the inn. And some mysterious disappearances."

Neville snorted. "Oh, that's probably just hype."

"No, it's real," Priscilla said, reading the history of
the place. "The first murder was a girl named Sally
Brown. Nearly a hundred years ago. They never found
her body, just her blood splattered all over the walls."

"Oh, goody, let's stay in that room," Neville quipped.
He was being facetious. But Priscilla really hoped they
got booked into Sally Brown's old quarters.

"Then there was this guy Andrew McGurk, whose
body was found, but not his head." She shivered. "And
then—oh, this is terrible—a little baby, who disappeared. The only thing they ever found of her was her
arm."

"I don't like baby ghosts," Neville grumbled. "I
imagine they cry all the time."

"And there's more," Priscilla said, glancing down at
the description of the Blue Boy. "Quite a bit more."

She looked over at Neville. "I think we've hit the jack-pot with this place. I mean, if we're looking for ghosts, this is the place that will have them."

"I can hardly wait," Neville said, as he drove the car north on 91.

5

The arthritis in Zeke's knees and hips burned like a thousand wasps stinging him all at once. Each step up the narrow stairs to the attic was agony. He couldn't do this much longer.

It was time to turn this job over to someone else.

And who better than young Mr. Jack?

Zeke lifted the old rusted iron key from the ring he carried on his belt, the one that had been jangling against his side all the way up the stairs. He slipped it into the keyhole on the door.

How many times had he done this particular job? Impossible to count. It seemed all his life. But it wasn't all his life. There had been a time before Zeke had come to this house, though he could hardly remember that life now, when his life had seemed full of promise. But that was a long, long time ago. Half a century Zeke had been tending to this place. And for almost half of that time, he'd been making this trip up to the attic, twice a day.

He turned the key in the lock.

Downstairs, Mr. Jack and his pretty wife were settling in, unpacking, freshening up. Oh, they had such
plans. They were going to clean the place up. Modernize it. The woman spoke of getting something called
"wireless internetting," whatever that was.

A little smile played across Zeke's lips.

They could plan all they wanted. They'd soon learn
it wasn't they who made decisions about the house.

He opened the door.

He listened.

He heard the sound then in the dark, cobwebby
room.

The panting.

Zeke stepped inside and closed the door behind him.

6

Annabel stood gazing out of her window into the cold bare limbs of the trees that surrounded the house. They looked like some sort of petrified aboriginal humans, frozen in the midst of some terrible cataclysm, staring up at the Blue Boy Inn with their arms outstretched to the sky.

"Lots of possibilities, don't you think, sweetheart?"

Jack had come into the bedroom behind her.

"I think if we knock this wall down here," he was saying, "we can open up the room to include the bathroom in a sort of master suite. That way we don't have to mingle with the guests in the hallway when we first get up in the morning."

Annabel didn't say anything. She just kept staring out into the trees.

"What do you say, baby cakes? Isn't that a good idea? You're the one with the artistic eye."

She turned around to face him. "I think it's a splendid idea," she said, trying to smile. "But I thought you wanted to respect tradition."

"I do, sweetheart, but you know I was mostly saying

that just to placate Gran." Jack smiled broadly, his cheeks indenting with dimples, and he took her in his arms. "This has been her home for a long, long time. I didn't want her to think that we were going to start pulling it down around her."

"It needs a lot of work, Jack," Annabel told him. "Much more than I thought. So many walls and floor-boards need to be replaced. The plumbing and electricity needs to be updated."

"I know, babe. One step at a time."

She shuddered and closed her eyes. She imagined she was at Fifth Avenue and Broadway, and the sound of honking taxicabs and police sirens filled her ears. It made her feel better, at least for a few moments.

She gently slipped out of her husband's embrace. "If I'm going to do this, I'll need your support, you know."

"You have it!"

"Are you sure?"

She looked at him. Jack's big blue eyes seemed filled with sincerity and purpose. They'd been madly in love once, five years earlier, when they'd met at a party and spontaneously married eleven days later, with no friends or family in attendance, just a justice of the peace and Jack's high school ring as a wedding band. Since then, some of the impulsivity of their union had faded, and Annabel's crises over the past year had severely strained their marriage. She didn't blame Jack for having a fling with Rachel Riley, one of her colleagues at *Orbit*. It had been just a one-night thing, when Annabel was locked away and Jack was lonely. He'd confessed to Annabel when she got out, apologizing profusely. She'd forgiven him. It was understandable.

But she could barely stomach looking at Rachel Riley, with her ridiculously blond hair and big boobs. She'd been Annabel's friend. Supposedly.

But in every other way, Jack had stuck by her. After the affair with Rachel, he had become even more devoted to making sure Annabel got better. So many other men might have walked away, but Jack didn't. Even during the period when she was coming home from fashion shoots strung out on coke, screaming and ranting and craving more blow, Jack had put up with her. He had calmed her down. He had brought her down from the high without letting her crash. When the time came for rehab, Jack had been right there, lending Annabel support and encouragement. Even as his own dreams of success had withered away, he hadn't given up on Annabel's.

Jack had thought he was on the fast track to the big time. In those heady first months after their hasty marriage, they'd imagined themselves the Next Big Power Couple. How excited he had been when a big publishing house bought the novel he'd been laboring over since college. It was a deep, involved story of a young man and his search for meaning in a world that was increasingly impersonal and commercial. Annabel thought that was ironic, given that Jack was always saying what he wanted most from his book was a contract for a Hollywood blockbuster so they'd get rich, rich, rich. When that hadn't happened—after much advance publicity, the reviewers had called the book "tedious" and "pretentious"—Jack had been devastated.

And it was just at that moment that Annabel's career had started its dizzying ascent. Her eventual crash was even more spectacular than Jack's.

Now here they both were, in the middle of the woods, miles and miles from civilization, in a place called the Blue Boy Inn.

Where Tommy Tricky lives, Annabel thought.

She smiled over at Jack.

"I didn't mean to doubt you," she said. "I know you support me. I couldn't have gotten through everything without you."

Jack beamed, leaned over toward her, and kissed her on the forehead.

"I'll see you downstairs, hon," he said. "You really ought to try Gran's rabbit stew. I know you don't want to eat bunnies, but, really, it's out of this world."

"I'll pass on it for now," she told him.

He winked at her and bounded out of the room.

Annabel looked around. How small the room was. So square and the ceilings were so low. The whole place smelled like old, wet wood. And rabbit stew. Annabel shivered.

She would never last here.

But she had to. There was nowhere else.

No other choice.

She would make the best of it. She would redesign this place. It was theirs, after all. The old woman was signing over the property to them. After that, they could do what they liked. Annabel needed a project. She could do this. She could bring in carpenters and painters and electricians. She still had some contacts over at the HG television network. Maybe she ought to pitch them a reality show set in the woods of western Massachusetts, as a former New York socialite tries to remake an old house. . . .

And her life.

No, Annabel didn't want cameras around for that.

She looked out the window again, at the gnarled branches so close to the house. *It's like they're trying to suffocate us*, Annabel thought.

When was the last time she and Jack had made love?

The thought struck Annabel suddenly and unexpectedly. She paused. She couldn't remember. Yes, wait, now she could. It had been three weeks ago. Right after he'd gotten the call from his grandmother. Jack had been so excited by the idea. He'd started kissing Annabel all over the face. "This is it, sweet cakes!" he had shouted. "The answer to our doldrums! Our new path! Our way out of the city! We're going to be huge successes there. Just you wait and see!"

The fact that Annabel hadn't wanted to leave the city was immaterial. She had been bulldozed by Jack's enthusiasm. And by his amorous advances. His big hands had suddenly been all over her. She hadn't wanted to make love that day, but Jack had insisted. Annabel had given in, and then, while he was inside her, she had started to cry, wanting to enjoy it, wanting to love sex the way she used to—wanting to love *Jack* the way she used to. How much Annabel wanted to love everything in her life the way she once had in days gone by—before the drugs and the breakdown and the humiliation.

"Baby doll," Jack had said, looking down at her, red-faced and puffing. "Why are you crying?"

She had replied that the tears came from her orgasm. That had been a lie.

That was also the last time they made love.

He might want to, tonight, she thought to herself. *To celebrate our first night here.*

Annabel dreaded the prospect. Not that she wanted to withhold sex from Jack. In fact, she wanted very much to make love to him, to feel his arms around her, to feel happy and content in his embrace the way she used to. She *craved* that feeling.

But she knew she couldn't feel that way. Not here. Not in this house.

A whiff of the rabbit stew reached her nostrils again, and nearly made her vomit. It smelled sickeningly sweet, like a dead mouse rotting under the stove.

This is never going to work, she thought to herself.

"Annabel, you have got to believe in yourself," her mother always used to tell her. "You're such a timid little kitten. You need to believe you can do whatever you put your mind to doing."

That had always been a challenge for Annabel. Even when she'd been on top of the world, New York's latest fashion and design darling, she'd doubted herself. It was why she had turned to coke and booze. She'd needed to feel confident—and she felt confident when she was high. But when she came down, she was right back to feeling unsure and timid again, so she had searched out more white powder to sniff up her nose. It had been a vicious cycle. No wonder she had burned out so quickly.

But she had to believe in herself now. She had to make this venture work.

She smiled as she looked at herself in the mirror. She tied her chestnut-colored hair back in a ponytail. Her big brown eyes disclosed her lack of sleep these past several weeks. Her face was a little fuller now than it had been during the worst of her addiction, but she could still stand to put on a few pounds. She wore no makeup. She reached into her purse and pulled out a lipstick, rubbing a very light pink on her lips.

"You can do this," she told her reflection.

Right away, she doubted her own words.

In rehab, they had tried pumping her with self-confidence, cheering her on. There had been therapists and psychologists whose jobs had been merely to instill in Annabel a sense that she mattered, that she was powerful. They were successful enough that she had been able to leave, to return home to Jack, to be able to handle the cravings when they came, and to finally feel free of them. Annabel didn't want coke anymore. She wanted something else, however, though that was harder to identify. Happiness, she supposed, but that felt like asking for too much.

She had an image then, as she gazed at herself in the mirror, of her mother's body hanging behind her.

She didn't jump. She saw it sometimes. Just like the day she had come in from school, aged sixteen, and found her mother hanging in the dining room.

The same mother who had told Annabel to believe in herself.

Annabel closed her eyes, opened them again, and the image was gone. That was the way it worked.

But now she spied something else behind her in the mirror.

Something that moved.

Annabel spun around. There was nothing there. Whatever she had seen was small, close to the floor, maybe a cat or a dog, moving quickly through the small, shadowy space between the bed and the dresser.

A squirrel? Annabel asked herself.

She took a step toward the spot where she had de-tected the motion. Had whatever it was gone under the bed?

"I wouldn't be surprised if this place is infested with vermin," Annabel said out loud, wondering whether she ought to stoop down and peer under the bed herself or go get Jack. She was a city girl, after all. In Central Park, she'd always been afraid of the squirrels.

"Believe in yourself, Annabel," she told herself, and laughed.

She knelt down on the old, warped wooden floor-boards. She lifted the bedspread and peered under the box spring.

Nothing. Just clumps of dust.

Annabel sighed.

She must have imagined she saw something. It must have been just the shadow of a tree branch moving outside. The day was becoming breezy, after all.

Annabel stood back up.

She looked over toward the door.

And there, grinning malevolently up at her, was the tiny blue figure of Tommy Tricky, gnashing his long, sharp, blue teeth.

7

Zeke heard the woman's scream as he was locking the door to the attic. He hurried down the steps as best he could, his arthritic joints screaming at him, and made his way to Annabel's room.

He hadn't expected it to start this soon.

The caretaker found the new mistress of the house standing up against the wall in the corridor, her face the color of flour, and her body shuddering as if she was having a seizure. Zeke reached out a hand to steady her.

"Miss Annabel," the old man said. "What's wrong?"

"I saw something," she managed to say.

"What did you see?"

"A boy. A little man."

Zeke narrowed his rheumy eyes at her. "There's no little boys here."

"I saw him," Annabel said, still trembling.

"What was he doing?"

"Smiling." She burst into tears and covered her face with her hands. "Teeth. His teeth!"

"A little boy smiled at you?"

Zeke kept his eyes trained on Annabel.

"Tell me exactly what you saw," he said.

But she was too overcome now. She just sobbed into her hands.

"What's going on?" came the voice of Mr. Jack, heading down the hallway toward them. He seemed more annoyed to be pulled away from his rabbit stew than concerned about his wife.

"Miss Annabel said she saw a little boy," Zeke told him,

"A little boy?"

"Oh, Jack," she said, and threw herself into his arms. "I saw him. The blue boy . . ."

"The blue boy?" her husband asked.

"You mean, the boy from our sign out front?" Zeke asked.

"And then he disappeared!" The color had returned to Annabel's face. Now she was all red and purple from crying. "He ran down the hall and somehow just disappeared. . . ."

"Annabel," Jack said, stroking her hair, "sweetheart, you had a hallucination. . . ."

She looked up at him. Zeke saw them exchange a glance that carried some meaning. Apparently, this pretty young lady had had hallucinations before.

That could prove convenient.

"It's okay," Mr. Jack told Zeke. "My wife has a vivid imagination sometimes."

"Imagination is good for the soul," the caretaker replied, "but not when it scares you half to death."

"She'll be okay, now, won't you, baby cakes?" Jack

asked, gently moving Annabel back into their room. He shot Zeke a glance. "Tell Gran I'll be back down in a minute."

"Yessir, Mr. Jack."

The old man shuffled down the hall back toward the kitchen.

Cordelia was waiting for him. Her intense blue eyes seemed to burn holes in her pale face. Her gnarled hands were opening and closing.

"What has happened?" she asked, in that voice that seemed so much younger than the face from which it came.

"She saw a little boy," Zeke told her.

"A little boy?"

"A little blue boy," the caretaker added.

Cordelia turned away. "I wish he hadn't brought her," she said.

"You can't expect a man to leave his wife behind."

She turned her eyes back to him. "Why not? My husband did. My son left poor Jack."

"That's what happens here," Zeke said, rather matter-of-factly.

Cordelia sat back down at the table. "By the way," she said. "You'll need to prepare one of the rooms." She paused. "We've got guests arriving."

8

Annabel started the car and backed out of the driveway. She wasn't very good at driving; there was never a need in the city. But she'd gotten her license because sometimes she'd needed to drive when they'd go out on photo shoots in the Hamptons or in Connecticut. She didn't necessarily enjoy being behind the wheel of a car, but right now the idea of getting on the road, away from the house, seemed blissful.

Jack had agreed it was a good idea for her to go down to the market and get some groceries. "It will clear your head," he'd told her.

As a vegetarian, Annabel was going to need some other provisions in the refrigerator besides leftover rabbit stew if she was going to survive. There was a market down at the end of the road, and Jack had told her to buy everything she wanted.

What she wanted was freedom. But Annabel couldn't figure out a way to buy that.

She steered the SUV down the twisting country lane. The misshapen trees on either side of the road terrified her. They reminded her of Cordelia's arthritic hands. She tried to concentrate on her driving, but Annabel's heart was still thudding in her ears from the scare she'd had.

I saw Tommy Tricky.

She let out a deep breath.

No, she told herself. It was not Tommy Tricky. It was another hallucination, like the ones she'd had during rehab and immediately after. Her therapists had found she was prone to hallucinations. She would begin to imagine that nothing was safe around her. Her therapist, Dr. Adler, had kept telling her, over and over, "You are safe, Annabel. Nothing can hurt you." But she had gone through periods where she had been absolutely convinced that she was unsafe—that everything and everyone around her was out to get her.

Getting off the drugs hadn't been easy. There were times she'd thought she was going mad. She saw snakes coming through the floorboards. She'd thought the apartment was on fire one horrifying night. None of it had been real, and the little blue boy she'd seen wasn't real, either.

Of course, I'd hallucinate about Tommy Tricky. I was upset and anxious, worried about the move. I was feeling claustrophobic. And I'd just seen that horrible sign out front.

Annabel was going to replace that sign no matter what anybody said. Screw tradition. She wanted it down.

Her stepfather had been a sadistic son of a bitch. How could he have terrified a little girl the way he did? Whenever he wanted to get a rise out of Annabel, he'd say, "Watch out for Tommy Tricky!" How she wished her mother had put a stop to it. But her mother was

weak. She had just let that horrible man continue tor-
turing her daughter. "Look behind you," Daddy Ron
would say. "I think I see ol' Tommy creepin' up on ya."

And then he'd laugh—a giant guffaw—as Annabel
would start to cry.

When Daddy Ron had been drinking, it was even
worse. He got angry so quickly after he'd had a few
beers. He looked for excuses to punish Annabel. One
time, when her mother had gone out, Annabel had
dropped the milk carton as she was putting it away. It
had spilled on the kitchen floor, an ocean of milk
spreading across the tiles. The next thing she knew her
stepfather was screaming at her. He grabbed her by the
shirt and dragged her down the hall to the linen closet.
He shoved her inside and locked the door. Annabel had
sat in the darkness, knees pulled up to her chest, sobbing as Daddy Ron taunted her from outside.

"Tommy Tricky is in there with you! He's got his
sharp little axe! He likes to chop up bad little girls and
eat them for lunch!"

Mom had let Annabel out of the closet when she got
home, hugged her briefly, and then told the little girl
not to make Daddy Ron angry anymore.

Up ahead, Annabel spied the market. It was a small
wooden structure fronted by big glass windows. A sign
above the door read FALLS GENERAL STORE. Annabel
pulled into the parking lot and cut the engine.

She took a deep breath, opened the car door, and
headed inside. A bell over the door rang as she passed
through.

"Good afternoon," the lady behind the counter sang
out.

"Good afternoon," Annabel replied.

The woman was large—not fat, just big-boned and tall, with broad shoulders and wide hands. Her hair was gray, worn long, and her face was friendly. She was probably sixty, but her skin was entirely smooth and un-wrinkled. Her eyes were periwinkle blue.

"May I help you?" she asked.

Annabel smiled. "Just moved in with my husband's grandmother. And I'm a vegetarian. Turns out there wasn't a lot in her fridge that I could eat."

The woman laughed. "Well, right now we don't have a lot of fresh produce. We tend to only sell what's grown locally, so you'll have to wait a few months be-fore we'll have tomatoes and corn and green beans and sweet peas and carrots. . . ." She smiled as she came around from behind the counter. "But I think we can stock you up with some of the best canned goods and preserves."

"Thanks," Annabel said, returning the woman's smile. "Even frozen is fine."

"I'm Millie," the woman said.

"Annabel."

"Pleased to meet you. Where did you move here from?"

She was pointing Annabel to an aisle filled with canned vegetables and fruits. Most of it was local stuff, preserved right here in western Massachusetts. Lifting a handbasket, Annabel began filling it up with various cans and jars. She tossed in a few boxes of whole wheat pasta as well.

"New York," she said, replying to Millie's question.

"The city?"

Annabel nodded.

Millie laughed again. It was a small, tinkly sound

for such a big woman. "Well, you're going to be in for some culture shock up here. How long you staying?"

Annabel sighed. "For good," she said.

Millie raised her eyebrows.

"My grandmother-in-law is rather frail. She can't keep up the place by herself anymore, so she's asked my husband and me to take over the house."

Millie folded her masculine arms across her chest. "So you're really okay moving out of cosmopolitan Manhattan for this little hole in the woods in the middle of nowhere?"

Annabel gave her the most convincing smile she could manage. "So long as I can find other things to eat than Gran's rabbit stew."

Something in Millie's eyes changed. Her brows furrowed as she studied Annabel.

"Something wrong?" Annabel asked.

"What's your grandmother-in-law's name?"

Annabel returned her odd stare. "Cordelia Devlin," she said.

Millie opened her mouth to say something, and then stopped. She tried again. "And the house you've taken over," she said slowly, "is the Blue Boy Inn."

"That's right."

"Well, well," Millie said, hugging herself tighter. "So the old place is going to be given a new lease on life."

Annabel smiled widely. "That's what my husband and I are hoping. We're going to fix it up, modernize it, get some new technology in there. . . ."

"Technology?"

Annabel placed a jar of peanut butter and some breadsticks into her basket. "Well, the place doesn't even have any flat-screen TVs, let alone any Internet. I think a guesthouse needs some amenities, even if it's out in the woods." She thought about it. "Actually, *especially* if it's out in the woods."

"Well, most of the people who still come to the Blue Boy aren't coming for cable television and Facebook." Millie unfolded her arms. "As I'm sure you're aware."

Annabel looked over at her. "You mean they come to get away from all that?"

"Maybe, but not necessarily," the storekeeper replied. "They come to the Blue Boy because they're looking for ghosts."

Just then, the bell over the door jangled. Annabel was still struck by what Millie had just said, so she didn't turn to look, but Millie did.

"Hello, chief," she sang out.

Annabel moved her eyes over to observe the newcomer. He was a tall, dark-haired man with a craggy, handsome face, maybe about forty, dressed in dark dungarees and a brown corduroy jacket. He gave Millie a little salute.

"What can I help you with today, chief?"

"Just a quart of milk, Mil," he said. "Ran out last night and had to eat my Cheerios dry."

Millie turned to look back at Annabel. "That's what he eats for breakfast and for dinner. Cheerios. The man needs a good woman who will cook for him."

The man laughed. "I've asked you a million times to marry me, darlin', but you always turn me down."

"And take a look at him!" Millie said, still talking to Annabel. "Movie star handsome. But still unattached."

"I'm married to my badge," he said, placing the milk down on the counter.

Millie moved around to ring him up. "And isn't Woodfield fortunate to have such a dedicated chief of police." She dropped the milk into a small paper bag. "Hey, chief, meet the new girl in town. Just arrived." Millie fixed him with a look. "She and her husband are taking over the Blue Boy Inn."

The chief looked around at Annabel for the first time. For some odd, unexplainable reason, she blushed.

"Is that right?" he asked. "Cordelia's giving the place up?"

"She's my husband's grandmother," Annabel explained. "And she's asked us to come run the place. She can't do it on her own anymore."

"Doesn't she still have Zeke around to help her?"

"Yes, he's still there. But he's rather old as well."

The chief smiled. "Older than the earth, it seems." He moved closer to Annabel and extended his hand. "Well, welcome to town. I'm Richard Carlson. If there's anything I can do for you or your husband, do let me know."

She shook his hand. "Thank you," she said. "I'm Annabel Wish." She was struck by how dark the chief's eyes were. Almost black.

"Enjoy the rest of your day, Millie babe," the chief said, heading out of the store.

The little bell over the door rang again.

Annabel watched him go through the large windows. He slid into a plain black car, probably a Ford. No cruiser. Annabel imagined he must have been off duty, since he hadn't been wearing a uniform.

She brought her basket of provisions up the counter.

"Oh, you'll like these," Millie said, lifting a couple jars of raspberry preserves. "I know the lady who cans these. Grows all her own berries on her farm. In the summer you can go up there and pick your own. Raspberries, strawberries, blueberries . . ."

"I'll keep it in mind," Annabel said. "But I'm not much of a berry picker, except from the display at Whole Foods."

Millie frowned. "You're going to have a lot of adjustments living here, sweetie."

"I know." Annabel paused. "Millie, what did you mean when you said people come to the Blue Boy to see ghosts?"

The storekeeper stopped what she was doing and fixed her with her blue eyes.

"You don't know?"

"Know what?"

"It can't be that your husband never told you about the murders."

Annabel's blood went cold.

"Murders?" she asked. "What are you talking about?"

"Well, if he hasn't told you, then it's probably best that you ask him."

Annabel suddenly felt frantic. "No, please, tell me what you know."

Millie shrugged. "It's not like I'm telling tales out of school. Everybody up here knows the history of the Blue Boy Inn. The only reason it stays in business is because of the ghost tourists. People think it's haunted because of all the deaths that have taken place there over the years."

"And these deaths were . . . murders?"

Millie was placing Annabel's groceries in a paper bag, one much larger than the one she'd just given to

Richard Carlson. "Well," she said, "not all, probably, but some of them definitely were. Like, for example, you don't accidentally get your head cut off."

"Oh, dear God," Annabel said.

"Look, honey, I'm sorry to be the one to break this to you. I can't believe you could move up here and not know. You should go right back up there and get your husband to tell you everything." Millie's eyes were kind, but also serious. "Because there's no way he doesn't know. One of the deaths up there, a long time ago, was Cordelia's young granddaughter. And if I'm figuring correctly, that would have been your husband's sister."

9

"It's up here, turn here!" Priscilla shouted at Neville. "That little lane, there!"

"Never would have spotted the bloody road," Neville grumbled, turning the car up the rutted passageway through the trees.

"Yes, very easy to miss," Priscilla agreed. "Hidden away in the woods. The way all haunted houses should be."

Her boyfriend smirked over at her. "Have I told you how excited I am to get to Florida?"

"Yes, six thousand times. Pull in over there. Next to the sign."

The Blue Boy stared down at him with his faded-paint eyes.

"Creepy, isn't he?" Priscilla said.

"I'd say the place is what's creepy," Neville replied, shutting off the car. "Looks like it hasn't been updated in decades."

"Perfect," Priscilla chirped, hopping out of the passenger seat. She stood gazing up at the old inn. "I can feel the vibrations, can't you?"

"All I can feel are hunger pains. You wouldn't let me stop at that McDonald's back on the highway. Hope this place has something to eat."

Neville withdrew their two bags from the trunk, and then clicked the remote to lock the car. A series of two quick, high-pitched beeps followed.

"I smell something cooking," Priscilla said, lifting her nose in the air.

"Probably human flesh," Neville muttered.

They headed up the walk to the front door. There were no other cars in the gravel driveway.

"Oh, there's somebody," Priscilla said. "Over there, coming out of the woods."

The trees had grown thick around the house. Only a few patches of sunlight shone through here and there. The deciduous trees might have been bare of leaves, but their gnarled limbs had all tangled together so tightly that they blocked out the sun in many places. And there were lots of tall pine trees as well, leaving the Blue Boy Inn mostly shrouded in shade and shadows.

So it was hard to see the person emerging from the woods about thirty or so yards away, but Priscilla was trying to wave whoever it was down. It was possibly the proprietor.

"Hello!" Priscilla called, taking a couple of steps in the direction of the figure. "Hello, we have a reservation to stay here!"

"Maybe it's just another guest," Neville said. "Let's just go up and ring the doorbell."

Priscilla frowned. "There are no other cars here. It can't be a guest! Hello!"

She waved her hand to catch the person's attention.

It was a woman, she could see now. The hair was long and possibly blond or gray. She was wearing some kind of white, diaphanous dress. . . .

"Hello!" Priscilla called again.

The woman finally turned in her direction.

And Priscilla let out a gasp.

The woman's face was covered in some kind of dark substance.

It could only be blood.

Priscilla screamed.

10

Annabel heard the woman scream as she steered the SUV back up the driveway. There was a small red car parked at the inn now, and a man standing near it holding two suitcases, and a woman a few feet away, screaming and pointing toward the woods.

Annabel hopped out of the car.

"What's wrong?" she called.

"She's covered in blood!" the woman was shrieking

The man was trying to calm her down. "Priscilla, come back here!"

Annabel looked in the direction the woman was pointing. She saw nothing.

She approached the woman. "Can I help you? What did you think you saw?"

The woman turned a pair of frantic but obviously exhilarated eyes to her. "Was she a ghost? Does she walk the property?"

"I don't know who you're talking about," Annabel told her.

The man had joined them. "We saw someone coming out of the woods. . . ."

"A woman," his companion added. "She's gone now. When I screamed, she bolted back into the woods." She frowned. "I shouldn't have screamed. I know better than that. We can sometimes scare ghosts as much as they can scare us."

Annabel looked at the couple standing in front of her. They were obviously guests arriving at the inn— "ghost tourists," as Millie had called them. They had English accents. They'd apparently come a long way to experience the Blue Boy's ghosts.

"Well," Annabel said, "I can't tell you anything. It's my first day here. My husband and I just moved here." Her gaze moved up to the front porch of the inn. "But I'm sure my grandmother-in-law can tell you whatever you need to know."

Cordelia was standing there, her face set like stone. She must have heard the woman's scream.

The couple hurried up to her, jabbering about ghosts. Annabel heard the old woman start to reply, but she didn't care to listen to what she had to say at the moment.

She decided she wanted to do a little exploring herself.

Her groceries would keep in the car for the moment. It was cold enough out. She started off across the grass in the direction the English woman had been pointing. If she had been alone in her claim of seeing something, Annabel would have dismissed her as a fanatic. When you come to a place *wanting* to see something, chances are you would. The human mind was susceptible to suggestion. Hadn't Annabel thought she'd seen Tommy Tricky earlier?

But the man said he'd seen somebody as well. So chances were they really did see somebody. Chances were it was a real person, and the woman's hysterical scream had indeed frightened the visitor away. Annabel hoped she found someone out there, so she could bring her back and introduce her to the English couple, and to Cordelia.

She wanted an end to ghost stories. She had no desire to be part of a place that depended on crazies coming to stay there. Annabel had been in a crazy house. She did not want to surround herself with lunatics and delusional people.

She'd had enough of that.

She pushed her way into the trees. A broken, brittle branch on the ground snapped as she stepped on it.

Jack was wrong not to tell her about the inn's reputation. Very wrong.

But if he had, she would likely have refused to come. It would have been too much for her. So he'd kept the knowledge from her, understanding how it would freak her out.

Annabel was going to tell him that he was wrong, and she was going to add that they were going to put a stop to the stories immediately.

Perhaps some terrible things had happened at the inn. But she and Jack were not going to make their livings from exploiting those tragedies.

Annabel stopped. There was something sticking out of a clump of dead leaves in a little clearing up ahead.

Something white.

As Annabel approached, she saw it was a stone.

A stone marker.

On which was inscribed a name.

CINDY DEVLIN

It must be Jack's sister.

This was her grave!

In that second of realization, a hand reached out from behind her and clutched Annabel by the shoulder.

11

"Welcome to the Blue Boy Inn," old Mrs. Devlin said, as she escorted them into the old house.

Priscilla was peeved. Mrs. Devlin had insisted they must have just seen a hiker. The Blue Boy Inn had no ghosts outside the house, she said, and certainly none that walked around with blood on their faces. Priscilla was deeply disappointed. She hoped this place, unlike so many of the others, wouldn't be a rip-off.

"Leave your bags there, by the door," the old woman said to Neville. "I'll have Zeke or my grandson, Jack, carry them up to your room."

"We'd like Sally Brown's room," Priscilla said.

Mrs. Devlin gave her a wan smile. "And you shall have it."

Neville returned the smile. "I suppose you get a lot of crazy ghost hunter types staying here."

Mrs. Devlin was nodding as she led them into the kitchen. "We're listed in all the guidebooks as a 'haunted inn.' It keeps people coming."

"And how often do guests see apparitions?" Priscilla wanted to know.

The old woman stopped at the roughhewn kitchen table, steadying herself against it with her hands. "Some of them report a sighting or two. I make no guarantees."

Priscilla snorted. "Well, there have been so many killings in this house. I'd imagine the spirits are very restless here."

Neville sighed. "She's a true believer, I'm afraid," he told Mrs. Devlin.

"A cup of tea?" the old woman asked.

Both accepted, and she gestured for them to sit at the table.

"I take it you're not a believer then, sir," Mrs. Devlin said, looking over at Neville as she poured steaming hot tea into two delicate china cups, balanced on saucers.

"Not really. I'm here for the fun of it, and because Priscilla would only go with me to Florida after a week of ghost hunting in New England."

Mrs. Devlin pushed the cups of tea toward them with her bony, spotted hands.

"Thank you," Priscilla said, taking hers and lifting it to her lips.

"Well," Mrs. Devlin said, sitting down at the table opposite them, "I suppose there must be restless spirits here. You're right, young lady. There have been an awful lot of deaths in this house. More than our share."

"So you've never seen any ghosts?" Priscilla asked, setting down her cup into the saucer and leaning slightly toward the old woman.

"I don't think I'd recognize them if I did. I've been here a very, very long time. Sometimes it takes someone unaccustomed to the place to pick up on things."

Priscilla nodded. "That's true. I've read about that

phenomenon. You live here with the spirits and so you're on the same vibration. You don't see them. But those who come in from the outside can pick up more easily on things."

Neville laughed out loud. "What a bloody rationalization! Fanatics like you, my dear, can come in and claim they see things simply because you're on a different vibration!"

Priscilla shot him an angry look.

Neville grinned, reaching over to pat her hand. On her pinky she wore an opal ring. It was supposed to attract spirits. "I use the word *fanatic* with great affection, my dear."

"Zeke has seen some ghosts," Mrs. Devlin told them.

Priscilla looked back over at her. "Who's Zeke?"

"Our caretaker. He's been here nearly as long as I have. He's seen things. You should ask him."

"Oh, I certainly will."

"I should also tell you," Mrs. Devlin said, standing up again, with some difficulty, "that my grandson and his wife have just arrived. They will be living here with me now, taking over the care of the place. Zeke and I have gotten too old to do it all by ourselves anymore."

"Is that the lady who drove up while we were outside?" Priscilla asked.

"Yes."

"She went off into the woods," Neville said. "I guess looking for the woman who was hiking." He smirked. "To apologize for Priscilla screaming her head off, I imagine."

"I tell you," Priscilla insisted, "her face was covered with blood."

"Perhaps she scratched herself in the thicket out there," Mrs. Devlin said. "Or it was mud. It gets very swampy a few feet into the woods."

Priscilla sniffed. She wasn't entirely convinced that what she'd seen had not been a ghost.

"Anyway," the old woman continued, "I haven't yet filled in my granddaughter-in-law about some of the more distressing chapters in the inn's history. I didn't want to frighten her too badly on her first day. And since you've obviously read everything there is about the Blue Boy Inn, I'd appreciate you not bringing it all up with her. At least, not quite yet."

Neville made a face in surprise. "You mean to tell me, her husband brought her to live here without telling her about the history of this place?"

Mrs. Devlin pursed her lips. "We decided it was best to tell her when she got here."

Neville laughed. "Because otherwise, no sane person would ever have come."

A tight smile stretched across the old woman's face. Priscilla took it to mean that Mrs. Devlin was saying, *Ah, but my granddaughter-in-law isn't sane*.

"You must be tired from your drive," Mrs. Devlin said, lifting an old copper key off a nail on the wall near the sink. "I'll show you up to your room."

Priscilla and Neville stood to follow her.

"So were the killers of any of those who were murdered here ever found?" Priscilla asked as they headed back out into the hallway.

"Most of the deaths here were simply tragic accidents," Mrs. Devlin said, leading the way through the narrow, musty corridor, not looking back as she spoke.

"Well, that poor man whose head was never found," Priscilla said. "That was no accident."

"No, I suppose it was not," the old woman replied. "Andrew McGurk died here before my time. My husband's father owned the place then."

"And the little baby who disappeared," Priscilla asked, "except for her arm?"

Mrs. Devlin paused near the stairs. "For the life of me, I don't know where Zeke or Jack are," she said, evidently done with speaking about murder and death and ghosts.

"That's all right," Neville said, grabbing their bags. "I don't mind hauling them myself."

The old woman frowned. "Not a good way to treat our guests. I apologize."

They started up the stairs.

"But please," Priscilla said. "Tell me about the baby."

"I had just arrived here," Mrs. Devlin said. "Had just married my husband. And I suspect, in that case, it was a kidnapping gone wrong. The mother was a rich heiress. She was running away from her father, and some goons were after her. I think they thought taking the baby might get them quite the ransom."

"But why would they cut off the poor thing's arm?" Priscilla asked.

"You'd have to ask them," Mrs. Devlin said.

They had reached the top of the stairs.

"Here's your room," the old woman said, unlocking the door.

They stepped inside. It was small, neat, low-ceilinged. Mustiness pervaded everything. The four-poster bed was small, carefully made. A three-drawer dresser stood beside the single window. Except for a straight-backed chair, that was all the furniture in the room.

"And Sally Brown?" Priscilla asked. "The girl who died in this room?"

"Before my time, too," Mrs. Devlin said. "But what my mother-in-law told me was that poor Sally got word that her fiancé had died in Germany. This was during World War I. And so she slit her wrists. That was the cause of the blood on the walls."

"But her body was never found," Priscilla pointed out.

"I was told Sally ran outside to bleed out," the old woman said matter-of-factly. "I suspect bears and coyotes finished off her remains."

Neville shuddered. "Such a delightful history."

"Even if they weren't all murders," Priscilla said, "these were very traumatic deaths. Suicides make for some of the most frequent ghosts." She looked over at Mrs. Devlin. "Do many people report seeing Sally?"

The old woman nodded. "Yes. Many do."

Priscilla smiled.

"Then I'll let you get settled," the old woman told them. "I've made some rabbit stew if you'd like some for dinner. Otherwise, there are some decent restaurants up in Sheffield."

"Thank you," Neville said.

Mrs. Devlin left them alone.

"It was a ghost I saw out in the woods," Priscilla said. "I know it. I'll bet it was Sally Brown!"

Neville flopped down on the bed. Dust puffed up into the air.

"I don't think I could eat rabbit stew," he said.

Priscilla was examining the wallpaper for blood-stains. "We're going to get what we paid for here, I'm certain of it." She looked over her shoulder at Neville. "We're going to have a major close encounter with the spirit world here. I can feel it in the air!"

Neville could only groan.

12

Annabel spun around to see who—or what—was behind her.

"Jack!" she shouted.

Her husband was grinning sheepishly. Standing beside him was the hunched-over figure of Zeke.

"I didn't mean to scare you, baby cakes," Jack said.

"Well, you did," Annabel replied.

"I'm sorry," he said, trying to take her hands, but she pulled them away.

"What is this, Jack?" Annabel pointed down at the ground. "This stone?"

The name seemed to glare up at them.

CINDY DEVLIN

"That's my little sister," Jack said, very quietly.

"You never told me you had a sister," Annabel said, her voice harder than she meant it to be. "Never, in all our years together."

He looked at her. His eyes shone with pain. "It's always been difficult to talk about Cindy," Jack told her.

"She was a very sweet little girl," Zeke offered. "Such a tragedy."

Annabel looked from them down to the grave marker in the leaves, then back to them again.

"Why is she buried here, in the middle of the woods?"

Jack smiled sadly. "She's not buried here. That's just a stone Dad put up to remember her by. To give us someplace to come to."

"Her body was never found," Zeke explained, his old yellow eyes finding Annabel's.

"What happened to her?"

Jack took in a long breath, and then let it out very slowly. "She just disappeared. She—must have gotten lost in the woods or something. There was no trace of her."

"Except—" Zeke began to say.

But Jack shot him a look that shut him up.

"Except what?" Annabel asked.

Jack hesitated. "We found blood. A lot of it."

"She was a sweet little girl," Zeke added. "The sweetest, really."

"I'm sorry to hear this," Annabel said. "I wish you had told me about her before."

Jack sighed. He made no response.

"In fact," Annabel went on, "I wish you had told me a lot of things before we came here. Such as all the deaths and murders that took place at the inn over the years. When did you think you'd tell me, Jack? You must have known I'd find out as soon as we got here."

"Who told you about all that?" Zeke asked.

Annabel shifted her eyes over to the old man. "The woman at the market."

"Ah, that Millie, she's a busybody," Zeke grumbled.

"I was hoping Gran and I could tell you, in our own way," Jack said.

Annabel looked down at the little white stone marker. "You knew I wouldn't come if I had known this place had such a lurid history."

Jack took her hand. "Babe," he said softly. "We're no strangers to lurid histories, you and I."

"What's that supposed to mean?" Annabel asked.

"Just that . . ." Jack seemed to search for the right words. "We needed a place to start over. And I think the Blue Boy Inn needs to start over, too. You and I . . . we want to put our pasts behind us. So does the Blue Boy."

She frowned. "That's not likely, with all these ghost tourists seeking the place out."

"It's true that there have been some unfortunate tragedies here," Jack admitted. "But the town made way more of them than they were. Over the course of more than a hundred years there have been some deaths here. Some perfectly peaceful. Some not so peaceful. That's to be expected anywhere that's been around for as long as the Blue Boy. But the locals like to tell stories, and every new death here has been woven into a never-ending tale. Legends of ghosts and death curses sprung up. And the tourists started coming."

Annabel was still looking at the marker for Cindy Devlin.

"If she got lost in the woods," Annabel asked, "why was there a lot of blood?"

Jack sighed. "The police chief thought maybe a bear got her. There had been sightings of bears not long before she went missing."

"And where was the blood?"

Zeke stepped forward. Annabel had almost forgotten he was there.

"On the back steps and down the path," the old man said. "I found it. We'd been calling for Cindy all morning, when she wasn't in her bed. And then I went around back and found the blood. . . ."

"My father speculated she got up in the night for some reason," Jack said, his voice thick with emotion. "And she went out back and that's where the bear spotted her. . . ."

"But why was her body never found?"

Jack shrugged. "The police scoured the woods for her. The bear must have . . ." He couldn't speak. "She was so little, you know."

Annabel reached up and touched his cheek. She had been so upset about not being told about all this history that she hadn't been very compassionate. This was his *sister* that Jack was talking about. This was a childhood tragedy that had apparently scarred him so badly he'd never been able to speak of it before.

"I'm sorry, Jack," Annabel said, stroking her husband's bristly cheek.

"We thought we'd find *something* of her," Zeke piped in. "But nothing. Just the blood."

"And then," Jack said, finding his voice, "the town went and turned it into another example of the murder curse on the Blue Boy Inn, adding poor little Cindy to their long list of ghosts that haunted the house." He shook his head. "I never told you, sugar cakes, because I've always hated that part of the Blue Boy's history. As far as I'm concerned, we're putting an end to it."

"Good," Annabel said. "We stop marketing the place as a haunted hotel. Get it out of those guidebooks. Debunk the ghost stories whenever anyone asks about them."

"That's a mighty fine sentiment," Zeke said. "But without those ghost tourists, I'm not sure you have a business. What else could bring people out to the middle of nowhere to a rundown old house?"

"So we change the place from rundown to fabulous," Annabel replied. "We modernize. We renovate from top to bottom. Make it comfortable and loaded with amenities. We are on some gorgeous property here. In the spring and summer these woods will be in full green bloom. And in the fall I can only imagine how magnificent the colors will be. I'd love to redo the gardens, make some paths, maybe put in a Jacuzzi. We'll make this place the perfect getaway destination. We won't need ghosts to sell it."

"I think you have the right idea, babe," Jack said.

Zeke gave them a crooked smile. "Not sure what Cordelia will think of ripping the place up."

Annabel felt her back stiffen. "She asked us to come here, didn't she? She wanted us to take over the place. If she wants this place to stay in business, she'll agree. Otherwise, none of us can afford to keep this house going. We'd have to put it on the market. . . ."

"Oh, no," Zeke said. "I know Cordelia wouldn't want to do that."

"Then it's settled," Annabel said. "We're going to make this an entirely new place, with an entirely new reputation, aren't we, Jack?"

"We sure are, sugarplum," he said, wrapping his arm around her and pulling her into him.

Overhead a crow screeched in the bare limbs of a tree.

13

Cordelia listened to her guests moving above her. They seemed like nice people. Strange, like all the ghost tourists were, but nice. She especially liked the man.

Nothing would happen while they were in the house. She would see to it.

She'd been seeing to it for a long time. Now she was old. She was giving the Blue Boy over to Jack and his wife. Could she sleep easy, knowing they would be the ones to take over from her in safeguarding the house?

Annabel was a wild card. Cordelia wasn't sure about her. She seemed obstinate. Defiant. Too independent.

That could prove problematic.

She wished once more that Jack hadn't brought a wife.

For a moment her thoughts wandered to Jack's father. Her son. He'd brought a wife to the Blue Boy Inn, too. And two little children.

But Cordelia pushed the thought out of her mind.

She heard the sound of her guests upstairs running

water. They were washing up. They would be downstairs again soon.

The old woman made her way into the living room. It was a big, open space, furnished with just a few antique wingback chairs and a long table in front of large bay windows. The windows were cloudy. How many years had it been since Cordelia had washed them? But what did it matter, really? The bushes outside had grown up so thickly in front of the windows that they nearly obscured the sunlight anyway.

It was better that way, Cordelia thought. This house—and especially this room—needed no prying eyes looking in from the outside.

The living room was dominated by the old stone fireplace in the center. The hearth extended four feet out into the room, and the mantel was a good six feet. But the fireplace was devoid of any tools hanging at its side. There was no pot hanging inside, even for show. In fact, the opening was bricked over. No fire could be built there. The bricks enclosed the path down to the firebox and sealed off the flue. They had been installed with care and precision. Cordelia knew this. Because she had helped lay the bricks.

She heard the back door squeak open.

"Gran, we're back!" she heard Jack call.

With a final glance at the sealed-off fireplace, Cordelia headed toward the kitchen.

14

Roger Askew was a mean son of a bitch.

He'd just told that busybody, dried-out old fruit Millie Westerbrook at the general store to stick it where the sun don't shine, and then added that since nothing had been stuck there in ages for her, she'd probably enjoy it.

Millie had been giving Roger a hard time because he smelled like whisky and dropped the F-bomb in front of some little kids. Why couldn't the bitch just mind her own business?

So Roger had just paid for his pack of smokes and slammed out of that goddamn place.

As he trudged through the path in the woods, he realized the reason he was in such a foul mood was all because of Tammy.

His girlfriend.

Rather, his ex-girlfriend. At least she would be, after today.

She was a lazy, good-for-nothing bitch. Roger had asked her to do one simple favor for him. Run down to the store and get him some cigarettes. And she'd said she had to pick up that brat of hers, Jessica, from school. Like the kid couldn't have waited five minutes? Tammy was just so goddamn selfish. She never did anything for Roger.

She hadn't even been putting out lately.

He stopped on the path, tore open the pack of cigarettes, shook one out, placed it between his lips, and lit it.

He sucked in the smoke. Ah, yes. He'd needed that.

Roger was going to be twenty-nine in a couple of weeks. It was time he made a clean break. He needed to give Tammy the old heave-ho. He deserved a girl-friend who appreciated him.

Not one who bitched at him all the time to find a job.

He'd had no choice but to quit the last one. The manager of the Jiffy Lube was a fucking prick. He'd had it out for Roger. Always on his case, making him take the worst of the freaking lemons that people drove into the place, the cars that were literally ready to die, and Roger was somehow supposed to get them purring smoothly again. Finally, he'd told his asshole manager to go fuck himself, and added that, since it had obviously been a long time since anyone had fucked his scaly self, he'd probably enjoy it.

That was one of Roger's favorite insults.

Up ahead on the path, he saw someone walking toward him.

Roger hoped it wasn't anyone he knew. He was in no mood to say hello to anyone. All he wanted to do, in fact, was punch someone. He had a temper. He knew that. He'd served time for beating up a few people, and Tammy had threatened to have him arrested the last time he'd hauled off and whacked her across the head. So far he had yet to smack that brat of hers, not that Jessica didn't have it coming. But Roger knew if he ever hit the kid, he'd have to deal with the freaking banshee her mother would become.

He hated kids. Even his own. His daughter was probably eight or nine years old by now. She lived with her mother up in Pittsfield. Roger hadn't seen her in three years, but still her bitch of a mother kept demanding he pay child support, and Roger was damned if he was going to fork over the little bit of cash he had to a kid he never saw and who he had doubts was really his, anyway. So now the mother-bitch had offered him a deal. Give up all parental rights for all time and she'd stop hounding him for money.

Roger figured that was a deal. Tomorrow morning he was heading up to Great Barrington to make that all legal.

He looked up the path again. Whoever he'd seen there was gone.

Where the fuck did they go? There was one straight path through these woods, from the store to the apartments along the river, where Roger lived. Must have been some goddamn nature explorer, heading off into the woods to scrounge for mushrooms or something freaky like that.

Above him, a crow in the bare tree branches suddenly screeched, making Roger jump a little.

He wished he could shoot the thing. Roger hated everyone and everything. Ever since he'd been born in this godforsaken little town, everyone had been against him. His parents. His teachers. The cops. That bitch who'd seduced him into getting her pregnant and then having his kid. Roger had told her to abort the thing, but she wouldn't.

Someday, really, he ought to just give in to his rage and get a gun and start shooting. Like those guys who finally snapped and mowed down theaters full of people or kindergarten classrooms. Roger could relate. They had just had enough of all the crap that they were dealt on a daily basis. If people only weren't so goddamn nosy—

Behind him, Roger heard a twig break.

He looked over his shoulder.

No, the sound hadn't come from behind him. It had come from off in the woods somewhere.

It was whoever had been on the path ahead of him, now moving among the trees.

The woods were a pale blue this time of day. The sun was low in the sky, hidden by clouds, and the cold, bare trees seemed to shiver before the coming darkness. The ground was hard. There wasn't a speck of green that Roger could make out anywhere.

Just blue. Deep blue shadows.

He took the last drag on his cigarette and dropped the butt to the ground. He picked up his pace a little.

From the other side of him, he heard another twig snap in two.

Why did his flesh crawl?

He'd been on this path hundreds, maybe thousands, of times. It was as familiar to him as his own living room. And Roger didn't scare easily. Rather, he scared other people. That had always been the way it was.

He was a big guy. Five-eleven, one-hundred-eighty-five. He was strong. He wore his hair long, down over his shoulders, and he brandished blue, red, and purple tattoos up and down his arms. Skulls and arrows and lightning bolts. When people saw Roger Askew coming, they didn't mess with him.

So why was he suddenly creeped out? Why did he want to get off this path as soon as he could?

The crow in the trees suddenly took off into flight, the sound of its giant wings flapping echoing down through the skeletal trees.

Roger began to walk even faster.

Up ahead, whoever he'd seen earlier stepped back onto the path from the woods.

"It's just a woman," Roger whispered to himself, instantly relieved, and even a little embarrassed that he'd been afraid.

A woman dressed in white. With long gray hair.

Who could be afraid of some old lady?

She stood there in the middle of the path, waiting for him.

Roger felt the fear return, flooding his body like a shot of Novocain. His limbs froze. His heart began to echo in his ears.

He wanted to turn back and run the other way.

But this was just some old bitch! Why should he fear walking past her?

Roger forced his numb legs to continue walking.

As he drew closer to the woman, he noticed a few things about her. She was watching him intently. Her face was dirty, caked with something. And she wasn't really that old at all.

When he was just a couple of feet away from her, the woman spoke.

"Are you from around here?" she asked.

"Yes," he told her.

"I seem to have lost my way," the woman told him.

Roger was now standing directly opposite her. Not only wasn't she old, but she wasn't half bad-looking, either. Out here in the middle of the woods, Roger realized he could do anything he wanted to her. He began to get excited.

A smile started to make its way across his face, like a worm.

He never even saw the knife, but he felt it. And the warm cascade of blood that flowed from his gut down over his groin and legs. He felt that, too.

Roger looked up in disbelief at the woman.

But she was gone.

His legs crumpled beneath him. And then everything went dark.

15

"I hope you slept well," Annabel said to Priscilla and Neville when they shuffled into the dining room for breakfast the next morning.

"Well, I might have," Neville replied, bleary-eyed, "but Prissy here was carrying on a conversation with somebody."

Priscilla looked exhausted but exhilarated. "She came to me!" she told Annabel. "Sally Brown! She was sitting in my room talking to me all night!"

"Yeah, and keeping me awake," Neville grumbled, pouring himself some coffee.

Priscilla held up her hand. "I wear an opal ring all the time that was given to me by a psychic. It's said to be able to attract ghosts!"

Annabel didn't want to encourage the woman's delusions. The sooner they ended this association with ghosts and weirdos the better.

"Well, what we hope for our guests is they get a good rest when staying here, so I hope tonight will be more peaceful," she said, laying out a tray of blueberry and corn muffins that she and Cordelia had baked that morning. The old woman had shared her recipe and showed her where all the ingredients were kept in the pantry. Eventually, when she retired, Cordelia told Annabel this would be her job. Annabel thought a better idea would be to hire a chef who could whip up some nouvelle cuisine breakfasts for their guests.

As Neville slabbed butter all over a muffin, Priscilla sat down and gushed about her otherworldly encounter.

"I opened my eyes and there she was, as real as you are," she said. "She told me that she had spent her life walking these hallways, trapped in these rooms. Oh, it was so thrilling!"

"Did you see her, too?" Annabel asked Neville.

He shook his head. He had butter on his chin. "I just heard Priscilla chattering away. A couple of times she prodded me to sit up and have a look, but each time I did, I saw nothing. She wouldn't turn on the light."

"Sally asked me not to," Priscilla said. "She doesn't like the light."

"Yeah, well, whatever," Neville said, returning to his muffin.

"I should tell you," Annabel said, "that I don't believe the stories of the ghosts in this house. Once my husband and I take over running the inn completely, we aren't planning on marketing that particular element anymore. We're going to upgrade the house and make it a real first-class destination. No more tales of ghosts and murders."

Priscilla looked horrified. "But you can't do that. The ghosts will still be here. Just because you don't want to promote them doesn't mean they'll just go away."

"I guess we'll cross that bridge when we get to it," Annabel told her.

"Seriously! Sally Brown can't cross to the other side! She told me so! She's trapped. We sat and talked for nearly an hour!" Priscilla smiled, remembering. "She's really quite sweet, you know."

Annabel smiled as well. "Well, I'm pleased that you got what you came here for."

The Englishwoman's face suddenly changed. "You're patronizing me. Just like Neville."

"No," Annabel protested. "Really, I'm not. . . ."

"Yes, you are. If you don't believe in the ghosts, then you think that I'm either making up what I saw last night, or that I'm mad."

"No, really, I just—"

"Of course, we believe you," came a new voice.

They turned around. Jack stood in the doorway of the kitchen. He was wearing jeans and a white ribbed tank top. Annabel could tell he'd just come from the shower. His hair was still damp.

"I was a child in this house," Jack said, coming into the kitchen and pouring himself some coffee. "My wife was not. So she doesn't know."

Priscilla turned to look over at Neville. "You see?" she asked.

In the moment she was looking away, Jack took the opportunity to wink over at Annabel. She realized he was only trying to pacify the guests. She said nothing more.

"Did you see many ghosts here when you were a boy?" Priscilla asked him.

"Oh, many, many ghosts," he said, sitting down at the table opposite her. "Some were pretty scary, but some were friendly ghosts, like Casper."

"Did you ever meet Sally Brown?"

"Sure, I did. Sally and I got to be good friends."

Annabel couldn't stand it. She walked out into the living room. She figured she'd start today with a good cleaning of the living room and dining room. She'd mentioned the idea to Cordelia this morning, who hadn't seemed to mind. Annabel wondered how long they'd have to tiptoe around Cordelia's feelings. She'd asked them to take over the place, so she couldn't very well stand in their way of modernizing it. Eventually, they'd have to just sit her down and explain that if the inn was ever to turn a profit again, they'd have to make some changes. Once the paperwork was complete, and the Blue Boy was in their names instead of Cordelia's, they could do what they wanted.

Annabel paused. It felt odd that the Blue Boy would be in her name. That she'd be an owner of a place that appeared from its sign to be the home of Tommy Tricky.

She was gripped by a memory.

Darkness. Stale air. The smell of mothballs.

She was trapped in a closet. She was banging on the door. She could hear her heart thudding in her ears.

"Help me! Mommy! Help me!"

"Your mommy isn't here, she can't help you," came the voice of Daddy Ron. "She can't save you from Tommy Tricky!"

"No!" Annabel screamed.

"He's right behind you! Can you see hear him breathing?"

Annabel could. The imp was panting, like a dog.

"And how he loves to eat bad little girls!"

"Miz Wish?"

Annabel jumped. A voice behind her. A real voice. Not the terrible daydream.

She turned around. It was Zeke.

"Sorry," the caretaker said. "I didn't mean to startle you."

"Oh, it's all right," she said. "I was . . . lost in thought." She tried to smile. "Zeke, will you help me take down these curtains? I want to wash them and air them out. I'm going to be giving the living room a deep cleaning today."

"Yes, sure, I can help you," he said. "But I wonder, first, if you've seen Miz Cordelia."

Annabel looked at the old man's face. He was clearly upset about something.

"Why, yes, I saw her earlier this morning. We baked some muffins for the guests. I told her about my cleaning plans, and she seemed fine with them."

"Do you know where she went afterward?"

"No, I don't. Isn't she in her room?"

Zeke shook his head. "I've looked everywhere for her. And there's something I need to discuss with her right away."

"Anything I can help you with?"

"No, ma'am."

"Well, Jack's in the kitchen. Maybe he can help—"

"Nobody can help but Cordelia," Zeke said. "If you see her, please tell her I'm looking for her."

"Of course."

The old man hurried off, as best as he could hurry, hobbling up the steep, narrow stairs.

That was odd. Where in this cramped old house could Cordelia possibly disappear?

Annabel stuck her head back into the kitchen. Neville had left. She could see him through the window out in the backyard, smoking a cigarette. Priscilla and Jack were still seated at the table, leaning in toward each other, discussing the ghosts of the house. Their faces were only inches apart. It made Annabel oddly uncomfortable.

"Another ghost I remember seeing was a little boy," Jack was saying. "He'd come riding a tricycle down Gran's path and then just disappear!"

"Oh, that's brilliant," Priscilla said, completely snookered and in awe.

She was pretty. Annabel hadn't really noticed before. Priscilla had just seemed too odd and eccentric to be pretty. But she was. Long blond hair and breasts much larger and fuller than Annabel's more modest pair. For a second she had a flash of Rachel Riley, and then pushed the thought away.

"Jack," she said. "Zeke is looking for your grandmother."

"Haven't seen her," her husband replied, before resuming the story of the ghost boy on the tricycle. Priscilla continued to give him her rapt attention.

Annabel stewed. It was one thing to mollify the guests, to not offend them—but he was actively encouraging all this ghost talk, after he and Annabel had decided they'd put that all behind them. She turned on her heel and strode back out into the living room.

She heard something then.

The slightest sound.

Scratching.

She listened closely.

It was coming from the other side of the room.

Annabel approached the sound.

It seemed to be coming from the fireplace. From

below it, to be exact. The sound seemed to rise from below the fireplace and from the floorboards surrounding it.

"Rats," Annabel murmured to herself.

Or maybe just mice or squirrels or chipmunks.

Either way, she thought, they'd need to exterminate.

16

"There you are," Zeke rasped, out of breath, as he spotted Cordelia, huffing nearly as much as he, coming down the stairs.

The old woman fixed him with an icy glare. "You're incompetent," she snarled.

"I did not leave the door unlocked, if that's what you're thinking," Zeke replied.

Cordelia glanced around. She could hear Annabel in the living room. She lowered her voice.

"Well, I certainly didn't leave it unlocked," she whispered angrily. "You were the last in there."

Zeke's old eyes looked as if they might burst into tears. "I was certain I locked the door! I always check, every time I leave."

"Well," Cordelia muttered, "it's all taken care of now."

He grabbed her bony wrist. "Are you sure? Everything is safe?"

Cordelia yanked away from him and moved toward the kitchen. "For now. But you better take care, you old fool. Jack has got to know soon. Don't let anything happen in the meantime."

17

At the little police station at the end of the one-block Main Street of Woodfield, Chief Richard Carlson was going over the day's schedule with his deputy, Adam Burrell. Carlson was drinking a cup of coffee and eating a cinnamon cruller he'd picked up at Deb's Diner. His fingers were sticky and sugary as he turned over the schedule's pages.

"Might be a bit of a traffic tie-up at the Route 7A intersection today," the chief told his deputy. "They're putting up a new light around noon."

"I'll be there," Burrell assured him.

"And tonight there's that meeting in the public works room at town hall. Can you be there as well?"

"Sure thing, chief."

Carlson smiled. "Thanks, Adam. Just not sure I can handle another one of those."

"Small town politics getting you down?"

Carlson sighed. "It seems everyone's got an agenda against everyone else. The town manager hates the board of selectmen, the board of selectmen hate the school superintendent, the school superintendent hates the town manager . . . it's a vicious circle."

Burrell smiled. He was a young man, redheaded and freckled. "Yeah, but everybody loves the chief of police."

Carlson knocked on the wood of his desk. "So far," he laughed.

"Hey, you've been chief for a decade and no one's tried to get you fired. That's a good run."

Carlson finished the last of his cruller. "I guess it is," he said.

Burrell left the office to start his morning's rounds. The chief sat back in his chair, sipping his coffee. Deb made it good and strong, the way he liked it. He drank it black. In the old days, when Amy had still been around, he'd taken cream and sugar in his coffee. But ever since Amy had died, Carlson had needed something stronger in the morning. Something to jolt him awake and keep him alert and concentrating all day.

The people of Woodfield had never known Amy. His wife had died two years before Carlson had come to this little town. He was the "new bachelor chief of police" and had attracted a great deal of feminine attention during his first few years here. Every single lady, and a couple married ones, too, had seemed to try to date him. He'd gone out on one date in his whole time here, just one, and it had been a disaster. Cora Coakley. Poor Cora. She'd seemed nice enough when she'd come into his office, bringing him homemade jams and apple pies. But when they went out to dinner, she'd sat across from him blushing so hard Carlson had started blushing in return, and every attempt at conversation had faded off to a few mumbled sentences. Now when Carlson saw Cora around town he just tipped his hat to her. He didn't want to say something to her and risk those cheeks of hers turning bright apple-red again.

The fact was he didn't want to date anyone. He had loved one woman. One woman only. Amy had been everything to him. He could never replace her. Even twelve years after her death, Carlson could not imagine loving another woman.

His phone buzzed.

It was Betty, his secretary, in the front office.

"Rich," she said, "Tammy Morelli is on the line. I tried to give her Adam's voice mail, but she insisted she wanted to talk to you."

"Okay, put her through," he told Betty.

Poor Tammy. She worked at Deb's Diner. Poor kid didn't have it easy, raising that little girl, Jessica, all by herself, with no help from that good-for-nothing boyfriend of hers, Roger Askew. Carlson had noticed that Tammy wasn't at the diner this morning. When he'd asked about her, Deb had just shook her head in exasperation.

"Hey, Tammy," he said when Betty switched over the line.

"Chief, I know what you're going to say, but I've got to tell you anyway," she said.

"Okay, shoot."

"Roger didn't come home last night."

"And what did you think I was going to say about that?"

"Well," Tammy said, "first I figured you'd say, 'Good. It would be better for you if he never came home.' Then I figured you'd say, 'Well, there's no cause for alarm. He's probably off somewhere sleeping off a hangover.'"

Carlson smiled. "You know, Tammy, you're psychic."

"And you're right on all counts," she replied. "The only thing is, this morning, he had a court date up in Great Barrington, and I know he really wanted to go because he hoped to get some charges dismissed against him. . . ."

"Failure to pay child support, wasn't it?" Carlson asked.

"Yes, he was agreeing to give up all parental rights to his kid in order not to have to pay another single cent to her," Tammy told him.

"What a great dad."

"Believe me, I think that little girl will be better off without him in her life."

"Maybe you ought to think the same about your own little girl," the chief told her.

Tammy started to cry. "I know, I know. I'm going to leave him. Really, I am. I just . . . right now . . . like this morning. I know Roger's a waste of a human being. But at least he can take Jessica to school for me. I pick her up in the afternoons when I get out of the diner, but Deb's got me working the breakfast shift, and so I can't take Jessica and she's scared of the bus. So Roger comes in handy once in a while."

"That's why you weren't at the diner this morning," Carlson said. "But even though you didn't call asking for my advice, Tammy, I'm going to say anyway that Roger's occasional chauffeur assistance really doesn't outweigh his drinking, his temper, his violent flare-ups. . . ."

"I know, I know! And believe me, if you find that he's dead in a ditch out there, I'm not going to cry one single freaking tear over him." She grew quiet. "But I thought I should at least report that he didn't come home. I'll let you take it from there."

"Okay, Tammy, I'll mark it down," Carlson told her.

"You're not going out looking for him?"

"Has he been missing for forty-eight hours?"

"No, just since last night, when he went out to get cigarettes at Millie's store."

"Okay, well, then, you just keep us posted on whether he comes home, or not."

"All right, chief."

"Take care of yourself, Tammy."

She promised she would, but Carlson doubted it.

18

"You've got to talk to her," Annabel said, alone at last with Jack in their room. "You've got to tell your grandmother that in asking us to take over the place, she has to give her consent to some modernizations."

"I'll talk to her, babe," Jack promised. "Gran's just sentimental. She's run this place a long time. She's attached to the way she and my grandfather used to do things. And then my dad and mom . . ."

Jack's voice trailed off.

"What about your dad and mom?" Annabel asked.

"Well, Dad took over after Granddad died. And I remember he wanted to make some changes to the place, too, but . . ."

Once again his voice trailed off. He walked over to the window and looked out into the tangled arms of trees.

"What is it, Jack?" Annabel asked, her voice becoming compassionate. "Has coming back here made you think of your parents' deaths?"

He nodded, still looking out the window, away from

her. "This was the last place I ever saw my mother. She was here one day, absolutely fine. Next thing I knew, she was gone, off to the hospital in Boston. I never even knew she had cancer until she was gone."

Annabel walked up behind him and placed her hand on his back. Jack so rarely spoke of his parents, especially his mother. She died when he was in his teens of breast cancer. Now that Annabel knew he had lost a little sister as well, she felt tremendously sad for her husband. His childhood had been filled with tragedy.

"I hadn't realized you had been visiting here when your mom was taken away to the hospital," she said softly.

He turned back around to look at her. "We had come up here to start the process of helping Gran after Granddad died. Mom had been pretty excited about the idea. She had lots of ideas, just like you." His voice thickened and he couldn't go on for a moment. "But it wasn't meant to be. Within a week of us getting here, she suddenly got sick and Dad took her to Boston. I never even had a chance to say good-bye. I just came downstairs one morning and Mom and Dad were gone. Dad came back late that night and told me Mom was in the hospital. She died a few days after that."

"I hadn't realized she died so quickly," Annabel said. "I mean, to seem so completely healthy one day, and then be rushed to the hospital and die a few days later . . . breast cancer is usually a far more lingering illness."

Jack's face darkened. "Well, that's what Dad told me she died from."

"You think it might have been something else?"

"I don't know. But it always did seem so fast and

strange. The last time I saw Mom, she was happy and singing and down there in the parlor supervising some workers who'd come to do renovations. She was excited to have a project. She had so many ideas about fixing the place up. And then she was gone."

"Obviously, your father didn't want to continue with her renovation plans after she died," Annabel said.

Jack shook his head. "He was too distraught, I guess. Cindy disappeared not long after that, too. So Dad was never the same." His face showed the sadness he carried. "That's when I was sent off to boarding school in Connecticut. Dad died a few years later himself."

Annabel took his hands in hers. "Jack, was coming back here a bad idea?"

His eyes met hers. "No. This is our chance to start over. To finally make something of our lives. To become successful."

"Well," Annabel said, "to do that, we'll need to honor your mother's wishes and redo this place like she wanted to do."

"Yeah," he said, nodding. "That would be a nice tribute to Mom." He smiled weakly. "Though, as I recall, Gran wasn't keen on her changing things, either."

"The only way to turn this old dump into a money-maker is to renovate it," Annabel told him. "That's the only way we can become successful here."

Jack nodded again. "You're right, babe. I'll speak to Gran and tell her she's got to let us do what we need to do."

"Thank you, Jack," Annabel said, reaching up and kissing him lightly on the lips.

The little kiss led to another, and then several more. In moments, they were kissing deeply, the first time in a long time. Annabel had feared this moment, had dreaded the idea of being intimate with Jack again, but now that the moment had arrived, she didn't push it away. She wanted things to be right between her and Jack. They'd embarked on this journey together. They needed to be united, committed. They were starting over.

She kissed Jack hard, fumbling with the buttons of his shirt.

He cupped her breasts with his hands.

In moments, they had tumbled backwards onto the bed. Jack had slipped off his shirt and was now pressing Annabel's over her head. She felt his hot, wet breath on her neck and shoulder. His hands were now pulling down her jeans. She heard the jangle of Jack's belt buckle unfastening. Annabel tensed and waited.

But then . . . nothing.

Jack flopped over onto his back beside her. His eyes were staring straight up at the ceiling.

"I'm sorry," he whispered.

"It's okay, Jack," she said.

Annabel didn't know how she felt. Disappointed? Relieved? She reached over and stroked her husband's face, but he gently pulled away from her touch.

"I guess I'm just too . . . I don't know . . . too worked up," he said, still looking at the ceiling. "It's all I think about. This has got to work, you know, baby cakes?"

"What has got to work?" she asked quietly.

He finally pulled his eyes away from the ceiling tiles and looked at her. "*This*," he said. "This house. This business idea. This taking over and making it ours."

"We'll do what we can, Jack. We aren't miracle workers."

He sat up, his face suddenly tense. "No, it's *got* to work! I won't take any failure! I tried so hard with that goddamn book, Annabel. I thought I had the whole success thing figured out. And I failed, sweetheart. I failed!"

"Jack, publishing is a tough business. You didn't fail. The company just didn't market your book the way they should have."

His eyes grew dark. "Bullshit. The book was crap. I'm a lousy writer." He suddenly grabbed Annabel by the shoulders, making her jump. "This is my last chance, angel pie. I've got to make this fucking guesthouse the most successful inn in all of New England! I've got to make us rich! This is my goddamn last fucking chance!"

"Jack, putting that kind of pressure on yourself isn't going to help."

He let go of her shoulders, his eyes narrowing at her. "What's the matter, sweet cakes? Don't you want to be successful? Seems to me, after all you've been through, you'd want a second chance to prove yourself, too."

"Prove myself to who?"

"Annabel," her husband said, "I don't want this house to blow up in our faces, leaving me to rot somewhere in the city and you back on the blow."

"I'm never going back on the blow, Jack," she told him. "No matter what happens."

He stood, shrugging. "You gotta hope not. That's why we need this to work, angel face. For both of us. Get a big glossy profile in *Travel & Leisure* magazine."

Annabel didn't stand. She just sat there in her panties

and her unhooked, crooked bra, looking at him. "I fully intend to do everything I can to make this place successful, Jack. That's why I wanted you to set some ground rules with your grandmother. But it's not life or death, Jack. I refuse to see it that way. If I learned anything in rehab it's that we always have choices. We always have options. If not this, there will be other things—"

"No!" Jack cut her off. "It's this, babe! This!" He suddenly looked defeated. "I don't have the strength to try again if this fails."

He buttoned up his shirt and buckled his belt and headed for the door.

"I'm going to go talk to Gran. Tell her we're going to start renovating the place." He smiled at Annabel. "First thing tomorrow morning."

She gave him a weak smile of consent. He left the room.

Annabel wasn't unhappy. This was what she wanted. She had some great ideas about how she could fix the house up. She'd start with the parlor, then the bedrooms.

But Jack's all-or-nothing attitude troubled her. She guessed that, in her own struggle in overcoming her addictions, she'd failed to see just how profoundly Jack had been affected by his own career troubles. Annabel had known how disappointed he was, but she now understood the disappointment had gone very deep. It had been publicly very humiliating for him to get such universally terrible reviews. It had called into question his whole life's game plan. Suddenly, she felt terribly sorry for Jack.

She fixed her bra, slipped her shirt back on, and pulled up her jeans.

The only thing to do was to get moving.

Annabel pulled out her computer and hit the power button, before suddenly remembering there was no Internet in this godforsaken place. How was she supposed to find the best local contractors to hire to start the work on the house?

The old-fashioned way, she told herself.

She dug out of her pocket the card she had picked up at the market yesterday. MILLIE WESTERBROOK, it read. *Proprietor*. And underneath was the phone number.

Annabel whipped out her phone. Not many bars, but enough. She entered the number of the market.

"Woodfield Market," a woman's voice chirped.

"Hi, this is Annabel Wish. I was in yesterday?"

A moment of silence on the other end.

"I just moved into the Blue Boy Inn."

"Oh, sure," Millie said, her voice filling with recognition. "What can I do for you, honey?"

"I'm wondering if you might be able to recommend a good contractor."

"Well, the best around is Charlie Appleby. He and his sons do good work."

"Terrific," Annabel said. "Do you think they'd be able to start work right away?"

Millie laughed. "Had enough of all that dust and gloom already, huh?"

"I figure if we can start now, maybe we'll be up and running by summer."

"Charlie's pretty busy, but he could probably get one

of his boys to start giving you a hand. Hold on. Let me get his number for you."

"Thanks, Millie."

Annabel smiled. It felt good to be taking the first step.

19

"Oh, I'm sorry," Jack said. "I didn't know anyone was in there."

Priscilla blushed a deep crimson, holding the towel as tightly around her as possible. She had just stepped out of the shower when the door to the little bathroom had opened and Jack had walked in. She didn't think he'd seen anything, as she'd already been wrapping the towel around herself. But she couldn't be sure.

Now he stood on the other side of the door, having closed it again, apologizing.

"It's all right, really," Priscilla told him. "I should have locked the door."

"I forgot there were no bathrooms in the individual guest rooms," he told her. "We're going to be changing that. When you come back next time, every room is going to have its own private bath."

"Wow, that's ambitious," Priscilla said.

"We've got a lot of big plans," Jack told her through the door.

Priscilla thought it was a little odd that he kept talking to her, knowing that she was naked and dripping inside here. But she kind of liked it. Jack was very handsome. He'd made her heart flutter as she was talking to him. That never happened with Neville.

She suddenly felt bold. Making sure her towel was firmly secured around her, Priscilla grabbed the door handle and walked out into the hallway.

Jack was still standing there, as if waiting for her. She noticed the way his eyes looked her over. Priscilla felt a tingle of electricity race through her body.

"It's good to have plans," she told Jack. "I can't wait to come back and see how you've remodeled the place."

He didn't reply immediately. His eyes were too busy eating her up.

Priscilla was being very naughty, and she knew it. Jack was a married man. But what harm could a little flirting do?

"Yeah, well, you won't recognize the place," Jack told her.

"I would hope you'd talk with me first before you start knocking down walls." It was a new voice. They both looked around.

The old woman, Mrs. Devlin, stood at the end of the corridor. Priscilla let out a little gasp.

"I was just heading back to my room," she chirped, and hurried down the hall.

20

"Come into my room," Cordelia told her grandson. She could feel her lips tightening into a scowl.

Jack obeyed. Once they were inside, Cordelia closed the door behind her.

"Now, don't worry, Gran," Jack was saying. "We're not going to start tearing down walls. Anything we do, we'll include you in on the plans."

"Now, listen to me, Jack," she said, her tiny frame standing up to him, her neck craned to look up into his face, her bony finger pointing. "This house has stood for more than a century. There is an integrity to this house. Your father believed so, and his father before him. You can't come in here with a wrecking ball."

"I told you, Gran. It will be nothing like that."

Her fingers curled into two tiny fists. "When I'm gone, do whatever you want. But for now, Jack, please, just leave things as they are."

"Gran, Annabel has some ideas. Good ideas. They'll make the place even better."

"Ideas!" She sniffed. "Other people have had ideas, and it's done them and us no good."

Jack made a face as he looked at her. "Are you talking about my mother?"

Cordelia wished she hadn't said that. She tried to backtrack. "Your mother was a dear, kind woman. She meant well. But if she had succeeded in tearing up the place as she had planned . . ."

"Mom wasn't going to tear up the place, Gran," Jack said. "And neither will Annabel and I. Maybe if Mom had succeeded in fixing the place up all those years ago, it wouldn't have gone into the red." He made another face, which Cordelia took to indicate sympathy, but which seemed simply idiotic to her. "I've gone over the books you gave me, Gran," Jack went on. "This place hasn't made any money in years."

"We get by," she told him.

"Gran, I've spent too much of my life just getting by," Jack said. "You asked me to come up here and take over from you. I plan to do that. And I plan on making a success of things. A success of me!"

Her gnarled old fingers gripped his wrists. "Jack, please, go slow. And please don't do anything without talking to me first."

"I told you we'd include you in everything," he said, smiling at her, lifting her hands to his lips to kiss them.

Cordelia's eyes stung with tears. Nearly sixty years ago she had come to this house a happy bride. How had it come to this?

21

"Help me!!"

Cordelia, aged twenty-five, had stood there, not believing what she was seeing.

The woman struggled. Her face was a mask of terror.

"Help me!" the woman screamed again.

Cordelia tried to run to her, but her husband stopped her.

And she had watched in sickening horror as the woman was pulled down into the darkness.

22

"Just please go slow," Cordelia said to her grandson, her voice low and whispery.

Jack pulled her in for a big bear hug. She practically disappeared against his chest.

"Don't you worry about anything, Gran," he said. "We'll respect the integrity of the house. You'll be pleased with the changes. You'll see."

23

Annabel was having a grand time, mapping out designs for the house. She'd found a little table in one of the ~~other~~, unused bedrooms and dragged it back to her own, making it into a desk for herself. She began sketching a rough blueprint of how she envisioned the parlor could look. One wall gone, the fireplace opened up, the windows enlarged . . .

This is just what I need, Annabel thought to herself. *A project.*

In New York, she had liked nothing more than to be immersed in a project. During her short tenure at *Orbit*, she had loved designing the look of the magazine, working with their graphics team to come up with a sleek, stylized presentation. She was always sketching, trying new ideas out. In those days, Annabel was at her happiest, most fulfilled.

Too bad her nights had been consumed with coke.

But that was over now. She had triumphed. She had made it through rehab, survived her breakdown, and emerged whole and healthy. She had not wanted to come to Woodfield with Jack. She'd felt pressured into doing so, as if she'd had no other choice. But maybe that was changing. Maybe the challenge of remodeling this place would be just what she needed.

Because Annabel needed something.

She needed to feel as if she mattered. As if she could run her own life. She needed to feel strong and capable again. She'd triumphed over the addiction, but what she still felt she hadn't regained was the self-confidence. She wondered if she'd ever really been self-confident, if maybe all her time as a hotshot New York fashionista and designer had been a sham, if she'd been fooling herself and everyone else. She wondered if she had ever really believed in herself, or if she had been putting on a show—if she had still been, at heart, the scared little girl Daddy Ron had locked in the closet.

Yet Dr. Adler at the hospital had told her that before she could believe that she was strong and capable, she needed to believe she was safe.

"Do you feel safe, Annabel?" Dr. Adler had asked her.

"I feel safe here," she had replied, meaning the hospital, "but I'm not sure I'll feel safe anywhere else."

She had hated the hospital—hated feeling confined and boxed in—but at least she had felt safe there.

I need to feel safe here, too, Annabel told herself. *And I can feel safe by making this place my own. So long as it doesn't feel like my own, then I won't feel safe.*

And feeling unsafe was a terrible way to live.

Already she had hallucinated since coming here. Her mind was sometimes going to play tricks with her—Tommy Tricky, as a matter of fact. Dr. Adler had warned her about that. But she couldn't succumb to

such tricks. She had to teach her mind to distinguish between reality and illusion. She had to make her mind
strong—working it out every day, the way people worked
out their bodies by going to the gym. And the best mental
calisthenics Annabel could do were the designs and blueprints for her renovation of the inn.

If Annabel could meet the challenges of living here
at the Blue Boy—if she could find her courage and her
strength and her self-confidence here—then all the
pain and struggle she had gone through would have
been worth it. But most important, she needed to do it
on her own. Jack had been a steadying influence during the worst of her ordeal. He'd been a great support.
But Annabel needed to do this next part on her own.
That was vital.

*I need to find a way to feel strong and safe again on
my own,* she told herself, as she sketched out the windows she had in mind to open up the parlor.

From a corner of the room, she heard scratching.

"I may need to find an exterminator as well," she
said with a long groan.

Damn it. The idea of vermin running around inside
the walls of the house creeped her out, made her flesh
crawl. She'd heard scratching downstairs in the parlor.
Probably mice. Or maybe chipmunks. Annabel hoped
it was nothing worse than that.

She stood and walked over to the wall. Crouching
down, she pressed her ear low to the wall. She could
definitely hear something, but in fact, she realized it
wasn't the same sound she'd heard downstairs. Up
close, Annabel wouldn't describe it as scratching. It
sounded more like . . . scuffing. Like someone was
scuffing along the floor behind the wall. . . .

"That's crazy," Annabel said out loud. "Mice and chipmunks don't scuff."

But it sounded bigger, heavier than a mouse or a chipmunk.

Pressing her ear harder against the wall, Annabel was surprised to discover that a part of the wall buckled just a bit. A sliver of the plaster actually moved. She looked down.

She saw a small panel, about two feet by three feet, where the wall met the floor.

Slowly, carefully, Annabel slid the panel back. If there was some animal behind there, she didn't want it jumping out at her. But the sound was gone now. There was utter silence. Still, Annabel moved very slowly, frightened that a skunk or a possum was about to poke its snout through the panel at her. With careful deliberation, she pushed the panel aside, trying to catch a glimpse of what was behind the wall.

It was too dark to see. Annabel stood and hurried over to her pocketbook, snatching up her phone. There might not be any reception up here, but she could still use her flashlight app. She pointed her phone into the panel and switched on the light.

She saw no animal or any sign of one. There was just a very narrow space that seemed to lead all around the room. No way was she going in there to explore. Annabel hated enclosed, tight spaces. She just wanted to close this panel and seal it shut—

But then her eyes landed on a small dusty pile of books just beyond the panel opening.

Hesitantly, Annabel reached in and grabbed the book on the top of the pile.

Bringing it back out into the room, she looked down

on its cover. The book seemed ancient. The binding was cracking and covered in mold. The mold made a pretty blue-and-white pattern across the black leather cover. Carefully, Annabel opened the book. She let out a little gasp when she read the words on the frontispiece.

DAEMONOLOGY

Invocations and Spells

The date at the bottom was 1862.

24

"Stay back," Chief Richard Carlson told the kids who had gathered along the trail. "Stay behind Deputy Burrell."

The call had come in about half an hour ago. Some kids had found something along the path through the woods. One of them, little Julie Chen, had run home to her mother screaming and then Mrs. Chen had called the police.

The kids claimed it was a body.

A dead guy, they said.

Richard had ordered the kids kept back. A group of curious adults had gathered by now, too, and Adam was holding them back as well while the chief made his way up the path.

"It's right over there," called one of the kids who had found whatever it was. "Just off the trail beside a log."

Richard could see something in the direction the kid was pointing. It looked like a clump of dark brown blankets from where he was standing. He continued toward it.

What if it was a body?

What if it was murder?

There hadn't been a murder in Woodfield since Richard had taken over as chief. The job was very different from his time working on the Boston police force, where he'd had to turn over a dozen dead bodies a year, all of them potential homicides until proven otherwise. During his years in Boston, Richard had seen his share of bloodshed. But since coming to Woodfield, his worst problems were those damn town meetings where everybody was fighting with everybody else. That and the occasional underage drinking down at the lake, or thrill riders going ninety down the old twisting back roads.

Woodfield was a quiet, peaceful little village. But Richard knew it hadn't always been so.

Before he'd come to town, there had been a string of unexplained deaths. Many of them were out at the Blue Boy Inn, but not all. On slow days, Richard sometimes went through the cold case files, lifting the bulging manila folders down from the shelf and leafing through them. For such a small town, there were an awful lot of unexplained deaths.

And from the looks of it, there had just been another one.

Richard turned back toward his deputy. "Adam," he called. "Get the EMTs here pronto."

He heard Adam make the call.

The chief knelt down beside what from a distance had looked like a brown clump. It was brown all right. Brown, hardened blood. The corpse was lying on its right side and its clothes were all drenched in blood. The poor guy's face was turned, pressed into the dirt, so Richard didn't recognize him as a local. At least not right away.

He felt for a pulse. He knew there wouldn't be one, but he did it anyway. The guy was dead. And cold. Richard guessed he'd been dead for a while.

"What is it, chief?" somebody called from the crowd.

He wasn't sure he could say exactly. From the looks of it, the guy might have been jumped as he walked down the path. Or maybe he'd been dumped here. But it was clear he must have been stabbed to produce so much blood.

Richard took out his phone and snapped several pictures. Then, carefully, he turned the corpse on its back.

That was when he recognized him.

Holy shit.

Roger Askew.

He heard Tammy's voice.

Roger didn't come home last night.

"He sure as hell didn't," Richard whispered.

"Hey, chief," Adam shouted over to him. "The EMTs are on their way."

Richard nodded.

His first thought was this was a drug deal or a gambling debt gone bad. Roger Askew had lots of enemies. It wasn't going to be easy to find his killer.

Richard was looking down at the corpse. Roger's right arm was twisted under his body at an odd angle. All Richard could see was his shoulder. Gently, the chief reached forward to examine the arm. The odd angle might be a clue as to how Roger died.

But as he felt under the cold, stiff body, Richard uttered a little sound in surprise.

There was no right arm!

It had been severed just below the shoulder. That was why there was so much blood.

Richard stood up. The sun was dropping a little lower in the sky and the woods were filling up with shadows, strange twisting shapes cast by the bare branches of the trees. Had the arm been cut off for some reason, and then tossed aside? The chief stepped away from the corpse, walking through the dead leaves, trying to see if he could discover the arm. But the leaves weren't disturbed for several yards around the body. There was no sign of any more blood.

He and Adam would do a more thorough search, and the state forensics team would likely be called in. But at the moment, Richard suspected that Roger's arm had been cut off and then his killer had taken it away.

But why?

25

"Well, Miz Wish," Zeke was telling her, "what can I say? It's an old house. There have been many people who've lived and stayed here over the many decades. And maybe one of them had some rather unique reading interests."

Annabel had told him about the books she had found behind the panel. "Well, they really disturbed me," she said, shivering.

"I hope you threw them away," the caretaker told her.

"No," Annabel admitted. "The others I left inside the panel. The one that I took out and examined, I placed outside, on the wood box. Would you take it down to the library and donate it, Zeke? It's so old that I thought maybe some historian would want it."

"Such blasphemy ought to be burned," Zeke said. "Don't worry. I'll take care of it."

"Good. I just want it out of the house." She rolled out the diagrams she had drawn up onto the parlor table. "And maybe nail shut that panel for me, too?"

"Happy to oblige, Miz Wish." Zeke smiled, looking

down at the plans Annabel was showing him. "What do we have here?"

"Some ideas I have about redesigning this room," Annabel said. "I've spoken with a contractor. He's coming by in the morning to help me get started. His name is Chad Appleby. His father is Charlie Appleby."

The old caretaker lifted his bushy white eyebrows. "I've known Charlie since he was a boy riding his tricycle. Can't believe he's got a kid old enough to do contracting work."

Annabel smiled. "He assured me that Chad is very good, that he thought he could give me a hand doing a few small jobs. When we move into the next stage, which will involve more intensive renovation, Charlie said he would come over to do the work."

"I see," said Zeke.

Annabel's smile changed into a smirk. "Charlie added that he only hoped he wouldn't find any bodies stuffed inside the walls when he starts tearing them down," she said.

The caretaker shrugged. "Well, those are the risks you take when you start moving things around."

"Look, Zeke," Annabel said, "I need to know that I'll be able to count on you. I know Cordelia is worried that we'll destroy the historical character of the house. But trust me, that's the last thing I want to do. In New York, I helped redesign many old buildings. Staying true to the character and the integrity of the place was always one of the most important motivations."

"What exactly do you plan to do to the house?" Zeke asked.

"For now, we're just going to start with this room," Annabel told him, gesturing around the parlor. "It's the first thing guests see when they walk into the house. I want to clean it up and give it a good polish. We're going to paint the walls, replace the windows, and sandblast the floor. Eventually get some new windows, and take out that wall over there."

She walked over to the fireplace.

"And we're going to open up the fireplace again," she added.

Zeke just looked at her.

"I have a mason coming by as well tomorrow," Annabel said, stooping down and examining the bricks that had been mortared over the fireplace opening. "I'll want to make sure the chimney is still sound. And I suspect we have mice or rats or squirrels living in there. I've heard a lot of scuttling. Up in my room, too."

"Listen, Miz Wish," Zeke said. "I don't think you oughta open up the fireplace. I can tell you that the chimney is no good. And the ash dump down in the basement is all cracked. Why don't you start on something simpler? Fixing the windows is a good idea, and I'll help you paint the walls."

Annabel shook her head. "We need a roaring fire in this room to ward off the cold this winter. How inviting will it be to walk into this room and feel the warmth of the fire, see the light flickering on the walls at night?" She smiled, standing up, and turning around to look back at Zeke. "In fact, I'd say fixing the fireplace is number one on my list."

Zeke stared at her. "Have you told Cordelia?"

"Jack spoke to her. Believe me, she's going to love how we fix the place up."

Zeke watched her as Annabel spread her plans out

on the table, looking up from them at the walls and the windows, then down at her blueprints again.

The woman was a fool.

She walks into this house and thinks she can do what she likes, Zeke thought. *She has no idea. None whatsoever.*

She's bringing in a mason to check out the chimney.

Zeke knew that, one way or another, he'd make sure that mason told Annabel to leave the fireplace alone.

26

"I think this calls for a glass of wine, don't you?"
Jack was asking.

They had all just come down to the dining room for
dinner. Normally, the inn only served breakfast to its
guests, but because a light dusting of snow was suddenly blanketing the roads, Annabel had offered to
make dinner for everyone. Priscilla and Neville had
thought that was a grand idea, since they weren't keen
on skidding along back roads in search of some restaurant.

Jack uncorked the wine as Annabel began chopping
vegetables in the kitchen.

"She's a vegetarian, you know," Jack told his English guests, pouring some merlot in a glass for each of
them. "Hope you don't mind a meal of carrots and
lentils."

"I'm sure it will be delicious," Priscilla said, accepting her glass and taking a sip. "Oh, this wine is divine."

It was just the four of them for dinner, plus Zeke, as
Cordelia had complained of a headache and disappeared into her room. The rest of them sat around the

dining table drinking their wine, Zeke sipping from a mug of beer.

"I should really go out to the kitchen and offer Annabel my help," Priscilla said.

Jack grinned over at her. "You just stay right there," he told her. "You're a guest. Annabel enjoys cooking." And he winked at her.

Priscilla could feel her cheeks redden.

"Annabel said she's going to open up the fireplace," Neville offered, apparently oblivious to Jack winking at his girlfriend. "A fire sure would be nice on a snowy night like this."

Jack was nodding. "We've got some good ideas for this place. I was telling Priscilla earlier that if you come back a year from now, you'll never recognize it."

"Now, look here," Zeke said, gazing up at them from over his mug. "You told your grandmother you'd go slow."

"Don't worry, Zeke," Jack assured him.

"And I'm not sure that chimney is fixable," the old caretaker said. "Not sure you want to spend four grand to fix it your first month here."

"What's a bed-and-breakfast in the woods without a fireplace?" Neville asked. "I'm with you, Jack. Get that chimney smoking again."

Jack was smiling and refilling everybody's glass of wine. "Absolutely," he said. "We could be toasting marshmallows as we wait for dinner."

They all laughed, except Zeke.

"What is that American custom of marshmallows and chocolate over a fire?" Priscilla asked.

"Do you mean s'mores?" Jack laughed. "Oh, sure,

it's very tasty. Melted marshmallow and chocolate between a graham cracker sandwich. Sticky, but good."

"Sounds delectable," Priscilla said, allowing her eyes to find Jack's again.

His eyes locked on to hers. "Gooey, sweet, and very satisfying," he told her, enunciating each word carefully.

Her cheeks reddened darker.

"Well," Neville said, "if we come back next year, I hope you'll have performed an exorcism on all the ghosts in the place."

Jack moved his eyes away from Priscilla and found her boyfriend. "Have they been keeping you up at night?"

"Only thing keeping me up is Priscilla jabbering with herself, thinking she's seeing spirits," Neville replied, before reaching over for the bottle of wine and refilling his glass.

"I *am* seeing spirits," she told him. "Two nights in a row now I've seen Sally Brown. Poor thing. She's very confused. Doesn't even know her name. But she comes into the room and sits at the end of the bed."

"Oh, does she now?" Jack said, smirking, winking this time at Neville.

"She *does*," Priscilla insisted. "I keep trying to tell her that it's okay to move on, that she shouldn't be trapped here between worlds. But she tells me she can't leave, that they're keeping her here."

Zeke sat forward in his chair. "Who's keeping her here?" he asked.

Priscilla shrugged. "She hasn't said," she told him, knocking back the last of her wine and setting down her empty glass, which Jack moved to quickly to replenish. "But if she comes by tonight again, I'll ask her."

"Just ask her quietly, okay?" Neville quipped. "I don't like being woken up."

"So you've seen nothing?" Zeke asked.

"I fall asleep as soon as my head hits the pillow," Neville replied. "She sits up waiting for her ghosts."

Jack stood, taking another bottle of wine out of the cabinet. "You know, if it were up to me, I'd keep the whole supernatural reputation for the place," he told the group as he uncorked the bottle. "I think it's a great selling point."

"It's a wonderful selling point," Priscilla said. "But it's more than that. It's truth in advertising. You can't rent out rooms without telling people they might be visited by spirits in the night." She smiled as she took a sip of wine. "Wouldn't be fair."

That brought another round of laughter.

"Well, Annabel doesn't like the idea," Jack said, sitting back down at the table, but this time taking the seat next to Priscilla, whose glass, though still half-full, he filled back up to the top. "Maybe we can work on her."

Priscilla giggled.

27

From the kitchen Annabel could hear them laughing.

She was glad they were having fun. It was good to hear laughter from real people in this gloomy old house.

The carrot-and-lentil soup bubbled on the stove. She'd also made rosemary popovers and an enormous salad. A good meal for a snowy night.

Maybe this wouldn't be so bad after all. She had the contractors coming tomorrow. Soon they'd be opening this place up, letting in light, sweeping out cobwebs, and drying out the mold. Maybe this little adventure would be just what Jack hoped it would be, a new start for both of them. A path to success.

The wind whistled against the house, rattling the glass panes in the windows.

Annabel couldn't wait until a fire was blazing in the parlor.

28

Tammy Morelli sat opposite Chief Carlson, her fingers massaging her temples. "Well, sure, Roger had enemies," she said. "Lots of people wanted him dead." She closed her eyes. "Including me, sometimes."

She opened her eyes again. They were bloodshot from crying. Richard didn't understand how a woman like Tammy, basically a good, decent, hardworking person, could actually grieve over a lazy bum who had beaten her and used her. But Tammy had sobbed like a baby when Richard had given her the news that Roger was dead.

Murdered.

"Anyone hate him enough to cut off his arm?" Adam Burrell asked her.

Tammy shuddered. "I have no idea," she said, massaging her temples harder.

Richard felt sorry for her. "I don't want to keep you any longer, Tammy. But if you can think of anything, like maybe the symbolism of his right arm . . . like maybe he did something to someone and they were cutting off his arm for revenge. . . ."

Her eyes snapped open and she was looking directly at Richard.

"But Roger was left-handed," she said. "If he did anything to someone, he'd have done it with his left arm."

The chief nodded.

After Tammy was gone, Richard and Adam sat in silence for a while. Outside the snow squall was ending. It had been a light winter so far, but that could change. It was still early. They could yet be buried in seven feet like they'd been last year.

"Tell me something, Adam," Richard said. "You grew up here. The cold case files tell me that there were a number of unsolved murders in this town before I took over as chief."

The deputy was nodding. "They stretch way back, more than a century."

"The last big flare-up was a little more than twenty years ago," Richard told him, remembering the files he'd perused. "So you must remember that."

"Sure do," Adam said. "I was around seven years old at the time. My parents were terrified. Kept me in the house, wouldn't let me go outside to play. There was even stuff on the news about the Woodfield Serial Killer."

"I seem to recall from the files that four people were killed in a matter of a few days."

"Well, four people went missing, never to be seen again. But only one body was found. The police chief at the time presumed there was a link."

"And why was that?"

"Because they'd all either been living or working at the Blue Boy," Adam told him.

The chief stood, walking over to the shelf and retrieving several folders. Placing them down on the table, he thumbed through the top file.

"Yes, here it is," he said. "A man and his wife had been staying at the inn. He reported she went for a walk and never returned. No body was ever found. But murder was suspected given the fact that the very next day Cynthia Devlin, the owners' granddaughter, also went missing. Although again no body was found, the little girl's blood was discovered all over the grounds. There was speculation a bear might have killed her."

"It wasn't a bear," Adam said. "Because there were two other guys as well."

Richard flipped forward a few pages in the file. "Yes, here they are. Contractors. They'd come up from New York to do some work on the place." He read further. "One would be reported missing by his wife. He never returned to New York. The other was found in the woods outside the Blue Boy, a bullet through his heart."

"Yeah, that sounds about right."

Richard couldn't figure it out. "There doesn't seem to be a pattern, except that they were all connected somehow to the Blue Boy Inn."

Adam shuddered. "My parents always told me to stay away from that place, that it was haunted," he said.

The chief was still reading through the file. "It says here that the owners were all questioned and were cleared of any suspicion." He read a little further into the report. "Cordelia had just taken over the place, her husband having recently died. Her son was questioned, it says here, but having lost his daughter, the poor guy was pretty shaken up, and he moved away soon after that."

"Hey, chief," Adam asked, leaning back in his chair, his hands behind his head, "are you thinking that Roger Askew's death might be somehow connected to those deaths twenty years ago?"

"I can't see how it's possible," Richard said, closing the file. "Roger was killed half a mile away from the inn. But I'd like to look into those cold cases regardless. The file left it all a complete mystery, saying no suspects or motives could be found, especially since only one body was ever found."

Adam smirked. "It'll give us something to do. It's been pretty boring around here lately."

"Don't let anyone know we're reopening those cases," Richard told him. "Officially, we're only investigating the death of Roger Askew. I have a feeling that one will be easy to solve as soon as we start talking to Roger's cohorts. But as you're talking to people, ask what they remember about the Blue Boy twenty years ago."

"Will do, chief," Adam said, bolting out of his chair, replacing his cap, and heading out the door.

Richard sat back down at his desk. He thought of that woman who'd just moved to the Blue Boy, the one he'd met at Millie's store. Such a pretty woman. Annabel, she'd said her name was. Richard hoped he wouldn't rattle her too much asking questions about the Blue Boy's bloody past.

29

Annabel wasn't pleased by how drunk everyone was. Even Zeke seemed to have had too much beer. The other three, including her husband, had polished off three bottles of wine. Her dinner had been a hit—Neville had asked for three helpings of the soup—but now Annabel wished she'd served something more substantial to soak up all the alcohol everyone had consumed. Everyone but herself, of course.

She was disappointed in Jack. He'd still had the occasional glass of beer or wine even after Annabel had come home from rehab. She didn't expect him to go sober just because she'd had an addiction. But he'd never gotten drunk in all that time.

Until tonight.

And he was flirting shamelessly with Priscilla.

Annabel stood. "I'm going to clean off these plates and make some coffee," she said, scooping up her plate and Jack's.

"Coffee?" Jack blurted. "I don't want coffee. How about we open another bottle of wine?"

"I think you've all had enough," Annabel said, piling the three other plates onto the two she held in her hand.

"Aw, come on, Annabel," her husband said, "don't be such a spoilsport."

"No, she's probably right, Jack," Neville said. "I've had plenty. And Priscilla is such a lightweight."

"Pretty girls usually are," Jack said, winking openly over at Priscilla, who blushed a bright scarlet.

Annabel carried the plates out to the kitchen.

All she could think of was Rachel Riley. Her bleached hair and big tits filled up Annabel's mind.

She placed the plates into the sink. Neville came in behind her, carrying soup bowls.

"Thank you," Annabel said.

"You're a marvelous cook," Neville told her. His cheeks were flushed from drinking, his mosaic of pimples redder than usual. "Really, I'm usually a meat-and potatoes sort of bloke, but this was superb."

"I'm pleased you liked it." She kept her eyes averted, focusing her attention on filling the sink up with soapy water.

"I do think it's a good idea to get the house fixed up and fireplace cleared. I wish you all the luck with that."

Finally, Annabel turned to look at him. She smiled. "I appreciate that, Neville," she said.

"You know, I've heard some rustling sounds from down there," he added. "I'm afraid you might have some vermin to deal with when you pull up those bricks."

"Yes," Annabel agreed. "I've heard it as well. Maybe just a couple stray squirrels. At least, that's what I'm hoping."

"Yes, well," Neville said, and he seemed suddenly at a loss as to what else to say.

They looked at each other awkwardly.

"Can I help you here?" he asked finally.

"No, thank you." Annabel nodded toward the door to the dining room. "I'm fine here. Please go back and keep Priscilla company."

Neville smiled, nodded a little, and then headed back into the dining room.

Hadn't he seen the way Jack had been flirting with his girlfriend? Was he blind? Clueless? Or maybe he didn't care.

Annabel sighed, dropping her hands down into the soapy water. She couldn't go back out there quite yet. She hoped that Neville would take Priscilla off to bed. Then Annabel would tell Jack that they, too, should call it a night. She wouldn't mention his obnoxious behavior. No need to play the jealous wife. She and Jack needed to be united in the morning, when the contractor arrived and Cordelia started throwing up roadblocks to the renovation. Besides, Neville and Priscilla were leaving in the morning. They had to get down to Hartford to catch a flight to Florida late tomorrow afternoon.

But as Annabel washed dishes, the laughter from the dining room only continued and got louder.

She brought out the coffee. Zeke's head had dropped down onto his chest and he was snoring lightly. Jack was regaling Neville and Priscilla with a story about the time he'd been at some fancy restaurant in New York right after his book came out, and people as diverse as Anna Wintour and Mayor Bloomberg and Lady Gaga were coming up to him to congratulate him. That had never happened.

"Here," Annabel said, pouring some coffee for her husband and pushing the cup over at him. "Drink this."

He ignored her, continuing on with his story, which now had turned into how he turned down an offer to write a Broadway show because they wouldn't pay him enough. He described the way he'd told off these imaginary producers and he had Priscilla and Neville laughing so hard that tears were popping out of their eyes.

Annabel sat back and watched them. Drunk people were so ridiculous. She hated to think she'd once been like that, at some public function and as high as a weather balloon. She kept noticing the way Jack winked over at Priscilla when he was finished with one of his stories. She decided she couldn't watch any more, so she got up from the table and walked out of the dining room and into the parlor.

And suddenly the whole room was different.

It was as if someone had slipped a mickey into her coffee. Some sort of hallucinogen. The room seemed to sway and vibrate. Annabel had to reach out and touch her hand to the wall to steady herself.

From behind her the laughter from the dining room continued, only now it got absurdly louder and then seemed to disappear entirely for a few seconds, as if the merrymakers were holding their party underwater. Annabel tried to clear her head. She stood in one spot, holding on to the wall, taking long, deep breaths. She closed her eyes.

When she opened them again, Tommy Tricky was standing in front of her.

Gnashing his sharp blue teeth.

Annabel let out a small scream.

But the creature was gone. A figment of her imagination. The room continued to spin. What was happening to her?

The laughter surged. Annabel felt as if her legs would give out from under her. She made her way across the room by holding on to the wall. She reached the fireplace and looked down at the bricks that sealed off the opening.

She heard scraping coming from below.

Scraping, scraping, scraping.

A hand was on her shoulder. Annabel gasped.

Turning, she saw Neville, as if in a dream.

"Vermin," he said, his eyes crazy. "Vermin."

Annabel thought she'd pass out. She nearly fell onto the fireplace, holding on to it to keep from falling to the floor. Neville was gone. Had he ever been there?

Once again, Annabel made her way around the room, her right hand against the wall to keep herself steady. She turned the corner back into the dining room.

And there was Jack fucking Rachel Riley on top of the table.

Annabel closed her eyes and opened them again.

No, not Rachel. Jack was sitting very close to Priscilla and they were about to kiss. Her husband looked over at her and smiled.

His mouth was full of sharp, broken teeth.

Annabel cried out and ran upstairs, shutting herself in her room.

But it wasn't her room. She was in a closet. A very small, cramped, dark closet.

Daddy Ron had put her in there.

"Turn around, Annabel," her stepfather's horrible, jagged, drunken voice rasped through the door. "Turn around and see who's behind you!"

"He's not real!" Annabel shouted, her hands in her hair.

"Aw, Tommy don't like it when people say he's not real. Gets him real mad."

Annabel spun her head from side to side, looking into the darkness.

"Hear him sharpening his teeth?" Daddy Ron asked.

She could. She could hear the devil's teeth gnashing, anticipating the moment he bit down into her flesh.

"He's right behind you, Annabel!" Daddy Ron shouted, and then he laughed.

She had to get out of there. All around her, linens were stacked neatly on shelves. Her mother's linens. There was a hamper beside her filled with dirty clothes. It was a tight space. So small. She was stuck there, using up all the air. Pretty soon there would be no oxygen left and Annabel would die.

She had to break free. She began pounding on the door, swinging her arms out, knocking all the linens off the shelves.

Annabel was trapped! Her claustrophobia took over and she screamed.

That was when she saw the little boy's hand resting upon her shoulder.

30

Priscilla staggered up the stairs to her room. What had happened down there? She was drunker than she had ever been before. She had allowed Jack to keep refilling her glass because he excited her. Excited her far more than Neville had ever done. More than any man had ever done.

But now she was lost in a fog of her own thoughts and desires. What had happened? Her blouse was unbuttoned. Where was everybody?

She took another step and tripped. She had to grab ahold of the bannister to keep from falling down.

"Neville?" she called in a small, whispery voice.

The stairs were moving. The whole house seemed to be swaying. Priscilla clung to the bannister for fear she'd tumble down the stairs.

"Neville?" she called again.

He had gone upstairs. She thought she remembered him saying good night, that he'd had far too much to drink himself and was calling it a night.

He had left her alone with Jack.

Zeke was gone, too, and Annabel.

It had just been Priscilla and Jack.

She tried to button up her blouse, but her fingers wouldn't work.

She reached the top of the stairs and stumbled into the hallway. It was very dark and very quiet. Priscilla could hear herself breathing. At least the house had stopped spinning. She took a step down the corridor. Her room was only a few feet away.

What had happened down there? She wished she could remember.

Ahead of her, a figure approached.

A figure in white.

"Sally," Priscilla said softly. "Sally, help me. . . ."

Sally Brown approached her. She looked at Priscilla with eyes that seemed both sympathetic and accusatory. Priscilla reached out to her.

Sally smiled, and grabbed hold of her hand. A glint of moonlight reflected off Priscilla's opal ring. She followed the ghost down the hall, and then began climbing some stairs. At the top of the stairs was a door. Sally opened the door and they passed through.

The attic. They were in the attic.

But then Sally was gone and Priscilla was alone.

She turned around a few times, got dizzy, and dropped down to sit on an old stuffed chair that smelled like dust and mold. She sat there for a while, breathing heavily, until her head stopped spinning again.

It had started to rain outside. At least, Priscilla thought it had. She could hear a soft tap-tapping on the walls and roof of the attic.

Priscilla looked around the room. A small lamp on the table provided a very dim light. "Sally," she whispered. "Sally, where are you?"

There was a small rumble of thunder off in the distance.

At least, Priscilla thought it was thunder.

The rain was hitting the house harder now. An icy rain, Priscilla thought. She imagined the long icy fingers that scratched the roof of the house. She shivered.

"Sally!" she called again. "Where have you gone? What have you brought me here to see?"

Despite her dizziness and confusion, Priscilla was excited. This was exactly why she'd come to the Blue Boy Inn. To see ghosts. And now Sally had brought her to a place where she'd see plenty of ghosts, Priscilla was sure.

All at once, a huge thunderclap made her jump, and the lamp went out.

"Oh, no," Priscilla murmured. She loved her ghost adventures, but she'd prefer not to experience them in total darkness. That was just a little too creepy.

She breathed a sigh of relief when the light flickered back on again.

On the table in front of her, Priscilla spotted a candle and an old book of matches. The candle was little more than a stub. Priscilla considered lighting it, but seeing that it was so small, she didn't want to waste the wax while the electricity was still on. Should the power go out again, she'd light it. She kept the book of matches near her hand so she could find it easily if the darkness returned.

She smiled. Despite all she'd had to drink, she was still thinking clearly.

The lamp flickered. Priscilla felt her heart flutter.

She looked up. And she saw in the darkness a hand holding a knife.

Priscilla screamed.

It took her several minutes to calm herself. "Well, that was a good one, Sally," she said out loud. "Who was that? The person who killed you? Does his ghost walk here, too?"

She had learned that ghosts could only hurt the living in very rare circumstances. Priscilla wasn't afraid of being hurt. She was afraid in a fun-house kind of way, the way she might feel watching a scary movie.

Thunder again, the loudest yet, directly over the house.

The light struggled to hold—

—shivered—

—and then went out.

Darkness.

Priscilla held her breath.

"Come back on," she whispered.

But the darkness remained.

"Oh, well," she said, feeling for the matches.

How terribly dark it was in the attic. Gripping the box of matches in her left hand, Priscilla felt around for the candle with her right. What if the power didn't return? The little stub would never last. . . . She moved her hand over the tabletop. Where was the candle? It had been sitting right there! The darkness was absolute. Deep and thick. The rain kept up its pummeling of the roof. She prayed for a flash of lightning just to show her the candle. But all she got was a low rumble of thunder.

There!

She felt something in the dark. The candle—

She moved her fingers to grip it.

And whatever it was that she touched—moved!

It was a hand! A human hand!

Someone was in the dark with her!

Priscilla gasped.

"Who's there?" she asked. "Who is it?"

Oh, this was exciting!

But she'd prefer it without the total darkness.

Finally, a flash of lightning. The room lit up for an instant. Priscilla saw she was alone in the room.

And there—there was the candle!

She grabbed it as the darkness settled in again. Fumbling for the matches, Priscilla found that her hands were trembling. But still she managed to strike a flame and shakily light the wick of the candle. A small, flickering circle of light enveloped her. She sat back in the chair, awaiting whatever vision Sally had to show her next.

The memory of the hand she had felt—

It was small, she thought. *Like a child's*.

She lifted the candle and stood. She was far too anxious to stay seated. As she moved into the center of the room, Priscilla realized she was stepping in something sticky.

Was rainwater dripping in from the walls?

She lowered the candle.

And she could see plainly that it wasn't water.

It was blood!

She looked up. And there, in the candlelight, was Sally.

"Oh, Sally," Priscilla said. "I'm glad you're back."

But then she saw that Sally was the one holding the knife.

"Sally," Priscilla said, "why are showing me this?

Sally took a step closer to her, pointing the knife at her.

"Sally! Please stop this!"

The ghost swung the knife, nicking Priscilla's arm. She drew blood.

Suddenly, Priscilla was terrified.

"Sally, no!"

The ghost kept coming closer. Priscilla turned and ran.

In her mind, still swimming from the wine, the small space of the attic suddenly seemed cavernous. She ran and ran, for many minutes it seemed, down an endless corridor that stretched farther and farther off into the distance. How could this be happening? How could she keep running for so long? What had happened to this room?

Behind her, Sally's footsteps echoed as she pursued her. Thunder clapped overhead. Priscilla just kept on running, down that impossibly long corridor.

And then she stopped, her head spinning as if she were riding an out-of-control carousel. She turned around. Sally was right behind her, smiling sweetly.

"Oh, Sally," Priscilla said. "You gave me such a fright."

Then the knife came plunging down into Priscilla's face.

31

"Wake up, you old fool."

Zeke opened his eyes. Sunlight was streaming into his room and Cordelia was standing over him, glowering at him, her arms akimbo.

"What time is it?" Zeke asked, sitting up, just as a headache pushed him back down.

"It's past time, you miserable man," Cordelia scolded.

"Oh, no," Zeke said, sitting up again, slower this time, rubbing his forehead.

"I've taken care of things," Cordelia said. "No thanks to you."

"Is everything all right?"

Cordelia's eyes darkened. "Everyone is sleeping off their hangovers in their rooms. After all that noise last night, I presume they'll sleep well past noon."

The old man got up out of bed. He was still wearing the clothes he had on yesterday. He smelled of beer and sweat.

"It's been so long, Cordelia," he told her. "So long since I just had a good time . . . unwound . . . had a few beers. Don't be angry at me."

"You had more than a few beers, apparently. I came in here two hours ago and couldn't get you to wake up for the life of me." She folded her arms over her chest. "So I had to take care of things myself."

"And everything was all right?"

Cordelia narrowed her old eyes at him. "I think she's figured out how to deal with that lock."

"The door was locked, wasn't it?" Zeke asked.

"It was locked," Cordelia said. "But I don't think it was locked all night."

"What makes you think so?"

She brushed her hand at him. "I don't have time to stand here jabbering with you. We have things to do today." She scowled. "Annabel has some people coming to see her."

"The mason," Zeke said, nodding.

"Make sure he stays far away from that fireplace," Cordelia said, before hobbling out of Zeke's room.

32

Annabel opened her eyes.

For a moment she had absolutely no idea where she was. She looked up at the ceiling and didn't recognize it. She sat up and looked around. The room made no sense to her.

Then she realized she was at the Blue Boy Inn, and Jack was snoring beside her. They both were wearing the same clothes they had worn the day before.

What had happened last night?

She'd hallucinated, that was what had happened. She'd thought she'd been locked in a closet by Daddy Ron. It had been horrifying.

You're safe, Annabel, she heard her therapists telling her. *You are completely safe.*

"I'm safe," she whispered to herself.

Annabel swung her legs off the bed and placed her feet—still in shoes—against the floor. Her hands covered her face and she felt as if she might cry. She hadn't had a childhood flashback like that in a very long time. During her breakdown and her time in rehab, such flashbacks had come frequently. Many a night she had thought she was back in the closet, locked there by Daddy Ron. But recently Annabel had begun to hope that she was finally free of such nightmares, that she had finally moved past those terrible memories.

Apparently not.

Dr. Adler had warned her that the flashbacks might come back if she was stressed or experienced some sort of trauma.

Annabel removed her hands from her face and looked over at Jack, snoring like a grizzly bear beside her.

She remembered the trauma of last night.

Jack had been flirting with Priscilla. He may have even had sex with her.

Annabel stood and pushed herself over to the mirror. She looked into her eyes. They were puffy and bloodshot.

What had she seen? Jack and Priscilla. What had they been doing?

She turned to look at her husband.

How she hated him.

No, she told herself. *You love Jack. He stayed with you through everything. You love Jack. You owe him so much.*

Annabel had to get out of that room. She felt boxed in. The air was stale and smelly.

Out in the hallway, she breathed better.

And suddenly she remembered the contractor and the mason were coming this morning. Yes! For some reason, the thought cheered her. She looked at her watch. They would be there in an hour. She hurried to the bathroom to get ready.

33

Chad Appleby was finishing up his breakfast at Deb's Diner.

"You want more coffee, Chad?" Tammy asked him.

"Sure, Tam. Just a splash."

She refilled his cup.

"You know, I can't say I liked Roger," Chad said, "but I'm sorry if what happened has left you upset."

Tammy gave him a wan smile. "I appreciate that, Chad. I suppose it's good that he won't be coming around anymore. Jessica was scared of him." She sighed. "But nobody deserves to get stabbed to death and get his arm cut off."

"Cops have no idea who did it?"

Tammy shook her head. "The chief has talked to all of Roger's friends and all of his enemies, and nobody seems to have had anything to do with it, or figure out any motive. I mean, why cut off his arm?"

Chad used his last piece of bacon to wipe up the egg yolk on his plate and then forked it into his mouth. "And they haven't found the arm yet, have they?" he asked as he chewed.

Again, Tammy shook her head. "The whole thing creeps me out," she said, before moving on down the counter to refill the next customer's cup.

Chad looked at his watch. Paulie was supposed to meet him here fifteen minutes ago. But Paulie was always late. Back in high school, Paulie got more demerits for showing up late to class than any other kid in their class. He was a stoner, but Paulie was also a damn good builder and mason, and that was why Chad had asked him to come out with him this morning to the Blue Boy Inn.

He couldn't believe that was where he was going. Dad had asked him, "Hey, Chad, you want to take on one very weird job?"

"And what would that be, Dad?"

"The Blue Boy Inn wants its chimneys inspected," his father had told him.

The Blue Boy Inn. Everybody in town knew that old place was haunted. Or at least had so much creepy history that it should be haunted. There was the time that little girl went missing but blood was found all around the place. And a guy was found shot dead in the woods a stone's throw from the place. Plus, there were stories that lots of people had died in the rooms over the last hundred years or had never been seen again after they'd gone inside. The Blue Boy was legendary in these parts.

And the two old people who ran it, that guy Zeke and that ancient Mrs. Devlin, looked like they were cast members of *The Addams Family,* all wrinkled and hunched over and dressed in black.

Chad had told his father that he was glad to take the job. He'd never been inside the Blue Boy, and he looked forward to finally getting a peek inside the spook house.

"Sorry I'm late, my man," came a voice behind him suddenly, a hand on his shoulder.

Chad looked around. Paulie had arrived, and his red, glassy eyes revealed he'd been four-twentying in his truck on the drive over.

"Sit down and have some coffee, Paulie," Chad told him.

Tammy brought him a cup.

"So you anxious to get a look inside the Blue Boy?" Chad asked.

Paulie grinned. He was a doughy-faced guy with floppy ears. They made an odd-looking pair, Paulie so soft and stout and Chad so chiseled, slender, and tall.

"Sounds cool to me, man," Paulie said, taking a sip of coffee. "Hope we don't run into any ghosts."

"Remember that Halloween you and me and Nicky Malone went up there and threw rotten tomatoes until the old lady came out and scared us away?" Chad laughed. "Jesus Christ, we were bad kids. I'm surprised the old lady didn't call the cops on us."

"Maybe she did," Paulie said, his floppy ears wiggling. "Maybe we were just too fast."

"Well, we're reformed now, aren't we, Paulie? Model citizens."

Paulie laughed.

In truth, antics like the one at the Blue Boy, tossing those tomatoes, bothered Chad to remember. He'd never been a bad kid, really, but there had been other pranks like that. Like the time he and Nicky had pointed a DETOUR sign down an old dirt road and caused half a dozen cars to get stuck in ruts. And another time he'd rigged up a bucket of water over the front door of the high school and pulled a string so it doused stuffy old Mr. Hillcrest, the principal. Nobody could ever pin any of those things on Chad and his friends.

Now he hated to remember them. He was twenty-four years old, and intended on doing Dad proud as his assistant in the family contracting business. His older brothers had no interest in taking over the company. They were lazy good-for-nothings. But Chad imagined a day when Dad retired and Appleby Contracting would be his own.

Maybe he'd even hire old Paulie to work for him full-time. Providing the wacky weed wasn't still a daily ritual.

"Well, come on," he said all of a sudden, getting up off his stool and plunking down a twenty and a couple of ones on the counter. It was a bigger tip than Chad was used to leaving, but he felt sorry for Tammy. "If we don't get a move on," he told Paulie, "we'll be late getting to the Blue Boy. I told the new owner we'd be there at ten."

Paulie downed his coffee and stood, a little shakily, to follow his friend out of the diner. Chad waved good-bye to Tammy and placed his hand on the door, but suddenly Paulie stopped him.

"You know," Paulie said, looking up at him with those bloodshot eyes, "maybe we oughta smoke a little something before heading up to that haunted house."

"I'm fine, Paulie," Chad told him. "And I think you're already higher than the Blue Boy's weathervane. In fact, why don't you ride with me? Leave your truck here."

Paulie smiled. "All right, captain. You're the boss."

34

Cordelia watched from the window of her room. There were men coming to the Blue Boy. Men who intended to knock down walls and pry up bricks. She wouldn't let them.

They must be stopped.

She remembered the day she and her husband had first sealed up the fireplace. Cordelia had laid many of the bricks herself. Then, years later, she'd had to lay those bricks again, this time with her son.

She hoped that old fool Zeke wouldn't fail her again, as he had failed her so often recently. Zeke's infirmities were the reason she'd had to ask her grandson to come up and take over. Otherwise, she never would have involved Jack.

But she was going to have to involve him completely soon. Especially if his wife persisted in her cockamamie schemes to renovate the place.

Jack's mother, Cordelia's daughter-in-law, had had similar ambitions.

And look what had happened to her.

"What are you doing?" Cordelia had asked the young woman, all those years ago.

"I'm taking the bricks out of the fireplace," Jack's mother had replied. "We should have fires in this room. It will make the place more inviting. Cozy and warm."

Cozy and warm.

The Blue Boy Inn had never been cozy and warm, not one day in all the years Cordelia had lived in the place.

She was going to have to speak to Jack. Soon. Very soon.

The way her husband had spoken to her.

"You're mad," she had said to him, when he finished.

His weary eyes told her that he was not mad. He was simply terrified.

In her mind, Cordelia heard again the screams of the mother whose baby had been taken from her. The little baby whose arm was found. Only the arm.

How that memory was seared into Cordelia's mind.

She pulled back the dusty old lace curtain and peered down onto the yard. She spied Zeke standing in the shadows of some tall pine trees. Good. He was there, at least. She prayed he'd be successful.

She was so intent on watching Zeke that she didn't hear the soft footfalls behind her.

But Cordelia certainly felt the sting of pain that suddenly seized the back of her head.

Without making a sound, the old woman crumpled to the floor.

35

Zeke heard the truck rattling up the dirt driveway before he actually saw it. The snowfall from the night before had mostly melted by now, and the tires of the truck were spraying stones from side to side as they crunched over the path through the woods.

The old caretaker watched carefully as the truck came into view and parked at the far end of the lot. Two young men stepped out. One was tall and blond and rather handsome; the other was shorter, darker, and stout. Without saying a word to each other, the men made their way up toward the house.

"Good mornin'," Zeke shouted, suddenly emerging from the shadows.

The men appeared to be slightly startled. They turned around to look at him. The shorter one seemed to sway just a little bit as he looked at Zeke, and his eyes were red.

"Good morning," the taller man said.

"May I help you?" Zeke asked. "I'm the caretaker here."

"We're here to see Annabel Wish," the man told him. "I'm Chad Appleby and this is Paul Stueckel."

"I see," Zeke said. "You're the contractors, I take it."

"Yes, sir, we are."

Zeke smiled with his crooked teeth. "Is she askin' you to do a big job?"

"I wouldn't know that yet," Chad told him. "I haven't seen what she wants to do."

"Say she asks you to take down a few walls and re-store a fireplace and chimney," Zeke said. "How much would that cost her?"

"I'm not sure," Chad said, seeming to grow a little leery of talking to him. He kept glancing up toward the house. "I'd have to see the actual work it entailed, and the condition of the house. . . ."

"How about if I told you," Zeke asked, drawing in closer to the men and speaking in a conspiratorial whisper, "that whatever you quote Miz Wish to do the job she's asking, Mrs. Devlin will pay you that plus half to *not* do the job?"

The men looked at him strangely.

"Mrs. Devlin is sort of sentimentally attached to the house as it stands right now," Zeke explained.

Chad frowned. "Well, from what Ms. Wish told me on the phone, it's she and her husband who are now the owners."

"Paperwork hasn't been signed yet," Zeke told him.

"But if it's going to be," Chad replied, "then I really ought to speak with the woman who asked me to come out here and give her an estimate."

"Mrs. Devlin will pay you double whatever you quote to leave the house alone," Zeke said, his voice hard as he upped the offer.

The two men exchanged looks.

"I think I need to speak with Ms. Wish," Chad said finally, heading off toward the house. His zoned-out-looking friend followed.

"Remember what I've offered you," Zeke called after him. "But the offer's no good if you tell Miz Wish about it."

The men didn't look back. They just continued on toward the house.

36

"Well," Annabel asked, after she'd given the contractors a tour, "what do you think?"

Chad looked around the place. "To really fix everything up, to do the kinds of things you've drawn up in your plans, will cost a lot of money. We're looking at six figures. I can maybe keep it under two hundred grand, but I can't guarantee it."

Annabel frowned. "That was what I was afraid you'd say."

Chad shrugged. "I wish it could be less. But the house is really falling apart. All the electricity is going to need to be updated. And the plumbing . . . from what I can see, I'm surprised you haven't had a major episode yet. The pipes are all rusted out."

"Well, we'll start slow," Annabel said. "A bit at a time."

Chad smiled at her. "That's what Dad and I usually tell our clients. Go room by room."

Annabel returned his smile. "And this is the room where we will start. The parlor."

Chad liked her. It helped, of course, that she was

pretty damn hot, with that shapely body and shiny auburn hair. But she was also real smart, having drawn up some blueprints like a real pro, and had some really cool ideas about how to fix this old place up. It would be a hell of a lot of fun to help her do it.

But if he refused, the old gnome in the parking lot said Mrs. Devlin would pay him *double*. That was possibly three hundred thousand smackers for sitting on his ass!

"So we'll do this room first," Annabel was saying, gesturing around at the walls. "Open it up. Bring in some more light." She strode over to the fireplace. "What did you guys decide about the chimney? Is it salvageable?"

Paulie had been doing his own inspecting. His sleepy face brightened now that it was his turn to show off his expertise.

"Well," he said, "from what I could see up on the roof and down in the basement, the chimney is in surprisingly good shape. Why did they brick it over?"

"I have no idea," Annabel replied. "The caretaker told me the chimney was broken."

"Why would he say that?" Paulie wanted to know.

Chad stepped forward. "Is the caretaker the little, hunched-over old man we met on the way in?"

Annabel nodded. "That's Zeke."

Suddenly, he felt he needed to do the right thing. "Ma'am," he said.

"Call me Annabel," she told him.

That just made him more determined to tell her the truth. "Look," Chad said, "I don't want to get anybody in trouble, but . . ." He hesitated. "That old guy told us Mrs. Devlin would pay us double whatever we quoted you *not* to do the renovation."

"What?" Annabel seemed aghast.

"I just thought you should know. I mean, if we're going to work together . . ."

Her eyes were blazing. "Cordelia asked us here, my husband and I, to take over the place. But then she tries to control everything we do."

Chad looked at her. "The old man said the paperwork hasn't been officially signed yet. He said the old lady still calls the shots."

"She's already put my husband on the deed," Annabel told him, "and my husband supports the renovation one hundred percent." She folded her arms across her chest. "Besides, Mrs. Devlin doesn't have that kind of money. She just told Zeke to tell you that to get you to back off."

"That's what I figured," Chad said. "Well, I just thought you ought to know."

"Indeed," Annabel told him. "Thank you."

"So, yeah," Paulie said, looking down at the fireplace. "I'd say that I could get this baby smoking for you in no time."

"Could you start right away?" Annabel asked.

"Sure," Paulie said. "I could come by later this week and get going. . . ."

"No," Annabel said. "I mean today. Could you start today? I'll pay you entirely upfront."

Her eyes were filled with fire.

"Well," Paulie told her, "I suppose I could. . . . I'd have to go back home and get some tools. . . ."

Annabel smiled. "I want Cordelia to come down those stairs and see the work has begun," she said.

37

But what puzzled Annabel was why Cordelia had not yet come down the stairs at all this morning.

As she watched the two men rattle off in Chad's truck, with Paulie promising to be back before noon, Annabel supposed that Cordelia might have gotten up earlier this morning and then gone back to her room. She did that sometimes. And Annabel had slept a little later this morning anyway, given her bad dreams all night long.

Everyone, in fact, was sleeping late this morning. Annabel tiptoed up the stairs and opened the door to her room. Jack was still sound asleep, flat on his back, still dressed in his clothes. Pausing outside the door of their English guests, Annabel could hear snoring from inside. Neville and Priscilla were apparently still sleeping off their drunks as well. They had a plane to catch later this afternoon, and the airport was at least an hour away. If they weren't awake soon, Annabel would have to wake them.

She headed back down the stairs.

Had something happened between Jack and Priscilla last night?

Settling down at the kitchen table with a cup of coffee, Annabel tried to make sense of what had happened last night. Jack had definitely been flirting with Priscilla. He'd been drinking too much. He hadn't had so much to drink in a long time, and apparently he'd lost his ability to handle his liquor. But had anything happened other than flirting?

Had Annabel caught them kissing? Fucking?

Why couldn't she remember?

It was all just an hallucination, she told herself, rubbing her temples with her fingers. And that, in some ways, was even more distressing than the idea of Jack fooling around with another woman.

She'd had hallucinations during the worst of her addiction. At rehab, sometimes they'd been overpowering. Sometimes they had been so strong that Annabel couldn't distinguish between illusion and reality.

"You're safe," Dr. Adler, her favorite therapist, had insisted to her, but Annabel hadn't bought it.

"I'm not safe!" she had screamed, as visions of demons walked through the walls. "I'm completely *unsafe!*"

How terrible those days had been.

Annabel prayed her hallucinations weren't coming back.

But ever since she'd come to this house, she'd had signs they were returning. She'd seen Tommy Tricky her first day here. And last night, after becoming upset with Jack, she'd thought the whole house was spinning. She'd thought she was a little girl again, put in the closet by Daddy Ron. Tommy Tricky had been in the closet with her. He had come at her. He had tried to eat her!

"Stop," she told herself.

She stood and looked out the window. Where was Zeke? She was furious with him. How dare he try to bribe the contractors? When Annabel found him, she'd let him have it. And when Jack woke up, she'd tell him exactly what his grandmother had tried to do. They wouldn't put up with such nonsense anymore. They needed to lay down the law. They were in charge now.

Annabel had to feel that she was in charge. Otherwise, she thought she might crumble into a million pieces and her hallucinations would take over again. Down into a black hole she'd tumble, and she'd never be safe again.

38

Paulie sat in his truck and lit his pipe. He inhaled the sweet, precious weed long and deep. He felt it fill his lungs. He'd parked far enough away from the house that nobody could spot him toking. In seconds, Paulie's mind was blissful and calm.

Bracing for the cold air outside, he opened the door of his truck and headed around to the back for his tools. Paulie slung them over his shoulder and then made his way back up to the Blue Boy Inn.

He didn't usually take jobs the same day. But Annabel had given him a check, payment in full, plus a fifty-dollar tip. How could he refuse?

He knocked on the door.

Annabel opened it quickly. She was very happy to see him. Welcoming him inside, she asked him if he wanted some coffee. Paulie declined.

"Thank you," he said, "but I never drink on the job."

They both laughed.

Paulie got down to work.

First, he covered all the furniture in the parlor with

drop cloths. Then he pulled on a pair of leather gloves and slipped some eye protection over his face. Finally, he got down to work with his chisel and his hammer. He began chipping away at the mortar.

39

Upstairs, Cordelia could hear him start to work.
Chip, chip, chip.
"No," she moaned.
But she couldn't move.
She couldn't stop him.
"No," she moaned again.
Behind her came the sound of soft laughter.

40

"I'm running to the market quickly," Annabel told Paulie. "We've run out of coffee, and our guests will be awake soon. I'll be back in a few minutes."

He lifted his eye protection to look over at her. "Sure thing," he said.

Annabel smiled. "Wow," she said. "You've already made progress."

Paulie stepped back from his work. He'd chiseled out a two-foot-by-three-foot opening so far. The removed bricks were stacked neatly off to the side. "I can feel the air from the flue," Paulie told her. "I might have this baby blazing in a couple of hours."

"Thank you so much," Annabel said. She gave him a big smile before heading out the door.

Paulie watched her leave. As soon as her car disappeared down the driveway, he stepped over the bricks and headed to the restroom.

A little more weed would make the rest of the job go by very pleasantly.

Safe inside the restroom, he lit up his pipe, making

sure to crack the window. Just a few puffs was all he needed to feel nice and happy.

He returned to the parlor.

And the first thing he noticed was that the bricks he had stacked so neatly were now knocked over. That was odd. He supposed he had disturbed them with his foot.

He got back to work. Another brick, and then another. The fireplace opening was gradually revealing itself. He chipped away at the bricks, stacking them up carefully at his side. Now the space was three feet by four feet. Once he'd removed all the bricks from the opening, he could see if any repairs were needed to the flue.

Paulie reached inside the opening, feeling for the chute to the ash dump in the basement.

His hand brushed against something warm and soft.

He yanked his hand out of the opening.

"Great," he mumbled. "A mouse or a rat."

He rummaged around in his tool bag for his flashlight. Switching it on, he shone the light into the opening.

A little face looked back at him.

A terrible little blue face, with a mouth full of fangs.

"Jesus!" Paulie shouted, stumbling backwards, the flashlight falling from his hands.

What was that?

It looked like a freaking little elf.

But maybe it was some kind of possum.

Calming his fluttering heart, Paulie grabbed ahold of the flashlight again and got down on his hands and knees in front of the fireplace. He got as close as he dared—he didn't want some mean old possum jumping out at him—and peered once more into the fireplace.

Just blackness now. There was nothing there.

What was in that weed he'd been smoking?

Paulie moved the flashlight around to examine the inside the fireplace. It was difficult to see, so he slowly, tentatively, stuck his face into the opening he'd made, the beam of the flashlight at his cheek.

That was when everything went red.

Excruciating pain filled Paulie's eyes.

The flashlight dropped from his hand, clattering onto the floor.

Paulie could feel sharp claws gripping his eyeballs like acorns, and then yanking them right out of their sockets. At the same time, other claws were clamping down onto his shoulders, easily slicing through his flesh and grabbing onto his collarbone.

Paulie screamed.

With uncanny swiftness, his body was pulled through the opening in the fireplace and down into the darkness.

If someone had been standing in the parlor watching, the last they would have seen of Paulie were his sneakers disappearing down an extraordinarily large ash dump. His muffled screams could be heard for a fleeting few seconds.

Then everything was silent.

41

Millie Westerbrook looked up as the little bell over the door tinkled. The woman who'd just moved into the Blue Boy Inn—what was her name again?—stepped inside.

"Good day," Millie called over to her.

"Good day," the woman called back, giving Millie a smile.

Annabel. That was her name. Millie didn't think her last name was Devlin, though. She had said something else. Something short and simple. Wells? No, it was something more whimsical than that. Mille thought it was amusing how so many of these young girls today didn't take their husband's last names. That was a good thing, Mille thought.

If she had ever have gotten married, Millie told herself, she would have kept her own name, too. But Millie hadn't gotten married. She'd never been asked. She'd waited and hoped, and finally given up. And back in Millie's day, women didn't ask men to marry them. So here she was, sixty-one and single. Millie supposed there were worse fates.

She was putting away some stock—canned vegetables—but she was also watching Annabel-from-the-
Blue-Boy meander down the aisles. She was an awfully
pretty girl. Nice figure. Lots of wavy, shiny auburn hair.

Millie sure felt sorry for her, living in such a place.

Millie had played cards with Agnes Daley a few
nights ago. They'd gotten to talking about the Blue
Boy, and all the terrible things that had taken place
there. Agnes was the town historian, so she knew the
inn's history. She told Millie that the first owner of the
place had been a priest—no, not a priest, Millie, thought,
trying to remember. It wouldn't have been a priest back
then. The house was built around the time of the Civil
War, and Millie didn't think there were all that many
Catholics in Woodfield back then. She supposed Epis-
copalians had priests, too, but she didn't imagine a
great big Episcopalian church out there in the middle
of the woods. No, the first owner had to have been a
minister, of some long-forgotten Protestant church.

But what Agnes told Millie about this minister—
well, Millie just couldn't believe it.

Seems he was a very bad man. Not a man of God at
all. This minister, Agnes said, was hanged for witchcraft!

"Now, that's just plain crazy," Millie had said to
Agnes.

"Read the history books," Agnes had replied.

"I don't know much about history," Millie had coun-
tered, "but I do know they weren't hanging men for
witchcraft at the time of the Civil War."

"They found other reasons to hang him," Agnes had
insisted. "But the whole town knew what kind of
witchcraft he practiced."

Millie had snorted. Agnes liked to act so superior, knowing everything about the town, all its past and its history. But maybe, in fact, there was something to the story, since a curse did seem to cling to the place.

All those murders. All those people seemingly swallowed up into nothingness up at that house.

"May I pay for this?"

Millie looked up as she heard Annabel calling to her. The pretty young woman was standing up by the cash register, holding a packet of coffee.

"Oh, yes, of course," Millie said, hurrying over to assist her.

That poor girl, she was thinking. *That poor girl up in that frightening house. . . .*

"Did you speak with Charlie Appleby?" Millie asked when she got behind the cash register, ringing up the coffee beans.

"Yes, indeed, he sent over his son Chad," Annabel told her. "We've got a man there making renovations now."

Millie raised an eyebrow. "And Cordelia's okay with that?"

The clerk remembered one of the few times old Cordelia Devlin had ever stepped into this market. She'd come in with that old handyman of hers, looking for duct tape to fix a leaking pipe. She had frowned deeply when Millie had asked if she ever thought about updating her plumbing. "It's got to be plenty old," Millie had said.

"The house is fine as it is," Cordelia had grumbled. "Nobody's touching it."

Annabel smiled. "Well," she admitted, "we did have to insist. She's very sentimental about the old place.

My husband and I had to assure her that we plan to do nothing that will hurt the integrity of the house. We really respect the architecture. We just want to make it more modern, more inviting to guests."

Millie dropped the coffee into a paper bag. "Have you had any inquiries about guests?"

"We have two guests right now!" Annabel said happily. "Please spread the word that we are open under new management and that soon the place will be a wonderful getaway, complete with all-modern luxuries and amenities."

Millie smiled tightly. "I'll let people know," she said.

"Thank you," Annabel replied, and then, with a little smile and wave, left with her coffee, heading back to her car.

Millie returned to stocking her cans. Why did she feel so worried for that poor child? Surely the stories that the townspeople told about the place were just old wives' tales—myths, legends, and rumors. There was nothing to them. Even if Agnes was right about the first owner being hanged—even if he had done some terrible things—that was a hundred and fifty years ago. Nothing that had happened up there since was in any way connected. It was just a series of unfortunate, random events.

Still, Millie worried for that poor, pretty girl.

42

Neville came staggering down the stairs. His head was pounding. Why on earth did he drink so much last night?

He noticed the drop cloths covering the furniture as he passed through the parlor. The fireplace was now open. Bricks were stacked alongside. A flashlight was on the floor, rolling slightly back and forth, shining its light toward the opening. But no one was around.

Neville made his way into the kitchen. Just as he entered, Annabel came through the back door, a bag in her hands.

"Well, good morning," she said, smiling. "Just went out for more coffee. I figured everybody was going to need it today."

Neville sat down at the table. "Yes, coffee might help," he said, rubbing his forehead.

"I was wondering when you'd get up," Annabel said, starting the coffee immediately. "I was going to wake you. You have a plane to catch soon."

"Oh, yes," Neville said, still massaging his head. "Florida awaits. Thank God."

"Give yourself at least an hour to get to Hartford," she told him.

"Yes," Neville replied. "I'll have a little coffee, then jump in the shower and then we're out of here." He looked around. "Has Priscilla already had her coffee?"

"No," Annabel said. "She hasn't been down yet."

"Well, she must have," Neville told her. "She wasn't in the room."

"She wasn't?" Annabel looked over at him oddly as the coffee began to drip. Its aroma made Neville feel a little better already. "That's odd, because I haven't seen her. I slept a little later this morning myself, but she hasn't been around for a least the past couple of hours. Could she have gotten up much earlier?"

"Not likely, given how much she had to drink," Neville said. "But come to think of it, I don't remember her coming to bed. I was pretty drunk, though. Maybe I just slept through it."

Annabel poured him some coffee. "Maybe she slept elsewhere in the house," she offered. "I haven't looked in the other rooms."

"Why would she do that?"

"Maybe you can tell me," said Annabel, sitting opposite him.

Neville looked at her. The coffee was reviving him, but he didn't know what Annabel was implying. "What do you mean?" he asked.

"Do you think . . ." She struggled with her words. "Do you think Jack was at all inappropriate last night? Could she have taken offense at anything he said? If so, I do apologize for him."

Neville sighed and took another sip of coffee. "Oh, you mean the way he was flirting with her? I don't think she would have been offended. From what I can remember, she seemed to enjoy it."

"It didn't bother you?" asked Annabel.

Neville shrugged. "Priscilla's a pretty girl. Men seem to go for the pretty, bookish types. The ones who look quiet on the outside. I've gotten used to it. I'm not much of a looker myself, so if some handsome bloke like Jack can give Priscilla a little attention, I don't mind." He leaned in toward Annabel. "But did it bother you?"

"A little," she said. "But Jack was right beside me all night, snoring like a bear."

"All night?" Neville asked.

Annabel sat back in her chair. "I assume so. He's up there now."

Neville shrugged again. "I'm not suggesting anything. But it's just curious that Priscilla isn't in our room."

"I'll go look for her," Annabel said.

Neville just nodded.

43

As Annabel passed through the parlor, she saw that Paulie was gone. She walked over to the fireplace and looked down. He'd gotten it opened, however. His flashlight was on the floor, its light still shining. Annabel reached down and shut it off. No need to waste the battery.

She glanced out the window. Paulie's truck was still in the driveway, as she'd observed when she'd driven up a few minutes earlier. So where was Paulie? Maybe out back, taking a break, smoking a cigarette? Or smoking something else, Annabel thought. She hadn't missed the fragrance of marijuana that clung to him.

Did she go looking for Paulie or for Priscilla? She figured it was more urgent to find Priscilla. If they didn't leave soon, they'd miss their flight.

But Priscilla was nowhere to be found. Annabel searched every room of the house and she wasn't there. She even opened the door to her own room again and all she saw was Jack, still sound asleep like a bear in hibernation.

She noticed the small narrow steps at the end of the hall that led up to the attic.

She hadn't been up there yet. Zeke had told her it was dangerous. Annabel was sure it was. The rafters were probably so rotted that they'd snap underfoot. But still, she should check. What if Priscilla had been so drunk she'd gone up there for some reason?

Maybe to get away from Jack?

Or maybe . . .

Maybe she and Jack had gone up there for a tryst. Jack had come down, but Priscilla had spent the night up there, passed out.

That was the thought going through Annabel's mind as she climbed the steep, narrow stairs. At the top was a door. She turned the handle.

But it was locked.

Well, if she couldn't get in there, then Priscilla wouldn't have been able to, either. At least that ruled out the attic.

Annabel came back down to the second floor. She had looked everywhere! Where could Priscilla be? Had she gone outside?

But her coat was still hanging on the hook beside the front door.

Annabel thought of something.

She hadn't looked everywhere. She hadn't looked in Cordelia's room.

Annabel paused outside the old woman's room. She knocked.

"Cordelia?" she asked softly.

There was no answer.

Had the two of them gone off together?

She knocked again and called the old woman's name once more.

Still no reply.

Annabel hesitated, and then turned the doorknob. The door was open. She went inside.

Cordelia was lying on her back on the floor. Her head was propped awkwardly against an old cast-iron figurine of a hawk, used as a doorstop.

"Cordelia!" Annabel cried, rushing to her fallen grandmother-in-law and kneeling beside her. She noticed the small pool of blood behind the old woman's head.

Annabel grabbed her by the shoulders.

"Cordelia!" she shouted. "Are you all right?"

The old woman's eyes flickered open. One clawlike hand clutched at Annabel's blouse.

"The fireplace," Cordelia croaked.

"What?" Annabel asked. "What are you saying?"

But the old woman said nothing more. Her eyes closed and her head fell back.

Annabel rushed off to call an ambulance.

44

Chief Richard Carlson watched the people of the house carefully as the body of Cordelia Devlin was carried out the front door on a stretcher.

Here he'd been thinking of coming by the Blue Boy Inn to ask some questions about the cold cases of a generation ago and now, here again, was another mysterious death at the old bed-and-breakfast. Examining the body of the old woman, the coroner had declared it might have been accident. She was frail, and she might well have fallen, hitting her head against the iron doorstop. But until he had a chance to better examine the body, the coroner was reserving judgment as to cause of death.

That was wise, Carlson thought, as there were some other mysterious developments that might end up having some bearing on the case.

Three people had disappeared that morning as well. Paulie Stueckel, whom Richard would see every morning at Deb's Diner, sipping coffee and eating a doughnut, looking as if he'd smoked a half-pound of weed as soon as he woke up. Priscilla Morton, a British tourist. And old Zeke, the caretaker of the place.

Any one of them might have slipped upstairs and whacked the old woman on the head, then taken off.

Chad Appleby was pulling up in his truck.

"What the hell happened?" he was asking as he hurried across the parking lot.

"Morning, Chad," Richard said. "Or I guess I should say, afternoon."

The sun was directly above them now, weakly shining down on the van as Cordelia Devlin's body was loaded inside.

"Where's Paulie?" Chad asked. "I left him here just a little while ago."

"We don't know where Paulie is," Richard told him. "That's why we asked you to come down here."

Chad looked absolutely befuddled. "Last I saw him, I dropped him back at his truck. He was planning on heading back here to start work on the fireplace."

The chief nodded. "And he did just that. He was hard at work when Ms. Wish left for the store, but he was nowhere to be found when she got back. She was gone less than fifteen minutes."

"And the old woman was dead," Chad said.

Richard nodded. "Tell me something," he said. "Was Paulie high this morning?"

"Chief," Chad said, looking at him as if he'd just asked the most absurd question of all time. "You know Paulie's always high."

Richard shrugged.

"Come on, chief," Chad said. "You know Paulie. He's harmless. A stoner, sure, but a pussycat. He swerves to avoid hitting squirrels. He wouldn't kill an old lady."

"I have to ask questions, Chad."

The young contractor seemed to think of something. "But, you know . . ."

Richard looked over at him. "What is it, Chad?"

"Have you spoken with Annabel?"

The chief nodded. "Yes, she's given a statement."

"Did she tell you what the old man told us?"

"What old man?"

"Zeke. The caretaker."

Richard's ears perked up. Chad didn't yet know that Zeke was missing as well. "No," he said. "What did Zeke tell you?"

"He told Paulie and me that Mrs. Devlin would pay us double of whatever we quoted Annabel to *not* to do any work on the house."

Richard raised his eyebrows. "No kidding. Why would she do that?"

"Beats me. And I told Annabel about it. Boy, was she pissed. That's why she had Paulie start the work today. She said she wanted the old lady to come down the stairs and see the work being started."

"Really now?"

"Yup. Crazy."

"So, what you're telling me is, Annabel Wish was very angry at her grandmother-in-law this morning."

Chad seemed to be uncomfortable with the implication Richard was making, but he couldn't deny the truth. "Yeah," he said. "She was angry."

The chief looked back at the house.

Now he didn't have just three suspects anymore.

He had four.

45

Jack sat at the kitchen table, blinking frequently, unable to fully comprehend what had happened here this morning.

"Gran," he kept saying. "Gone. And I slept right through it."

"Jack," Annabel said, pouring him more coffee, "there was nothing you could have done. She fell and hit her head. She didn't suffer long."

His eyes shot up at her. "The police chief seems to think there might have been more to it than that."

"Yes," Neville said, sitting across from him, "he was questioning all of us as if we'd killed her." He paused. "Or rather, as if Priscilla had killed her, and taken off."

"That's crazy," Annabel said. "Why would Priscilla kill Cordelia?"

Neville fixed her with his eyes. "It does seem crazy. But then where is Priscilla? She's nowhere in the house!"

"Her coat is still hanging in the foyer, and it's too cold to go outside without it." Annabel turned to Jack. "Where is the key to the attic?"

Her husband looked at her without comprehension. "The attic?"

"It's the only place I wasn't able to check. It's locked." She met Jack's eyes and held them. "Did you and Priscilla go up there last night?"

"Me . . . and Priscilla?" he asked.

Neville stood. "Yes," he said. "Come on, man. This is no time for games. Whatever happened last night happened. For now, who cares? Just tell us what you know about Priscilla!"

"Indeed," came another voice. "I'd like to know that, too."

They all looked up. Chief Richard Carlson had just walked into the kitchen.

"I let myself back in through the front door," he said. His deputy was behind him, and behind him was Chad Appleby. "I'd like your permission to search the house," the chief said. "I'd like to see if we can find some clue to the three missing persons."

Jack, still sitting at the table, glowered.

"Do you have a search warrant?" he asked.

"Jack!" Annabel was horrified. "We have nothing to hide! If they can find something to explain where Priscilla and Paulie and Zeke went, then let them search!"

"I'd have to add my encouragement to that as well," Neville said. "It seems highly unlikely right now, but if they can find Priscilla up in that attic, she and I might still make a plane bound for the sunny skies of Florida later this afternoon."

Jack just shrugged. "Sure, go ahead. Search the place."

Richard Carlson stood looking at him. "When I came in, you were being asked what you knew about Priscilla Morton. Is there anything you can tell us?"

Jack covered his face with his hands. "Why is everyone badgering me? My head is killing me!"

"Mr. Devlin," the chief said, "we are just trying to understand what happened here this morning, and to locate three missing people."

Jack stood. His hands were running through his hair. "Okay, so maybe Priscilla and I had a little too much to drink last night. That's not a crime, is it?"

"No, it's not," the chief assured him.

"But then she went one way and I went another," Jack said, not looking at any of them. Instead, he stood at the back door, gazing out into the woods.

"You didn't take her up to the attic?" the chief asked.

Jack spun around, his face furious. "I don't even know how to unlock the goddamn attic door!"

"Zeke usually carries the keys," Annabel said. "But it's the one place I was unable to check this morning."

"We've got to get in there," Neville said. "Maybe Priscilla is in there."

"And Paulie, too," Chad Appleby said from behind the chief.

"We might have to break the door in," the chief told Annabel.

She nodded.

"Go right the fuck ahead!" Jack shouted, turning around to look out the back door again.

"All right, let's go," Chief Carlson said, and the five of them, minus Jack, made their way across the parlor toward the steps to the attic.

No one thought to examine the fireplace further, or to look down its ash dump.

46

Richard found everyone in this whole house suspicious.

As they climbed the steep narrow stairs to the attic, all sorts of thoughts were running through the chief's mind.

Jack Devlin was sure acting questionably. He seemed to know more than he was telling about the missing Priscilla Morton. And it appeared that both his wife and Priscilla's boyfriend suspected something had happened between the two of them the night before.

But that meant that both Annabel and Neville might be suspects as well. They would both have had a motive for doing harm to Priscilla, if indeed they had discovered she'd been fooling around with Jack.

Just why they would have followed that with an attack on the old woman, however, did not make any sense.

And where the hapless Paulie Stueckel fit into all of this, Richard as yet had no idea.

But he did know that Annabel had been very angry

at both Cordelia and Zeke. Had she killed both of them, but only had time to hide Zeke's body?

If that was the case, her enthusiasm for searching the house didn't make any sense at all.

The chief had to admit he was stumped.

He reached the attic door and gripped hold of the knob. It was locked, all right.

"Adam," he said to his deputy. "Give me a hand."

The two policemen pressed their shoulders up against the door.

"Stand back," Richard shouted down to the others on the steps behind him. He turned to Adam. "Okay, on the count of three."

Adam nodded.

"One, two, three!"

They both rammed their shoulders against the door. It rattled but did not pop open. Strange, for such fragile old wood.

"Again!" Richard shouted.

They positioned their shoulders once more.

"One, two—"

But just at that moment, the door opened. And there, standing in the doorway, grinning up at them, was Zeke.

47

"What's going on here?" the old man asked.

Annabel pushed forward on the stairs. "Zeke! Where have you been? We've been looking all over!"

The wizened little caretaker shrugged. "There was all that noise coming from the parlor and I couldn't sleep." His eyes twinkled as he looked around at all of them. "I often come up here when I need some quiet for my nap."

Stepping out of the room, he closed the door carefully behind him.

"Now," Zeke asked, "what are all these people doing here?"

Chief Carlson looked at him intently. "We're trying to find out what happened here this morning," he said, "and locate a couple of people. We thought maybe they might be in the attic. We've checked everywhere else."

Zeke looked from him over to Annabel. "Seems a lot has happened since I went in to take a nap," he said.

"Zeke, Cordelia's dead," Annabel told him.

She watched his reaction. He placed a hand over his chest and declared, "It can't be!"

Quickly, Annabel detailed how the old woman had been found. Zeke kept shaking his head in surprise and grief, but Annabel didn't believe him. She thought he'd already known that Cordelia was dead before he went into that attic.

"But that's not all," Chief Carlson added. "A guest in this house and a young man doing work down in the parlor can't be found. I'd like to go up into the attic and look around."

"Oh," Zeke said, "I was just up there. I can assure you no one is there. It's just an empty, dusty, old attic."

"Still, I'd like to see for myself," the chief said.

Annabel watched Zeke. She saw the unease in his old yellow eyes.

"Well," the caretaker said finally. "If you insist."

He turned around, opened the door, and led the group inside.

"Maybe the rest of you should stay back," Carlson said, turning around to the others.

"No way," Annabel told him. "This is my house now. I'd like to see what's in here."

The chief shrugged his consent.

Annabel followed him into the dark, musty space. The deputy was close at her heels, and Neville came last. The room was fit into the point of the roof, so that it was impossible to walk up straight except in the very center. Moving off to the far ends of the room necessitated lowering one's head as the slant of the roof decreased. The place stunk of mold and something else—sweat, Annabel thought. There was only one dim, unshaded lightbulb hanging from the ceiling, which cast a pale amber light over the room. Annabel scanned the darkness, allowing her eyes to adjust.

The first thing she discerned was a small cot tucked into the far corner. Everywhere there were boxes and chests. An old dressmaker's dummy gave her small fright when she looked at it, thinking it for a second to be a person. And then her eyes alit on something very strange. A small, cracked toilet in plain view.

She looked over at Chief Carlson. She saw that he was taking it all in as well.

"My little hideaway," Zeke told them. "Sometimes, when all our guest rooms are booked, I'll give up my own room and come up here to sleep. Or when there's too much noise downstairs, I'll retreat up here to nap."

The chief and deputy were looking around the place, lifting boxes, moving crates. It was clear that there was nowhere to hide, and that no one was up here.

So where were Priscilla and Paulie?

If Zeke was telling the truth, and he'd retreated up here to nap after confronting Chad and Paulie in the driveway, then he wouldn't have seen anything. But why did Annabel feel certain he wasn't surprised when she told him about Cordelia's death?

From the way Chief Carlson was looking at Zeke, it seemed he shared Annabel's suspicions.

"All right," Carlson said. "I'm going to have my men search the woods surrounding the house for any signs of Paulie and Ms. Morton."

"I'll help," Chad volunteered.

"So will I," Neville echoed.

"As will I," Zeke added.

"Just a moment," Annabel interjected. "I think Zeke needs to explain why he accosted Chad and Paulie in the driveway and tried to bribe them into not taking the renovation job."

"Ms. Wish," the chief said, "I'll question Zeke on my own about that."

"Well, I have nothing to hide," the old man added. "Cordelia is—was, I mean—very sentimentally attached to this house. She felt very strongly that it shouldn't be changed and butchered up."

"But she asked Mr. Devlin and Ms. Wish to come up from New York and take the place over," Carlson said, eyeing him. "Wouldn't she have expected them to make some changes?"

"She felt they were moving too fast," Zeke said simply.

"You and I will talk more about that," the chief said. "For now, it could very well be that Mrs. Devlin's death was a tragic accident and that Paulie and Ms. Morton had nothing to do with it, and that their disappearances have a logical explanation."

"Maybe they're off in the woods enjoying a little romp," Zeke offered.

"It's twenty-one degrees outside," the chief said. "And Ms. Morton's coat is still on the hook."

The old caretaker just shrugged.

"Come on," Carlson said to Deputy Burrell. "Call into the station and get a couple of other men down here. We'll divide up the woods."

The men began trooping back down the stairs. Annabel hung back, so she could say something in private to Zeke.

"Are you telling everything you know?" she whispered.

"Honest to goodness, Miz Wish."

She held his eyes for a long time. Then she, too, made her way back down the stairs.

48

Neville's mind was racing.

As he clomped across the frozen earth, brittle twigs snapping under his feet, he struggled to make sense of how much everything had changed in the course of just a few hours. Yesterday he'd been thrilled that they'd soon be on their way to Florida. He'd only made this pit stop because Priscilla had wanted to see some ghosts. She had, and she was happy and satisfied, and Neville looked forward to a good, relaxing, fun time in Disney World, riding Space Mountain, and lying around the pool.

Now Priscilla was gone, and no one knew where she was.

Some worker was gone, too.

Had they run off together?

It was possible. After watching Priscilla flirt with Jack last night, Neville supposed it was possible that Priscilla was bored with him and might take up with another man she deemed more exciting. Ever since they'd started dating, Neville had known Priscilla was out of his league. She was far too pretty for a plain, acne-scarred guy with a gut who was nearly ten years older than she was. It had been three years, but Neville had fully expected Priscilla to throw him over for some hotter guy at some point.

That she had not done so, Neville figured, had less to do with any feelings she had for him than for the simple reason that she just simply couldn't be bothered. Priscilla was never man-hungry. She didn't really like sex all that much—which was a shame, Neville thought, with that killer body of hers. Priscilla would have much rather been out kayaking, or bird-watching, or hunting for her stupid ghosts. Neville had a feeling that she stayed with him only because he grudgingly went along with her quirky interests, not because she much cared about him, or the whole concept of having a boyfriend.

But maybe there were times she longed for something more. Maybe she secretly ached for a big, strong, virile man to come after her—which hardly described Neville. But it did describe Jack Devlin, and maybe he had awoken a passion in Priscilla that she herself had never known was there.

Only one thing didn't fit. She hadn't disappeared with Jack.

Jack was very much in evidence. He insisted that they'd gone their separate ways after doing whatever they did last night.

The person who'd gone missing with Priscilla was a mason, this Paulie Stueckel guy, who, from the descriptions Neville had heard, was hardly what one would call virile. He was pudgy and kind of goofy-looking, and perennially stoned on pot.

That didn't sound like the sort of man who could turn Priscilla's head. Still, both of them were missing.

But the man's truck was still there. If Priscilla had left with him, they'd gone by foot, or somebody else—a taxi?—had picked them up. But why wouldn't she have taken her coat? Her wallet? Her money? Her passport?

It was all very strange.

Looking behind bushes and clumps of cold, hard, bare trees, Neville had a sense that something terrible had happened. Priscilla wasn't going to be found. At least, she wasn't going to be found alive.

He dreaded calling her mum and dad. They'd never liked Neville all that much. Thought he was too old, and not good looking enough, for their daughter. They'd sneered at the idea of this holiday to America.

Suddenly, his thoughts were shattered by the sound of voices up ahead.

It was Deputy Burrell. He was calling to the chief.

"Come here! Quick! I've found something!"

Neville ran.

49

Richard Carlson knew what he was looking at the moment he peered down into the box of firewood on the side of the house.

The gray, splotchy thing lying on top of the wood that looked like a deflated balloon was in fact Roger Askew's right hand.

"Call forensics back here," Richard shouted over at Adam. The deputy immediately began pressing keys on his phone.

Staring down at the hand in the wood box, Richard considered the fact that Roger's entire arm, not just his hand, had been hacked off. So if this was indeed Roger's hand, someone had also taken the trouble, at some unknown point, to sever the arm at the wrist.

Richard didn't know for sure that this was Roger's hand. But it likely wasn't from one of the two missing people. The thing in front of him was a few days old, and starting to decay. Richard's gut told him that this was Roger's hand, and that he'd been right to wonder if Roger's death was somehow connected to the cold murder cases at the Blue Boy Inn.

Annabel came around the corner and peered down inside the wood box. She let out a gasp and covered her face with her hands.

It was that little gesture that told Richard that Annabel was guiltless in all this. She was genuinely horrified. Sometimes Richard experienced what he called "psychic moments," in which he seemed to get a direct line into people's thoughts. He figured lots of cops would know what he was talking about, the moment it becomes obvious some witness is either innocent or guilty. His training as a police officer had left him sensitive to the slightest tic in a person's expression, or a gesture of their hands, or the way they said a word. Sometimes he couldn't put his finger on exactly what had swayed him one way or another. It was just as if, in that moment, he saw inside their heart and knew their truth.

Of course, he'd never base an arrest or an acquittal on such intuition. He would continue to gather hard, direct evidence before making any kind of final decision. But he'd never known his gut to be wrong when he experienced one of his "psychic moments." And what his gut was telling him right now was that Annabel Wish had nothing to do with Cordelia Devlin's death and knew nothing about the locations of Paulie Stueckel and Priscilla Morton.

She was looking up at him, distress and revulsion and despair written on her face.

"This will just bring all the stories about murder and death back to the Blue Boy," she said, near tears. "We were trying so hard to put all that behind us. . . ."

"I'm sorry, Ms. Wish."

She looked in again at the hand and shuddered. "Whose hand is it?"

"I . . . I don't know." Richard closed the lid of the wood box until the county forensics team could get there. "But I think it's safe to say it's neither of our missing persons."

Neville had arrived and seen the hand for himself. "Well, thank God for that," he said.

"Find anything else in the woods?" Richard asked the Englishman.

Neville shook his head. "Not a thing." He furrowed his brow as he looked at the police chief. "I don't have a good feeling about any of this."

Richard didn't reply. But he didn't, either.

In fact, he had a very bad feeling. A very bad feeling indeed.

50

"Mr. Jack?"

The new master of the house was standing at the window, looking out at the people gathered around the wood box. He barely lifted an eyebrow as Zeke approached him.

"Mr. Jack, may I speak with you a moment?" the caretaker asked.

Jack turned around to look at him. Zeke watched him carefully. Jack seemed distracted, angry. Of course, that might have been grief. His grandmother had just died. But it seemed to Zeke to be something more, too.

"What is it?" Jack asked, his voice cold and hard and small.

Zeke steadied himself. He had long anticipated that this conversation would be led by Cordelia, that it would have been Cordelia to tell Jack what he needed to know. But now Cordelia was gone. Zeke was on his own.

"Now that you're in charge here," the caretaker began, "now that the house belongs to you . . ."

He stopped. He couldn't go on speaking.

"Out with it, you old fool," Jack said impatiently. It was almost as if Cordelia was now inhabiting her grandson's body.

"I've lived here a long time," Zeke said. "I've seen many things—"

"I expect you have," Jack said, cutting him off. "And I expect that you will assist my wife in everything she wants to do to fix this place up. Do you understand?"

"But that's what I need to talk to you about, Mr. Jack. . . ."

Jack pushed past him and headed into the parlor. "There's nothing to talk about! I want this place to be a destination that people seek out from all over the world! Do you understand, Zeke? I want to be a success!"

He jabbed a finger against the old man's chest, his eyes wide and wild.

"But you will be, Mr. Jack," Zeke said. "I'm sure of it."

Jack looked away from him. His gaze fell onto the fireplace with all the bricks piled around it.

"You've just got to hear what I have to tell you," Zeke went on. "There's things you need to understand. Things you need to do. Your grandmother was going to explain them all to you, but now it's up to me."

Jack turned back to look at him. He was scowling.

"What are you talking about?" he asked.

"After everybody is gone from outside, after you and I are all alone, there are things I need to show you, Mr. Jack."

"What kinds of things?"

"I can't show you now, not with people still in and out of the house. But you need to know, Mr. Jack."

Jack looked at him suspiciously. "Why the great mystery, Zeke?"

"For now, please, just trust me." He drew closer to Jack. "Help me put the bricks back into the fireplace."

Jack grimaced. "You mean seal it back up?"

Zeke nodded.

"But why? Didn't you hear what I said, Zeke? I want my wife's renovations to go forward. I want this place to become a popular resort." He leaned down close to Zeke so as to make himself clear. "I want to make a lot of money," Jack enunciated.

"That's good, but we need to brick up the fireplace. . . ."

Jack laughed at him. "My grandmother is dead! I don't have to worry about her foolish sentiment anymore! We need a fireplace, Zeke! This is a goddamn New England bed-and-breakfast! Guests expect fireplaces!"

"But, Mr. Jack, you've got to listen to me!"

Just then, Zeke heard the back door open and the sound of people coming inside the house. Chief Carlson was speaking with Annabel.

"Please, Mr. Jack," Zeke whispered, "will you let me speak with you privately later?"

Jack glared at him. "Yes," he said finally. "All right. But don't you dare touch those bricks in the meantime."

He strode off toward the kitchen.

Zeke turned around and looked at the fireplace.

He heard the scurrying down below.

51

That night, Annabel slipped under the sheets beside Jack. What a terrible day it had been. They hadn't had much time to talk about anything with the cops and the forensics team in and out of the house. Neville had decided he couldn't leave without knowing what had happened to Priscilla, so he was staying on at the house. Around five o'clock, Paulie's brother had arrived with spare keys to Paulie's truck and drove it off the property, but not before insisting he look around the house himself for any clue as to what had happened to his brother. And Richard Carlson had been there until the sun went down, scouring the place with his eyes, seeming to commit every inch of the house to memory.

Annabel just wanted the day to be over, hoping that when she woke up the next morning she'd realize it had all been a bad dream.

Jack lay there beside her, eyes open, just staring up at the ceiling.

"Oh, Jack," Annabel said. "I worry now that the

Blue Boy will never shake its reputation of being cursed and haunted."

"Don't you worry, sugar babe," her husband told her, still staring at the ceiling. "We are going to do just fine."

"What were you and Zeke talking about earlier? After the chief finally left?"

Jack didn't take his eyes off the ceiling. "Just a few things that needed to be done around the house."

"You seemed to be very intent. And when I came in, you both stopped speaking." She pulled closer to Jack. "Is there anything going on that I need to know?"

He turned his eyes abruptly to meet hers.

"No," he said. "Nothing you need to know."

"I feel so badly about Neville," Annabel said. "Not knowing about Priscilla, whether he should stay here or go back home. . . ."

"He's paying for his extra night here, isn't he?"

Annabel spun on her husband. "Jack! How unfeeling of you! Of course, he's not paying. He offered, but I said he could stay here as our guest."

Jack grunted.

Annabel settled back against her pillows. "I know it was uncomfortable when the police chief kept asking you about Priscilla," she said. "But that was just his job. He had to ask those questions. Now hopefully he can find out what happened and we can move forward."

"You'll keep going on with the renovations?" Jack asked.

Annabel looked over at him. "Do you think I should?"

"Yes." He smiled at her. "In fact, I'm going to help finish the fireplace myself."

She returned his smile.

"Where do you think they went?" Annabel asked him.

"Who?"

"What do you mean, who? Priscilla and Paulie."

Jack shrugged. "They ran off together. She was kind of trampy, wasn't she?"

Annabel frowned. "Not at all. How can you say that?" She thought Jack was being awfully cavalier and insensitive.

"Besides," she said, "Paulie's truck was still in the driveway . . . and Priscilla left her things. . . . Jack, something bad happened here today. The chief speculated that whoever killed Roger Askew may have come by here, disposed of the hand, and then taken Paulie and Priscilla away, maybe at gunpoint or something."

"So he was certain that the hand in the wood box was this guy Askew's?"

"Yes," Annabel replied. "There was a tattoo or something that clinched it."

"Well," Jack said. "It's as good a theory as any."

Annabel shuddered. "If I hadn't run to the market at that particular moment, he might have taken me, too."

Jack reached over and stroked her hair. "It's okay, baby," he said.

"But Jack," Annabel went on, "I worry about the publicity. I mean, with everything . . . the hand in the wood box, Cordelia's death, the missing people . . . We'll never break free of the macabre reputation the Blue Boy has had for so long."

"Well, I wouldn't worry your sweet little head about it, angel baby," Jack said, rolling over toward Annabel. "We are going to be a huge success. Trust me."

"I hope you're right."

"I know I'm right."

He began to kiss her. Annabel tensed. She didn't feel like making love. Not after everything that had happened today.

But unlike last time, Jack was rock hard.

She couldn't stop him. She felt him grab hold of her pajamas and yank them down. He mounted her, and without any foreplay at all, he clamped his lips onto hers and entered her, roughly and abruptly. Annabel shuddered. She surmised that Jack was acting as quickly as he could, before he went limp again like last time. He thrust into her four or five times, then reached orgasm. He withdrew and rolled over onto his back again, breathing heavily.

Annabel just lay there. She felt dirty and violated. Their sex life hadn't been good in some time, but it had never been like that, so quick and so rough. Soon Jack's breathing turned into snores. Annabel slipped out of bed and took a long, hot shower.

More than ever, she wanted to run. Run as fast as she could and as far as she could, far, far away from this strange old house and these dark, cold woods, until she was safely back among the skyscrapers, bright lights, and taxicabs of New York.

52

"Thanks very much," Neville said, accepting the mug of coffee and gratefully bringing it to his lips.

The morning sun was streaming into the kitchen. The Englishman watched as Annabel sat opposite him. Neither had said more than a few words since getting up. Neville had been unable to sleep much. He'd tossed and turned all night, and one glance in the mirror had shown him just how tired he looked.

"What will you do?" Annabel asked. "I mean, how long will you wait?"

"Well, the chief wants me to stick around for a while. He said he might have to ask me more questions." Neville grinned sheepishly. "I guess I'm a suspect."

"We all are," Annabel said, "but there's no evidence any crime was committed."

Neville sighed. "Well, I'm not scheduled to fly back home to England for another week, but Florida is certainly no longer in the game plan. I'll stay here a few more days, if that's okay. I'll be glad to pay for my room—"

"No," Annabel said. "I wouldn't hear of it."

"Please, I can't stay for free."

Annabel shook her head. "After all we've been through, I insist you stay as our guest."

"You're very kind," Neville told her.

They exchanged small smiles.

"It must be so hard for you," Annabel said after a pause. "Worrying about Priscilla. We've got to just continue to hope that she's okay."

Neville frowned. "I suppose that's the way to look at it, but I must be honest and tell you, I think she's gone for good. Whatever madman stabbed that man on the trail in the woods has taken her, as well as that man who was here working on the fireplace. And given how he butchered his first victim in the woods, I don't suspect he's going to go any easier on these two."

"But if he *has* taken them, as the chief suggests," Annabel said, "then maybe he's using them as hostages. Maybe he'll release them unharmed. This Roger Askew was occasionally a drug dealer. It was probably a revenge killing, and the murderer will try to use his hostages to negotiate with police. We've got to keep believing that Priscilla and Paulie will be returned safe and unharmed."

"I like your optimism," Neville said, taking another sip of his coffee and then setting it down on the table in front of him.

Silence resumed. Nobody had mentioned breakfast.

"Is Jack still sleep—" Neville began to ask, but at the same moment his coffee mug flew off the table, shattering on the floor and spraying the hot brown liquid everywhere.

"Oh!" Annabel exclaimed.

Neville jumped up. "Dear Lord, did I do that?" he asked, flustered and surprised. "My arm wasn't anywhere near it, I swear! It just fell off on its own!"

"It doesn't matter," Annabel said. She had sprung to her feet and grabbed a dish towel and was now soaking up the spilled coffee. "We're all jittery this morning."

Neville was squatting down beside her, collecting the shards of pottery from his mug. "But, really, I didn't do it. It was the strangest sensation. It almost seemed as if a child ran by and knocked the mug from the table. A child—a little person."

Annabel stopped what she was doing and looked over at Neville. Their eyes met just a few inches apart.

"A little person? What do you mean? Did you see something?"

Neville stood, carrying the shards over to the trash and dropping them inside. "No, not really. It was just how you sometimes have a sense—see something very briefly in your peripheral vision, maybe, and you get a sense of something. It felt like someone ran by the table and knocked the coffee to the floor deliberately. Someone small."

Annabel stood, dropping the coffee-soaked dish towel into the sink. She seemed struck mute by what Neville was saying.

He tried to smile. "Well, don't I sound like a lunatic. I suppose you're right. We're just jittery. I'm sure I did it myself, and I apologize."

"No need . . . to apologize," said Annabel, though she continued to seem very distracted.

Neville watched her as she walked out of the kitchen toward the parlor. She seemed to be looking for something. He poured himself more coffee into a new mug and sat back down at the table. Annabel returned in a matter of minutes.

"Everything all right?" he asked her.

"Yes. I was just . . . listening for Jack."

"He's still asleep then?"

"No," Annabel told him, sitting back down. "When I awoke, he was already up and getting dressed. He said he was going to work with Zeke this morning repairing some broken eaves in the attic. He said we were losing a lot of heat through there."

"Yes," Neville said. "I think I heard them banging around up there this morning."

"I'm sorry if they disturbed you."

"Not at all." He cupped his mug in his hands, careful to keep it away from the edge of the table. "So no more guests arriving?"

"No," Annabel replied. "There had been a couple scheduled for next week, but I called and canceled, refunding their money. Until all of this is over—in fact, until the renovation is done—I think it's best not to have anyone staying here."

"That's smart," Neville said.

Suddenly he felt compelled to say something.

"You know, I'm not sure why I need to tell you this, but here goes." He paused for just a second. "I don't think I'm in love with Priscilla. I think maybe that's why her behavior toward Jack the other night didn't really bother me."

Annabel lifted her eyebrows. "I see," she said.

"Of course, I want her to be found," Neville went on,

"and to be safe and unharmed and all of that. But I'm not in love with her. If I were, her behavior would have been very troubling to me."

Annabel gave him a tight smile. "I think what you're telling me is that I ought to have found Jack's behavior troubling."

"No, I would never presume to suggest—"

"It's okay," Annabel said. "I did find it troubling. Jack was the aggressor, not Priscilla. But, you know, I'm not nearly as troubled by it as I might have been."

They shared a small smile again.

Neville liked Annabel. He suspected her marriage was not very good. Almost as if he were reading her mind, he saw the Blue Boy Inn as their last, best try to make things work. And now, to be hit with all this . . .

Annabel excused herself. She needed to call Chad Appleby. She was determined to press on with the renovation, and she hoped Chad would be as well.

Neville sat at the table looking across the room, staring out the window into the gray winter day. Where was Priscilla? What had happened to her? Would she come back?

And if she did, would he tell her what he had just told Annabel?

53

"No trace of anyone or anything," Adam told the chief. "We've scoured those woods. Except for Roger's hand in the wood box, there's been no evidence of anything suspicious. Certainly no sign of the two missing persons."

Richard sat back in his chair, propping his feet up on his desk.

"This just doesn't make sense," he told his deputy. "How could whoever killed Roger Askew force his— or her—way into the Blue Boy Inn, take off with two hostages, likely on foot, and not leave a single trace?"

"Are you certain they made off on foot?" Adam asked. "I mean, a car could have pulled in there during the time Ms. Wish was out at the market. . . ."

"Didn't you read the report, Adam?" Richard asked him.

The deputy stiffened. "I glanced at it. I've been out interviewing so many people . . ."

Richard smiled. "It's all right. Well, when you do get around to reading it, you'll see that I interviewed Ted Cassidy, from the Department of Public Works. He was filling in a pothole around the corner from the inn. He saw Annabel go to the market, and he saw her come back. He was certain no other car came by in that time."

"Jeez," Adam said.

"We've searched the house, we've searched the grounds, and nothing," Richard said.

"It just doesn't make sense how three people could disappear so completely."

"And you still think whoever killed Roger also killed the old lady?"

"It's a working theory. Maybe he wanted to hide out at the inn, Cordelia gave him a hard time, and he whacked her over the head."

"But why would they be in her bedroom?" Adam asked.

The chief shook his head. "Good question. That's what I mean. None of this adds up."

"Well, here's another monkey wrench to throw into your theories," said Richard's secretary, Betty, walking into the room and placing a sheet of paper on the chief's desk.

"What's this?" he asked.

"Fax just came in from the county coroner's office," Betty told him.

Richard snatched it up and read it quickly.

"Christ," he grumbled.

"What is it?" Adam asked.

Richard laughed. "The coroner is ruling Cordelia's death an accident. Her head injury is entirely consistent with a fall, during which she struck her head on the iron doorstop."

"So then we don't have a murder investigation," Adam said. "Just a couple of missing persons."

"I don't buy it," Richard said. "The old woman's skull was cracked. She'd have to have come down to the floor at a superhuman rate to hit that doorstop and crack her head that severely."

"Can you contest the finding?" Betty asked.

Richard sighed. "Sure, I can. But it'll take time." He pounded his fist on his desk. "That coroner is old and out of it. This isn't the first ruling of his I've disagreed with. But there's not much I can do at the moment."

He hesitated.

"I'm going to have to tell Neville Clarkson he's free to go back to England." The chief picked up the phone. "If he takes off immediately, that would be a sign he knew more than he was saying. If he sticks around, waiting for news of his girlfriend, then he's innocent of anything. Let's keep close tabs on the place, okay?"

Adam told him he'd visit the Blue Boy twice a day for the next week. The chief gave him the thumbs-up as the phone started to ring at the inn.

54

"Thank you for coming back," Annabel said, greeting Chad Appleby at the door.

The young contractor offered her a small, sad smile as he stepped inside. "I could either listen to the village idiots at Deb's Diner bleating about the curse of the Blue Boy, or I could say, hey, I've got a job to do," Chad told her. "And if I didn't come back here, I'd be forever branded a chicken all around town."

"I'm sorry to have put you in this position," Annabel said.

"It's okay," Chad told her.

Annabel looked genuinely unhappy that her inn had such a sordid reputation. "You do know that the chief called yesterday and told us that the coroner had ruled Cordelia's death to be an accident, don't you?"

Chad nodded. "Seems a strange coincidence, though, given Roger Askew's hand being found out back and Paulie and your guest disappearing at the exact same time."

"I know," Annabel said, "but we have to believe it. Who knows? Maybe Cordelia saw something from her window, and in her hurry to call the police, she tripped and fell. That's what Chief Carlson suggested as a possibility."

Chad shrugged. "I guess it *is* a possibility."

Annabel smiled. "Yes," she said, "it is."

"Well, let's move on," Chad said. "Like I said, I have a job that I was hired to do. And we were planning to start in the parlor, right?"

"Yes," Annabel said, leading him inside. They stood in the center of the room. The bricks Paulie had removed from the fireplace were still piled off to the side. "Tell me what I need to do to prepare for you to start."

"Well, we'll have to move all this furniture out of here."

"I can do that. Jack will help me put it in the basement."

"Then you and I need to pick out some tiles, and some paint. You said you want that wall knocked down there, correct?"

Annabel was nodding. "That's right. It will open the room up into the dining room. Make the flow a lot smoother."

Chad walked over and knocked on the wall. "That should be easy enough. But that's the only structural change you want, right?"

"Right. Well, except for the windows."

He walked over to the windows and inspected the wood. "That's not really structural, though you do want to make them a little bit bigger."

"Yes, to bring in more sun."

"We can do that." He peeled off a piece of wood that was flaking off the sill. "Okay, so new windows, the wall removed, and we'll sand the floor and the moldings . . . really restore everything."

"And the fireplace," Annabel added. "We'll need to finish it."

Chad was nodding. He approached the fireplace and looked down. "Paulie said the chimney was sound. I can finish removing any last bricks that are needed, then we can paint the rest white, as you suggested."

"I think that will brighten up the room," Annabel said.

"You might want to clean out the ash dump down in the basement," Chad told her. "There should be a door on the chimney underneath the fireplace. You can hire a chimney sweep, or maybe just have your caretaker do it, if he's familiar with it."

"I'll ask him," Annabel said.

Chad smiled at her. He liked Annabel. He felt sorry for her, too, trying to get this place in shape, battling its reputation and now confronted by the inn's latest streak of bad luck. He didn't blame her for whatever happened to Paulie. Chad still hoped his friend would turn up alive, but he didn't have a good feeling about it.

"I can start the actual work in a couple of days," Chad told Annabel. "But I'll be back tomorrow to take measurements. Maybe later in the week we can take a drive up to Great Barrington to pick out some tiles and paint."

"That sounds like fun," Annabel replied. "I'd like nothing more than to take a drive out of town."

Chad smiled. "Then it's a plan." He shook her hand. "I'll be here tomorrow afternoon with my measuring tape."

"Thank you for sticking with the project," Annabel said.

"Don't mention it," Chad told her, as she escorted him back to the door.

55

Annabel watched from the window as Chad drove away. She was glad he'd be coming back. If he had backed out of the renovation, Annabel would have been devastated. The renovation was her reason for staying here.

It certainly wasn't Jack.

If Chad had not agreed to continue fixing up the place, Annabel really thought she would have called a taxi to take her to the nearest bus terminal and returned to New York. She had no idea where she would have stayed in the city, but she would have had found something. If it had meant continuing to live in this stark, musty house without any hope for change, Annabel would have bolted.

Because she had never felt so alone. Not even during those harrowing days in rehab, when at least she'd had doctors and therapists rooting for her, surrounding her with support.

Here, she felt increasingly she was on her own.

Jack had been distant and strange these past two days. Thankfully, he hadn't tried to force himself on her again. Annabel would have kneed him in the groin if he did that again. In fact, when they slept, they stayed to their own sides of the bed. That was fine with Annabel.

She tried to keep hope alive, however. This was just a bad stretch. They could either give in to the tragedy of Priscilla and Paulie's disappearance, or they could move forward. Richard Carlson had been by and told her that he was having his deputy come by at least twice a day, just to make sure the kidnapper had not returned, and that made Annabel breathe easier. She liked seeing the police car come up the driveway in the mornings and the afternoons, and Officer Burrell get out and look around. She knew that a patrol car came by at night, too.

They could get through this. And she hoped that as the house started taking shape, Jack would start acting more normal again. This was a stress on all of them. If they could survive this, they could survive anything.

Annabel was pleased that Neville had stuck around. His warm, calm presence made things easier. Annabel could talk to him in ways she couldn't talk to Jack at the moment. In fact, she could talk to Neville in ways she'd never been able to talk to Jack. She knew he'd be returning to England soon; the chief had said he was free to go. But he said he didn't feel right leaving without knowing anything about Priscilla. He told Annabel he'd wait until at least the week was out. And she was glad about that.

At the moment, Neville was out, taking a ride to clear his head. Annabel wished she'd been able to go with him, but she'd had to wait for Chad.

And Chad had asked her to have the ash dump

cleaned. Zeke must know how to do it. He'd lived in the house so long.

But Zeke was upstairs again, working with Jack in the attic. Annabel would go up and ask him, and take a look around at the work they'd done.

One by one, she climbed the steep, narrow steps to the attic.

At the door at the top of the stairs, she turned the knob. But just like the other day, the door was locked.

She could hear them inside, muffled voices and the occasional pounding of a hammer.

Annabel rapped on the door. "Jack! Zeke!" she called.

No answer.

She knocked harder. "Jack! Why is the door locked?"

The muffled voices inside fell silent.

Annabel knocked again. "Jack! Zeke!"

The door suddenly opened without warning, with Annabel's hand still poised in the air. She gasped a little in surprise.

Her husband glared at her.

"We're in the middle of patching the roof," he grumbled.

"Why was the door locked?"

"For your own safety," Jack told her. "We've had to tear up some of the floorboards. You could have tripped."

"Okay," Annabel said, miffed at his tone of voice. "Sorry to have bothered you."

"What did you want?"

She was already turning to leave, heading back down the stairs. "Never mind," she said.

Jack grabbed her by the shoulder. "Wait, honey babe," he said, stepping out of the attic room and closing the door behind him. "I didn't mean to be gruff. I just had to get down from a ladder. I'm sorry."

"It's okay," Annabel said, extricating herself from his grip and continuing down the stairs.

"Did Chad come by?" Jack asked.

"Yes. He'll get started on the renovation the day after tomorrow."

"Great," Jack said. "I'll be down shortly."

"Okay," Annabel said.

She didn't turn around. She heard him go back inside the attic and shut the door. And then she heard the faint click of the lock being slid back into place.

He's different, she thought. *Ever since the night when he came on to Priscilla . . . and even more since his grandmother died. . . .*

Annabel recalled Neville's admission that he wasn't in love with Priscilla.

Was she in love with Jack?

She wasn't sure. She thought her feelings for him might return—she *hoped* they would—but at the moment, she was just not sure how she felt about her husband. All that she could detect was numbness when she thought of him.

Once again, Annabel felt like running.

She wanted to run out the front door and down the driveway and down the road to Millie's store. She'd call the taxi from there. She just needed to get out of this dark, stuffy house. She felt closed in. She felt as if she couldn't breathe. She was trapped. She couldn't get out! She would die in here!

Annabel gripped the post at the bottom of the stairs.

"Stop it," she scolded herself.

As Dr. Adler, her therapist, had trained her to do, she took three long breaths, feeling the air as it filled up her lungs, then as it flowed back out through her nostrils.

"I'm going to turn this house into a showcase," she said out loud.

She didn't need Zeke. She could clean out the ash dump herself.

Annabel made her way around to the stairs that led down into the basement. Since moving in, she'd managed to avoid the place pretty much. She and Chad and Paulie had taken one quick peek the other day, but Annabel had let them go ahead of her, and she hadn't stayed long, leaving them to do their inspection. The basement was dark and cobwebby and the ceiling was very low. It smelled of dank earth and mold and mice. For someone with claustrophobia, the Blue Boy's cramped basement was a place to be avoided at all costs. But Annabel pushed on. She was determined to ignore her fears.

Reaching the bottom of the stairs, she moved her hand upward, feeling around in the darkness above her for the string that hung from the light. Her fingers brushed through sticky cobwebs and she recoiled. When she found the string, she pulled hard, and suddenly the dark basement was illuminated by a pale white light.

Unlike the attic, which was littered with junk, the basement was mostly empty. Letting her eyes adjust, Annabel glanced around to find the base of the chimney.

It stood some feet away, directly underneath the fireplace in the parlor. The chimney base squatted in the middle of the room, looking like an old man hunched over under a blanket of old bricks. Annabel approached. A black iron door, about two feet by three feet and even with Annabel's waist, had been cut into the brick. As she got closer, Annabel noticed an old, rusted padlock had been secured onto the door.

She lifted the padlock in her hands. It was an old thing, but it still held the door shut. A key was needed to unlock it.

Why on earth would someone padlock the door of a fireplace ash dump?

Annabel tugged at the lock. As old and rusted as it was, it still wasn't going to budge. She'd have to ask Zeke for the key. Until they had cleaned out God-only-knew how many decades of ashes that had collected inside, they wouldn't be able to get the fireplace blazing again. And Annabel felt that until the fireplace was crackling with wood, she wouldn't be able to call the Blue Boy her home.

Her eyes glanced up the length of the chimney that protruded through the floor above. There, on a small nail blasted into the mortar, hung a key.

It had to be the key for the padlock. But it was out of reach. Why was it hung so high? She really wanted to get a look inside the ash dump to see how much work cleaning it out would entail. If it was packed with ash and debris, she might have to call someone to clean it for her. But if there wasn't so much, she could maybe brush it out herself, into a pail, and dump it in the woods.

But that damn key was so high that not even Jack, who was six feet tall, could have reached it easily.

Annabel looked around the basement for something to stand on. Her eyes fell on an old wooden chest, one of the few items in the vast dark space. She hurried over to it, grabbed ahold of its sides, and pulled it back toward the chimney. The chest was surprisingly light. When she'd gotten it to where she wanted it, she decided to peek inside.

She discovered moth-eaten little girl's clothes and a couple of moldy plastic dolls.

These must have been Cynthia's, Annabel thought, her heart breaking for Jack's little sister who'd been killed by some wild animal, her body never found.

Carefully replacing the clothes and the dolls, Annabel set the lid back down on the chest. Now she needed something else. A rusted old rake, leaning against the wall, would do the trick. Holding the rake in one hand, Annabel climbed up on top of the chest. Then she lifted the rake over her head and knocked the key off its nail. It went flying through the air, landing somewhere on the earthen floor in the dark.

"Oh, great," Annabel grumbled, getting down off the chest and dropping to her hands and knees, feeling around for the key.

She found something else instead.

A furry mouse—or maybe a rat—squeaked as Annabel's hand closed around it. She heard it skittle away. She let out a gasp and felt the gooseflesh crawl up her arms. She was about to go upstairs and find a flashlight when, miracle of miracles, her fingers touched metal. It was the key.

Gripping the key tightly in her hands, Annabel stood. She returned to the padlock on the door of the ash dump. Bending down, she inserted the key. It fit perfectly. With a slight turn, the padlock fell open.

Annabel hoped there was enough light. The one bulb

on the ceiling was directly behind her. She thought she'd be able to get a good sense of what was inside.

She opened the door of the ash dump.

And immediately a dark brown liquid dripped off from the inside of the door.

Some kind of oil?

Hunched down, peering through the door, Annabel tried to make out what was inside. She couldn't see much. But it was clear there wasn't a surplus of ashes. What was inside seemed more solid. With great reluctance, Annabel reached her hand inside.

What she felt was soft and pulpy.

She let out another short gasp and withdrew her hand.

It was covered in the same dark liquid that dripped off the door.

With a growing sense of horror, she walked slowly backwards, coming to a stop directly underneath the lightbulb hanging from the ceiling. Stretching her hand up overhead, she brought it as close to the light as possible.

One look told her what was on her hand.

Blood!

Annabel screamed.

56

Neville heard Annabel screaming as he came through the front door. He bolted toward the sound.

"Annabel!" he called. "Are you all right?"

She came bounding up the cellar steps. "Blood!" she shrieked. "Blood!"

And she held up her hand, coated in a thick, purplish goo, for him to see.

"Dear God, are you hurt?" Neville asked.

"The chimney!" Annabel was shuddering. "The chimney!"

She wasn't making any sense.

"I've got to wash this off my hand!" Annabel cried, hurrying toward the kitchen. Neville followed.

Annabel had already plunged her hand under the hot water at the sink by the time Neville made it through the kitchen door.

"Did you cut yourself?" he asked.

"No!" Annabel's eyes were wild. "There's blood in the ash dump! At the base of the chimney!"

She was scrubbing furiously, squeezing gobs of dish detergent all over her hand. The steam that rose from the gushing water from the faucet revealed just how hot it was.

"Careful you don't scald your hand now," Neville told her.

"I don't care," Annabel said, near panic. "I want to get all of that off me!"

Neville heard movement behind him. Jack had come through the kitchen door.

"What's going on?" he asked. "We could hear you shouting all the way in the attic."

"There's blood in the chimney," Annabel told him.

Jack looked at her as if she were crazy.

"Go downstairs to the basement and see for yourself," Annabel said. "I'm never going down there again!"

"Zeke's down there now," Jack told her. "We saw the door was open and the light was on, so he went down there to check."

Something in the way Jack spoke seemed to unnerve Annabel.

"Go down there!" she shouted. "Please, Jack, see for yourself."

He gave her a small smile. "I'm sure Zeke will be able to tell us what it was you thought you saw."

Neville saw the sudden fear in Annabel's eyes. It was a different fear, not the panicky terror that had sent her rushing to the sink to wash her hands. This was very different. She turned her terrified eyes to Neville.

"You go down!" she begged him. "Please! See for yourself."

"You want me to go down to the basement?" Neville asked.

"Yes! There's blood! I think that's where the killer put Priscilla's and Paulie's bodies!"

"Oh, dear God," Neville muttered, horrified now himself, turning and heading out of the kitchen.

But before he could make it through the door, he ran smack-dab into the old caretaker Zeke.

"What's all this shouting for?" Zeke asked.

"Annabel thinks she saw blood in the chimney downstairs," Jack said.

"Blood?" Zeke displayed his hand. "It's just wet soot."

His hand was indeed black with soot. He walked calmly past Annabel over to the sink, where he washed his hands just as she had done, but without any of the mania that had gripped her.

"I saw the door to the ash dump was open, so I closed it," Zeke said.

"There was blood inside!" Annabel insisted.

"Wet soot can look like blood," Zeke told her, not looking around.

"But it was on my hand," Annabel said, lifting her now pristinely clean hand in front of her face. "I know what I saw. . . ."

"Sugar cakes," Jack said, "you know sometimes you see things that aren't there. . . ."

"You saw my hand," Annabel said to Neville. "You saw it was blood!"

"Well, I . . ." Neville tried to think. He'd seen Annabel's hand covered in something. But was it blood, or wet soot as Zeke claimed? "I didn't really get a close look at it. You washed your hands so fast."

"Anyway," Zeke was saying, drying his hands with a

dish towel, "I looked inside and there wasn't much of an ash buildup. I'll clean it out later today so you can continue on with your renovations, Miz Wish."

"No, don't clean it out," Annabel said. "I want the police chief here to inspect the chimney. . . ."

"Sweetheart," Jack said taking her by the shoulders, "you're getting hysterical. You know your doctors told you that you might have flashbacks. . . ."

She shoved him away. "I'm not hysterical!"

But her face, so contorted and upset, made Neville think she might be.

"Annabel," Jack told her firmly, "I think you should go lie down."

She glared at him. She seemed to accept that she was beaten.

"All right," she said, her voice quiet now. "Maybe I will go lie down."

"That's a good girl," her husband said.

He moved over to the refrigerator and popped it open. "Think this bowl of Gran's rabbit stew is still good?" he called over to Zeke.

"Sure it is," the old caretaker said. "I'll heat some for both of us."

As they were distracted by the stew, Annabel turned to leave. Neville watched her with fascination. As she passed him, she paused for just a second, and spoke in a whisper that he could barely make out.

But he heard her.

"Go down there," she said. "Key on a nail up above."

Then she was gone.

Zeke was pouring the stew into a pan on the stove. Jack had settled down at the table, reading a newspaper.

Neville slipped out of the kitchen.

Every nerve in his body trembling, he found the door to the basement steps. He opened it slowly, hoping it didn't creak. Then he scampered down into the darkness. Yanking the string to light the bulb overhead, he saw the base of the chimney. A chest and a rake were positioned in front of it. Right away Neville knew this was how Annabel had gotten the key that was on "a nail up above."

But the door to the ash dump was securely padlocked.

And while Neville could see the nail protruding from the bricks above, there was no key hanging from it.

Somehow that fact confirmed for him that Annabel had been right.

There was indeed blood in that chimney.

Behind that small iron door, Neville was convinced, lay Priscilla's body.

57

"You're really going to keep working at that scary old place?" Tammy asked, sliding Chad's scrambled eggs and home fries in front of him on the diner counter.

"I was hired to do a job," Chad told her, "and I'm gonna do it." He brought a fry to his mouth and took a bite. "My way of paying tribute to Paulie."

"Well, I think that's pretty brave of you," Tammy said. "I feel bad for that couple that just arrived to fix up the place. Now they're forever haunted by Roger's hand." She shuddered.

Chad smiled up at her. "How you doing with that, Tam? You dealing with his death okay?"

"I made a resolution when I got up this morning," the pretty, dark-eyed waitress told him. "I was moving on with my life. I'm going to be just fine on my own."

"Hear, hear!" Chad said.

"I'm going back to school, and I'm going to get a degree," Tammy told him, before smirking. "If I can afford it on my tips from this place."

Chad thought a moment. "You know, if I recall, you

fixed your place up pretty nice. Refinished the floor yourself. Laid down some new tile."

Tammy beamed. "That I did. With good advice from you."

"I could use an assistant like you," Chad told her. "It would mean going out to the Blue Boy Inn, but I could help you make a few extra bucks."

"What would I do?" Tammy asked.

"Help me with painting and sanding, to start," Chad told her, bringing a forkful of eggs to his mouth and afterward wiping his lips with the paper napkin. "Would it creep you out too much, going to a place where Roger's hand was found?"

"Not at all," Tammy answered. "When do I start?"

"Come with me this afternoon when you get off here," he said.

"All right. I'll have my mom pick Jessica up at school and watch her until I get home. She's been after me to get a better job anyway. She'll be happy to do it."

"Then welcome to Appleby Contracting, Ms. Morelli," Chad said, extending his hand across the counter.

They shook.

58

Annabel lay in bed. She hadn't left her bed since coming up here yesterday afternoon, shaken by her discovery of blood in the chimney.

She was certain the blood wasn't there anymore, however.

Zeke had cleaned it out. She knew that in her gut. That was why he'd locked it back up and taken the key, as Neville had reported to her late last night, so he could go back later and clean it all out. He would destroy the evidence of any body ever being stuffed into the chimney.

Since Annabel's cell phone didn't have reception, and she didn't dare use the house phone, Neville had promised that he would drive into town this morning and tell the police chief what Annabel had found.

She realized the significance of the fact that she didn't dare use the house phone.

It was because she was afraid of being overheard.

Jack and Zeke knew something. They were hiding something. Somehow, they were covering up the murders.

Might they—Annabel trembled to think it—have committed them?

She'd thought Jack was sound asleep that morning. But had he snuck out while she was at the store? Zeke had claimed to be in the attic. But he, too, could have come downstairs while Annabel was gone.

But why?

Annabel felt frozen. She lay there immobile on the bed. All night, she had been awake, listening as Jack breathed beside her. When he'd come in the night before, she'd pretended to be asleep. They hadn't spoken a word. All through the night, Annabel had had the sense that Jack, too, was awake, lying beside her, waiting and listening for her to make a move. So Annabel had kept as still as she could, breathing shallowly but regularly, hoping he believed her to be asleep. In the morning, when Jack had finally risen and left the room, Annabel had let out a long, relieved breath.

It was unbelievable.

She was frightened of her husband.

Jack—who had stood with her through all her trials in the past.

Annabel felt as if she was going mad.

She smelled coffee brewing downstairs. She had yet to hear a car crunch across the gravel driveway, so Neville had not yet left for the police station. If he didn't leave soon, she would jump up when she heard Officer Burrell make his daily drive-through checking on the place. She'd scream from the window for him to come in and arrest Jack and Zeke!

But for what?

Maybe she was going mad.

Annabel tried to focus, to make sense of what was

happening. She was fearful that Jack was involved in murder—or that he was covering it up. But such an idea was crazy! She couldn't think straight. Jack and Zeke were hiding something in the attic. That much Annabel knew. And then they had prevented her from exposing the blood in the basement.

Sugar cakes, you know sometimes you see things that aren't there. . . .

Was that it? Was she was just imagining things?

Maybe Jack and Zeke really had been fixing the rafters and the floorboards in the attic. Maybe that really had been wet soot in the chimney.

Annabel heard a sound.

She sat up on her bed. Looking across the room, she watched in disbelief as the panel on the far wall slid back. The same panel where she had found those terrible books. Zeke had never nailed it shut.

From the darkness behind the wall within emerged two little blue feet.

"No," Annabel murmured, pulling her legs under her and wrapping her arms around her body.

Tommy Tricky crept out of the hole in the wall.

He looked up at her, his blue eyes shining.

He gnashed his sharp little teeth.

But then—even worse—his twin emerged from the dark space, following him out into the room.

The two little creatures stood there looking up at Annabel. She was so terrified she couldn't make a sound.

Then they gave a little laugh and dashed across the room, under her bed.

Annabel screamed at the top of her lungs.

Her fear turned everything white. Blindingly white.

The next thing she knew Jack was standing over her, trying to hold her down on the bed, telling her to calm down and stop screaming. Zeke was there, looming over her as well. And Neville, too! They were all in on it! They were all out to get her!

Annabel passed out.

59

Neville left Annabel's room completely mystified. "What happened to her?" he asked Jack and Zeke. "She seemed fine earlier."

"She has a history of hallucinations, of histrionics," Jack said, peering in at her one last time, making sure she was resting comfortably before he shut the door. She had seemed to calm down, but Neville thought she might start thrashing about again anytime, so great had been her distress. "Her doctors told us she could occasionally have relapses," Jack continued, and he looked sincerely worried about his wife.

If that was so, Neville thought, perhaps he'd been wrong to believe Annabel's story about blood in the chimney.

He would wait for a while before talking with the police. Jack seemed perfectly reasonable; it was Annabel who was the raving lunatic at the moment. Neville didn't want to start trouble.

In fact, all he wanted to do was leave. He was certain now that Priscilla wasn't coming back. He just wanted to get on an airplane and go home, get back to work, visit his parents and his brother and his nieces and nephews. Neville just wanted some normalcy in his life again. The past few days were enough fear and confusion and chaos to last a lifetime.

But he couldn't leave. Not quite yet. He liked Annabel, and he wanted to make sure she was all right. Tomorrow, he figured. If she was up and about tomorrow, talking sensibly, he'd leave tomorrow.

"I'm going to the store," Jack announced. "Not Millie's market, but the supermarket in Great Barrington. I want to get some real groceries. Frankly, I need some meat. Some steak and potatoes, since all that's in the fridge are Annabel's vegetables." He smiled over at Neville. "Can I get you anything, buddy?"

"No, thank you," Neville told him. "I've come to quite enjoy carrot and cucumber sandwiches."

"Have it your way," Jack said. He turned to Zeke. "You'll look in on Annabel? If she wakes up, tell her I'll be back in about an hour."

"Will do," the old man replied.

Neville watched from the window as Jack drove off.

"I'm going to finish some work in the attic," Zeke told him. "If the telephone rings, you can let it go to the answering machine."

"I'm happy to answer it and take a message for you," Neville said. "I'm just going to settle down here in the parlor and read a book."

"Very good."

Neville took a chair opposite the fireplace. How he wished there was a fire crackling in front of him, sending off waves of heat across the room. The day was so terribly cold. Neville shivered a little, buttoning his wool cardigan sweater all the way down. Opening his book, he began to read.

60

Upstairs, Annabel was awake. She lay rock still, listening to Tommy Tricky and his twin whisper under her bed.

"Let's get her."

"No, not yet."

"But I want her."

"Leave her!"

I'm going mad, Annabel thought. *Stark raving mad.*

There was no such thing as Tommy Tricky. But here she was, listening to his voice. And there were two of him.

Knowing that she had gone insane gave her a weird sense of peace. She just lay there, not moving, listening to the little men scuttle around under her bed.

61

"Hello?"

A man's voice startled Neville awake. He had fallen asleep reading his book. His head was down on his chest. He leapt from his chair.

"Hello?" the man called again.

Two people had let themselves in and were now standing in the foyer. The man who'd been calling was Chad Appleby, the contractor. The other was a pretty, dark-haired woman Neville had never seen before.

"I'm sorry to just barge in on you," Chad said, "but we knocked and no one answered the door."

"Oh, it's quite all right," Neville told him. "But I'm afraid Jack has gone up to Great Barrington and Annabel is . . . taking a nap. She wasn't feeling so well, you see."

"No problem," Chad replied. "I'm just here to take some measurements. This is my assistant, Tammy Morelli."

"How do you do?" Neville asked, smiling over at the woman, who nodded hello.

"I'll need to go down into the basement," Chad said.

"I need to make sure the floorboards are going to be strong enough for when we take out that wall."

"I'll walk down with you," Neville offered. "I know where the string for the light is."

"Thanks." Chad turned to Tammy and tossed her a measuring tape. She caught it expertly. "In the meantime, start measuring the windows and moldings like I told you, okay? Not just the ones on the first floor, but on the second floor, too. We're going to order all the new windows at the same time."

"Aye, aye, captain," Tammy said.

The two men set off down the stairs into the basement.

"Here's the light, right here," Neville said, when they reached the bottom. He pulled the string.

"Thanks," Chad said. "I can find my way from here." He switched on his flashlight. "I just want to inspect the floorboards."

"Actually," Neville went on, "I came down so I might ask you a question."

"What's that?"

"Annabel was a bit concerned earlier when she found a dark, brownish-purplish substance inside the chimney down here. Apparently, when she opened the ash dump, it was full of the stuff."

"Brownish and purplish?"

Neville nodded. "She thought it looked like blood."

"Oh, Jesus."

"Given everything that happened here, to your friend and my girlfriend, well, I thought you ought to know. And if there was any way you could take a look at it . . ."

Chad swung his flashlight over to the door to the ash dump. "Why the hell is it padlocked?" he asked.

"I don't know," Neville said. "And the key has been missing ever since Annabel looked inside. Zeke said what she saw was wet soot."

Chad made a face. "Who ever heard of purple wet soot?"

"Well, I guess that's right. I was going to mention it to the police . . ."

They had reached the base of the fireplace. "I'd say that would be a good idea," Chad said. "I mean, if it's a clue to what happened—" He stopped speaking abruptly. "Hey," he said. "Listen."

They put their ears close to the ash dump door.

"Something's in there," Chad said.

Neville listened. There was indeed something in there.

And it was eating!

The sound of chomping and chewing came from inside the old brick chimney.

62

Tammy stretched the measuring tape across the windowsill on the second-floor landing. She noted the length and jotted it down in a little pad. Then she did the same for the height.

This place wasn't so creepy. All her life Tammy had heard stories about the Blue Boy Inn. There had been lots of deaths and disappearances up here. Kids in school called it a haunted house. Her mother used to say the place was "cursed." She hadn't even liked to drive by on the road on the way to Millie's market.

But the English guy who'd greeted them had been pleasant enough. And once Chad was through with his renovation, the place was going to be real bright and sunny. It would be like a modern showplace, according to the plans Tammy had seen. She was excited to be in on it. This would be good for her. A real change, and Tammy needed a—

"I told you, no more!"

An old man's voice suddenly cut through the stillness of the upstairs corridor.

Tammy tried to ignore it, but the voice came again.

"Get back here!"

The voice was coming from the steep, narrow stairs at the end of the corridor. Tammy assumed they led to the attic. She took a few steps in that direction, pausing at the foot of the stairs to listen.

She could hear people moving about. There was some kind of struggle, it seemed. The old man spoke again, but softer this time.

"Stop this," he urged. "There are people in the house." And then he added, insistently, "Shhh!"

Now Tammy was distracted by a sound behind her. She turned away from the stairs and looked back down the hallway. A woman was emerging from one of the rooms. She was dressed in blue jeans and a wrinkled oversized T-shirt. She looked a wreck, as if she hadn't slept in days. Her long auburn hair was all mussed up. Her eyes caught Tammy's.

"Who are you?" the woman asked.

"Tammy Morelli. I'm working with Chad, the contractor."

The woman's eyes softened. "Then you're real," she said, a small smile fluttering across her face. "Good. That's good."

She made her way down the stairs.

How very strange.

Tammy thought she might have to revise her earlier impression of the Blue Boy. It was indeed pretty creepy after all.

63

"Annabel!" Neville exclaimed. "You're up! Are you all right, my dear?"

"I need to take a walk," she said. "Clear my head."

He thought she looked terrible. "It's very cold out," he told her.

She didn't reply, just yanked on her coat. Behind Neville, Chad now appeared, emerging from the basement stairwell.

"Hello, Annabel," the contractor said.

She grunted a reply.

"Are we still on for tomorrow morning?" Chad asked. "To take a drive up to Great Barrington and pick out some tile and paint?"

Neville watched as Annabel turned to look at him. Her eyes seemed dull and gray. It seemed almost that she didn't recognize Chad. She stared at him for several seconds, as if she was trying to process what he was asking her.

"Yes," she said at last. "Take a drive. Get away from here. Yes, we're still on."

"Great," Chad said. "You know, I should tell you that we were just down in the basement—"

Neville quickly and subtly moved his foot over to the other man, whacking his shin.

Chad stopped speaking. He exchanged a look with Neville.

"Do whatever you need to do," Annabel said softly. "I need to take a walk. Get some air."

"All right," Chad said. "See you tomorrow then. I want to get an early start. The weather report says we might get a pretty big snowstorm tomorrow afternoon."

Annabel didn't answer. She just headed outside.

Chad looked over at Neville once she was gone. "Why did you stop me from telling her about what we heard in the chimney?" he asked. "If she's got raccoons living in there, she's going to need an exterminator before we can finish repairing the fireplace."

"She's had a rough day," Neville replied. "She doesn't need to start worrying about raccoons."

Chad wasn't satisfied with that answer. "But that might explain the blood she found in there. If those coons have been eating squirrels and mice . . ."

Neville gave him a cold look. "I doubt it's squirrels and mice they're eating."

Chad shivered. "Wait. Are you . . . ?" His face blanched. "Are you thinking that the killer stuffed Paulie's and Priscilla's bodies inside the chimney, and that's what we heard the raccoons chomping on?"

"It did cross my mind."

"That's just too freaky." Chad looked back down the stairs. "But you just may be on to something. That's one really wide chimney. You could fit a body in there, sure."

"Especially if the killer was adept with a butcher knife, as the hand in the wood box would seem to indicate," Neville added.

"Jesus." Chad shuddered. "We need to tell Annabel, or her husband."

"I promised Annabel last night that I would tell the chief of police. She did not, for her own reasons, want her husband to know."

"Why the hell not?"

"It doesn't matter." Neville headed toward the door, grabbing his coat from the hook on the wall. "All I know is I need to fulfill the promise I made to Annabel. I'm going down to the chief's office now."

"I'll go with you," Chad said. "He'll want a statement from me, too, about what I heard."

"All right."

Tammy had come down the stairs. "What's going on?" she asked.

"Listen, Tam," Chad said, "I'm going to run Neville here into town for a moment. I'll be back in two shakes. You almost done?"

"I've measured every window upstairs," she said, "except for the attic. It's locked. There's somebody in there."

"It's Zeke, the caretaker," Neville told her.

"He seemed a little upset."

"That's just Zeke," Neville assured her.

"Okay, listen, Tam," Chad said. "Get the windows in the kitchen and dining room measured. We might as well plan for everything now. We're going to be replacing all the windows eventually."

"All right, boss."

Chad turned to leave, and then looked back at Tammy. "You going to be okay by yourself? I'm just going to be gone a little bit."

"Well," Tammy said, "I've discovered there's some weird people in this house, but I haven't seen any ghosts yet."

Neville saw the smile the two of them exchanged.

Operative word being yet, he thought, as he and Chad left by the front door.

64

It was the thought of driving up to Great Barrington that revived Annabel. The thought of getting away from here, on the road, driving miles and miles away. The idea appealed to Annabel almost as much as a Caribbean vacation.

The cold afternoon air rushed into her nostrils. It functioned as she had hoped. Her mind felt clearer, more alive.

As she walked into the woods, leaves and twigs crunching under her feet, Annabel told herself she had allowed her imagination to run amok. It had happened before, when she was in the hospital, when sometimes she hadn't known where she was, when the orderlies had looked like deformed monsters and her room like a dungeon. Jack was right. Her doctors had warned her she might have flashbacks. The delirium that had set in as her body withdrew from the drugs had been intense. It was still there, buried deep down in her brain.

It had taken being raped by Jack to bring it out again.

He wouldn't call it that, of course. He'd say they had

just made love. Annabel hadn't fought him. She hadn't resisted. But still she felt raped just the same.

He had just tried to do it as fast as possible, fearful he'd lose his erection again, she argued with herself. *It wasn't rape. That's not fair to Jack.*

But what about fair to her? She couldn't deny how she felt.

And that horrible feeling had led to some horrible hallucinations. Annabel had to find a way to deal with it, to get it all out of her head—the anger, the fear, the sense of violation. Otherwise, she wouldn't be able to go on. She would always feel unsafe here.

Annabel paused at the little white stone marker. She looked down at the words carved across its surface.

CINDY DEVLIN

Poor little girl. How had she died? Her death must have been terrible, given how much blood was found.

Annabel wondered what kind of memorial Jack would want for his grandmother. They'd been notified that her body had been taken from the morgue to be cremated. Jack had told her that his grandfather's ashes had been scattered in these woods; Annabel assumed that was what he'd want to do with Cordelia's as well. They should have a little service, she thought. Maybe ask a minister to come in and say a prayer. Annabel could get some fresh flowers from Millie's store and carry them as the old woman's ashes were scattered. Afterward, they'd put the flowers on the mantel over the fireplace.

Annabel walked on into the woods.

How she wished she was walking down Fifth

Avenue, or through busy Times Square, taxicabs honking, sirens wailing, lights flashing. She yearned to be
surrounded by masses of people—thousands of them,
all moving past her, rubbing shoulders—and away from
this stark, gray, silent place. Some claustrophobics hated
being in the city, and longed for the empty countryside.
Annabel was different. The city made her blood race. It
filled her up.

She missed New York like an old, comforting friend.

Above her, a crow cawed. She heard the flapping of
its wings, but could not spot it through the network of
interlacing, bare, blue limbs.

Annabel didn't want to get lost. She kept turning
around, making sure she could still see the outline of
the house.

What had she been thinking? Had she really been so
angry at Jack that she believed him capable of murder?
How crazy was that? What motive did Jack have to kill
those two people? Even if something had happened between him and Priscilla that night, Jack had had absolutely no interaction with Paulie that mattered. It was
just crazy. In her confused state of mind, subcon-
sciously blaming Jack for hurting her—violating her—
Annabel had seen sinister motivations behind every
action Jack took, every statement that he made.

She'd been seeing other things as well.

Like blood in the chimney, when it was clearly just
old soot and debris.

Like a pair of Tommy Trickies, whom she had
stopped believing in a long time ago.

I've been decompensating, as Dr. Adler would say.
She still remembered the definition he'd given her of
the term after he'd used it to describe what was hap-

pening to her. *The failure to generate effective psychological coping mechanisms in response to stress, resulting in personality disturbance or disintegration.*

That was what she had felt. That she was disintegrating.

She had to get it together. She was stronger than this.

She stopped and sat down on a log, breathing in the cold air. She could see her breath in front of her.

Off in the woods, she heard the snap of a twig.

She wondered what kind of animals might be out here. Jack had said they'd feared little Cindy had been killed by a bear all those years ago. Were there still bears prowling these woods? There were also coyotes and foxes and bobcats, Zeke had told her. The bobcats could be particularly vicious.

And they'd seen that big, terrifying moose on the ride up, too.

She laughed a little then, remembering the moment. Annabel felt as if she had tumbled down the rabbit hole into a very strange, topsy-turvy world.

Another snap of another twig, closer this time.

Annabel stood. She shouldn't have come out this far. What if what she heard moving out there was a bear or a bobcat?

She looked around. She couldn't see the house. *Damn it!*

But she could hear something approaching, crunching through the leaves.

"Okay, Annabel," she whispered to herself. "It's time to go home."

She started walking back in the direction she'd come. At least, she thought it was the same direction.

All at once she heard something.

The tweet of a bird?

But it sounded different than that. . . .

She paused.

The sound came again.

Annabel's blood ran cold.

It was no bird.

It was also not a bear or a bobcat, either.

What Annabel heard was a short, two-note whistle, made, she was certain, by human lips.

It sounded again.

As did the crunching of the leaves, very close to her now.

So maybe it's a hiker, Annabel thought. *Or a hunter.*

A hunter with a gun. Who might mistake her movements among the trees for a deer, and shoot to kill.

I've got to get home.

Annabel began to walk faster. And as she did, the sound of whoever was crunching through the leaves toward her accelerated at the same pace.

This was no hunter, no hiker, she told herself. It was also not a wild animal.

She walked even faster. The sound behind her also sped up.

Annabel realized she was being pursued.

She started to run.

65

Tammy stretched her measuring tape across the windowsill in the kitchen. But before she could make a note of the length, she suddenly had the distinct sense someone was behind her. With a start, she looked over her shoulder.

She was right. There was a man there. A tall, handsome man with two paper bags full of groceries in his hands.

"Oh, hello, I wasn't aware someone came in," Tammy said, turning to the man.

He set the groceries on the counter. "It's always a pleasant surprise to come home and find a beautiful woman in your house."

She blushed. "I'm Tammy," she said. "I'm working with Chad, taking some measurements of the windows."

"I didn't see Chad's truck out front," the man said, taking some steaks out of the bags and putting them in the refrigerator.

Tammy shook her head. "He took the Englishman who's staying here into town."

To this, the man lifted his eyebrows. "Did he now? Why couldn't Neville have driven himself? He has a car."

"I'm not sure. I don't know what their errand was. But Chad said he'd be back shortly."

The man nodded. "I'm sorry, I've been impolite," he said. "I haven't introduced myself." He walked across the room and extended his hand. "I'm Jack Devlin. The owner of the place."

"Hello, Mr. Devlin," Tammy said, accepting his greeting.

To her surprise, he brought her hand to his lips and kissed it. "It is a pleasure to make your acquaintance, Tammy. A very fine pleasure indeed."

He didn't let go of her hand.

"Have you seen my wife?" Mr. Devlin asked.

Tammy felt uncomfortable that he was still holding her hand. He was also standing a little too close for comfort. She could smell him. Man sweat and after-shave.

"Um, I actually didn't meet your wife yet, but I saw her," Tammy said awkwardly. "I believe she went out to take a walk."

"I see." Mr. Devlin smiled and took a step even closer to her. His grip on Tammy's hand tightened. "That means we have the house to ourselves."

"No," Tammy said quickly. "I heard a man in the attic. . . ."

"Oh, that's just Zeke," said Mr. Devlin. His eyes seemed strange to Tammy. His pupils were dilated. "He won't bother us."

Mr. Devlin leaned down toward her as if he was about to kiss her.

"No!" Tammy shrieked, yanking her hand away from him and hurrying across the kitchen. "You had no right to do that!"

"To do what?" Mr. Devlin asked her with a smirk. "I didn't do anything."

"I have a job to do, Mr. Devlin," Tammy told him.

His smirk stretched into a wide smile. "Then by all means," he said, "don't let me keep you from it." He winked at her, and then headed out of the kitchen.

Tammy had to sit down, she was shaking so much. *Hurry up, Chad*, she thought. *Get me out of here.*

66

Annabel ran.

Blood raced through her veins. She could feel it pulsing in her ears. She caught sight of the house up ahead, still too far away for comfort. She ran as fast as she could.

A broken branch on the ground proved her undoing. She tripped over it and fell facedown in the leaves.

A hand was gripping her arm. Whoever had been pursuing her had caught up to her.

"Annabel, are you all right?"

She looked up. It was Richard Carlson.

"Oh, Chief Carlson," she said, nearly bursting into tears. "I thought . . ."

He helped her to her feet. "You thought what?"

"I don't know," she said, brushing leaves off her coat. "A bear, maybe. I guess I thought you might be a bear."

He smiled. "Why would you think that?"

"Well, the way you were coming after me."

His face creased in puzzlement. "I wasn't coming after you. I just spotted you a few moments ago. I saw you from the parking lot, running through the woods. I was concerned."

Annabel looked at him. "You didn't whistle? A little two-note sound, like this?" She demonstrated what she had heard.

"No, that wasn't me," Richard told her.

"Then somebody was chasing me," Annabel said, looking back out into the woods and shivering.

"Are you certain?"

She moved her eyes back to the police chief's. "No," she admitted. "I'm not certain about a lot these days."

"Do you want to talk about it?" he asked.

Annabel thought his eyes looked kind. A little tired, and there was sadness in there, too, but they were kind.

"I didn't want to come here," she said, surprised at herself. The words just tumbled out; she hadn't planned to say them. "Jack thought it would be a good idea to leave New York and start over here at the Blue Boy Inn when his grandmother called and asked him to take over. So I came along."

"Have you changed your mind since arriving?" Richard asked.

She shrugged. "I was hoping the project of restoring the place would give me some purpose, something to focus on. But then Priscilla and Paulie went missing, and that hand was found out back. . . ." She shuddered. "It makes me long for the safe streets of Manhattan."

They both laughed and started walking slowly back to the house.

"If it's any consolation," the chief said, "I believe the killer is long gone. I don't know why he came through this way, or why he either killed or kidnapped Priscilla and Paulie. But I don't think he stuck around. We've been through here several times a day. I've had officers searching these woods half a dozen times. There's been no trace. I think you're safe here."

"Do you?" Annabel asked. "Honestly?"

"Safe from whoever killed Roger and possibly the other two," Richard told her. "Whether there are other dangers here for you, only you can know that."

She thought of Jack, and for a second, she wanted to tell Richard all of her doubts about him, but then realized how ridiculous that would sound. The chief of police was not a marriage counselor.

But he *should* know about the chimney. . . .

"Did Neville speak with you?" Annabel asked. "About what I found . . . ?"

Richard was nodding. "That's why I'm here. I came out right away. He and Chad came to my office and told me about the blood."

"Maybe it wasn't blood," Annabel admitted. "I may be getting a little hysterical."

"Well, it's worth a look, anyway," the chief said. "Especially after what else they told me."

"What was that?"

"They said that they heard some sounds down there today. Chad described it as a pack of raccoons eating very noisily."

"Raccoons?"

Richard's face became serious. "If the killer dismembered Paulie and Priscilla and disposed of their remains in the chimney, it could be that animals smelled their decaying flesh and decided to creep down the chimney for a meal."

"Oh, dear God!" Annabel was repulsed.

"I'm sorry, I didn't mean to upset you."

"It's okay, chief. I just . . . well, it's hard to imagine."

He placed a hand on her shoulder. "You can call me Richard."

Her eyes flickered up to his. "Oh, well, thank you."

"Tell me something. Has anyone else looked into the ash dump since you discovered the blood?"

Annabel found herself shuddering. Richard tightened his grip on her shoulder.

"Zeke and my husband both, I think," Annabel told him. "Zeke locked it up again."

"Do you know if he looked inside before doing so?"

"I don't."

Richard nodded. "I've got a forensics team on its way. But we ought to go down there ourselves first and take a look."

"Of course," Annabel said.

The chief removed his hand from her shoulder and they started walking back toward the house. "I'm sure this isn't how you imagined your new life in Woodfield would be."

"You know," she told him, "I had no idea what it would be like. I'm not a country girl. I've got the city in my blood. Born and raised in Manhattan. I miss the sounds of the city, the rush, the hustle, the constant energy. . . ."

He smiled. "My wife was originally from Manhattan. She loved the city as well."

Annabel paused. "Richard, I can't help but notice you speak of her in the past tense."

He nodded sadly. "She died. I've been on my own for a while."

"You miss her a great deal," Annabel observed. "I can tell."

"Every moment of every day," Richard admitted.

"How hard that must be for you." She looked over at him. "But how very wonderful it must be to have loved someone that much, and for her to have loved you as much in return."

"Yes," acknowledged the chief. "Yes, indeed it was."

They were close enough now to the house that they could see the driveway. Chad's truck was just at that moment pulling in.

"Chad and Neville didn't come back with you?" Annabel asked.

Richard shook his head. "Chad had to pick up some things at his office. But I came out straight away after they told me what they knew."

He pointed out another vehicle in the driveway.

"I see your husband is at home," Richard said.

"Yes," Annabel replied. "And for some reason, I don't think Jack is going to be very pleased that I'm taking you down into the basement to look at the chimney."

67

Tammy headed down the basement steps. Chad had said to measure every window, and she assumed that to mean the basement as well.

Besides, she wanted to get away from that horrible Jack Devlin, who was lurking around the parlor and dining room. Every time she cast a glance in his direction, he was looking at her.

Of course, Tammy thought, as she pulled the string to illuminate the overhead bulb, *he could corner me down here more easily.* But if he tried that, he'd have quite the surprise. Before making her way down the steps, she'd slung her purse over her shoulder. And inside, she carried a can of Mace. Being involved with a man as volatile as Roger, Tammy had learned to take precautions. And that prick Devlin would get a faceful of it if he tried anything again.

Once in the basement, Tammy saw that the windows were too high for her to easily reach. She realized she'd need something to stand on.

Over by the chimney, she spotted a small chest. She could pull that over.

But as she approached, the dim light above revealed something leaning against the chest.

A large doll of some sort, she thought. Propped in a sitting position.

But then—the doll's head moved.

Tammy gasped. She heard sounds. Teeth gnashing.

All at once, the thing sitting against the chest turned its face to look at her. It was a little man—and in his hands he held a bloody arm. He was gnawing at the bones of the fingers as if he were chewing on a chicken drumstick. Catching sight of Tammy, the little man hissed at her like a cat, baring a mouthful of bloody fangs.

Tammy screamed.

68

Annabel had just come inside the house with Richard when she heard the scream from the basement. It seemed to rise up like a physical thing, pushing itself through the slats in the floorboards, causing the whole house to tremble. It caused Annabel and Richard to stop cold in their tracks.

Chad and Neville were likewise frozen for that split second of time, standing a little ahead of them in the foyer. The two men hadn't even yet taken off their coats when the scream cut through the quiet afternoon.

Richard was the first to burst forward, heading toward the basement stairs, his hand on his gun. But he didn't have to go far. The young woman whom Annabel had seen earlier—Tammy something, she thought, Chad's helper—suddenly came bounding up the stairs.

She was as white as if covered in flour.

She bypassed Richard to run straight into Chad's arms.

"Get me out of here!" she said in the highest pitched voice Annabel had ever heard. The poor woman was shaking so badly it looked as if she had epilepsy.

"What happened, Tammy?" Chad asked.

"Down there!" was all she could say, burying her face against his chest. "Down there!" Then she broke free of Chad's embrace and bolted outside, Chad following.

"I'm going down," Richard announced, gun drawn, heading down the stairs.

"I'm coming, too," Annabel said.

The chief turned to her. "Stay up here," he barked.

"I've got to see whatever is down there," Annabel said.

Richard made a face. "Then stay well behind me," he told her.

They made their way down the creaky old stairs.

The light was still burning. They saw nothing. Annabel lifted the flashlight from the floor and shone it around the near-empty basement. Still nothing. All they could see was the chest near the chimney. The door to the ash dump was still padlocked, and the key was nowhere in sight.

"I've got to go out and interview Tammy about what it was she saw down here," Richard told Annabel. "Whatever it was appears to be gone now. In the meantime, I'll need your permission to search this place, to pry open that ash dump door. . . ."

"What the hell is going on here?"

They spun around.

Jack had come down the stairs. He was angry, eyes blazing. "What was all that screaming about? And exactly why do you need to search this house?"

Richard looked at him. Annabel tensed.

"Mr. Devlin," the chief explained, "Tammy Morelli

just ran out of this basement a terrified wreck. She saw something down here. I'm going out to interview her now. I don't know what she saw, but there have been enough reports about this house to warrant a complete search."

The chief pushed past Jack to head back up the stairs. Annabel attempted to follow him, but Jack grabbed her arm.

"I'm not letting anyone search this house," her husband growled.

"Jack, we have to cooperate with the police."

"Yeah, I think you've been cooperating a little too closely with that guy," he grumbled. "I saw you out walking with him, taking a little romantic stroll through the woods."

"Jack!" Annabel was nearly flabbergasted. "You are talking crazy!"

"I'm not letting him search this house. You said yourself that we needed to stand up against this reputation as being haunted and all that."

"Jack, this is no time to argue," Annabel said, hurrying up the basement stairs. In truth, she had become afraid of him, and didn't want to be in the basement alone with him.

Upstairs, she found Neville sitting forlornly in the parlor. "They're outside," he told Annabel, gesturing with his head toward the front door.

She stepped outside onto the porch. She could see Tammy sitting in the passenger's side of Chad's truck, her arms wrapped around herself. Richard was speaking with her intensely through the open door. Annabel headed toward them.

Chad stopped her halfway. "Look," he said. "Tammy's always been a bit hysterical. You know Roger Askew was her boyfriend."

Annabel was stunned. "The guy whose hand was found in the wood box?"

"Yeah. So she's easily spooked. She's had a hard time the past few years, and I was trying to help her out. But I wouldn't necessarily take what she says as gospel. I think she's clean now, but she used to do a lot of drugs. . . ."

Annabel bristled. "Just because someone once had an addiction shouldn't mean we discount their intelligence or reliability."

"No, no, of course not, I just meant—"

Annabel cut him off. "What has she been saying?"

"It's crazy talk, Annabel. She says she saw a little man in the basement—like an elf—eating a human arm."

Annabel couldn't speak for a moment. "A . . . little man?" she finally asked.

"Yeah. I think she was upset about something else, though." Chad looked over his shoulder, and then drew closer to her. "You should know about this. She might be making a complaint. She claims your husband sexually harassed her earlier."

This was all too much for Annabel to take in. She felt light-headed, as if she might pass out.

"I'm sorry to have to tell you that," Chad said. "But it's what Tammy is saying. And like I said, she can get hysterical at times."

"She's not hysterical," Annabel managed to say.

Richard had left Tammy's side and was now approaching them. "Take her home, Chad. She's very upset." The chief looked at Annabel. "I'd like to get a team out here this afternoon to inspect that chimney," he told her.

Annabel glanced over at the front porch. Jack stood there, legs spread apart, arms crossed over his chest. He was scowling.

"I don't think he's going to let you," Annabel said sadly.

"Then I'll have to get a court order, and that could take a couple of days."

"I'll try talking to him," Annabel said, looking over at Jack, "but he's . . . different."

"What do you mean?"

"I'm not sure," she replied, as she headed back toward the house. "I'm not sure of anything anymore."

69

Neville didn't think he should be listening to Annabel and Jack argue on the front porch. He stood up from the couch in the parlor and started to head up to his room, but then decided on a different destination.

What had Tammy seen down in the basement?

Perhaps he was being foolish to go back down there by himself. If there was some mad killer loose, the same one who'd cut off that bloke's hand and kidnapped and/or killed Priscilla, Neville might run smack into him down in that dark, dusty space.

But he had to go down there. He had to find some answer to give Priscilla's parents.

Her mum's voice still rang in Neville's ear. How upset she'd been when he'd finally called to give them the news of Priscilla's disappearance. She had blamed Neville, saying her poor darling daughter must have run off because of something he had said or done. It was the only way the distraught woman could make sense of the whole thing. Neville hadn't had many facts to give her to refute her theory. He was scheduled to return to England in a few days, and he didn't want to fly back over the pond without some understanding of what had happened to Priscilla.

He made his way down the stairs.

He saw nothing. What could possibly have spooked that poor girl so terribly? Neville tried to yank open the ash dump, but the padlock held firm. He hoped the police could get in there soon and inspect what was inside.

He was moving away from the chimney when he stepped on something on the floor. In the darkness he hadn't seen it. Evidently no one had.

He stepped down and scooped up the small object in his hand.

It was a ring.

Priscilla's opal ring. The one she used to attract ghosts.

He slipped the ring into his pocket.

Given the tension between Annabel and Jack, he wasn't going to bring the ring to them. He didn't trust what might happen. Instead, he was going straight to the police station and give the ring to Chief Carlson.

70

Richard pulled up in front of Millie's store, turned off the ignition, and just sat there for a while. Such strangeness at the Blue Boy Inn. He had no idea what to make of it.

In his head, he was running through all those cold case files again. What was it about that place that had resulted in so many deaths and disappearances?

The first strange death had occurred more than a hundred years ago at the place. And they had kept coming. Richard had been especially repulsed by the story of poor old Andrew McGurk, whose body had been found up there decades ago, but not his head.

And the most heartbreaking story was the little baby whose arm was found. The child's poor mother had been so distraught. That case, too, had remained unsolved for decades.

Richard got out of the car and headed inside Millie's. The little bell over the door jingled.

"Well, if it isn't our hardest working public servant," Millie sang out from behind the counter. "What can I do for you today, Richard?"

"Just come to pick up some supper, Mil," he told her. "It's going to be a late night at the station tonight."

He headed down the cereal aisle.

"Hey, chief," Millie called over to him. "Do yourself a favor and at least buy some ground beef. Enough with the Cheerios."

"There's nowhere to grill a burger at the station, Millie," Richard said. "I'll stick with my cereal and milk."

"How about some ham and cheese at least? I've got some nice hard rolls. . . ."

"Too much trouble," Richard said, the box of Cheerios under his arm as he headed over to the coolers to fetch a half-liter of milk.

"You must have a microwave there," the clerk said. "How about a nice Lean Cuisine? They've got some new ones. The salmon's pretty good. I've had it myself."

Richard lifted the milk out of the freezer. "Thanks, Millie, but my taste buds are in kind of a rut."

She shook her head. "What you need is a good woman to cook for you."

He smiled as he set the milk and cereal down on the counter. "Like I've said, you keep turning me down." He winked at her.

Millie smirked as she rang up the items. "How are things out at the Blue Boy?"

The chief shrugged. "Not sure. Lots of questions."

"What is it about that place?" She accepted Richard's ten and gave him back his change. "I've been here since I was fourteen, and that was a long time ago. And ever since, there's always been something weird up there."

"That's true, Millie. We're looking into it."

She placed the milk and box of Cheerios into a paper bag. "I sure feel bad for that sweet girl who came all the way up here from New York to live at the place. Annabel. That was her name, right?"

"Yes," Richard said. "That's her name."

"What kind of husband doesn't tell his wife about the unsavory history of the place he's taking her to live?"

"I don't know, Mil," Richard said, taking his dinner.

"I mean, that Jack Devlin had to remember how his poor little sister disappeared, and how his father went crazy. . . ."

Richard lifted an eyebrow. "His father went crazy?"

"Well, that was the rumor. He'd come up here, too, just like Jack is doing now, to take over the place after his father died. I remember he was a very nice man. But then he changed. Started acting all weird and secretive. Then, of course, when his wife died from breast cancer and his daughter disappeared—well, people who saw him said he went completely off his rocker."

"That can happen, Millie," Richard said, "when you lose someone you love."

He waved good-bye to her and headed back out to his car.

Driving to the station, Richard didn't think there was anything unusual about Jack Devlin's father "going crazy" after his wife died.

After all, Richard had almost gone crazy after Amy died.

So many specialists he'd sought out. So many second, third, fourth, and fifth opinions. And still Amy had died. Richard was a police officer, sworn to defend the public, to protect lives—but he had been unable to find a way to save the woman he loved.

For a while after Amy's death, Richard had blamed himself. He had thought he might go mad. He understood exactly what Jack Devlin's father must have gone through.

How very much Richard still loved his dead wife. He still physically ached for her presence beside him in bed at night. He could still smell the fragrance of her hair on his pillow, could sense her energy in the rooms of his house—even though Amy had never lived here in Woodfield with him. Even though she had been gone for so many years.

Could he ever love another woman? Could he ever allow another woman in his life again?

His mind flickered to Annabel Wish.

Richard couldn't deny that he'd been attracted to her. The first woman he'd felt that way toward in a very long time. She had looked so pretty, so vulnerable and yet so strong, too, standing there in the sunlight in the woods. Those were qualities Amy had had as well. Strength with vulnerability. Richard had found Annabel extremely attractive as he'd walked beside her, crunching through those fallen leaves. He had been filled, in fact, with the desire to kiss her. He had resisted the urge, of course.

But a momentary attraction to a woman did not mean he could love another woman. It did not mean he was ready to fall in love again. It only meant he was still alive, still a man, still with very natural desires. The chemistry, in other words, still worked.

He couldn't deny that he'd found Annabel Wish a very beautiful woman.

He thought of her up at that house. She was going to
need his help, and Richard would be glad to offer it.
That husband of hers was not to be trusted.

Richard had been extremely frustrated by Tammy
Morelli's refusal to bring harassment charges against
Devlin. "No, Richard, no," she'd kept repeating. "I
can't do that. Already half this town thinks I'm a slut.
They'll blame me."

"That's crazy talk, Tammy," Richard had told her.
"You did nothing wrong! That man tried to take advan-
tage of you. He shouldn't get away with it."

But Tammy had kept shaking her head. "I just want
to start living my life. I don't want anything dragging
me down. Roger is gone and I'm starting new. Me and
Jessica. I don't want any court cases or newspaper
headlines. I just want to get on with things."

Her eyes had narrowed as she had looked at Richard.

"And I don't want anything more to do with that
place. The legends are true, Richard. After what I saw,
I believe them!"

And what had Tammy seen?

Richard pulled his car into the station lot. The reason any case Tammy might bring against Devlin might
fail was because she also said some other things had
happened at the Blue Boy. And if people questioned her
about those things, they'd question her claims about
Devlin as well.

Tammy had claimed she'd seen a little man eating a
human arm.

Richard had dutifully taken all the details down in
his report. The little man, Tammy estimated, was no
more than three feet tall, maybe less. He was slender,
and had a bluish tint to his skin. Kind of like the blue

boy on the sign out front. Richard understood the power of suggestion when under distress. Clearly, that was the explanation for Tammy's little blue man. She was upset and anxious after the harassment from Devlin and imagined she'd something horrifying. Richard thought psychologists called it "counterprojection."

Still, he worried about Annabel in that house.

He got out of the car and headed inside. He'd been right when he'd told Millie he had a long night ahead. He needed to get the ball moving on a search warrant. If he had to drive up to see the judge personally tonight, he'd do it. He needed to arrange a forensics team to check out that chimney. And he needed to finish going through all the cold case files relating to the Blue Boy Inn.

There was something very odd about that place, and Richard aimed to figure out what it was.

He was surprised to find the Blue Boy's English guest waiting for him when he reached his desk.

"Chief," Neville said, "I have something very important to tell you. And *show* you."

He opened his hand to reveal an opal ring.

71

"Maybe I'm crazy to be going out with you to the tile store, as if everything back home is all peachy keen," Annabel told Chad, sitting beside him in his truck as they rattled north on Route 7. "But after yesterday, I just had to get out of that house."

"I don't blame you," Chad said, looking over at her. "A little time away will do you a world of good."

She smiled over at him.

"Seriously," Chad continued. "Think to the future. Someday this crap will all be over. They will have caught the guy who killed Roger and maybe killed Paulie and Priscilla, and you can go back to making the Blue Boy a first-class destination."

That was what she needed to do, Annabel thought, watching from the window as the countryside flew past her. She needed to focus on the renovation. She needed to throw herself into it—transforming that house from its gruesome past to something new, something she could call her own. She had to think ahead, and not dwell in the past, or wallow in her delusions.

Annabel ran the risk of decompensating again. She

couldn't let that happen. During her time in rehab, she had been told over and over again how important it was to stay strong in her mind. She had a tendency to retreat when things became difficult. It was sort of like the way some people curled into the fetal position to take shelter from the hard realities of the world. Annabel called it her "black hole." She'd sink down into it and her mind would go berserk. She'd imagine things. She'd hallucinate. She'd fall into a world that wasn't real, that existed only in her mind. She'd believe nothing was safe.

She supposed it had started all those years ago when she was a little girl, locked in the closet by Daddy Ron. The young Annabel would fall down into a rabbit's hole of illusion, imagining Tommy Tricky and all the terrible things he would do to her. This had been her tendency ever since, when she became afraid or anxious. She'd withdraw, decompensate—tumble down into her black hole where nothing made sense.

But she could no longer allow that to happen in her life.

Despite what Tammy Morelli claimed to have seen, Tommy Tricky *did not live* at the Blue Boy Inn. Annabel had to believe that. Tommy Tricky was a childhood fantasy, told to her by Daddy Ron to frighten her. Tammy had been frightened by Jack, and then she had hallucinated, much as Annabel had done herself. To believe anything else, Annabel was convinced, would have been to admit madness.

And she was not going to do that.

Last night, Jack had been conciliatory. He'd taken Annabel in his arms and kissed her tenderly, explaining how much he, too, wanted to start over, to make the

Blue Boy theirs, to free it from its lurid past. That was
why he was so resistant to the police searching the
place. Annabel was cool and reserved, remembering
what Chad had told her about Tammy. Once again, she
chose not to confront Jack. She planned to do so—she
wasn't going to just let this slip by—but not just yet.
Annabel wasn't sure she could trust her husband anymore. In fact, she'd become a little bit afraid of him.
She worried that Jack would blow up at her, or try to
control what she did, and if Annabel had learned anything during her time in rehab, it was how to stay safe.
Nothing was more important than that. So until she felt
safe with Jack again, she was not going to bring anything up with him that might set him off.

Of course, things couldn't stay this way. This was no
kind of marriage. Annabel knew she and Jack were at a
breaking point. Either they got through this, or they
didn't. Not for much longer would she live with Jack's
volatility, or stand for his continued flirtation—and
maybe more than that—with other women. She would
see how the next few weeks went. If things only got
worse—if Jack remained hostile to a police investigation, for example, or if he continued to seem angry and
distant—Annabel would suggest they needed some
time apart. She had no family other than Jack, so she
had no idea where she'd go. But surely there must be
some old friend in New York who would take her in.
Or, if necessary, she'd go deeper into debt and stay at a
hotel. If she needed to get out of here, she'd find a way.

But Annabel wasn't running just yet. For the moment, she would stay on course. One of the other
things she'd learned in rehab was to resist the urge to
flee. She learned that she was strong enough to face

anything. So she would persevere for the next few weeks, keeping her mind clear, resisting the hallucinations, rejecting the fear. She would resist feelings of paranoia. She was safe here. *Safe!*

And so she would push on with the renovation, the plan to make the house her own. She had no other choice. Otherwise, she might decompensate again and wind up nearly catatonic, as had happened yesterday morning. Annabel would not go down that road again.

"Kind of lost in thought over there, aren't you?" Chad asked, interrupting her reverie.

"Oh, I'm sorry," Annabel said.

"No need." He smiled over at her, revealing dimples in his cheeks. "I know you've got a lot on your mind."

"Well, maybe it's time I put some of it *out* of my mind." She returned his smile. "So, tell me, Chad. Do you plan someday on taking over your father's business?"

"That's the goal. My brothers aren't into it. But for me, I've loved remodeling houses ever since I built a loft in my bedroom when I was nine."

"Nine!"

Chad nodded, his eyes on the road ahead of him. "I've always been good with my hands."

Annabel laughed. "I'm sure your girlfriend appreciates that."

Chad looked over at her and smirked. "Annabel, was that a double entendre?"

She blushed suddenly. "I guess it did sound that way. But not what I meant. I just meant a woman likes to have a handyman around the house."

"Still sounds dirty," Chad said, laughing. "But the point is moot. I don't have a girlfriend. Not anymore."

"What happened?"

"Not really sure. I was dating this girl Claire ever since junior year of high school. I guess she just got tired of waiting for me to marry her, and she gave me the old heave-ho a few months ago."

"Oh, I'm sorry.'

"It's okay, really. If I'd have really been in love with her, like she said, I would have asked her to marry me a long time before that."

Annabel frowned. "Well, did she ever ask *you* to marry *her*?"

"Oh, plenty of times." Chad switched on his turn signal. "I'm just not the marrying type, I guess."

They headed off the highway.

"That's okay," Annabel said, looking off into the miles of bare, shivering trees on the side of the road. "Marriage isn't for everybody."

Chad looked over at her. "Is it for you?" he asked, and then quickly added, "I'm sorry. That was too personal."

"No, it's okay," she said. "To be honest, I'm not sure."

They were silent after that.

"Here we are," Chad announced a short time later, steering the truck into the lot outside a shop called BERKSHIRE TILE & PAINT. "Let's go in and let our imaginations run wild, shall we?"

Annabel smiled.

But as she headed into the shop, her own imagination was already racing far ahead of either of them. It was something Neville had said to her, late last night.

"I suspect this will all be cleared up in the next few

days," he'd whispered, out of earshot from Jack, after he came back into the house from some trip into town.

Annabel had asked him what he meant, but he'd just smiled enigmatically, his finger to his lip.

What had he meant? He'd appeared so certain. He'd still been asleep when Annabel left with Chad this morning, so there had been no chance to question him further.

But Annabel prayed he was right. *All be cleared up in the next few days.*

Passing through the lot, Annabel noticed a few tiny snowflakes swirling through the air.

"We're supposed to get a big storm tonight," Chad said, sticking out his tongue to collect some of the flakes. "Guess these are the first arrivals."

Laughing, they made their way inside the well-lit shop. With music playing and cash registers jangling, people laughing and cell phones ringing, Annabel felt her anxieties evaporate. She was comforted that, at least for the moment, she was back in the real world, far away from the dark warrens of the Blue Boy Inn.

72

"I told you," Jack Devlin growled, standing at the front door of the inn, blocking their way, "I won't have you tramping through this place, making us any more notorious around town than we already are."

Richard Carlson had anticipated this. Calmly, he reached into his jacket pocket and withdrew the court order that he'd just gotten from the judge. After Neville had paid him a visit last night, revealing the ring he'd found on the basement floor—the ring Priscilla Morton never, ever removed from her finger—Richard had made a special request of the judge to issue an immediate warrant for a search of the Blue Boy Inn. He had picked it up this morning, and showed it now to Jack Devlin.

"You'll see that this is a court order signed by a judge," he told Devlin.

The man's face darkened as he read the document. Behind Richard, Adam Burrell and two other deputies stood ready as backup, in case Devlin resisted. They would arrest him if they needed to.

Jack's dark eyes lifted from the paper to meet Richard's.

"Well, then," he said, his voice even. "I guess I'll have to let you come in then."

"Thank you for being reasonable, Mr. Devlin," Richard told him.

Jack stepped aside to allow the officers to enter the house.

"You two start in the attic," Richard directed two of his deputies, "while Adam and I will start in the cellar."

The chief looked around to see that the old caretaker, Zeke, had come into the parlor. Richard did not miss the look he exchanged with Devlin.

"Do you have the bolt cutters?" Richard asked Adam.

"That I do," the deputy replied, producing them from his pocket.

Richard nodded. With a flashlight showing the way ahead of him, he started down the basement stairs.

The padlock was easily dispatched with the bolt cutters. It fell to the earthen floor with a thud.

Richard opened the old iron door of the ash dump. It creaked in the stillness of the basement. Pointing the beam of the flashlight through the door, he looked inside.

"This thing has been recently cleaned," he said.

"How can you tell?" Adam asked.

"I can see the marks of whatever sort of brush that was used," the chief said, snapping photographs of the interior of the chimney. "Wind and condensation would have dissolved them after a few days. But now they're plain as day. This was just cleaned this morning, in my opinion."

He brought the light closer to the floor of the ash dump.

"But there's still some residue that doesn't look like soot," he pointed out. "You see?"

Adam peered inside and nodded. "It's a different color," he offered.

"That it is." Richard swung the beam of the flashlight out of the ash dump. "When forensics gets here, make sure they take a sample of that stuff."

"Will do, chief."

Richard made his way around the rest of the basement. He saw nothing. He was hoping to find something else besides the ring that had belonged to one of the two missing persons. But there was nothing in the basement other than an old chest, which, when Richard opened it, turned out to be completely empty.

He hoped his deputies in the attic were having more luck.

73

Neville was steaming mad. He stomped down the stairs behind the two officers who had let him out of his room—*rescued* him, in his opinion! He was bursting to give someone a piece of his mind—and he expected it would be Jack Devlin.

But in the parlor he found the Blue Boy's owner speaking with Police Chief Carlson. Well, that was convenient!

"I want to report an assault!" Neville shouted, rushing into the room and interrupting the two men's conversation.

The chief turned to look at him. Neville noticed the cagey expression that crossed Jack's face.

"An assault?" the chief asked.

"Yes, indeed," Neville replied. "I consider it an assault to be locked in one's room, unable to get out! What if there had been a fire?"

"You were locked in your room?" the chief inquired, looking from Neville back over at Jack.

Neville nodded. "That I was! I have been trying to get out for the past two hours, banging on the door and calling, but no one came to my assistance until these two officers here."

"We heard him calling on our way back down from the attic," one of the two deputies told Carlson.

Jack's face turned compassionate. "Oh, Neville, I'm sorry to hear this. Zeke and I were shoveling snow off the walk and must not have heard you. Annabel is up in Great Barrington with the contractor, so none of us were here to respond. I'm so sorry."

"There was a key in the lock outside the room!" Neville shrilled. "I was deliberately locked in there!"

"No one here would do such a thing," Jack assured him.

Neville swung his eyes to Chief Carlson. "He's lying!"

The chief said nothing, just studied both men.

"Look, Neville," Jack said, trying to sound reasonable, "you must have left your key in the lock last night. The doors are old. Sometimes if you don't remove the key, the door will lock again when it's closed."

"That's not true, chief," Neville said. "Someone came into my room while I was sleeping, found the key, and then locked me in there!"

"For what purpose would someone have done this?" Carlson asked.

"I don't know," Neville admitted. He looked over at Jack. "To be free to hide evidence, perhaps? Or look for it?" He opened his fist, which until now had been tightly clenched at his side. "Were you looking for this, Jack?" Neville asked, revealing Priscilla's ring.

"I don't know what that is," Jack said calmly.

"The night before Priscilla disappeared," Neville told the chief, "Jack was putting the moves on her. He was very aggressively getting her drunk. I don't know what happened, because I was too drunk myself."

The chief's eyebrows lifted. "How come you didn't tell us this before?"

Neville frowned. "I didn't think it had any relevance. But mostly because I didn't want to offend Annabel, who has been very kind to me."

Jack was smiling. "We all had a little too much to drink. I told you that, chief. But I was certainly not putting the moves on Priscilla, as Neville says. I think he might just be a little jealous because Priscilla clearly was coming on to me."

Neville saw the way the chief looked at Jack, the deep suspicion in his eyes. "Just like Tammy Morelli was putting the moves on you, too?" He smirked. "Seems every woman who comes into this house gets the Jack Devlin treatment."

"I don't think that's fair, chief," Jack told him, looking wounded.

"Look," Carlson said, turning his attention back to Neville. "You may well have locked yourself in by mistake. There's no way to prove otherwise. I'd just suggest you pack your things and leave. But before you do, I'd like you to come down to the station and give us an amended statement. Tell us everything you left out the first time."

"Gladly," Neville sniffed. "I leave tomorrow for England, but I think I'll head down to Hartford this afternoon and stay at a hotel outside the airport tonight."

"If flights are taking off," the chief commented, and they all looked up at the window. The snow was coming down heavier now. "We're supposed to be getting a nor'easter tonight."

"Well," Neville said, "I'd rather brave snowy roads than spend another night in this place."

He turned and headed back up the stairs. He could feel Jack's eyes on the back on his head until he was out of sight.

74

"Surely, you don't think I'd lock him in his room, do you?" Jack asked Richard once Neville was gone.

"I don't know what to think," Richard replied. "All I know is . . ."

He was distracted by the sound of people coming through the front door.

"The forensics team is here," Adam announced.

"What's that for?" Jack asked, his eyes narrowing as he watched Adam direct the two women and one man down the basement stairs.

"Just taking some samples," Richard told him. "I'm sure you want to find out what happened to Priscilla and Paulie as much as anyone, don't you, Mr. Devlin?"

The man's eyes darkened. "Did you find any sign of them at all? Your men have been crawling all over this place from top to bottom for the last hour."

"Not yet," Richard admitted. "But we'll keep looking."

In his mind, he cursed the snow. It could obscure or obliterate any clues outside. Thankfully, they'd already searched most of the surroundings.

"How much longer will you be here?" Jack asked. "Not that I'm trying to hurry you. I want to be completely cooperative." He smiled insincerely. "I'm just curious."

"We'll be out of here in a few minutes, I'd think," Richard told him. "Just long enough for the team downstairs to scrape a little gunk out of the ash dump." He smiled. "But the court order allows us to return if need be."

"I ought to just give you a key to the front door," Jack said, smirking.

"No, we're happy to knock," Richard assured him.

One of the two deputies who had searched the attic came up behind the chief. "We did find one thing that we can't account for," he said.

"What was that?" Richard asked.

The deputy held up a plastic Baggie. Inside was a tampon. Used, slightly pink.

"The old man says he sleeps up there from time to time," the deputy explained. "But I doubt this is his."

Richard turned to Jack. "Any ideas?"

Jack sneered. "Well, it certainly isn't mine, either."

"Have it analyzed," Richard told the deputy. "See if it matches the DNA we took from Priscilla's hairbrush."

"Maybe it's my wife's," Jack offered helpfully, though the insincerity was still evident in his voice. "It looks a little too fresh to have been my grandmother's."

"When is your wife back?" Richard asked.

"Who knows, with this storm?"

The two men locked eyes for several seconds.

"Okay, chief," Adam said. "Forensics got what you wanted."

"All right, then," Richard said, nodding in Jack's direction. "We'll leave you alone for now, Mr. Devlin."

"Be careful on those roads," Jack said, walking with the officers to the door, doing little to disguise his contempt for them. "Looks like it's getting slippery out there."

75

For the past hour, Annabel had managed the impossible. She had forgotten all about the nightmares back at the inn. Just as she used to do when she was working in New York—on a magazine photo shoot, maybe, or organizing a fashion show—she had focused in, laserlike, on the task at hand. Looking at tiles, comparing paint colors, she allowed herself to shift into creative mode. In her mind, she could see the parlor designed as a sleek, contemporary room, with lots of glass and exposed brick and mirrors on the walls. The kitchen would sparkle with new appliances and the bedrooms would be painted throughout with a soft, comforting blue. The bathrooms would be lined with brilliant Italian tiles.

"I'm really into bringing out the brick," Annabel said, looking at a sandblaster. "If we offset the brick with some glass and metal . . ."

"Sounds good to me," Chad agreed. "Maybe even knock some of the brick out and replace it with glass blocks to bring the light through."

"Oh, excellent idea!" Annabel beamed. "This place will make *Architectural Digest*. I know people there."

"Here are some of the paint samples you requested," said a stocky clerk with thick glasses, worn low on his nose.

"I like the blue," Annabel said, examining them, "but the yellow is a bit too bright. Can you subtle that a little more?"

"Sure thing," the clerk said, returning to his paint mixer.

"This is so much fun," Annabel gushed to Chad.

"It's nice to see you smile," the contractor told her.

Annabel felt herself blush. Chad was awfully sweet, and cute, too. "Well," she said, "I must admit it feels good to smile."

At that moment, her phone buzzed in her purse.

It had been so long since her phone had worked— the cell reception at the Blue Boy was the next problem they needed to address—that she almost didn't recognize the sound. She dug the phone out from among the lipsticks and tissue and tampons in her purse. The number was that of the inn. It had to be Jack. Oh, God, what was he going to say?

"Hello?" Annabel said into the phone, walking over to a quiet corner of the store.

"Annabel. It's Neville."

He was whispering.

"Neville. Is there anything wrong?"

"I had to call you from the house phone because my mobile doesn't work here." He sounded anxious. "I don't want anyone to hear me."

"What's wrong?"

"I wanted to let you know I'll be gone by the time you get back. Someone locked me in my room this morning. I expect it was Zeke, on Jack's orders."

"Why would they do that?"

"Because they were cleaning the house of evidence. I'm sure of it. Chief Carlson was here, searching the place."

Annabel was stunned. "So he got a warrant?"

"Yes. And he found nothing. That's why I expect Jack and Zeke cleaned things up."

"The ash dump?"

"They opened it, and it was as dry as a whistle."

"None of that wet soot?" Annabel asked.

"Nope. Though they did scrape out something from the bottom for analysis, but it wasn't very much." Annabel could hear Neville shudder at the other end of the line. "I've never been happier to leave a place, no offense to you."

"None taken."

"I'm leaving now, heading down to Hartford before the snow gets too bad. Even if my flight's canceled tomorrow and I'm stranded at Bradley Airport overnight, it'll be better than spending another night here."

"I understand."

Neville sighed. "I'm supposed to fly to New York to catch a connecting flight to London. Pray that I make the connection. I'll be in touch, Annabel. I may have to return to testify if they find whoever took Priscilla."

"So you spoke with the chief?"

"I'm heading there now to give him a final statement before I head out."

"Oh, Neville . . ." Annabel thought she might cry.

"Thank you for your kindness, my dear," he said, "and good luck with everything."

"Yes, Neville, good luck to you, too."

"If you don't mind me saying so," the Englishman said, "I think there's something very sinister going on in this house. Take care of yourself."

"I will, Neville."

"Good-bye."

"Good-bye."

Annabel clicked END on her phone. She suddenly felt endlessly sad.

"Everything okay?"

She looked up. Chad had approached her.

"I don't know," she said. "Neville just called to say good-bye. He's leaving. But he told me the police had been by with a warrant and searched the place."

"Did they find anything?"

"Apparently not," Annabel replied. "But who knows? They took a sample from the ash dump. Otherwise it was clean."

"That's odd," said Chad. "Hard to imagine that thing being very clean after all the chomping I heard in there. Raccoons aren't the neatest eaters."

"It was clean," Annabel said, her mind suddenly very far away.

"Look," Chad said. "The snow is getting heavier. I've put everything on order. We should head back."

"Yes," Annabel agreed. "We should."

The happiness she'd felt just a few moments earlier had now completely evaporated. The idea of going back to that place depressed her thoroughly.

I've got to hold on, she told herself. *I can't allow*

myself to fall down into a black hole again. I have to stay clearheaded. Strong. Resist my tendency to hallucinate and catastrophize. I have to keep my head, not lose it.

But Neville's words kept echoing in her mind.

I think there's something very sinister going on in this house.

Annabel followed Chad out to his truck.

76

Neville hung up the phone. Glancing around to make sure that neither Jack nor Zeke was around, he hurried from the kitchen.

In the foyer, his bag was packed and waiting by the door. A hush had settled over the house. Outside, giant snowflakes were floating down from the gray sky, blanketing everything in white. Neville realized he was going to have to brush off his car. He wished he had brought gloves.

"I'm *not* packing any gloves," he'd announced to Priscilla with a smirk, as they'd left their flat for Heathrow—which now seemed an eternity ago. "I am packing as if we are not making any ridiculous ghost-hunting side trips and going straight to Florida."

Florida. Neville had always wanted to go there. He'd been looking so very much forward to those sandy beaches, that warm water, that cool margarita in his hand. *Maybe another time*, Neville consoled himself with a sigh.

"Neville."

His name came from the parlor in a whisper. He didn't

recognize the voice. But it might have been Jack or Zeke, speaking very softly.

"Neville," the whisper came again.

He stepped around the corner and peeked into the room. He saw no one. The house seemed so quiet, as if every sound ceased. No hum from the electricity, no ticking of any clock, no wind from the eaves.

"Hello?" Neville called.

He walked into the parlor and paused in front of the fireplace. Had he imagined what he'd heard? No, that hadn't been his imagination. He had heard someone whisper his name. Twice. And the only people in the house were Jack and Zeke.

"Neville."

He spun around. "Who is there?"

Suddenly, Neville felt afraid. There was a killer loose, after all. Someone who had chopped off a man's hand, and who had surely killed Priscilla as well, if her ring was any indication. Was it the killer who called to Neville now?

He bolted for the door, planning to grab his suitcase and his coat and hurry off into the snowstorm outside.

He was almost to the door when he tripped. Just what he tripped over, he wasn't sure. But he went toppling over face-first to the floor.

He braced his fall with his elbows and forearms. The pain shot up through his shoulders. He might have broken something.

But he didn't have time to check. He looked around and saw what had caused him to fall.

A little man, no more than three feet tall, with a little blue face wearing rags for clothes.

"Can I get him?" the little man asked in a soft, whispery voice.

"Yes, you can get him," came another voice, and before the startled Neville could react, another little man, looking nearly identical, came hurrying around the corner. And then another little man appeared, and another and another, until five of the loathsome creatures had piled on top of Neville, grabbing at the back of his shirt and up and down his arms with their very sharp hands.

"Get off me!" Neville managed to shout, trying to shake them off.

But the little men were incredibly strong. They kept him from standing by clamping their clawlike fingers into his calves, ripping through his pants and puncturing his skin. Neville screamed.

"Help me!" he shouted, hoping that Jack or Zeke would hear. "Help me!"

The little men began pulling him across the floor. As much as Neville tried to fight them, he found he was powerless to escape their clutches. Three of them were at his feet, clawing and biting his calves and shins. The two others were positioned at each shoulder, grabbing ahold painfully and dragging him back into the parlor.

This can't be happening! This can't be real!

Neville could see the creatures on either side of him. They were laughing, thoroughly enjoying their task.

Twisting from side to side, still unable to break free of them, Neville looked up ahead. What he saw was even more unbelievable.

Two more of the creatures had popped their heads up from the ash dump panel at the bottom of the fireplace. They were waving their sharp little fingers—they looked like squirrel claws—motioning to their comrades to bring Neville closer.

"Nooo!" Neville screamed.

But he couldn't fight back. All he could manage to do was writhe from side to side. The creatures seemed to have complete power over him. Neville began to whimper.

This was how he would die, he realized.

The little men thrust his head into the fireplace. The creatures waiting inside the ash dump suddenly clamped their claws into his neck and Neville shrieked out in pain. The others behind him were pushing his butt and legs now. With one final thrust, Neville's head and shoulders were crammed down through the trapdoor into the chimney.

This is what happened to the others! This was how they died!

The creatures behind him kept pushing and shoving, while the creatures ahead of him kept pulling him down. Neville's body was now wedged halfway down the chimney.

That's one really wide chimney, Chad had said. *You could fit a body in there, sure.*

Neville felt his feet pass through the opening in the fireplace and he fell about a foot, becoming lodged in the darkness of the chimney.

Below him came the sound of gnashing teeth.

I doubt it's squirrels and mice they're eating, Neville had told Chad.

He was about to learn just how right he was.

77

The scream from inside the chimney echoed through the house. Suddenly it was cut short, and Zeke knew the man was dead.

The old caretaker stood in the parlor, staring at the fireplace. He was crying.

"How many more?" he asked the quiet house. "How long will this go on?"

No answer came, of course. There had never been an answer, for as long as he had lived at the Blue Boy Inn.

Damn that woman for opening up the fireplace. They had had it contained. They had had it under control.

He wiped his tears with the back of his hand. He knew what he needed to do.

He grabbed Neville's suitcase and headed outside. He'd hide the dead man's car in the woods. The police would think that he'd left for the airport in the midst of this blizzard in order to try to make it home.

But Zeke neglected to take Neville's coat. It remained hanging there on the hook.

78

Chad drove his truck back toward Woodfield, Annabel seated beside him. The snow was still light, but it was starting to stick to the roads. The state trucks were already out, spraying salt and sand from side to side.

"Could be a nor'easter," Chad said. "You're in for quite the experience, if the storm turns out to be as big as they're predicting it might be."

Annabel visibly shivered. "I've been worrying about being snowbound at the inn ever since we decided to move up here."

Chad smiled over at her. "But you've had big snowstorms in the city, too. I remember reading about that big one a few years ago where days later they found people in cars that had been piled over by snowplows."

"Oh, sure," Annabel told him. "But you see, in New York, you have other people in your building. You can go next door, talk to someone. You're not isolated. You can go down to the sidewalk and you can crunch through the snow to a market that's managed to open.

Even in the worst storms, some enterprising shop-keeper always manages to open his doors."

Chad sighed. "Okay, I hear you. That's certainly not the case here. In Woodfield—in a lot of western Mass, in fact—things just shut down during a nor'easter. Power can go out and stay out for a week."

Annabel groaned. "Oh, great."

"You ought to maybe think about getting a generator as part of your renovations," Chad suggested.

"Yes. That's a good idea. A very good idea."

They were quiet for a few moments as they drove.

"You know, Annabel," Chad said, breaking the silence, "whatever's going down back at the inn, if you need my help . . ."

She looked away, out the window. "Of course, I need your help, Chad. I can't rewire electricity and knock down walls myself."

"No, what I mean is . . ." Chad struggled to find the words. "With everything that's happened, you know, with the police being there and conducting a search, well, if I can do anything . . ."

Annabel turned back and looked at him. She offered him a small smile.

"Thank you, Chad," she said softly.

He liked her. He found himself really liking her a lot. Chad had never been attracted to a married woman before. He wasn't quite sure what to do with his feelings. Since the breakup with Claire, he hadn't had much interest in dating. He hadn't had much interest in women, period. A really gorgeous woman could walk right by him and Chad would barely notice. He remembered not so long ago, Paulie—poor old Paulie—looking at him as if he were crazy. Chad had been reading the newspaper, oblivious to anything around him. "Dude," Paulie had said. "That was a major babe who just passed by and you couldn't even pull your nose away from the Patriots' score long enough to notice."

But he sure noticed Annabel.

She was hot, no doubt about that. Her shiny auburn hair, her tiny waist, her perfect figure. And she was married to a major-league asshole, if Tammy's story was true—and Chad believed it was. What if Jack Devlin had something to do with Paulie's disappearance, and the disappearance of that English lady? Annabel could be in real trouble in that house.

"Listen," Chad said, as he switched on the blinker to take the exit toward Woodfield, "I'm serious. You have no idea what you're dealing with up at that old house. Too much weird shit has gone down there over the years. I'd like to be around to take care of you if—"

"You are very sweet," Annabel said, cutting him off, "and more than chivalric. I appreciate your offer, Chad. I really do." She looked away again, back out the window. "But I think I've got to learn how to take care of myself."

"Well, sure, but if things get rough . . ."

He could see that she was smiling, though she didn't look back at him.

"Oh," Annabel said, "things have been rough for a while. Jack said they'd get easier here, but they haven't. I'm not surprised." Finally, she looked back at him, giving him a smile and a flash of her pretty eyes. "So I'm used to things being rough."

"As rough as all this?" Chad asked, as the truck rattled onto the main road leading into Woodfield. "A dead man's hand being found on your property? Two people going missing from your house? The cops searching the place? Can you handle all that?"

Annabel's smiled faded and she looked away again. "We shall see," she said softly. "We shall see."

79

From his desk, Richard could hear the special weather bulletin on the television warning of an impending major winter storm. "Snowfalls possible of up to four to five feet," the woman in the bright pink jacket was saying, doing her best to look suitably concerned.

Richard was worried, but not about snow. He turned another page in the collection of cold case files on his desk. His predecessor as chief of police, Thad Arnette, had been on the job when Jack Devlin's father had "gone mad," as Millie described it. Arnette had left a fascinating note about the episode.

> I questioned Devlin at length, both about his wife and his daughter, because some things just did not add up. Investigating the little Devlin girl's disappearance, we discovered the mother had also recently died, reportedly of breast cancer. But no death certificate could be located for her, and no hospital in the state had records of her being a patient. Devlin explained this by saying that there was a paperwork mix-up and

that the death certificate would be issued shortly.
He seemed very uneasy, easily distracted, and
sometimes did not make complete sense. We
need to follow up with him, and see when that
death certificate is filed.

Richard ran his hand across his short-cropped hair.
Arnette suspected Devlin's father of something, he realized. Perhaps some complicity in, or knowledge of
his wife's death and daughter's disappearance.

But soon after that note came another.

Devlin has left town, returning to New York with
his son. Have not received death certificate for
Mrs. Devlin.

And then that was it. Most likely, other cases took
precedence and after a while, with Devlin gone, Arnette forgot about him. Out of sight, out of mind. Not
the best way to run a police department, Richard acknowledged, but it happened. The questions Arnette had
about the death of Mrs. Devlin and the disappearance of
the little girl—Cindy, her name was—were filed away
among the rest of the cold case files.

What had happened to Jack Devlin's mother if she
didn't die of cancer?

Richard buzzed for his secretary. "Betty," he said,
"could you come here in a moment?"

She was promptly bustling through the door. Betty
was a good scout. Utterly devoted to the department.
She'd been there twenty-one years. She'd started right
out of high school as a file clerk, working her way up
to secretary to the chief. She was thirty-nine years old,

a little plump, with short bronze-colored hair. She was always smiling, or smirking.

"You rang, master?" she quipped.

"Betty, tell me what you remember about Jack Devlin's parents."

She was biting the end of a pencil. "The parents? Didn't really know them. They weren't here very long. The grandparents, of course, were here for decades. . . ."

"Yes, but do you remember when his parents came to Woodfield? His father was going to take over the inn, I believe, just as Jack is doing now."

Betty was nodding. "Yes, that's right. I do remember when they came, but they were gone in a flash, it seemed, right after the little girl got eaten by a bear."

"That was never proven."

"It wasn't?"

Richard shook his head. "No, it wasn't. Do you remember that the mother died of breast cancer?"

"Oh, that's right, I do remember that. Poor thing. I saw her at the market a few times. Seemed very pretty, full of life. Then all of a sudden she was gone."

Richard pursed his lips. "So," he said, "she didn't ever appear sickly?"

"No. I remember being real surprised hearing that she'd died, especially of cancer. It surprised everyone. One day, she was just gone."

Richard sat back in his chair. "According to the official story, she was taken to a hospital and died there."

Betty grinned. "And you don't believe it."

"I'm just questioning it."

"What does that have to do with what's happening at the Blue Boy today?"

Richard shrugged. "Maybe nothing. I'm just trying

to get a history of everything that's gone down there. It's had more than its share of tragedy and mystery."

"That's for sure. You know who would know a lot about the Blue Boy?"

"No, who?"

"Agnes Daley. She's at the library. She's the town historian, but really she's the town gossip. Knows everything about everyone." Betty shuddered. "Probably knows a few secrets of mine, too. I wouldn't get on Agnes's bad side."

"How long has she lived in town?"

"All her life. And she's got to be seventy-five, at least. She can take you way back."

"Thanks," Richard said. "I think I'll give her a call."

"I'll get you the number for the library," Betty told him.

Within a few minutes, Richard was punching in buttons for the Woodfield Public Library. As the line rang, the chief's eyes glanced off toward the window. The snow was coming down lightly, little spirals of white. He hoped the accumulation wouldn't be too heavy. That always meant a nightmare for police work, with people snowed in on their streets, businesses unable to open, and fender benders all over town.

"Public library, Agnes Daley," a raspy, efficient voice suddenly announced.

Richard introduced himself.

"Chief Carlson!" the town historian exclaimed. "It's not every day that the chief of police calls me. What can I do for you?" Her ragged voice bore the unmistakable sound of someone who had smoked cigarettes all her life.

"I'd like to talk to you about what you know about the history of the Blue Boy Inn," Richard told her.

"The Blue Boy Inn?" Agnes snorted. "Oh, not you, too, chief."

"What do you mean, not me, too?"

"At least once a week the library gets a call from some far-flung corner of the world—Arkansas or Oregon or New Zealand or East Timbukistan—asking about that place. Ghost hunters, you know. They want details and pictures and otherworldly accounts."

Richard laughed. "Well, I'm interested in the history of this world, Ms. Daley."

"Call me Agnes, or we'll never get along."

"All right, Agnes."

"Is this about the latest disappearances?" she rasped. "And Roger Askew's hand? Because if so, I don't have any idea how—"

"Well, that's what has prompted my investigation," Richard said, interrupting her. "But I'm more interested at the moment in the inn's previous history. How well did you know Cordelia Devlin?"

Agnes chortled. "As well as anyone could know her. She was a recluse. Barely ever left that house since her husband died. She always sent that strange old man, Zeke, she had working for her on errands into town."

"Was she more social when her husband was alive?"

"I suppose she was. Then the husband died, and the son came up to take over the place . . ." Agnes's voice faded off as she spoke.

"Did you know the son?" Richard asked. "That would be the current owner's father."

"I met him a few times. Seemed a nice enough man. Until the tragedies with his wife and daughter."

It appeared Agnes knew little more about Jack's father than Betty had. Richard tried a different tack.

"What about Cordelia's husband?" he asked. "What kind of man was he?"

"Well, he was kind of an ambitious sort, as I remember, when he first took over the place from *his* father. But after that little baby died up there, he, too, became a recluse."

"The one whose arm was the only thing found?"

"Oh, yes," Agnes said. "How sad that was. Poor little thing. They said the child must have been eaten by a bear, just like what was supposed to have happened to little Cindy Devlin years later, though they found nothing of her."

"Sounds like you don't believe these were bear attacks."

Agnes snorted again. "Well, they fit so well into the haunted house narrative—you know, the curse of the Blue Boy Inn. So many deaths up there."

"Do you remember any others?"

"I remember that man McGurk. I was a little girl then. Freaked me out, as the kids say today. They found a body with no head. How outrageous is that? In the middle of the parlor yet! Never found the killer, either."

"Yes," Richard said. "I've been reading up on that case. The investigators eventually closed the case. Everyone in the house had an alibi, and the head was never found, so they never made an arrest."

"There have been other deaths and disappearances, too," said Agnes.

"I have them all here in my files," Richard told her. "How far do the stories of a curse go back?"

"Well, right back to the beginning," she replied.

"And when was the beginning?"

"Well," Agnes said, thinking, "the Blue Boy was built around 1865, I think. Right after the Civil War. It's been extensively remodeled several times, and the integrity of its original architecture is gone, but I think you can still see some of the original structure. I haven't been up there in an awfully long time, so I can't say for sure."

"Was it always an inn?"

"Oh, no. In the beginning it was a pastor's house. That's where the stories of the curse began."

"Care to fill me in?" Richard asked.

"Its original owner was the Reverend John Fall. He was the head of a little church that once stood on the property as well. But in 1869, John Fall was hanged."

"Hanged?" Richard asked. "For what?"

"Murder," Agnes replied. "One of his pretty young parishioners was found with her throat slit from ear to ear. But word around town was that the deeper crime of Reverend Fall was witchcraft. According to the rumor, he'd killed the poor girl in some kind of satanic ritual. His church, these stories insisted, was merely a cover for his black arts."

"Any proof of that?"

"Nope. Just the legends that persisted for decades after his death. The official line was that Fall had killed her because she was going to tell his wife they were having an affair."

Richard sighed. "I can see why stories of a curse would begin, if the original owner had been suspected of witchcraft."

"But there's no denying, chief, that ever since, lots

of people have died or disappeared up there," Agnes told him.

"No," he agreed. "There's no denying that."

"The church was torn down, and the house sat vacant for many years, until someone got the idea to open it up as an inn. Soon after the turn of the twentieth century, the Devlin family bought it, and they've owned it ever since."

"The current owner is the fourth generation of the family then," Richard said.

"Yes, sir. And he's already seeing the curse at work."

Richard laughed. "Surely you don't believe in it, Agnes."

"I'm a confirmed agnostic in all areas of my life. That doesn't mean I don't believe. It means that I neither believe nor disbelieve." She laughed. "It's the only path for a historian, unless you want to bring your own biases to your study of history."

"That sounds like the smart approach," Richard told her.

"I hope I've been of some help to you, chief."

Richard told her she had, and thanked her for her time.

"No problem," Agnes replied. "If you want to show your appreciation, you can make sure my street is plowed first thing in the morning, before anyone else's when this blasted blizzard simmers down."

Richard laughed. "I'll speak with public works," he told her.

"Much obliged," Agnes said.

After he had had hung up the phone, Richard thought he could hardly base an investigation on rumors of a nearly two-hundred-year-old charge of witchcraft. How foolish people were. Maybe they just couldn't believe a man of the cloth could succumb to the desires of the flesh and cheat on his wife, so they had concocted a tale about satanic rituals to account for it. He had learned little of use, it seemed, from town historian Agnes Daley.

But there's no denying, chief, that ever since, lots of people have died or disappeared up there.

Nope. There was no denying that.

Richard stared out the window. The snow was coming down heavier now. The snow made him think of Amy. But everything made him think of Amy.

80

Annabel and Chad came through the front door shaking snow off their coats and boots. "Gosh, it's really coming down!" Annabel exclaimed.

"Sure is," Chad agreed. "In another hour those roads won't be passable. The storm has come earlier than they were predicting. We got back just in time."

"I'll make some hot tea," Annabel offered, "if you don't have to rush right off."

Chad nodded. "I want to take a look at the fireplace to make sure the flue isn't damaged. When you've got this bad of a storm, you should really keep the flue closed."

"Oh, good idea, thank you."

Chad headed off into the parlor while Annabel made her way to the kitchen.

She turned the corner and walked straight into someone standing there. She gasped out loud.

"Jack!" she cried.

Her husband smiled down at her. "I heard you say you wanted tea. I've already got some ready, baby cakes. I figured you'd come in chilled to the bone."

"Oh." Annabel was flustered for a moment. "Great, thanks."

"Shall I pour you a cup?" he asked.

"Yes, please, Jack, thanks. And pour a cup for Chad, too. He's just checking the fireplace."

Jack smiled as he lifted the steaming pot off the stove. "The fireplace?" he asked.

"Yes. He's making sure the flue closes. With the storm coming, we'll want to make sure."

"Of course. Smart thinking."

He handed Annabel a mug, the steam rising from it in waves.

"Careful, sweetie pie. Don't burn your tongue."

She accepted the mug and held it in her hands.

"I'll pour one for Chad and set it here on the table for him," Jack said. "Let it cool off just a little bit."

Annabel cupped her mug between her two hands and stared at her husband. How sweet he seemed all of a sudden. He reminded her of the caring man he'd been during her hospitalization, how supportive he had been, how thoughtful. Jack had stuck by her through the worst of times. She had been so grateful to him.

This was the real Jack, she wanted to believe. The Jack of the past few days—mysterious and defensive—had been simply the product of stress and fear. And grief, over losing his grandmother. And worry, over the disappearances of Priscilla and Paulie and what that might mean to their business venture.

"Have a sip of tea, sugar babe," Jack said. "Take the chill off."

"Still too hot," she said, blowing on the mug. "I sure hope we don't get snowbound. I don't like the idea of being trapped."

Jack smiled. "Your old claustrophobia. Don't worry, angel heart. I'll dig a path from the front door to the street. You won't be trapped."

A smile bloomed on her face despite her misgivings. "Thanks, Jack. So, Neville's gone? I didn't see his car."

"Neville's gone," Jack told her. "Drink your tea, baby doll."

She blew on the mug again. "He called me, you know, before he left."

"Neville did?"

"Yes." She locked eyes on Jack. "He said he'd been locked in his room."

Jack frowned. "Yes, he told the police chief that, too. Sweetheart, the key was in his door outside. He must have left it there himself, and then the door locked again when he closed it. It's a problem of these old doors."

"You don't think he had any cause to say he was locked in?"

Jack laughed. "Who would have locked him in, and why?"

Annabel sighed. "I don't know, Jack. But we need to talk. Some very strange things have been happening. I understand when the police searched the chimney downstairs, they found none of the gunk that I put my hands into the other day. How did that all that get cleaned out?"

Jack looked mystified. "I don't know. Maybe . . . Zeke cleaned it out?"

"I'm wondering that myself."

"I'll ask him." Jack appeared as if a light suddenly went off in his head. "That could explain why the police found nothing." He smiled over at Annabel. "You know, I was very cooperative with them. I figured it was better to show that we had nothing to hide than to act as if we did."

"Oh, I'm glad, Jack."

His smile broadened. "Drink your tea, honey. You're still shivering."

Annabel returned his smile. Then she lifted the mug to her lips and drank.

81

"Christ," Chad said in a low voice, checking the fireplace one more time to be sure.

That's blood, he thought to himself.

He was squatting down, inspecting the floor of the fireplace, specifically the ash dump opening. It was a big panel, a good three feet by two feet, and all around its edges there was a sticky brownish-red liquid. When Chad touched his finger to it, he felt certain it was blood. Still fresh. Not dried.

Chad stood. He could hear Annabel and Jack talking in the kitchen. His first thought was to rush in and tell them what he found, but something stopped him. He didn't trust Jack. He was better off finding out what he could and taking the information directly to Chief Carlson.

He glanced over at the basement stairs.

Annabel said that the police had been here this morning and checked the ash dump downstairs. They'd found nothing.

But that blood's fresh. . . .

Chad surmised that the door to the ash dump at the

base of the chimney would still be open. The cops surely didn't lock it up again.

He needed to take a look. Then, depending on what he found, he'd hightail it out of this creepy old place straight down to the police headquarters. And he might just take Annabel with him, just to be safe. He liked her. He wasn't going to abandon her if, as he was starting to think, somebody in this house was a murderer.

And that somebody was very likely her creepy husband.

Listening as Annabel and Jack continued to talk in the kitchen, Chad made his way stealthily across the parlor and out into the hallway.

He paused, listening. He didn't want that weird old guy Zeke to spot him.

Chad made a dash for the basement stairs. He hurried down as quickly as he could without making too much noise.

He yanked the overhead light on.

He could see the chimney across the room, hunched over like a crippled Atlas, the sagging floorboards of the first floor the world on his shoulders.

Chad approached slowly. The dim light overhead outlined the small metal door on the side of the chimney. He could see that the door was shut tight. But there was no longer any padlock dangling from its handle.

He reached over to pull the door open, but then stopped. His hand hovered in midair.

What are you afraid of? he asked himself.

He wasn't sure. But suddenly Chad was very, very afraid.

He forced his hand forward and gripped the door.

He tried to pull it open, but the old metal was stuck. Chad shook it a bit, and then gave it a good hard yank, and all at once the door swung open in his hand.

He had uncorked a river.

A cascade of blood burst forward, splashing out from the chimney onto the floor, wetting Chad's shoes and turning them red. The flow only stopped when the doorframe became wedged with pale white human flesh.

Neville's head, in fact, severed from his shoulders.

He stared out at Chad with wide, terrified eyes, his dead mouth in an eternal silent scream.

Chad, however, wasn't nearly so silent.

He let out a scream and turned to run, only to be met on the staircase by a woman.

A woman he'd never seen before.

A beautiful woman with long gray hair, dressed in a long, flowing white dress.

"Hello," the woman said calmly.

Chad opened his mouth to ask her to please get out of his way, to run as fast as she could out of this house, when he felt the pain in his abdomen. He cried out, then looked down and saw blood collecting behind his shirt.

The woman had just stabbed him with a knife.

82

Annabel heard the scream below her and spun around.

"What was that?" she called out.

Jack just smiled. "Don't be so jumpy, baby cakes."

"Didn't you hear—?" She turned to run out of the kitchen toward the basement stairs, but suddenly her knees buckled. Her legs were too weak to hold her. She started to fall, but grabbed the table to steady herself.

"You okay, sweetheart?" Jack asked, his voice eerily calm.

"My head," Annabel murmured.

The room was spinning. She was passing out. Something was happening in the basement, and she was losing consciousness. . . .

Drink your tea, honey.

Annabel looked over at Jack. He was watching her compassionately, but not moving a muscle to help her.

"You . . . drugged the tea," she managed to say.

She heard a second scream from the basement.

"Chad," said Annabel, just as she crumpled to the floor and blacked out.

83

The light was different when Annabel woke up. She had the feeling that she'd been out for a long time. She realized she was in bed, in her room. She was alone.

She tried to stir, to sit up, but found her body was numb. She could barely move her hands or feet. *What did he give me?* That monster!

A monster she had once loved—and who, until a very short time ago, she had still been willing to give the benefit of the doubt.

Jack drugged me. He may be trying to kill me.

Just as he may have killed Priscilla and Paulie.

Annabel's mind was racing. She thought she could see things clearly now. Jack had killed Priscilla the night they got drunk. He had stashed her body somewhere—the fireplace!—and Paulie had found it the next morning. That was why he'd had to kill Paulie, too. Jack had stuffed both their bodies into the chimney. Annabel had gotten their blood on her hands! And maybe—the idea hit her like a lightning bolt—maybe Jack had killed Cordelia as well. Richard had seemed to doubt the coroner's ruling of accidental death. Had his grandmother discovered his crime as well?

Another memory suddenly struck Annabel. She gasped out loud.

Chad! Right before she'd blacked out, she'd heard Chad scream.

"Oh, no," she moaned.

Please don't let Chad be dead, too.

At least Neville had gotten away.

She had to get out of there. She had to run. She had to get Richard.

With great effort, Annabel managed to sit up in bed. It was morning. That much she knew. Although they'd lost power, leaving the electric clock on one side of the bed dark, the batteries in the clock on the other side had kept it ticking. The time was 10:15. Annabel realized she had been unconscious all night.

She needed to move. But she doubted she had the strength to swing her legs off the bed, let alone stand and walk. She was breathing heavily from the exertion. She looked helplessly across the room. Through the window she could see the storm was still raging outside. While she'd slept, the snow had piled up at least three feet. The whole world outside her window looked white. She could barely see the trees. Everything was just a washout of glaring whiteness.

"That means I'm trapped here," Annabel said out loud. "I can't get out and nobody can get in." She shuddered. "It's just me and Jack."

And Zeke. Unless Jack had killed him, too.

But even if he was alive, was Zeke friend or foe?

Annabel began to sweat. She wasn't sure what scared her more. Jack—or the claustrophobia of being snowbound in this house. The two together threatened to push her back over the edge.

Don't worry, angel heart. I'll dig a path from the front door to the street. You won't be trapped.

He'd been lying to her. Playing her. He'd known what he was doing. Lulling her into a false sense of security. Then he'd drugged her.

But why? What was Jack's plan?

What had turned him so insane?

"I've got to get out," Annabel said, and summoned every fiber of her being to move her legs off the bed and touch her bare feet against the cold wood floor.

He undressed me, she realized. *Jack took off my clothes and put me in my nightgown.*

Had he done other things to her?

She shuddered, remembering the night he had raped her. Yes, that was what it was. Her husband had raped her. She had tried to deny it to herself, but no more.

Jack was a monster.

But why? How? What had turned him into something Annabel no longer recognized?

She grabbed hold of the bedpost and pulled herself to her feet. She let out a groan doing so. Whatever she'd been drugged with still had a heavy grip on her body.

Standing, she had a better view of the outside. The snow had covered Jack's car in the driveway. She couldn't even make out its outline in the parking lot. The driveway was completely inaccessible. She had thought earlier that there were at least three feet of snow out there. Now that she could see the ground better, she revised that estimate up to five feet. From her second-floor vantage point, Annabel could see that the snow had drifted across the front porch, completely covering the front door. If she tried to leave by that route, she would be faced with a solid wall of snow. There was no way she could walk out of this house, even if she got her legs to move more freely than they did at the moment.

The snow was still coming down, too.

Annabel realized with a cold certainty that she was trapped.

Her palms started to sweat again. She began to shake uncontrollably. Stiffly, she wrapped her arms around herself.

"I've got to try," she said out loud. "Maybe I can go out the back door."

But what then? Maybe, despite the drifts and the blowing snow, she could make her way to Millie's store, the closest inhabited place to the Blue Boy Inn. Annabel thought she had cell reception there. Even if not, she could just hide out there until someone came by, as she didn't imagine the store was open in this blizzard.

She'd need to be dressed more warmly if she was going to try walking through that snow. With great effort she shuffled over to her dresser. With even greater effort, she pulled open the drawers. She let out a gasp. All her clothes were gone.

"No," Annabel cried.

Her cell phone. Her gaze swung around the room. She didn't see it.

It's in my purse downstairs, she remembered. *Jack surely has it.*

If she could get downstairs without Jack stopping her, she could call 911 on the house phone. It was an old model, with no cordless handsets that required electricity. If the phone lines weren't down, it should still be working.

She took a deep breath. With superhuman exertion, she put one foot in front of the other and walked. Steadying herself against the dresser, she made her way to the door.

She tried the handle. Of course it was locked.

He locked Neville in. Of course, he'd lock me in, too.

But at least Neville had managed to escape. Annabel suddenly felt she wouldn't be as lucky.

She began to hyperventilate. Her knees threatened to buckle, dropping her to the floor. She leaned up against the door to keep herself upright. She began to cry.

"You'll stay in there until you learn to be a good girl," came a voice through the door.

Annabel pulled back.

It was Daddy Ron.

"Look around, Annabel. Look around and see who's in there with you."

"No," she whimpered.

"Go ahead. Turn around. He's right behind you. Can you hear him?"

Annabel listened. Yes, there he was. She could hear Tommy Tricky behind her, gnashing his sharp teeth.

"He's not real," Annabel cried in a terribly small voice.

"Oh, don't say that," hissed Daddy Ron through the door. "That gets him mad. He doesn't like it when little girls don't believe in him."

She was crying like mad now, her body heaving.

This is crazy, Annabel thought, trying to get ahold of

herself, to stop her plunge over the edge. *This can't be happening. I'm an adult, not a little girl locked in a closet.*

There is no such thing as Tommy Tricky!

She turned and looked over her shoulder, just in time to see something scurry under the bed.

"No!" she screamed.

She was hallucinating again. That was the only explanation. She had to get out of this house! Even if it meant trudging through the blizzard. She'd rather freeze to death out there than go mad inside this house!

She walked slowly, awkwardly, over to the bed. Summoning all her strength, she grabbed hold of the side of the bed and shoved. It took a second, but then the bed slid across the floor.

And sitting there, underneath, his blue face alive with a mouthful of teeth, was Tommy Tricky.

Annabel screamed.

84

Richard Carlson stood at the window of the police station staring out into the snow. It had been snowing like this the day Amy had died. His wife had looked like a little rag doll in her bed at Massachusetts General Hospital in Boston, weighing just eighty-odd pounds. Richard had stood by the window, watching the snow blanket the city, looking back every now and then over at Amy. Her breathing was so shallow. The thin white sheet drawn up to her neck barely moved. Richard had known Amy was dead even before the nurses came in to examine her. There was no dramatic ending to sweet Amy's life. She never opened her eyes. There was no last look between her and her husband. Her faint breathing just stopped and she was gone. Richard had sat at her bedside for three hours after she was gone, just holding her rapidly cooling hand.

"All the roads are blocked throughout the county," Adam told him, coming into his office behind him. "There's no way the plows can get through this."

"I've lived in these parts all my life," said Betty, the

police secretary, "and I've never seen a snowfall like this."

"We've got reports of drifts up to nine feet," Adam said.

Richard looked back out into the swirling white. Why was he thinking of Amy? Maybe because of how badly he had wanted to save her. Maybe because he'd vowed to her that he wouldn't let her die, and he had. He could stop a bank robber in his tracks, but Richard and all his police training had been no match against cancer.

And now he was worried that another woman's life was in danger, and he might not be able to do a thing about that, either.

"Have you gotten an answer out at the Blue Boy Inn?" Richard asked Adam.

"Negative on that, chief. I suspect the phone lines are down. Power's out all over the western part of the state."

The station was being powered by a generator. Richard sat down at his desk and turned on his lamp as he looked again at the report that had come back from forensics late last night.

The substance they'd scraped from the base of the chimney at the Blue Boy Inn was definitely dried blood. The DNA tests weren't yet back, and they'd likely be delayed due to the storm, so Richard didn't know if the blood belonged to Priscilla or Paulie, or if maybe there was some from both. But the very fact that there was blood in the chimney warranted him to take Jack Devlin in for questioning.

"There are lots of logical explanations as to why we

might have found blood in there," Adam said, seeming to read Richard's mind.

"Name one."

"Somebody could have been cleaning out the ash dump and cut their hand."

"According to Annabel, there was enough blood in there to coat her own hand with it. If somebody had bled that much cleaning the damn thing, wouldn't we have been told about that? And this blood was recent. Seems to me somebody would have mentioned it if it was just a simple case of cutting their hand."

Adam smiled. "I don't doubt you're right, chief. I'm just playing devil's advocate. Because you know the lawyers are going to jump all over you if you try to arrest Jack Devlin on such flimsy evidence."

Richard stood, returning Adam's smile with a smirk of his own. "You younguns, all fresh from the police academy, think you know all the answers, don't you? Well, I'll tell you something, Adam. When you've been a cop as long as I have, you listen to your gut. And my gut tells me that Annabel is in danger out there."

"But we have no real evidence that her husband committed any murder."

"Nope, we do not. But you see, Adam, my gut also tells me that Jack Devlin is not our culprit." He smiled again as he saw his deputy lift his eyebrows in surprise. "In fact, I think Devlin might be in almost as much danger as his wife."

"From who? That old geezer the caretaker?"

"No, I don't think Zeke's our culprit, either. You see, this is where I'm stumped. To make any sense of this, I need to go over there. I need to get a plow to make a path for me."

Betty laughed. "Chief, even the county's biggest plows can't get through this stuff. All the roads are closed throughout the county."

Richard frowned. "Well, we've got to find a way as soon as we can."

"You could call in the National Guard," Adam suggested, not entirely seriously.

"Well, there's where your analysis would be right, Adam. The Guard would take a look at the evidence and say, 'We're supposed to send tanks out to the Blue Boy Inn because you found a little blood at the bottom of its chimney?'" He laughed. "No, we have to find a way to get over there ourselves."

"Do you really think it's that urgent, chief?" Betty asked.

Richard sighed. "We probably have a little time. But even if Devlin isn't the killer, he seems to be covering up for somebody. He may suspect we found blood in the chimney, and he may be waiting for us to respond. But he knows that we can't respond right away, due to the storm, so he's likely waiting this thing out as much as we are. He doesn't expect we'll get there until the storm lets up, so if we could get there sooner, we could take him by surprise."

"But you just said he wasn't the culprit," Adam said, "and that he might be in as much danger as his wife."

"Right. Whoever committed these murders is not rational. He or she could strike out at Jack as easily as Annabel." Richard sighed. "And as we saw when we discovered Roger's body, our killer is pretty handy with a knife."

Betty shuddered. "Do we know for certain that Annabel is there at the house?"

"Well, I think it's a fairly safe bet to assume she is," Richard replied. "I saw her in Chad Appleby's truck yesterday as the storm was just starting. They were heading up toward the Blue Boy. I presume he was driving her back after picking out supplies for the contracting job."

"Have you spoken with Chad?" Adam asked.

Richard shook his head. "No, but I've left him three voice mails. I presume in a storm like this, he's out trying to clear driveways. He's got a plow on his truck."

Betty snorted. "Chad's truck isn't big enough to make it through this."

"That's true," Richard said. A thought struck him. "Adam, did our English friend ever come by yesterday on his way out of town to give another statement?"

"Nope," the deputy replied. "Never saw him."

"That's odd," Richard said.

"Maybe he wanted to beat the storm," Adam suggested. "The snow had already started falling, and he wanted to get to the airport."

"Well, there's no way he's flying out in this," Richard said.

He settled back down at his desk. This whole situation was very difficult to figure out. If Roger's killer was somehow holed up at the Blue Boy—despite their apparently thorough searches—how did he get such a hold over Jack Devlin? Jack wouldn't have been so adamant about keeping the police from searching if he wasn't trying to hide something. That seemed to indicate Jack was somehow involved.

Yet Richard didn't think Devlin was the killer himself. Jack had an alibi for the night Roger was killed, and the chief believed that he really was sleeping when Paulie and Priscilla went missing. Annabel was out of the house at the time—Millie vouched for her—and Zeke was simply too frail to kill three people (Richard still believed Cordelia had been murdered) and dispose of two bodies in such a short time. The old caretaker certainly didn't have the strength to shove them down into the chimney, which now seemed to be the case.

So their culprit had to be someone else. But had it been the killer who had cleaned out the chimney and disposed of the remains? Or had Jack and Zeke done that much themselves? If so, why were they colluding with a killer?

Richard could see no motive that linked the deaths of Roger, Cordelia, Priscilla, and Paulie. None. It seemed entirely random. The act of an insane person. A serial killer who killed for no reason whatsoever.

Or for a reason none of them yet understood.

"Chief," Betty called over to him. "I've got Charlie Appleby on the line. He's asking about Chad."

Richard picked up the phone. "Charlie," he asked, "how you faring in this storm?"

"My boys and I have been out there trying to break through it with our plows, but we can't do a thing," Appleby told him. "We've given up. Staying home with some coffee and a shot of Jack Daniel's."

"Good for you. Chad with you?"

"Nope, and that's why I'm calling you. He didn't come around with the other boys and he doesn't answer his phone. My eldest made it through the snow over to Chad's apartment on Green Street and he reports Chad isn't there. As far as he can tell, his truck isn't, either, though it's hard to tell with the snow drifted so high."

"Any idea where he might be?" Richard asked.

"Well, last I knew he was going up to Great Barrington with that woman from the Blue Boy. I've been calling over there, too, and getting no answer."

"I know they made it back," Richard assured Chad's father. "I saw them yesterday afternoon."

"But where's he been since?"

"That I don't know."

Richard could hear Charlie shudder over the phone. "I had reservations when he told me he'd taken that job. That place is cursed. The people are no good. Something bad happens to whoever steps foot up there."

"As soon as we can get out there, Charlie, I'll inquire about Chad. For now, don't worry. He's probably out trying to make his way through this. Nobody's getting through."

"But why doesn't he answer his damn phone? It's one thing for a landline to be down, but far as I know, cell phones are still working."

"Cell reception can be affected by storms like this," Richard told the man honestly.

"I'm talking on a cell now, Richard, and it's working fine. All my other boys, their cells are fine, too."

"You know I'll do what I can to find him, Charlie."

"I know that. Keep me posted."

"Will do."

Richard hung up the phone. This was not good news. Now he had Chad to worry about as well.

And what about Neville? Had he skipped out on giving them a statement?

Or had something happened to him that had prevented him from getting here?

Richard needed to find a way to get out to the Blue Boy Inn. But how? He stood once more, returning to the window, which was now more than half covered with accumulating snow. There had to be seven feet, maybe eight, outside the station, and reports were coming in that drifts were sometimes double that.

He closed his eyes and saw Amy's face. When he opened them, it was Annabel he was seeing. Richard knew she was in danger. He had to find a way to get to her.

85

Zeke unlocked the door to the attic and stepped inside. He placed the tray he was carrying down on a table and let out a long sigh.

"I'm so disappointed in you," he said, looking across the room at the figure hunched down in the corner. "So very, very disappointed in you."

The figure didn't make a sound, nor did it move.

"I'm an old man," Zeke said. "I've done what I could. This can't go on. You need to understand that. It just can't go on."

Still the figure was quiet and still.

Zeke walked over to the little round attic window and peered out. The snow blew furiously. The whole first floor of the house was buried by now. The windows in the kitchen and the parlor were solidly white. It was getting cold, bitterly cold, in the house. The heat was off. And, of course, they couldn't build a fire in the fireplace to warm them.

Behind Zeke came the sound of scurrying across the floor, then the sound of eating and drinking, as if the partaker were famished.

"You just need to understand," Zeke said, turning around, "that I'm not doing this anymore. I just can't. I'm an old man. You need to understand that."

He said nothing more, just turned and left the attic, locking the door behind him.

86

Annabel sat in the corner, her arms wrapped around herself. Where did Tommy Tricky go? He had scampered away. He was hiding in the room somewhere. He was watching her, waiting to jump out and eat her.

Tommy Tricky eats bad little girls.

That was what Daddy Ron told her, and Annabel believed him. She started to cry.

The door opened. Annabel's mother came into the room, looking down at her daughter with sad, defeated eyes.

"Oh, Annabel," her mother said, "you got Daddy Ron angry again."

"Mommy, Mommy, you've got to save me from Tommy Tricky," Annabel cried, running to her mother, throwing her arms around her neck.

"Oh, baby," her mother told her. "Tommy Tricky isn't real. He's just something Daddy Ron tells you about so you'll behave."

"No, Mommy, Daddy Ron says Tommy Tricky gets very, very angry when you don't believe in him."

Her mother stroked Annabel's hair. "Oh, baby, I'm

so sorry he does this to you. But I don't know how to
make him stop."

Annabel realized her mother wasn't really there.
She was sitting by herself, in a corner of her room at
the Blue Boy Inn.

My mother failed me, Annabel realized. *She let that
monster torment me because she was too scared to
stand up to him.*

Annabel began to cry harder.

But then she wiped her eyes with the sleeve of her
nightgown. She had to get ahold of herself. She wasn't
back in her childhood home; she wasn't a little girl.
She was an adult, and she was in the Blue Boy Inn, and
she had to find a way out. She was hallucinating again.
She'd thought she'd seen Tommy Tricky. But Tommy
Tricky wasn't real.

Except—except—

Annabel thought of Tammy Morelli.

*She says she saw a little man in the basement—like
an elf—eating a human arm.*

Tommy Tricky eats bad little girls.

All Annabel knew was that she had to get out of
there.

She stood. Her legs were moving better now, more
easily, with less pain. Whatever drug Jack had given
her appeared to be wearing off. Annabel glanced
across the room. The clock now read 11:30. She must
have been huddled in that corner for about an hour. Her
eyes shot over to the window. She couldn't see anything outside. The snow had collected against the win-
dowpanes. Annabel shuddered. She felt more closed in
than ever.

"I can't give in to my fear," she whispered. "I have to keep moving."

Carefully, she walked toward the door. These old doors were flimsy. She could maybe rattle it enough that it would pop open. It was a slim chance, perhaps, but it was all she had.

She tried the knob. And to her great surprise and gratitude, it was no longer locked.

Maybe I'd only imagined it was locked before, she told herself.

Annabel opened the door and stepped gingerly out into the hallway.

The house was eerily quiet. The muffled sound of the storm outside was the only thing she heard. Annabel made her way to the top of the stairs. She had no idea what her plan was. She was barefoot and wearing only a nightgown. But she could think of only one thing to do. Make a mad dash for the front door and—

And what? She had seen the drifting earlier. It came up halfway over the door. Even if she could reach the front door without Jack stopping her, she would run straight into a solid wall of snow on the other side.

She really was trapped.

No. She wouldn't accept that.

All right then. She'd still make a mad dash down the stairs. But she'd run to the kitchen. Maybe Jack would be in there, waiting for her. But maybe he wouldn't be. She had to take that chance. Because the phone was in the kitchen. She could call 911. Even if he caught her, if she could just press those three numbers and have the call go through, they'd send someone out. Annabel had to pray that the phone was still working.

She took a deep breath and started down the stairs.

Her bare feet flew over the steps. She seemed to make no sound at all. It was almost as if she were running on air. She made it to the bottom of the stairs. But that was only half the challenge. She continued on without stopping to the kitchen. She could see as she rounded the corner that the kitchen was empty. Yes! Maybe Jack had left. Maybe she was alone in the house after all. She would call the police and—

But when she turned to lift the phone off the hook she saw something terrible.

The phone was no longer there.

It had been taken clean off the wall. All that remained was an empty jack.

"No," Annabel moaned, and then put her hand to her mouth. She didn't want to make a sound.

Face it, she heard Daddy Ron's voice tell her. *You're trapped in there.*

Trapped.

Except—

Annabel could almost hear the gears in her mind turning.

Except—she might not be able to get out of the house from the first floor, but the snow had not reached the second. She could jump from a second-floor window. The snow would cushion her fall. If it was packed hard enough, she wouldn't sink completely into it, and she could, she hoped, trudge through it into town.

Right. With bare feet. With winds that seemed to want to rip the roof off the house.

But what other choice did she have? Wait for Jack to come back and kill her the way he'd killed Priscilla and

Paulie? That much Annabel was certain she didn't hallucinate. She firmly believed she was right about that.

She hurried back into the hallway. Hanging on the hook beside the door she spotted a coat. It was Neville's, she realized.

Oh, no, Annabel thought. *I had thought Neville escaped. But why would he leave his coat?*

His car had been gone. That much Annabel was sure of. But he wouldn't have left in a blizzard without taking his coat.

Not knowing what to think, she grabbed Neville's coat and slipped it on. She'd need it if she was going to take a plunge into the snow. She could smell her friend's scent on the coat. It both comforted her and saddened her. Was he alive? What about Chad?

Annabel had never felt so alone, or so frightened.

She made her way back upstairs.

She decided she would go out the window in Cordelia's room. That was over the small roof that covered the front porch. Annabel could hop to the roof, and then take her leap into the snow. But she needed something on her feet. She'd never make it even as far as Millie's store if she had to do it barefoot.

She realized that although her own clothes were gone, Jack's clothes might still be in his closet.

Back inside their room, Annabel paused, looking over at the bed, now pushed aside at an angle. Was Tommy Tricky under there?

Stop it, she scolded herself.

She took a deep breath and pulled open Jack's closet door.

Yes! His clothes were still there. And a pair of work

boots! They would be big on Annabel, but if she tied the long laces several times around her foot, she should be able to keep the boots on during her trek through the blizzard. She sat down on a chair as she pulled the boots onto her feet. For the first time, a real sense of hope filled her. She would get away from here! She would not be trapped!

But then she sensed someone was watching her.

She spun her head around.

Jack stood there, leaning in the doorway, looking down at her with his arms folded over his chest and an enormous smile on his face.

"Where you goin', baby cakes?"

87

Chad woke up, only gradually becoming aware of his surroundings.

He was in the basement of the Blue Boy Inn. And he'd been stabbed.

He looked down at his body. He was drenched in blood. He'd lost a great deal. But his shirt and heavy sweater had acted to stanch the flow, becoming wedged in the open wound in his abdomen almost like a bandage. Chad knew that if he pulled his shirt and sweater off, he'd release the dammed-up blood again. He couldn't let that happen. He had to keep pressing against the wound until he could get to a doctor.

Who was the woman who had stabbed him? He'd never seen her before. Another guest at the inn? Chad didn't think they'd taken in any other guests after all the trouble began. But who she was didn't matter right now. He had to get out of there.

How long he'd been out cold, Chad couldn't be sure. His head ached. From the throbbing he felt at his right temple, he guessed he'd hit his head after being stabbed. Probably when he'd fallen, he'd hit the bottom rung of the basement stairs. Yeah, that must have been what happened. Chad was lying in a heap at the bottom of the stairs.

Was the woman with the knife still around?

Carefully, Chad managed to sit up. He didn't know if he could walk. But he had to try. That woman might well have been the killer of Paulie and Priscilla, and she could come back to finish him off. Who knew if she had killed the others in the house? Last Chad knew, Annabel and Jack had been talking in the kitchen. Were they dead or alive?

He made it to his feet. His head began to spin, and he had to lean against the concrete basement wall to keep from falling down.

He had to get up those stairs and out of the house, but he couldn't do anything until his head stopped spinning.

Above him, he thought he heard laughter. A man's laughter, from far away. Probably from the second floor.

He recognized the voice as that of Jack Devlin.

88

"Look at you!" Jack guffawed. "New York fashionista! Style arbiter of *Orbit* magazine! Wearing a ratty old corduroy coat and my scuffed-up work boots!"

Annabel said nothing, just sat there staring up at her husband.

"Really, sweet baby angel, you could do better than that," Jack said, laughing.

"My clothes are all gone," Annabel said. "I didn't have much of a choice."

"Yes, my darling, I took all your clothes." Jack's smile faded and his voice fell into a paternal, scolding quality. "Because I wanted to discourage you from going outside. I just knew you'd want to go out and play in the snow. But it's too nasty outside for little girls."

"I'm not a little girl," Annabel said.

Jack ignored the comment. "Come on, now, pumpkin pie, take off that coat."

"No," she said.

Jack took hold of her hands and forced her up from

the chair. He walked her over to the bed and sat her down. He took a seat next to her.

"Listen to me, Annabel. We're about to have something very wonderful happen here in our new home. You have to cooperate."

She just looked at him. His eyes were wide, the pupils dilated. She thought Jack had gone certifiably mad.

"We are going to be so successful here at the Blue Boy," he told her, still holding her hands in a tight grip. "And that's what we want, isn't it? That's what we came here to be, right? Successful? At long last? After all our disappointments?"

Annabel remained silent.

"You have no idea how hard it was for me, sweetie babe, when my novel tanked. I really thought I was a literary wunderkind." He laughed out loud, a strange, unhinged sound that seemed to bounce up to the ceiling and ricochet through the house. "But I was a fool. I let myself get so depressed over that, but in fact, I just missed my calling." He smiled, showing his straight, even teeth. "I've found it here, Annabel. Here I can really be a great, great success. The money is just going to come rolling in."

"Why do you think that, Jack?" she asked.

Annabel thought if she could engage him, ask him questions, appear to be interested in what he was saying, she could prevent him from hurting her.

"When my grandmother died," Jack said, "Zeke told me the secret of this house. I'd always known it, really. But I had blocked it out of my mind. But Zeke brought it all back. If we are good to the house, the house will be very, very good to us. It will make us rich."

Annabel studied his crazy eyes. "But, Jack," she said, softly, not wanting to upset him, "your grandmother wasn't rich. The inn had been losing money for years. She was one step from bankruptcy when we took over."

Jack smiled, nodding his head. "That was because Gran stopped being good to the house."

"What do you mean?"

Jack sighed. "A long time ago, my grandparents ran a very successful inn. They had learned the secret from those who had owned it before, and they carried on, doing what was right and good for the house. But then—"

His face darkened.

"But then what, Jack?"

"Then my father came. After that, they stopped being good to the house."

"Your father?"

"Yes. You see, darling baby angel cakes, that was what I had forgotten. How my father changed things during that short period when we were here."

"The period when your mother and your sister died?"

Jack frowned. "My father let his emotions overrule his better judgment. He gave in to his heart and didn't listen to his head." He smiled. "Now, my *mother* had the right idea, only she never lived to see it. *You* had the right idea, too, my darling Annabel, but unlike my mother, you can live to enjoy the fruits of your labors."

"I can . . . live?" Annabel asked.

"Of course, baby cakes. But not if you go out into that terrible storm."

Annabel allowed him to slip his boots off her feet. "So you're saying," she asked Jack, "that the house will make us successful because of some idea *I* had?"

"Yes, honey baby lover." Jack tossed the boots, one by one, across the floor. "You wanted to do the place over!"

He gripped her by the shoulders and stared at her with his insane eyes.

"You removed the bricks!" he said triumphantly.

"The bricks," Annabel repeated, "from the fireplace."

"That's the secret of the house, baby. Where all its wondrous power comes from."

"And . . . removing the bricks will make us rich?"

"Yes." Jack beamed. "Annabel, my dearest love, I know what a terrible year you've had. You want success as much as I do. You want to be able to show those assholes back in New York that no one can keep Annabel Wish down for long. Annabel Wish is going to come back, better than ever! She's going to run the most popular, successful inn in New England! No—in America! Maybe even the world!"

"I don't understand, Jack."

He laughed. "What don't you understand? Didn't we envision making this place a success? Didn't we see it as a first-class destination?"

"Yes," Annabel said. "That was what we talked about. . . ."

"Well, it can be." He narrowed his eyes at her. "So long as we are good to the house."

"And how can we be good to the house?"

He smiled again. "We give it what it needs!"

"And what does it need?"

"I'll take care of that part, Annabel," Jack said, standing now, apparently assured that he had gotten through to his wife, convinced her to do things his way. "You needn't worry yourself about that."

"Jack," Annabel asked, "did you kill Priscilla? Paulie? Your grandmother?"

He looked at her with a kooky grin on his face. "Me? Of course not, angel pie. Why would I kill them?"

"Who did, then?"

He sighed. "The house killed them."

"The house?"

He nodded. "It had to. Because we weren't giving it what it needed. We could have handled it on our own. But now that I understand what we need to do, I'll take care of things. We won't have any more guests going missing." He laughed again, that terrifying yelp that sounded like a fox caught in a trap in the woods. "That wouldn't do very well for business, would it?"

He's mad. Insane. No question about it. He killed them, and he's blaming it on the house. I've got to get away from him.

But . . .

Annabel realized she was safer if she just went along with Jack for now. He saw some kind of life together in this crazy house. She needed to act as if she shared his hopes and dreams. She needed to patronize him, placate him, get him to trust her again. And then, when the storm subsided, maybe she could find a moment to make a run for it.

"So, I'll take care of the house," Jack was saying, stepping over to the window to look outside at the still roiling storm, "but you'll have your own responsibilities, sweetheart."

"Whatever I need to do, Jack, I'm willing," she told him. "You know that."

"I *do* know that, angel cake." He smiled over at her before returning his gaze out the window. "You've had as bad a time as I have. We both need a new start."

"That's why we came here," she said.

"Yes, it is. But I had no idea the kind of success we could have here, if we were willing to do what was necessary." He frowned, looking back over at her. "I'm not sure if we'll be able to trust Zeke for much longer, sweetheart. So you'll have to take over from him. Your job will be the attic."

"The attic?" Annabel asked.

"Yes. Sweetheart, it's time you learned about the attic. You see—"

Suddenly a voice from downstairs interrupted him.

"Annabel!"

She recognized the voice. It was Chad.

"Annabel!" he was calling. "Are you here?"

Annabel saw Jack's eyes change. They had calmed, become almost sane. Now they were suddenly wide with rage. Her husband spun on her.

"You've been fooling around with him, too, haven't you?" he snarled.

"No, no, Jack, I—"

He leapt at her, clamping his hand over her mouth. Dragging her off the bed, he brought her back to his closet and shoved her inside.

"You stay in there, you bad girl," he spat. "I'll deal with your lover!"

"No, Jack, no!" As the door closed against her, Annabel screamed, in a last desperate warning and call for help, "Chad!"

The closet door slammed shut, leaving her in darkness. She heard Jack turn the lock.

"No, Jack, no, please, don't lock me in here—"

"Turn around," came the voice of Daddy Ron, seeping through the door. "Turn around and see who's behind you."

Annabel screamed.

89

"Annabel!" Chad shouted.

She'd called his name. She was somewhere upstairs.

Perhaps he'd been a fool to call for her. But the house had been so deathly quiet when he'd finally made it up to the top of the basement stairs. Chad had assumed he was the only one here. Maybe they'd all left, not knowing he was wounded in the basement. He could have tried going out into the storm on his own, trudging to a spot where he might have better cell reception, and calling his father or Chief Carlson. But he couldn't have left without calling to Annabel, just in case she was still in the house.

And, it appeared, she was. She had called back to him. But now she was silent.

"Annabel!" Chad called again.

The trip up the basement stairs had disturbed the makeshift bandage his shirt and sweater had provided over his wound, and he was bleeding again, pretty profusely. Chad didn't think he'd make it up the stairs to the second floor, where Annabel's voice had appeared to come from. He should just take his chances going outside and making his way through the snow, calling the cops as soon as he could. He'd already seen that the phone was gone from the kitchen wall. The only hope to get help was to get out of the house.

But as he neared the front door, Chad clearly saw there was no way he could get out. The snow was packed solid against the door and all the windows.

The only way out would be through a second-floor window.

And he couldn't leave without checking on Annabel. Maybe she'd been wounded, too, and had passed out after trying to call to him.

He had no choice. He had to go upstairs, or he'd stay here on the first floor, bleed out, and die.

But first, he ripped off a tablecloth from a hall table and wrapped it around himself as best as could, making a tourniquet to stanch the bleeding once again. It wasn't going to last long, but it would have to do for now. Chad didn't have a lot of options.

He began making his way up the stairs.

90

"Sorry, chief," Adam told him, hanging up the phone. "The county has none of its largest plows to spare. They said they'll get down here as soon as they can, but that might be days. The storm has completely immobilized everyone."

"This is crazy," Richard grumbled. "When this is over, I'm demanding bigger plows at the town meeting. The selectmen better go along with it. I don't want to hear any noise about money. Winters are just going to keep getting worse around here, and we need to be prepared."

"Hey, chief," Betty called. "Were you expecting a fax from the town library?"

"No," he said, barely hearing her.

"Well," the secretary said, approaching him with a thick stack of papers, "they just sent you over twenty-seven pages of town history."

"Just put it in my in-box," Richard told her.

Betty complied.

Richard was trying to think of an excuse to convince

state officials to send them one of the massive snow-plows they kept up at Great Barrington. But even if he said somebody up at the Blue Boy had some major health issue and needed help right away, they'd no doubt insist there were people all over western Massachusetts in the same position. If only he could—

Twenty-seven pages of town history.

All of a sudden he remembered his conversation with Agnes Daley.

But there's no denying, chief, that ever since, lots of people have died or disappeared up there.

Richard reached over and grabbed hold of the stack of papers Betty had placed in his in-box. Sure enough, they were from Agnes Daley.

Making use of being snowbound here in the library, Agnes had written in her careful penmanship on the cover sheet. *So glad the board of directors installed a generator. You were asking about the history of the Blue Boy the other day. You seemed dismissive of what I told you. Here's some newspaper coverage from back in the day, chief. Give it a read. A.D.*

Richard glanced over what Agnes had sent. They were microfilm printouts of old newspaper pages. The date on the first was from 1869.

REV. FALL HANGED FOR MURDER, the headline read.

There was an illustration of a man dressed all in black dangling from the end of a noose.

Richard looked at the next page. It was from a year later.

WOMAN FOUND DEAD, DISMEMBERED
NEAR FALL'S CHURCH

The murders up at that place really *did* stretch back a long time.

Another headline:

FORMER CONGREGANTS CLAIM
REV. FALL PRACTICED
BLACK ARTS, SATANIC RITUALS

The piece seemed like bad gothic horror fiction to Richard, but he read it anyway.

> Former congregants of the late Rev. John Fall, hanged here three years ago for murder, now claim that the disgraced pastor forced them to participate in the black arts. Fall's goal, these congregants insist, was to cast a spell that would open a portal into the netherworld, where he could harness the daemonic beings within to do his bidding. He possessed books filled with spells and incantations for such a nefarious purpose.

"Ridiculous," Richard murmured.

The rest of the pages were more recent—coverage of the deaths of the various people at the Blue Boy Inn, including the reports of Jack Devlin's missing sister.

But at the very end of the pile was another piece, dated December 26, 1915. It was one of those humorous little items newspaper editors often used as fillers. Agnes's neat, precise handwriting ran across the top of it.

This little item wasn't about Rev. Fall or any mysterious death, but the headline jumped out at me. What do you think?

Richard looked down at the article.

CHILD CLAIMS TO HAVE SEEN BLUE ELVES

Richard read the piece.

> Little Millicent Collins of Bangor, Maine, five years old, visiting the Blue Boy Inn in Woodfield with her parents, claimed to have seen "three little elves with blue faces" poking their heads out of the parlor fireplace. Could Santa have left behind some of his helpers on Christmas Eve?

Somehow the image of those three blue faces looking out of the fireplace unnerved him even more than tales of opening portals to the netherworld. All of this talk of witchcraft and spells and demonic rituals was absurd, of course. But, nonetheless, Richard was even more disturbed and anxious after reading it.

"I've got to get over to the Blue Boy," Richard said, banging his fist on his desk. "There's *got* to be a way!"

"I've got a pair of snowshoes," Adam said, shrugging.

"I'd give it a try," Richard said, "but I doubt I'd get very far."

"What you need," Betty said, poking her head around the corner from her outer office, "is a snowmobile."

"Of course!" Richard said. "Where can I get one?"

"Well, my son has one, but it's at our house."

Richard jumped to his feet. "Have him ride it over here!"

"In this storm?" the secretary asked.

"Betty, that's what snowmobiles are for!"

She scowled. "Maybe the kind the Navy uses in the Arctic, but Richard, my kid uses his just for fun."

"Then find me a better one," the chief barked. "Why doesn't the department have snowmobiles for our regular use anyway? We're living in the goddamn Berkshire mountains, aren't we?"

"I'll make some calls," Betty said.

"You, too," Richard ordered Adam.

"Yes, sir!" his deputy said, picking up his phone.

Richard looked out the window. It was becoming increasingly difficult to see outside. The snow had nearly walled them in. Only at the very top of the window could Richard see a bit of sky, and that was just a furious flurry of white.

I have to get over there. He had never felt so sure about anything. His gut was telling him something terrible was taking place. *I've got to get over there or Annabel is going to die.*

He couldn't get the image of those three little blue elves in the fireplace out of his head.

91

In the darkness of the locked closet, Annabel tried to keep her wits about her, but this was too much. She tried to hang on to the reality of the present, but she was fast sliding down a very slippery chute into the past. She was a little girl, locked in the closet by Daddy Ron, and Tommy Tricky was somewhere in the darkness behind her, waiting to devour her with his sharp blue teeth.

She saw a little man in the basement eating a human arm.

"No, no, no," Annabel moaned, and commenced banging on the door. "Jack! Let me out! Let me out! Oh, please, let me out!"

Behind her, she heard something scurrying in the darkness among her husband's shoes.

"He's not real," she said out loud.

"Don't get him mad," came Daddy Ron's voice through the door.

The closet seemed to be getting smaller. It was closing in on her. It was like that time she'd been trapped in the elevator. The walls had been moving in on her from all sides, and Annabel had feared she would be squeezed to death. She had utterly decompensated then, ending up in a puddle on the floor. She needed to fight that—stay clear in her mind—if she was to survive this. Because being locked in the closet wasn't the worst horror. Beyond the door her husband had become a madman, and surely he would kill her like the others.

But it was hard to resist panic when she heard the scuttling behind her.

The closet was almost completely dark. Annabel could not even see her hands in front of her face. The only light came from the small space between the door and the floor. She got down as close to the space as she could, irrationally terrified that she'd breathe up all the air in the closet and suffocate. She could see out into the room through the space. She could see one of the boots on the floor that Jack had removed from her feet. She could see the bottom of the dresser.

Annabel leaned in close to the space to gulp in some air.

What was Jack going to do to Chad? Maybe Chad had gotten away. Maybe he'd gone to get help.

That wasn't likely. Not in this storm.

Annabel heard the scuttling again. Except this time it wasn't behind her. It was right beside her. Right beside her face as she pressed it to the bottom of the door, gulping in air.

She moved her eyes.

Beside her own hand was another. A very small hand, with fingers that resembled the claws of a squirrel or a raccoon. It was hard to say for sure in this darkness, but Annabel thought the hand was blue.

She screamed.

92

Richard slammed down the phone. "Nothing," he grumbled over at Adam. "The town doesn't have any snowmobiles and the county can't get any to us until the storm lets up. We won't need them then!"

Adam shook his head. "I haven't had any luck, either. A friend of mine has one, but I can't reach him."

"Do you even know how to ride one?" Betty asked the chief.

"I've been on one," he told her.

She smirked. "That doesn't mean you know to steer it."

"We didn't have much need of them in Boston. But several years ago we were helping search for a missing girl up in New Hampshire. I . . . I rode a snowmobile then."

Betty's smirk deepened. "You rode one?"

"Yeah." Richard sighed. "Right into a tree."

Betty laughed. "Our great hero to the rescue."

"Is your son good with his?" Richard asked her.

"Sure. But as I said, it's just a beginner's model. Frank and I bought it for Danny last Christmas. It's just a small Ski-Doo."

"Ask him if he knows who else might have one in town," Richard said.

"I'm one ahead of you there, chief," Betty told him. "I already called him, and he's trying to find you a good-size one."

"Thanks, Betty."

The window of the police station was now completely covered with snow. A couple of officers were out front, digging a passage out the front door. It felt as if they were inside an igloo.

"Have you tried the Blue Boy's phone again?" Richard asked Adam.

"Yup. Still no answer, chief."

"The phone at Millie's store still works. I just called her. So why wouldn't the Blue Boy's still be working?"

"Beats me, chief."

"He's disconnected it," Richard said.

Adam looked up at him. "Who has?"

"Jack Devlin. I feel certain of it."

In his mind's eye he saw Amy, so small in her hospital bed. The snow had been piling up outside the hospital much as it was accumulating outside the station now. Richard couldn't shake the feeling of déjà vu helplessness. The longer he remained trapped in the station, the greater likelihood that he would let Annabel die.

Outside, he heard the whirr of an engine. It sounded like a buzz saw at first, then like the spinning of tires in snow. He hurried over to the front door, Betty at his side.

"It's Danny!" the secretary exclaimed.

A teenage boy in a bright green wool hat and orange parka riding a yellow snowmobile was stuck in a snowbank in the station lot. The officers who'd been shoveling out the front entrance were rushing over to assist him.

"That boy," Betty said, shaking her head. "He's so impulsive. When I told him you needed a snowmobile, he offered to come over. I told him under no circumstances did I want him venturing out in this storm. But he came anyway."

Richard was grinning. "I'm glad he's a disobedient child."

Betty looked up at him. "But take a glance out there, chief, will you? He's stuck! That's not a very powerful machine. If Danny got stuck in our parking lot, how are you going to make it all the way out to the Blue Boy Inn?"

"Danny made it all the way out here from your house, didn't he?" Richard asked, his eyes on the boy.

With a shove from the officers, Danny was able to maneuver the snowmobile out of the bank, then hopped back onboard and steered it over toward the front door, where he brought the machine to a stop. He waved a big blue-mittened hand when he noticed the chief and his mother watching from the glass door.

"I'm giving that boy a medal," Richard said, beaming.

"If he wasn't so tall," Danny's mother said, "I'd give him a spanking."

93

Chad climbed the stairs to the second floor.

He'd thought he'd heard Jack's voice, and then someone walking toward the stairs. But no one had come down, and now the house had fallen silent once more. Chad didn't like going up the stairs. He was afraid of what he might find. He was also afraid the exertion would cause him to lose more blood. But he had no choice, really.

The only possible way out of this house was from a second-floor window. And besides, in all good conscience, he couldn't just leave Annabel up here after he'd heard her call his name.

He reached the top of the stairs.

Chad looked around. There was no one. But peering down the hallway, he could see the door to Annabel's room was open. He had to go in there and look for her. If she wasn't there, then he was throwing open the window and making a jump for it. The snow was so high out there, Chad figured he might actually be able to just step out onto it, if it was packed hard enough.

He took his first step down the corridor. Under his foot, the old floorboards creaked.

Chad paused, listening. He heard nothing, so he continued on down the hall.

At Annabel's door, he paused again.

"Annabel?" he whispered, looking inside.

He heard the sound of crying. It was coming from the closet. He hurried to the closet door.

"Annabel!" he called.

If that was her behind the door, she was sobbing uncontrollably. She couldn't speak.

"Hang on, Annabel," Chad said, grabbing the closet door handle and finding it locked. "I'll get you out of there. I'll get you out and then we are getting out of this house."

He began to shake the door handle as hard as he could.

94

Annabel heard Chad's voice as if from a very far distance.

"Hang on, Annabel," he was saying. "I'll get you out of there if I have to break this door down."

She focused. She brought herself back to the present. She yanked herself out of her childhood, where she was a tiny girl, curled up in a ball in the closet, crying her heart out. Now she was back here, an adult woman, and she was going to get through this.

The door in front of her suddenly shuddered as Chad, outside, threw his weight at it.

Through the space at the bottom of the door, Annabel could see his feet. The black rubber soles of his boots.

"Oh, Chad!' she cried. "Oh, Chad, get me out of here!"

"I will, Annabel," he called in to her. "Just hang on."

The door shuddered again.

Through the space, Annabel saw droplets of blood raining onto the floor all around Chad's boots.

She turned her eyes. The little hand that had been beside her was still there. And now a little face emerged from the darkness to join her in peering out through the space under the door.

Annabel was face-to-face with Tommy Tricky.

He licked his blue lips with a snaky blue tongue.

"You're not real," Annabel told him.

Tommy just smiled, and then withdrew back into the darkness.

For a third time Chad threw himself against the door. It shook in its frame, and Annabel heard something crack. But still it did not open.

She could hear Chad breathing heavily outside. And she could see now another pair of feet. They appeared to be a woman's feet, in fuzzy pink house slippers. They had come in behind Chad. Facing the closet door, he wouldn't have seen whoever it was come into the room.

Annabel had to warn him.

"Chad!" she screamed. "Behind you!"

"Annabel, I'm—"

But whatever he was about to tell her became a scream.

Annabel watched as the pink fuzzy slippers came up right behind Chad's boots. She heard the sound of a knife plunging into flesh. Chad screamed again, and then dropped to his knees. Annabel could hear the knife, plunging in and out of him, making a horrible suction sound each time. Chad was screaming. Suddenly, as Annabel peered through the space, she saw a river of blood rushing across the floor toward her. Her hands, pressed close to the space, were quickly covered in it. Annabel leapt to her feet and screamed.

The sound of stabbing—suction in, suction out—continued for the next several minutes. Annabel covered her ears, but she could still hear the terrible noise. Chad's screams softened into moans. Finally, after agonizing minutes, he was silent.

Annabel dropped her hands from her ears. She heard the sound of slippers scuffing out of the room.

"Oh, Chad," Annabel cried, the tears dropping off her cheeks as she leaned against the door. The young man's blood continued to flow into the closet all over her bare feet. Annabel realized she had just listened to Chad's murder.

And now she was certain that hers would be next.

95

"Okay, so you grab the handlebar like this," Danny was shouting over the wind, as Richard watched him closely. The seventeen-year-old's hands closed over the bar tightly and he pushed it up to demonstrate. "Once the key is in the position, you pull the cord out and push the handlebar up. You follow?"

"I think so," Richard said. "Seems easy enough."

"It's more than easy. This is a really light footed sled. You should be able to glide over ungroomed snow without any problem. Just watch out for trees or bushes or anything that's covered that you can't see."

"That could send me flying, I guess," Richard said.

"Well, maybe not flying, but it could get you stuck." Danny turned his red-cheeked face to him. "That's what happened to me on the way in here, when I got stuck. I was fine all the way to the station from my house because I stayed on the roads. The minute I came over the station's yard I didn't know there was a hedge underneath me, and I ran smack into it. If you stay to the roads, you should be okay, because all that's under you is six or seven feet of snow."

"That should be easy then," Richard said, his breath freezing in front of his face.

Danny shook his head. "You haven't seen it out there, chief. Sometimes you can't tell where the road starts and yards begin. And not everyone got their cars off the street in time. There are lots of cars buried under drifts of snow. You don't want to run into one of them."

"No," Richard said. "I sure don't."

"How far you got to take this?" Danny asked.

"Up to the Blue Boy Inn."

The teenager grinned. "That haunted house? What's going on up there now?"

"That's what I aim to find out." Richard put his gloved hand out and Danny grabbed it. "I can't thank you enough for bringing this over, Danny. If I cause any damage to it, the department will pay for a new snowmobile for you."

"It's cool, man," Danny said, getting up off the seat and gesturing to Richard to take his place. "If you crack this one up, I've got my eye on a more advanced model."

"I think the department may be buying a few of those," Richard said, straddling the snowmobile and grabbing the handlebars. "If we're going to have more snowstorms like this, we need to have them in store."

"Oh, we're going to have a lot more of these kind of storms. Lots of extreme weather ahead of us. The climate's changing, chief. Hope you're not a denier."

Richard smiled at him. "Nope, no denier here, Danny. I've learned that we deny reality at our own peril."

He checked that his gun was safely secured at his

side, and then he revved the motor as Danny had showed him.

Behind him, Adam was shouting over the noise. "As soon as I can round up some more machines, we'll be up to join you, chief!"

Richard gave his deputy a thumbs-up with his right hand. Then he pulled on his goggles, tightened his scarf around his neck, gripped the handlebars, said a little prayer, and took off across the snow.

96

Annabel sobbed against the closet door. Chad was dead. The poor man . . . he had come into this house on her request. He had come up here, trying to rescue her. And now he was dead.

The door shifted as she leaned against it.

Annabel pushed. The door creaked open. Chad had succeeded in breaking the lock.

Slowly, fearfully, Annabel stepped out of the closet. She had no idea who might lunge at her as she did so. Tommy Tricky? Daddy Ron? The woman in the pink slippers who had killed Chad?

His body lay crumpled on the floor in front of her. She tried not to look at it. She feared she would start to cry so hard she'd never be able to stop. Poor Chad. She thought of him at the tile store, telling her it was nice to see her smile. Oh, poor, poor Chad.

She couldn't afford to break down. Not yet. She had to find a way out of the house.

She had no idea where Jack had gone to. Or the woman who had stabbed Chad. Who was she? Annabel thought she knew. She was the same woman she'd seen her first day at the inn. The woman in the woods. Perhaps she had been the killer all along.

But even if so, Jack was helping her. Jack was somehow under her sway.

Annabel knew she didn't have much time. At any moment, one of them could come back into this room. She had to get out.

But first she had the presence of mind to reclaim Jack's boots. If she was going out in that snow, she'd need them.

To get them, however, she had to step over Chad's body. The very act of doing so nearly sent her over the edge again. She was shaking uncontrollably as she pulled on the boots, both of them sticky with Chad's blood. It was all over the floor, coating the soles of Annabel's feet.

She then headed for the door. Zipping up Neville's coat, which she still wore, she hurried into the hallway, pausing only briefly to make sure the coast was clear.

Then she ran down the corridor toward Cordelia's room.

Her plan was the same as before. She would go out the window onto the small roof over the front porch. The snow was at least as high as that. From there she would trudge off, as best she could, hoping the snow was hard enough that she wouldn't sink too far. Hoping, too, that she could brave the cold and the wind until she got to Millie's.

She made it to Cordelia's room. Once again she had the presence of mind to close the door behind her. She didn't want Jack to come walking past and spot her as she went out the window.

Annabel's heart was thudding in her chest. She could see the window. She could see freedom!

But then she heard a two-note whistle. The same sound she'd heard that day in the woods.

Annabel stopped and looked frantically around the room.

And all at once, the woman who had killed Chad, crouching behind Cordelia's bed, stood up.

They locked eyes. The woman had long gray hair and was wearing a diaphanous white dress and fuzzy pink slippers. Her dress and hands were splattered with blood.

"Hello," the woman said, emotionlessly.

Annabel turned to run, but was stopped in her tracks when, directly in front of her, two little blue men suddenly ran past, scurrying under the bed.

Annabel screamed. This couldn't be happening!

The woman was now directly behind her. Annabel felt the cold blade of the knife pressed against the back of her neck. She didn't dare breathe.

"Where are you going?" the woman asked in Annabel's ear. Her voice didn't sound angry or threatening, just curious. "It's really bad outside."

Annabel didn't answer.

"You have to stay here," the woman told her. "You have to take care of the house."

"Who are you?" Annabel asked in a little voice.

She felt the knife move away from her neck and she breathed a little easier.

"Zeke is very angry with me," the woman said. "I can't find him. Have you seen him?"

She moved away from Annabel, but not very far. She still held the knife upright in her hands. Annabel saw that, despite her long, stringy, unkempt gray hair, the woman was not that old. She was quite pretty, in fact. Her skin was pale but very smooth.

"I haven't seen Zeke, either," Annabel said, latching on to an idea. "Maybe we can go out looking for him."

The woman smiled. "No. You'll try to run away."

"No, I won't."

"Yes, you will." The woman touched her fingertip to the blade of the knife. "I don't want to have to do to you what I did to that young man."

"No, no, please don't," Annabel said, shrinking back. "I won't run away."

"I had to kill him, you know."

"I know," Annabel said, desperate to appear cooperative and understanding. "You had to, because he was trying to run away and take me with him."

"That's not why I had to kill him."

"No?"

The woman shook her head, her long gray hair swinging from side to side. "I had to kill him to feed the house."

"Feed . . . the house?"

Now the woman nodded vigorously. "That's my job." She looked intently at Annabel. "It was supposed to be yours, as well."

"Mine?"

"Yes," the woman insisted. "You have to feed the house for me, because no one is supposed to see me."

"Okay, okay," Annabel said. "I'll do whatever you say."

The woman's eyes narrowed as they studied her. "You're afraid of the house, though, aren't you?"

"No," Annabel lied. "I'm not afraid of the house."

"Then crawl under the bed."

Under the bed. The little men had run under there.

"No," Annabel muttered.

"Prove to me that you aren't afraid of the house." The woman thrust the knife in Annabel's direction.

"Please, don't make me go under there. I know . . . I know what's under there!"

"Do it!" the woman commanded, waving the knife back and forth in the air.

I've got to overpower her. I've got to jump her, wrestle the knife away from her, Annabel thought.

But the blade was suddenly at her throat. Annabel had no choice but to drop to her knees.

"Good," the woman said. "Now crawl under the bed. They're waiting for you."

Annabel looked under the bed. Two pairs of eyes blinked in the darkness.

"No," Annabel cried, trembling uncontrollably.

"Come join us, Annabel," a little voice called to her. "It's time you learned that we are real."

97

Richard thought he had the hang of this. He was cruising pretty easily along Main Street on Danny's Ski-Doo, taking the kid's advice and staying strictly to the middle of the street. It was easy for Richard to do that here, since the buildings of the town center were on either side of him and it was clear exactly where he was. But when he had veer off and follow Route 7A up into the woods, it became increasingly difficult, with all these mountainous drifts of snow, to know what was road and what was not.

The chief did the best he could, squinting to see through his goggles, occasionally having to reach up and wipe the snow off them with the back of his glove.

The weather report had said the blizzard was winding down, but it sure didn't feel that way to Richard. Even in his thermals and heavy parka, he shivered against the deep chill. And the snow was blowing and drifting as fiercely as ever.

He needed to get to the Blue Boy before it got dark. After nightfall, it would become impossible to make it through these woods. On the back of the Ski-Doo, there was room for one other person. If Annabel wasn't the only one in need of help—if, as Richard feared, Chad was trapped there as well—then they might have to make several trips back and forth, and that could take the rest of the afternoon. Richard hoped Adam could scrounge up some other snowmobiles fast.

He glided over the snow. What would he find at the Blue Boy?

What he knew for a fact was that human blood had been found in the chimney. Chad reported that he'd heard animals eating something at the base of the chimney. But the space had been nearly cleaned out when Richard inspected it. Neville had reported that he'd been locked in his room shortly before that inspection, suggesting that someone in the house didn't want him to witness the cleaning of the chimney. And the only two people in the house, as far as Richard knew, were Jack Devlin and the caretaker, Zeke.

Devlin, of course, had been desperate to prevent a search of the house. The scenario had all the hallmarks of Devlin being guilty, of at least covering up a crime.

But he was very possibly guilty of much, much more.

He could be using this storm to finish what he started, Richard reasoned. *He thinks we can't get to him, so he's free to continue killing the rest of the people in the house*.

He prayed that Annabel would still be alive when he got there.

Richard turned the handlebars, steering the snowmobile up the narrow, wooded road that led to the Blue Boy Inn. He thought he was safely in the middle of the road. But apparently he had strayed off the path.

He felt the machine suddenly shudder beneath him. The snowmobile stopped, churning up a geyser of snow and throwing Richard clear over the handlebars.

Plop! The chief found himself head-and-shoulders deep in cold, fluffy snow.

Moving his arms as if swimming, he managed to pull himself upright. He stood, with some difficulty, as the snow was not packed all that hard. In this case, that was a good thing. The snow had cushioned his fall. If it had been hardened with ice, Richard might have cracked his head open. His goggles had stayed in place, but he'd lost a glove as he'd flown through the air, and his scarf was askew, allowing a cold draft to slip down his sweater.

Breathing heavily, Richard assessed the situation. The Ski-Doo was about four feet away, no longer spitting snow. Caught on some bush below the snow, it appeared to have stalled out. Richard said a silent prayer that he could get it started again.

Just getting back over to it was a chore. Every step he took, he sunk to his knees, and sometimes up to his hips. The wind was blowing so fast and furiously that even his goggles couldn't keep his eyes from welling up. His exposed left hand was freezing. There was no way he'd ever be able to walk the rest of the way to the Blue Boy. He had to get that snowmobile moving again!

Finally, he reached the machine. The first thing he needed to do was push it away from the spot, so it wouldn't get stuck on the branches of the bush again. It took some muscle, but finally Richard shoved the snowmobile farther out into the clearing, where he was certain that the only thing beneath him, some five or six feet, was the dirt road. Hopping onboard, Richard started the ignition as Danny had showed him. But the Ski-Doo was unresponsive. No matter how many times Richard tried, the motor remained silent.

"Goddamn it!" he shouted into the wind.

Had it been damaged in the accident? Had Richard damaged it pushing it off the bush? What could he do to fix it? He had his cell phone, carefully stowed in an inner pocket of his coat. But what was he going to do? Ask Danny to trudge on out here? Even if he made it, it would take hours. And hours Richard did not have.

His mind was racing, trying to calculate the risks and the possibilities of heading up to the Blue Boy on foot. He'd have to try. He couldn't just give up. He'd have to walk. If there was danger up there, however, he wasn't sure how he and Annabel or anyone else might escape it without the snowmobile.

Richard was ready to slide his leg back over the machine and start on his trek when he decided to try the ignition one more time.

Below him, the Ski-Doo hummed back to life.

"Hallelujah!" Richard shouted into the blowing wind.

In moments, he was back to gliding over the snow, heading up into the hills toward the Blue Boy Inn.

98

"Please don't make me go under there!" Annabel cried, as the little eyes under the bed blinked at her in the dark.

"Get up off your knees, Miz Wish."

Annabel's head snapped up. The woman with the long gray hair was gone. Standing in her place was Zeke, looking very weary and sad.

"Zeke!" Annabel jumped to her feet. "Please let me go! Please don't keep me here!"

He placed his finger to his lips, a sign for her to keep quiet. Looking over his shoulder, he said, "Keep your voice down. I'll take care of things."

"That woman," Annabel whispered. "She killed Chad."

The old man nodded with great sadness. He looked as if he might cry.

"Where did she go?" Annabel asked, terrified she'd come back with her knife.

"I sent her away," Zeke told her. "For now, you're safe. I'll see to that."

Annabel pulled back from him. "How do I know I can trust you?"

"You don't. But you don't have any other choice." Zeke looked at her coat and boots. "If you were thinking of going out there, forget it. You'd get swallowed up alive by this nor'easter. I've seen many of these storms in my day, and this is by the far the worst."

"But I can't stay here," Annabel said, wrapping her arms around herself. "Where is Jack?"

"Walking through the house, muttering to himself." Zeke shuddered. "The house has gotten to him. Just as it did his father and his grandfather."

"What do you mean?"

"His grandfather fed the house for years in exchange for great success. Cordelia finally made him stop, but then young Mrs. Devlin showed up—Jack's mother— and like you, she had grand visions for the house. Even her death wasn't enough to keep Jack's father from falling under the spell of the house. But when they came for Miz Cindy . . ."

"Who came for her?"

Zeke looked at her. "The house. And when Mr. Devlin saw what happened to his precious little girl, he finally woke up, and sealed over the fireplace once again. It stayed that way for many, many years." The caretaker's ancient yellowed eyes found Annabel's. "Until you arrived, Miz Wish."

"The . . . fireplace?"

Zeke suddenly held up his hand, as if he'd just heard a sound. "I will be back," he told Annabel. "Stay here. I will lock the door so no one can get in."

"No, please, don't lock me in again. I can't bear it! Not with that thing under the bed."

Zeke looked at her uneasily. With great difficulty, he bent down. "There's nothing under there now," he reported as he stood back up, breathing heavily.

"I don't believe you," Annabel said.

"Then don't. I don't really care if you do. But if you want to be safe, stay in this room. If you go out the window, that's your choice. But you'll never make it off the hill."

Zeke hobbled out of the room. Annabel heard him turn the key in the lock.

She hurried over to the window. She could see the way the snow was blowing. Ten-foot drifts were forming right before her eyes. Zeke was right. She'd never make it down the hill to the road, let alone all the way to Millie's. The snow was too soft, too unsettled. It would swallow her up alive, as Zeke had said.

But stay here? Out in the storm, she risked death from cold and exposure. Here in this house, she risked death from an insane woman roaming the halls with a knife.

Or worse—she risked death from her worst childhood nightmare.

She would be eaten alive by Tommy Tricky.

99

The soles of his shoes making sticking sounds as he walked through the blood on the floor, Zeke draped a sheet over Chad's dead body.

The poor man. *But he was a fool, too*, Zeke thought. He should have accepted the offer Zeke and Cordelia had made him. They might not have been able to make good on the offer, but Chad would be alive today, sitting at home with a mug of coffee, riding out this storm.

Zeke stood looking down at the body. He'd draped many sheets in his years in this house. The first had been over the headless corpse of Andrew McGurk. Zeke had been just a teenager then. He and old Mr. Devlin had managed to pull McGurk back out of the fireplace, but the house had already gotten his head.

It was that episode that had finally convinced old man Devlin to brick over the fireplace. But eventually his son, Cordelia's husband, had unbricked it. The pattern repeated itself every generation.

The worst had been the baby. That poor woman, hiding out here from her rich father's goons, had thought she was safe. From her father, yes. From the house, no.

Zeke had found the baby's arm in the ash dump. That was all that was left of her.

All his adult life he'd been covering up corpses, wiping up blood. Ever since he'd taken this infernal job, he'd been enslaved to this house, a prisoner of its terrible secrets. No more. He wanted an end to this before he died.

And bricking up the fireplace was no longer enough.

He sighed and turned to leave the room.

And walked directly into Jack, who had been standing there in the doorway, unknown to Zeke, watching him.

"What are you doing in here?" Jack asked him.

"Giving the dead a little respect," Zeke replied, his voice surly.

Jack grabbed the old man by the front of his shirt. "Don't interfere, Zeke. You must give the house what it needs."

Zeke struggled, but couldn't break free of Jack's grip. "Oh, Mr. Jack, please try to see things as they are! We can't do it anymore! The house will take us all. Don't you care?"

"The house will make us successful," Jack told him, tightening his hold on Zeke's shirt. "That's what they've promised. My father, my grandfather, my great-grandfather—they all understood that!"

"Until they died broken men, the ones they loved destroyed around them!"

Jack's hand loosened its grip, and Zeke took the opportunity to move away from him.

"Your mother, Jack! Don't you remember?"

Jack's eyes clouded over.

"The house took your mother! She didn't die of cancer. She didn't die in a hospital. Your father lied to you, Jack. She died here—horribly—"

Jack's arm suddenly swung out. The back of his hand connected with Zeke's face, and the frail old man went flying across the room, hitting his head against the wall. He slid down into a clump on the floor.

"Think of your wife," Zeke managed to whimper, as his head throbbed and the room around him began to spin. "Think of Annabel."

But Jack just stalked out of the room.

Zeke put his face in his hands and cried. Eventually, everything went dark.

100

Annabel thought she heard shouting from another room. She steadied herself, bracing for the worst. Then she heard footsteps clomping down the hall. Jack's footsteps, she thought. Hard, heavy, angry. Was he coming in here? Was he going to kill her? Annabel began to tremble violently. But the footsteps went right past the door and up the steps to the attic. Annabel heard the door to the attic open and close.

For the moment, she let out a sigh of relief.

But she was not out of danger. Far from it. Zeke had told her to wait for him, but she was no longer willing to wait. For all she knew, the shouting she heard from the other room had been an altercation between Jack and the old man, and Zeke was never going to emerge the winner from a fight like that. He might even be dead.

Annabel had to get out of the house. She'd take her chances outside. Better to freeze to death than get hacked up like Chad.

Or worse.

She flew to the window. But when she tried to lift it, the stubborn thing wouldn't budge.

She tried again. Still it didn't move.

It hadn't been opened in years, Annabel figured. It was painted shut decades ago. Cordelia had never brought fresh air into this room. Suddenly, Annabel panicked. Her palms got sweaty again. She was trapped.

"No!" she screamed.

She looked around for something with which to smash the window. The iron doorstop would have worked, but the cops had claimed it as evidence after Cordelia's death. There wasn't anything in the room that looked strong enough. Finally, Annabel ran over to the bed, hoping the little man would not leap out from under it and grab her ankle. She snatched the pillows off the bed and removed their cases. Then she opened Cordelia's drawer and yanked out one of the dead woman's lacy old slips. Annabel proceeded to wrap the slip around her right hand, and then pulled both pillowcases over that. Balling her hand into a fist, she walked back to the window.

She whacked the pane of glass as hard as she could.

"Oww!" she yelled.

But still it didn't break.

She tried once more. The glass in the old window didn't shatter, but it did pop out of the pane, tumbling down into the snow as a gust of cold air rushed into the room. But that wasn't good enough. The window had twelve panes, each separated by wooden frames. Annabel couldn't fit through the one pane that she'd removed. She'd have to pop out at least four of them, and she'd have to also break the wooden frames.

And try as she might, that old wood was impervious to her blows.

"Owwww!" Annabel cried out on her fifth attempt to break the wood. Even a second pane remained resistant to her assaults. She was making a great deal of noise. Jack would hear her. Or he'd be attracted by the sound of the wind gusting through the open space in the window. Snow was swirling into the room, encrusting the wall and the floor.

But she had to try. It was her only chance.

Annabel pulled her hand back to swing it once more against the window. But just as she did so, she spotted a sight she could not believe—something she hadn't dared let herself hope for.

A man was barreling up through the trees on a snowmobile.

It was Richard Carlson!

101

I n the other room, Zeke was struggling to regain consciousness.

He dreamt. He was fifteen years old again, standing on the front porch, asking old Mr. Devlin for a job.

It was 1949. Back in those days, the Devlins maintained a farm out in back of the inn. A brood of hens clucked all around the place, and a rooster crowed from somewhere out in back. Old Mr. Devlin told Zeke he'd hire him to feed the chickens and cut the corn.

The young man ended up doing a lot more than that.

"Where is my baby?" the woman was screaming at him.

In his hands Zeke held the bloody pink arm. It looked as if it had come from a doll. The woman fainted dead away.

"Help me! Help me!" McGurk shrieked, as he was carried toward the fireplace.

Zeke grabbed hold of one leg, Mr. Devlin the other, but they were too late.

The sound of those creatures munching on McGurk's head haunted Zeke's dreams for the rest of his life.

But the worst, for him, was the attic.

In his dream, he walked those stairs, just as he had every day for the past twenty-three years. Everything that had come before had been terrible enough. But the attic these last two decades had been even more wicked.

She had been beautiful once.

Until the house had gotten to her.

The craziest thing of all, she loved the house. She would do anything for the house. The house that had tried to kill her.

In his dream, Zeke saw her as she once was. So beautiful. So innocent.

And then he saw her as she was today.

The knife—slashing Chad over and over, the way she had slashed others.

All for the house.

Zeke opened his eyes.

"No more," he said to himself.

He would end this. He would do what successive generations of Devlins had failed to do. He would destroy the Blue Boy Inn.

102

"Richard! Oh, thank, God, Richard!"

He heard Annabel's voice as soon as he switched off the engine of the Ski-Doo. He lifted his goggles and looked up at the inn. There she was, shouting from a second-floor window over the front door. She had popped out a pane of glass, and was waving what looked like a pillowcase to get his attention.

"Annabel!" he shouted through the wind in response.

The snow had covered nearly the entire first floor of the house. From the second-floor window, it was only a matter of a few feet to jump to the little roof over the front porch, and then another couple of feet to the surface of the snow.

But given the wind, the cold, the softness of the snow, and the instability of the snowdrifts, Richard knew it was still going to be very difficult to get up there to Annabel and then get her back here to the Ski-Doo.

He started off across the snow.

"Annabel!" he called again.

Her face appeared at the open pane in the window. She placed her finger to her mouth, telling Richard to be quiet. He figured she was in danger. She didn't want someone else in the house to know that he was coming. He nodded and kept on approaching.

The snow, thankfully, was somewhat harder here. Richard sunk only to just below his knee with each step. He made it to the front porch, mostly buried in snow. By grabbing on to the trellis that was attached to the side of the porch, he was able to haul himself up onto the little roof, dislodging a couple of feet of snow as he went. His gloveless hand was freezing. He was pretty certain he'd end up with frostbite.

He was just grateful that it was his left hand. He'd need his right for shooting his gun, if necessary.

Standing on top of the porch roof, Richard could see Annabel's face much more clearly. She looked terrified. Her hair was disheveled, and Richard believed he could discern blood on her hands and clothes. She was wearing a coat. Apparently, she'd been thinking of going out the window herself.

He grabbed hold of the ledge that ran above the porch and out under the windows of the second floor. It was only about six inches wide, but once he'd knocked the snow off it, Richard figured the ledge would be sufficient to get him over to Annabel's window. He hoisted himself up. For a second, his bare hand slipped, and he dangled precariously over the snow. But he steadied himself, and scrambled up onto the ledge. He took a deep breath, and then began inching his way toward Annabel.

"Can you break the window frame?" she was asking him in a desperate whisper as he got closer. "Break it and we can get out of here."

"Yes," he told her. "I think so."

He positioned himself outside the window and tried to punch it in. The wood was too strong. He would have thought such an old house would buckle easily under his fist.

"Oh, please," Annabel was begging. "Jack's in here! He's gone mad! And there's a woman—with a knife!"

Richard tried punching through the window again, but still it held firm. Finally, he reached down and grabbed his gun. It wasn't easy to do. His gun had been encased in a protective pouch to shield it from the snow. He should have unsnapped it before climbing up here. Richard cursed himself for being too hasty. He had to get the gun out of the pouch while managing to remain balanced on the six-inch ledge outside the window.

He was successful. He gripped the gun by its barrel and used the grip to whack the window. On his second try, he heard the wood crack. On the third, it smashed inward, the glass panes popping out, one of them smashing onto the floor inside.

Richard swung himself inside. It was the only way he could help Annabel out.

She threw her arms around him. "Thank God!"

"Anyone else in the house that needs help?" he asked. "Is Chad—?"

Annabel began to cry. "He's dead. The woman killed him."

"No one else then?"

"Well, there's Zeke," she said. "He tried to help me.

I don't know what's happened to him. Last I heard, he was in the room down the hall."

"Stand by the window," Richard said. "Be prepared to jump onto the porch roof, then follow the tracks I made back to the snowmobile. Do you know how to ride one?"

"Me?" Even under such distress, Annabel seemed to find the idea humorous. "No, not at all!"

Richard frowned. "If Zeke needs our help, I can't just leave him. If something happens to me, I want you to be able to escape on your own." He handed her the keys. "I'll be right back. Just hold these, just in case."

"I'll never be able to drive it . . ." Annabel said, but she zipped them inside the pocket of Neville's coat nonetheless.

"I can't just abandon a man who might be in danger here," Richard said, looking over toward the door. "Tell me. Does Jack have a gun?"

"No, there's no gun in the house," Annabel said. "But that woman has a knife—"

"Who is this woman? Do you know?"

Annabel shook her head. "I've never seen her before. But I think she's been living in the attic."

Richard approached the door and listened intently through it. "I've got to go out there and see if I can spot Zeke. If he's not within sight, we'll beat it. But I have to at least give him a chance." He turned the knob carefully.

"The door's locked," Annabel told him.

But it wasn't. The door creaked open under Richard's grip. "Stay by the window!" he ordered Annabel, as he stepped out into the hallway, his gun held high. "And use the keys to get away on the snowmobile if you need to."

The corridor was empty. Richard took three large steps down toward the only other room with an open door and glanced inside. All he could see was a tremendous amount of blood on the floor. A bloody sheet was crumpled in one corner, as if someone had tried to mop up the blood.

He couldn't go searching the house for Zeke. He might risk Annabel's life if he did so. He ran back down the hallway, throwing open doors as he went. The rooms were all empty. He'd done what he could

"Come on," Richard said, holstering his gun and hurrying back into the room where Annabel awaited. "Let's get out of here. I'll send in reinforcements as soon as I can."

Annabel gripped him by the shoulders. "I can't believe you made it here," she said. "I really thought I was going to die."

Richard gave her a small smile. "You can buy me a cup of coffee later to thank me. For now, let's just get the hell—"

103

Annabel screamed as Richard suddenly went flying against the wall.

Jack had come charging into the room through the open door, shoving Richard hard, taking him by complete surprise.

"No!" Annabel screamed again.

Richard was quickly back up on his feet, hauling off and landing a hard punch against Jack's jaw. Annabel's husband staggered backwards, but regained his balance quickly. He lunged at Richard, just as the chief was going for his gun.

"You're not going to destroy my success!" Jack shouted.

With superhuman swiftness, he lunged at Richard, sending him toppling out of the open window. The gun in his hands went flying through the air, clattering across the floor and coming to a stop under the bed.

Running to the window, Annabel watched in horror and disbelief as Richard plunged to the ground, smashing headfirst into the snow. Only his feet remained sticking out from the surface.

"Nooo!" Annabel screamed into the wind.

She saw Richard's feet twitch once, and then go still. The snow around him slowly turned pink.

Annabel turned around to face her husband. "You killed him," she said in a low voice.

"I had to," Jack said. "He was going to destroy everything we've built up here, sugar cakes. He was going to prevent us from getting the success we deserve!"

"You're insane!" Annabel shouted, running over to him and beating her fists on his chest. "You have gone completely insane!"

She didn't care anymore what he might do to her. In that instant, Annabel lost control, giving vent to all her fear and despair. Richard had been her last hope. No one was going to save her now. She dissolved into tears, covering her face with her hands.

Jack grabbed her by her arms and forced her to look up at him. "It's up to you, Annabel," he said, his voice calm but firm. "You can join me in a successful life, or you can turn your back on all the house has to offer us. I'll forgive you for your indiscretions with these other men—"

She yanked away from him. "There have been no indiscretions, Jack! Why do you talk that way?"

He arched an eyebrow at her. "That policeman—he meant nothing to you?"

Annabel started to cry harder. "He was trying to save me."

"Save you from what? From a glorious life here, with me, at the Blue Boy, where everything we touch will turn into gold?"

Annabel wanted to scream. "Who told you that, Jack? Why do you believe that?"

He smiled. It was a terrible, frightening smile. "The house told me," he said simply. "Once I learned the secret, I could listen to the house. I could understand what it was telling me."

"You're mad," Annabel spat out.

She just couldn't pretend anymore. She couldn't make it seem that she was going along with Jack's demented plans. She just had to get out of there. She had to find a way. Her mind started to race, to calculate.

She'd make a run for it. Yes, that was what she'd do. She'd go out the window in her room. It was a longer drop from there, but Annabel had seen how Richard had trudged through the snow. It was passable, not so soft that she'd sink. And the window in her room opened easily. Annabel began to believe that she could run in there, throw open the window, and be outside in less than a minute. She had to believe she could. It was her only hope.

And in her pocket she had the keys to the snowmobile. She would have to believe that she could drive it. She would have to believe that she could save herself.

But for her plan to work, she'd need to incapacitate Jack, even temporarily, just to give her enough time to get out the window and run—or, rather, trudge—to the snowmobile. Otherwise, he'd be out the window right after her, and there was no question he'd be able to catch her. Annabel had just witnessed how strong Jack had become, sending Richard flying through the window with very little effort. Her husband was a tall, well-built man, but in recent years he'd grown a bit squishy from too much time on his hands, watching sports on television, and drinking too much beer. Where had this sudden burst of power come from?

The house, Annabel realized.

The house was making him strong.

Now I'm thinking crazy like Jack, Annabel admonished herself. *What we have here is one very deranged man—nothing supernatural about that.* Those visions of little men, Annabel told herself, were just her mind playing tricks, her hallucinations coming back under stress.

But then how to explain the woman with the knife? Annabel was certain she was very much real, after watching what she did to Chad.

For the moment, what was real and what was illusion didn't matter. Annabel just needed to get out of there. She needed to gain some kind of power over Jack so she could get away.

The gun. Richard's gun. It was under the bed. She needed to get it.

But Tommy Tricky was under there.

No, stop it, he's not real.

He doesn't like it when you say he's not real.

Annabel was suddenly overwhelmed with the feeling that if she reached under the bed, a little blue clawed hand would grab her.

She tried to calm herself. What she needed to do, she knew, was buy a little time from Jack. She took a deep breath and looked over at him.

"All right, Jack," Annabel said, wiping her eyes and looking over at him. "I have no choice but to go along with you. I don't understand what you mean about the house, but maybe . . . maybe you'll teach me."

"That's it, baby cakes. That's the spirit!" He wrapped his arms around her and squeezed her tightly. "We're going to be very successful here, you and I."

She gently extricated herself from Jack's grip. "I feel so light-headed," she said. "All this blood . . . this death, Jack . . . I don't know how to deal with it."

"You've never known how to deal with bad stuff, angel sweets," Jack said. "Sit down. Take a few breaths."

That was just what Annabel wanted him to say. She sat down on the bed.

Please let the gun be within reach, she prayed.

"I feel like I might faint," Annabel said.

"Bend down and put your head between your legs," Jack told her, as he walked over to the window with a blanket, trying to find a way to block the snow blowing into the room. "Let the blood run to your head. That will bring you out of it."

Perfect. This was perfect. He had just told her to do exactly what she needed to do to be able to look under the bed. And his back was to her. Perfect. This was working perfectly.

Annabel leaned over. She peered into the darkness. What she saw made her gasp, though she retained enough presence of mind to suppress it.

The gun was right there, all right. Within reach.

But lying right next to it, on his stomach, his chin in his sharp little hands, was Tommy Tricky. He smiled at Annabel, licking his lips with his blue tongue.

She steeled herself.

You little fucker, she thought. *You're not going to keep me from getting this gun.*

She reached under the bed. The imp's eyes followed her hand.

He's going to bite you, Annabel heard Daddy Ron tell her in her mind.

But she didn't pull back. She closed her fingers around

the gun. Tommy Tricky watched her. His eyes were all
that moved.

Annabel sat up all at once, the gun in her hand.

To her great relief, Jack was still at the window, trying to stuff the blanket into the space between the broken wood frames and shards of glass.

"I've got to get a piece of plywood and patch this
thing," he was saying. "Else we will have a foot of
snow in here before long."

He turned around. Annabel saw the surprise and disbelief on his face when he saw her standing there,
pointing the gun at him.

He knew she could use it, too. In New York, she'd
taken a self-defense class. She'd learned how to fire a
gun.

He stood there, mouth open, staring at her.

"You threatened to kill me, Jack, but I'm not going
to kill you," Annabel told him. "At least, I don't want to
kill you. I will if I have to. I could as easily aim this at
your head or your heart as your leg. So come on along
with me. Put up your hands."

Her husband sneered at her, but he obeyed.

"Come on," she said. "Walk in front of me."

"Where are we going?"

Annabel smirked. "Let's see how you like being
locked in a closet."

"If you lock me up," Jack asked, "you won't have to
shoot me, too, will you?" He shuffled slowly across the
room, Annabel behind him, the gun pressing against
the small of his back.

"Sorry, Jack," she replied, "but I'm not taking any
chances. You've got an accomplice running around
here somewhere, and she could let you out. So unfortu-

nately you'll have two legs full of gunshot wounds in addition to being locked in the closet. But don't worry. I'm heading back to town, and I'll send an ambulance for you." She shoved him toward Cordelia's closet. "As soon as the storm lets up, that is."

"Annabel," Jack said, "don't so this. We can be so happy—"

At that moment, a wail came from above them. From the attic. It was a terrible sound, a cry of grief and despair. It was enough to distract Annabel for half a second—which was just enough time for Jack to spin around with that superhuman speed he now possessed and knock the gun out of her hands. It fell to the floor with a thud.

Annabel saw the rage that suddenly filled Jack's eyes.

She ran. She bolted out into the hallway, but Jack was fast on her heels. She'd have to go past him if she were to try jumping from the window or running downstairs. There was only one option for her, and she took it without even consciously realizing she'd done so.

She ran up the stairs to the attic.

The door was open. She bolted inside, no longer thinking, just reacting, driven solely by an instinct to survive.

She didn't even realize that Jack had not pursued her up the stairs.

Yet despite her desperation to get away, Annabel came to a skidding halt when she came upon the scene in the attic.

The woman with the long gray hair stood there. Her white dress was now soaked with blood. In front of her various body parts were scattered around the room.

Legs and arms, a portion of a torso, with the rib cage sticking out. And Chad's head, looking up at Annabel with lifeless eyes. At the moment, the woman was sawing an arm off a shoulder.

Annabel screamed, and then got sick, before fainting this time for real.

104

Zeke heard Annabel's scream from the attic and, with a heavy heart, started up the stairs. He was unprepared for the gore that he found there.

"Oh, what have you done, Cindy?" he asked, in utter despair and horror, looking around at the carnage. "I have told you and told you that you must not do this. . . ."

"But I must," the woman in the bloody dress told him. "I promised them. You know I promised them."

"It is too much," Zeke said, his face a mask of anguish and grief. "We can't go on."

He saw Annabel slumped on the floor.

"I must get her out," he said. "And then . . ." He looked back at the woman. "Then we must all pay the price for what we have done."

"I promised them," the woman said, sulking now. "They let me go, because I promised them."

Zeke walked over to her, cupped her face in the palm of his hand.

"It's not your fault, Cindy. You were just a little girl. It destroyed your mind. You poor sweet little girl."

"I promised them," she said, a broken record.

"They get nothing more," Zeke said, angry now. "Nothing more."

He bent down to Annabel. "Wake up, Miz Wish. Come with me. Can you walk?"

She stirred.

"Get to your feet," Zeke said. "It's all a bad dream. You'll wake up in the morning and it will all be gone. But come with me now. Walk with me."

"What—?" Annabel mumbled, as she got to her feet.

"Don't look over there," Zeke told her. "It's just a bad dream. Come with me. You'll be safe with me. Walk with me down the stairs."

Annabel, like a zombie, obeyed.

He took her all the way down to the first floor, into the kitchen. He sat her down at the table.

"Listen to me, Miz Wish," Zeke said. "I've cleared a path from the back door. You can get out that way. I've also cleared the way to your car. Here are your keys."

Annabel looked at him. The old caretaker could see that her mind had shut down. It was a defense mechanism against the horrors she'd seen upstairs.

"Listen to me, Miz Wish. Annabel. Here are your keys."

He pressed them into her hand.

"You are to walk out and get into your car. Do you understand? The snow is stopping, but you still can't drive out. But I've cleared the snow off it, and you can start it. You can keep warm there. Keep the window cracked, as I left it for you. That will keep you safe from any fumes. But just a crack."

Annabel said nothing.

"Do you understand? You will be safe there until someone comes for you. Someone will be coming. The police will come looking for the chief, and they'll find you."

Annabel stared at him blankly.

"Do you understand, Annabel?" Zeke asked, growing concerned.

"I . . . understand," she finally said. "I can go to the car . . . and wait there . . . be safe . . . someone will be coming soon."

"Yes, yes, that's right. And Annabel. Do not come back inside the house, under any circumstances." He shivered. "No matter what happens. I think, when you see it, you'll know it's for the best."

Annabel's eyes moved around the kitchen. She seemed to smell something.

"Yes, that's gasoline you smell," Zeke told her. "I've sprinkled it all over the house. Upstairs and downstairs. Every room."

He walked across the room and lifted the can, shook some more of the liquid onto the floor.

"It's the only way," he told Annabel.

"The only way," she echoed dully.

He heard the scuttling then. The sound of dozens of little feet running toward him.

"No!" Zeke shouted, frantically running across the kitchen for the box of matches.

But the old man couldn't run very fast, and he slipped on the floor, falling flat onto his stomach, knocking the wind out of him—just as thirteen little men came scurrying around the corner from the parlor and crawled all over him.

"Nooo!" Zeke screamed.

But it was too late.

105

Annabel watched the events unfold as if from some faraway place.

The little men—so many Tommy Trickies everywhere all of a sudden—grabbed on to the old man on the floor. With uncanny strength for their small size, they lifted him and carried him off. Zeke writhed and kicked, but the little men paid him no mind as they carted him out of the kitchen and back in toward the parlor.

Annabel stood. She followed them, as if in a daze.

"No, no, please, no!" Zeke was screaming.

The little men marched him in front of the fireplace.

"Nooo!" Zeke shouted.

They pressed his feet into the ash dump door.

Annabel watched. Only gradually did she come back to her senses, and begin to comprehend what was happening.

When she finally understood fully, she screamed.

But her scream was drowned out by Zeke's, as the old man was pulled down inside the fireplace by several sharp tiny blue hands sticking up out of the ash dump.

The last to disappear were Zeke's outstretched arms and hands, frantically twisting and opening and closing as the creatures below ravenously consumed his body.

When finally he was completely gone, the thirteen little men who had delivered him leapt into the air, cheering and laughing over a job well done.

They'll come for me next, Annabel realized.

She also realized that she still had the keys to the car in her hand. She turned and bolted out of the parlor, back into the kitchen.

And ran right into the arms of Jack.

106

"I really appreciate this," Deputy Adam Burrell said as Danny's friend Melvin started the snowmobile for him. "You guys are the best."

Melvin gave him a freckle-faced smile. "Hey, dude, anything to help out the Woodfield finest. When Danny called me to say the cops needed a snowmobile, I didn't hesitate to hop on mine and zip right over here." The teenager leapt up off the seat so that Adam could slide on. "Remember that, okay, next time you catch me with a little weed."

"I'll look the other way one time only," Adam said, taking the handlebars, "and then we're even."

Melvin gave him a little salute.

Unlike the chief, Adam knew how to handle a snow-mobile. Growing up in these parts, he'd been riding the machines since he was a kid. Adam wished Richard had let him go in his place. He would have been able to handle the Ski-Doo with ease. As it was, they were all wondering if maybe the chief had had an accident. It had been a couple of hours now since they'd heard from him, and Adam was beginning to worry. Had he crashed?

But maybe a snowmobile crack-up was the least they should be concerned about.

Setting off down the road, Adam didn't know what he'd find at the Blue Boy.

The snow had stopped, but it was still blowing pretty fiercely. It would be days before everything was plowed. The department was definitely going to need to invest in its own snowmobiles, if storms like this were getting more frequent. As it was, their call to various private citizens had rounded up three more Ski-Doos. Their owners were riding them in even as Adam headed across town. They were coming from a bit farther out in the woods than either Danny or Melvin, so it would still take some time for them to get to the police station. But at least Adam knew he'd have some backup of more officers at the Blue Boy eventually, if it turned out he needed it.

And need it, he might. He'd gone over everything they'd learned about what had been taking place at the inn. The disappearances, the blood in the chimney, the sounds that had been heard, the fact that the Englishman had been locked in his room. Something really weird was going down at that place. The fact that there had been no word from the chief unnerved Adam the most.

He sped on across the snow.

107

"Give me the keys to the car, Annabel," Jack said, holding out his hand.

Annabel had no choice but to obey.

"What am I going to do with you?" he asked, stuffing the keys down into his jeans pocket. "First you threaten to shoot me and lock me in a closet, and then you try to run off."

"Those things—" Annabel could barely speak. "Those things that took Zeke—"

Jack smiled. "They're real, Annabel. And they don't like it when you say they aren't."

He was deliberately mocking her. She had told him all about Daddy Ron.

"How is it possible?" Annabel asked, gripping the back of a kitchen chair to keep herself from falling down. Her head was throbbing. She couldn't make sense of all that she had witnessed this afternoon.

"Sit down, angel cakes," Jack told her. "Take a load off. I'll make you some tea."

"No," Annabel said.

Jack laughed. "Afraid I'll poison you? I suppose you should worry. You've been a very bad girl."

Annabel thought she might faint. She pulled out the chair and sat down in it, holding her head in her hands.

She was going to die here. Jack was going to kill her.

Or worse—he was going to put her down the fireplace. She would die crammed into a tiny space, unable to move, eaten by a dozen Tommy Trickies.

Her childhood nightmare come true.

"Please, Jack," she cried.

"I should take no pity on you after everything you've done," Jack said, and Annabel could hear the teakettle whistling on the stove. "I should really punish you, you know."

"No," Annabel sobbed.

"But success would be no fun on my own," Jack continued. His wife could hear him pouring some hot water in a mug. "Do you want chamomile or Earl Grey?"

"No, no, no," she muttered.

"I guess I'll give you chamomile. It's more soothing. And you need to calm down."

He placed a steaming mug in front of her, the tab of a tea bag dangling from its side. Annabel didn't touch it.

Jack sat opposite her at the kitchen table. "Sweetie, I want to do this together with you. The only reason my father didn't have the heart to go on was because he lost my mother. If they'd been a team, they would have had so much success here."

Annabel wouldn't look at him.

"I want you to remake this place into a grand destination, just as we planned. You'll redo this kitchen, make it all sparkling and modern." He leaned toward her. "And maybe you could learn how to make Gran's rabbit stew. You don't have to eat it, sweetie, but it could become the inn's signature dish. Carry on a little tradition, you know, for our guests."

Finally, she snapped her eyes up to look at him. "Our guests? Who'd be picked off, one by one, dragged down screaming into that pit of hell?"

"No, you see, sweetheart, that's why I need your help. We can control the house." He chuckled. "I admit, right now, it's a bit out of control. But if we give it only what it needs, it will take care of us. It will make us successful. That was the promise given to my great-grandfather when he bought the house over a hundred years ago."

"By whom?" Annabel asked.

"By the house." Jack looked at her as if she was being thickheaded. "And the house keeps its promises."

"And kills those who live here." Annabel's eyes hardened. "Or it does worse things to them. Like your *sister*." She spat the word, watching Jack's face to see how he reacted. "Look what it's done to *her*."

"My sister," Jack said softly. "Yes, you're right, Annabel, Cindy's a problem we have to deal with. Again, this is why I need your help."

Annabel saw an opening, maybe a way to appeal to whatever reason and sanity Jack might have left. "Cindy needs help, Jack. We need to get her help."

He stood and began pacing the kitchen. "Gran thought she had everything under control. With the fireplace bricked over, the only way to feed the house was through the door in the chimney in the basement. She kept it padlocked, but Cindy—well, she's very strong. And she kept breaking the lock, and feeding the house through the door."

"Feeding it with what?" Annabel asked.

Jack shrugged. "Whatever she could find. Rabbits, mice, dead raccoons, skunks." He made a face of disgust. "But the house was starving for something better than that. Cindy understood this, and of course, she would do anything to please the house. The house had spared her, and she was grateful."

"Spared . . . her?" Annabel asked.

"Yes, sweetheart. Drink your tea. And I'll tell you the story."

108

Jack was just a little boy, he told Annabel, when he came down the stairs to find his father sitting in the parlor, his head in his hands, sobbing.

"They took her," his father was saying.

His grandmother had been standing over him.

"Brick it up," she was telling him. "Brick it up now!"

Jack had been so young he couldn't understand everything that was happening. He had just stood there watching and listening.

Cordelia had approached the fireplace. "You filthy monsters! Do you think we haven't read the books? Do you think we don't know how to put an end to this?"

Jack's father stood. "Don't, Mother. Don't provoke them. They'll come back. . . ."

"Brick it up!" Cordelia shrieked.

"Stop, Mother! They'll hear you! They've taken my wife and they've taken Cindy! They'll come back—for us—for Jack!"

Jack had shrunk back at hearing his name, suddenly terrified.

His father had rushed to the fireplace then, speaking into it.

"Give her back if it's not too late," he pleaded. "Give Cindy back and I will make sure we give you what you need, always! We had a bargain! You would make me successful if I gave you what you needed. I will keep my end of that bargain. Just give me back Cindy!"

Jack had watched from around the corner of the parlor.

He had heard a rustling sound. Scratching.

And then he had seen a small pink hand reach up from the ash dump in the fireplace. . . .

109

"They . . . they let her go?" Annabel asked, unable to truly comprehend what she was hearing.

"Yes," Jack told her. "They made the bargain with my father—which he failed to keep. But I intend to make up for what he did wrong!"

"Jack, all of this is madness!"

He still seemed miles away, lost in his memory. "I had blocked it all out. Because, you see, when Cindy came back to us, she wasn't the same. She was wild, uncontrollable. My grandmother decided to keep her here when my father and I left. She bricked up the fireplace because the house was very angry at being deceived." He smiled over at Annabel. "And it's no good to have the house angry at us, as you have witnessed."

"Jack, please, listen to what you're saying. . . ."

He sighed. "Poor Cindy. The house had let her go, but it still had her mind. If my father had reneged on his promise, she was determined to make it up to the house. She fed the house, gave it what it needed. . . ." He looked over at Annabel sadly. "Until recently. She kept sneaking out of the attic—Zeke was getting far too old to control her, and Cindy had become far too cunning—and finally she went out and killed that man, chopped him up, fed him piece by piece to the house."

Annabel thought she might be sick again.

"Jack," she said, when she was finally able to form words, "this is crazy talk. Can't you see that? It makes no sense!"

"It makes perfect sense, Annabel, if you *let* it make sense."

She struggled to show him how absurd his words were. "If Cindy could open up the door in the basement, then why didn't those things get out that way? Why did they have to wait until the fireplace was unbricked?"

"That's just the way it is, Annabel. That's what it says in the books. They can only come out through the fireplace."

"What *books*?" But then suddenly she remembered. The books she'd found—those books about demons and witchcraft hidden in that secret panel—the same sort of panel that must exist all through the house, Annabel realized, allowing the creatures free rein. "No," she mumbled. "It can't be possible."

Jack remained calm. "You only think it can't be, because you don't believe in the house."

Annabel ran her hands through her hair. "You think this house—those terrible things—those creatures—they can somehow make you successful? Why do you think that?" She thought of those hideous books once more. "Is it like some terrible pact with the devil?"

"Call it what you like, Annabel."

She shook her head. "And success comes through *feeding* the house?"

"Yes, now you're getting it." Jack sighed. "But

here's the dilemma. Cindy is determined to keep giving the house what it craves, yet the truth is, she doesn't need to, anymore." He laughed. "The house has been freed to take what it wants all by itself!" He smiled broadly over at her. "*You* freed it, Annabel."

The tears were running down her cheeks.

"But you're right, angel cakes." Jack was nodding, as if he were thinking things over. "We're going to need to find a way to control Cindy. We can't allow her to disturb our guests. We need to find something productive for her to occupy her time with."

This was utter madness. Annabel put her head down on the table and cried.

Jack wandered across the kitchen, lost in thought. "She was such a sweet little girl," he said dreamily. "You know, I had blocked all of it out . . . all of what happened to her. I was so young and my father told me that I was mistaken. I hadn't seen Cindy climbing out of the fireplace, all bloody and sooty. Dad insisted that she'd wandered off into the woods."

Annabel looked up at him. "Jack, you have to help your sister. All these years, the way your grandmother hid her in this house, it wasn't fair to her."

"But Cindy *wants* to be here," Jack insisted. "She belongs here. So do I." He took a step toward Annabel. "So do you."

"Jack, please—"

They heard the sound of a motor out in front of the house.

Jack rushed to the window.

"Another cop on a snowmobile," he seethed.

"Jack," Annabel pleaded, "let me talk to him. I'll tell

him that none of this was your fault, or Cindy's. Please, just let me talk to him—"

"You think I'm a fool?" Jack growled. He grabbed Annabel, pulled her up from the chair, and clamped his hand over her mouth. "You'll say nothing, you hear? You won't make a sound, baby cakes, or I'll have to break your neck. I won't like doing it, but I will."

He dragged her across the kitchen toward the pantry.

"Cindeeee!" he called.

Then he banged open the door to the pantry with his shoulder and took Annabel inside.

110

Pulling into the snow-covered driveway of the Blue Boy Inn, Adam could see Richard's snowmobile, already nearly covered by drifting snow. He could also see a path that had been dug out from around the side of the house, leading to an SUV, which had also been cleared of snow. *That's convenient,* Adam, thought, as otherwise, he'd have to try to gain access to the house by crawling up the side and going through a second-floor window. The first floor was almost completely covered in snow.

I'll bet the chief shoveled out this path, Adam thought, steering the snowmobile over to the clearing. *I'll bet I'll find him inside, having coffee with Annabel. Everything's going to be fine. The only reason we haven't heard from him is because there's no cell reception out here.*

For some reason, the shoveled path reassured Adam. He thought he'd find everything peaceful inside. They'd been wrong to worry.

He didn't look too closely at the front of the house, or the pink snow near the front door.

Adam brought the snowmobile to a stop. He dismounted and headed over to the path that led to the kitchen door.

"Chief?" he called as he approached the house.

He peered through the one window that had been cleared of snow. He looked into the kitchen. He didn't see anyone. But there was a steaming mug of what looked like tea on the table. Things couldn't be too bad if they were sitting around drinking tea.

Adam rapped on the door.

There was no sound, no movement, from inside.

He rapped again. "Hello!" he called. "Chief! Are you there? Mr. Devlin! Ms. Wish!"

Why wasn't anyone answering?

Adam tried the door. It was open. He let himself in.

Something wasn't right. He felt it as soon as he stepped inside the kitchen.

He held his gun in front of him with both hands.

"Chief!" Adam called. "Hello! Anyone here?"

A woman suddenly appeared in the doorway that led to the parlor. She was pretty, but her hair was long and gray. She was wearing a long blue dress.

"Hello," the woman said.

Adam lowered his gun. "I'm Officer Burrell. I'm looking for Chief Carlson."

The woman looked at him as if she didn't understand.

"Who are you?" Adam asked her.

She just smiled and took a step into the room.

111

In the pantry, Annabel and Jack watched from a crack in the door.

"Mmm," Annabel moaned, Jack's hand still pressed over her mouth.

"Shh," he growled at her.

Annabel watched in despair as Cindy approached the policeman. She could see the knife she carried behind her back, even if the poor man did not. How Annabel wanted to warn him. But Jack would break her neck if she made a sound. She truly believed he would.

But the policeman had a gun. He could shoot Cindy if she tried to attack him. Jack, too. He could put an end to all of this madness.

What did it matter if Annabel died? She was going to die in this house anyway. If she made some kind of a sound, there was a chance that the policeman could shoot Jack before he had a chance to kill her. Staying silent simply prolonged her misery. Making noise gave her a chance—a slim chance, but a chance nonetheless. And if she died, so be it.

She couldn't live in this hellhole much longer.

Jack held Annabel in a vise grip in front of him, preventing her from moving her arms. His hand was secured over her mouth.

But he hadn't counted on her feet.

She was still wearing his clunky boots. They were loose. If she could shake one off . . .

Annabel lifted her right foot up to the side. She kicked.

The boot remained on her foot. If she tried again, Jack might notice.

But she had to try. She lifted her foot again. And kicked doubly hard.

The boot flew off her foot and crashed into a low shelf of glass jars containing Cordelia's preserves. Apricots and strawberries smashed all onto the floor.

112

Adam heard the sound and swung his gun around in the direction of the pantry. As he did so, the woman in front of him lunged at him with a knife.

He fired wildly, pumping the kitchen ceiling full of lead.

The woman's knife made contact with his arm, cutting through his coat and slicing into his flesh.

Adam spun back around, slugging the woman, sending her flying and the knife skittering across the floor.

He kicked open the door to the pantry.

"Ms. Wish!" he exclaimed.

Jack let her go.

"Mr. Devlin," Adam said, trying to make sense of things. "Come on out of there, please. I'd like to know what's going on here."

113

Annabel's relief and gratitude were short-lived. Behind Adam she saw Cindy stand up. Dear God, what kind of strength did she have? Adam had just knocked her out cold.

What kind of power did this house give to people?

Annabel saw Cindy stand and grab her knife off the floor. . . .

114

"No!" Ms. Wish suddenly screamed, looking behind him.

Adam turned in time to see the woman back on her feet, coming at him with the knife. He swung his gun around—

But it was too late.

The knife plunged deep into Adam's gut. He gasped and buckled forward.

Devlin began punching him. Adam fell to the ground.

The last thing he saw was the knife above him, coming down at his throat.

115

Annabel saw Cindy bring the knife down onto the policeman, then pull it up again, then plunge it down again, repeating this several times, each time dripping more blood.

"Okay, honey, enough now," Jack was saying to her gently.

"I have to cut him up," Cindy said, like an eager child.

Jack tenderly lifted her off the twitching, bloody corpse. "No, Cindy, you don't have to do that. From now on, I'll take care of feeding the house. Do you understand, baby?"

Cindy looked up at him with sad eyes. "They don't need me anymore," she whimpered.

"Oh, honey baby, the house will always need you." Jack pulled her into an embrace, stroking her stringy gray hair.

"They're my only friends," Cindy cried against his chest.

"No, baby, I'm your friend, too. And Annabel—"

But Annabel had just bolted.

She ran out of the kitchen into the parlor. She couldn't have gone out the back way. Jack would have gotten her. Her only hope was to go out through her window upstairs, as she'd originally planned. She still had the snowmobile keys zipped in her pocket. Even if she couldn't get very far on it, Annabel was certain now more policemen were on their way. She just had to get out of the house before Jack or Cindy could get her.

Or worse—she could be caught by Tommy Tricky and his brothers.

She ran up the stairs and turned the corner into the corridor.

But she didn't get very far.

A hand suddenly reached out and clamped itself over her mouth. Before she knew what was happening, she was pulled into a dark closet by a very strong pair of arms.

116

Richard kissed her to make sure she didn't scream out.

Annabel shuddered in his arms, still full of terror. He moved his lips off her.

"It's okay," he whispered in her ear. "It's going to be okay."

In the very dim light of the linen closet, Richard saw Annabel's eyes sparkle with sudden surprise and relief. "Richard," she said, as the tenseness in her body relaxed. "You're alive!"

He grunted. "Well, my face is never going to be the same, and I think I broke my ankle, and I can't feel my left hand, but yes, I'm alive."

He smiled.

"Thank God," Annabel said, looking up at his face. "Oh, Richard, you're all cut and swollen."

She tried to touch him and he flinched. The pain was quite severe now. Only as his body had warmed did he begin to feel just how injured he was.

He had come to under the snow. How very peaceful it had been down there. On some primal level, Richard had wanted to stay right where he was. He was fading in and out of consciousness, and he wasn't unhappy. He wasn't uncomfortable. But he would die if he stayed where he was. He was, in fact, slowly freezing to death. The thought had startled him back to full consciousness, and Richard had begun to scrape his way out of the snow.

It hadn't been easy. The snow was hardening, and he was stuck headfirst in it. At first, it had been almost impossible to move his arms. He pushed and elbowed as best he could, and kicked as hard as he could muster with his legs. Finally, he created enough space around him to move, to shift his position. He swallowed a lot of snow in the process.

He was bleeding from his face and neck. The impact had cut and scraped him pretty badly, but he hadn't felt much pain at first. He was too cold. He was too numb. Clawing his way out of the snowbank, he had stood up and looked around. That was when he felt the first pain—in his ankle. He didn't think it was the fall that had done it, but rather the way Devlin had slammed him into the wall.

The man was going to pay.

Richard noticed another snowmobile was now parked out in front. Could it be one of his officers, come looking for him? Or was it someone else?

He could take no chances. Knowing that Devlin might be watching him, Richard crunched through the snow to the back of the house, where he spotted a rainspout. He tested it, determined it was strong enough, and he began to climb. The angle made it impossible to be seen from any window of the house. Once he was close enough to a window, Richard used the butt of his gun to smash his way in.

He always traveled with a spare gun.

Stepping through the broken window, aware that the sound could bring Devlin running, Richard steadied himself, his weapon in both hands, raised in front of him. He was aware that Devlin might have his other gun, the one he'd lost when he'd been taken unawares. That had never happened before to Richard, ever, in his career. He was known for being very swift, very agile, able to turn on a dime. But Devlin seemed to possess some kind of strength that Richard had not expected.

So he was extra cautious as he made his way down the hall.

That was when he had heard the screaming and crying from downstairs and the scampering of feet. He'd backed into the open linen closet so he wouldn't be seen. In seconds, Annabel had come running by. Now he held her, trembling in his arms.

"Does he have the gun?" Richard whispered in her ear.

"Not at the moment," Annabel told him. "But I'm sure he'll get it."

"Where is it?" he asked. "Do you know?"

"I had it for a while, but he knocked it away from me. It was on the floor in the bedroom."

"Let's go," Richard said. "If it's there, we'll get it. If not, well, he can keep it. Shoot himself with it, for all I care. Either way, you and I are going out the window." He looked down at her. "You still have the keys to the snowmobile?"

"Yes." Annabel gripped his coat and looked up at

him. "But Richard, you need to know what's happened here. Terrible things."

"What kind of terrible things?" he asked.

She shuddered. "Adam's dead."

"Adam—?"

"Cindy killed him."

"Cindy?" Richard looked down at the terrified woman in his arms. "That was the name of Devlin's sister, the little girl who died. . . ."

"She's alive. She's the woman I told you about. She's been living here. Completely insane."

"So she's the killer."

Annabel looked as if she'd cry. "Yes, but no . . ."

"Annabel, what do you mean?"

"Oh, Richard, it's the house. There are things that live in this house . . . creatures who come up through the fireplace. . . ."

She was delirious. And who wouldn't be, after everything she'd been through?

"Come on, Annabel," he said. "We're getting out of here."

"They'll get us, Richard! The little men! Tommy Tricky and his friends!"

"Calm down, Annabel. Stay behind me at all times." He nudged the door of the closet open just a crack, getting a look down the corridor. "We're just going across the way and into the bedroom, then out the window."

"But Richard . . ."

"Listen to me. We're going out the window and then onto the little roof over the porch. From there it's an easy jump to the snow, and at that point we can move pretty quickly to the snowmobile in the tracks that I made getting here."

"Richard, they're not going to let us leave. . . ."

"You mean Jack and his sister?"

"No. The little men."

Richard looked at her. It was best not to argue with her at this point.

"Come on, Annabel," he said, pushing open the door. "Let's go."

117

Annabel followed Richard out of the closet.

Where were Jack and Cindy? Lurking somewhere, Annabel was certain. They would pounce on them. But even worse—

The little men.

They'll put us down the fireplace!

"Come on," Richard urged in a harsh whisper, and they ran across the hall.

As they rushed into the bedroom, they could see the window. There was no gun in sight, but all that really mattered was that they reach the window. The window meant freedom. For half of a second, Annabel's spirits leapt. She believed they would escape.

But then Tommy Tricky dropped from the ceiling onto Richard's back.

He must have been sitting on the top of the opened door, waiting, watching.

He plunged his long sharp claws into Richard's neck. Richard screamed.

"I don't like it when you don't believe in me,

Richard," the little imp said in his high-pitched doll's voice.

Annabel screamed at the same time Richard did. Blood squirted from the chief's neck like water from a leaky pipe.

Richard grabbed his neck and in doing so, he knocked the little man from his shoulders. Tommy had only a second to look up at him and hiss through his sharp, clenched teeth when Richard aimed his gun at him and fired.

The little man exploded in a mess of blue blood and plasma.

"Richard, are you all right?" Annabel said, rushing to him.

"I think so," he said, more dazed and shocked by the creature than the attack itself. He kept looking down at the bubbling ooze on the floor.

"It's not possible," he said. "That thing—"

Finally, he pulled his eyes away and grabbed Annabel by the wrist.

"Come on, let's go!"

But when they looked toward the window they saw little men were now crawling all over it. The creatures were coming out of the woodwork. Literally. Floorboards raised. Panels in the walls opened. And the little men stepped out, their fierce blue eyes trained on Annabel and Richard.

"Through the other window!" Richard shouted, pulling Annabel out of the room and into the corridor.

The moment they stepped out of the room, however, every door along the hall slammed shut. They were left in semidarkness. Richard tried the door to his left. It was locked. Annabel tried the one opposite. That one, too, wouldn't budge.

"Look, Richard!" Annabel suddenly shouted.

Marching up the stairs and into the hallway was an army of six more little men. They all looked nearly identical, with little blue pinched faces and blue teeth and blue rags as clothes. They were all gnashing their teeth.

"Shoot them, Richard!" Annabel screamed.

He was firing even before the words were out of her mouth. The first two creatures exploded like their fallen comrade, but those in the back suddenly leapt to the walls, crawling like spiders, still coming toward their prey. Richard fired again, but the creatures easily darted away, and the bullet simply tore open a portion of the wall. Another of the little men was now on the ceiling, and as Annabel looked up at it, it dropped down on her.

Clinging to her shoulders, face-to-face with her, Tommy Tricky laughed. "I like eating bad little girls," he hissed.

Annabel screamed.

Richard knocked the thing to the floor with the butt of his gun, and then shot it. Once more, Annabel watched it bubble into a blue goo.

But the other three were now clawing up Richard's leg. He shook one off, sending it flying through the air. He shot it before it hit the wall, a messy blue explosion in mid-flight.

But the other one was now crawling up his torso. And the final little man had jumped off Richard and onto Annabel's arm.

Suddenly she got angry.

"You filthy bastard!" she bellowed, and whipped her arm around, crashing the creature into the wall. She took delight in seeing the way its blue teeth smashed on impact. The thing fell in a dazed lump to the floor.

Richard swatted the thing off his torso, shot it, and then did the same to the creature Annabel had dispatched.

"What are these fucking things?" he asked.

"I told you. They're the—"

"Yes," he said, finishing her thought. "From the fireplace." He looked over at her. "Do you think this is all of them?"

"No," Annabel said. "There are more. I don't know how many, but there are definitely more."

"Well, at least we know they can be killed," Richard said. He seemed to realize something. "So the stories of old Reverend Fall were apparently true after all. He found his portal."

"What?" Annabel asked.

"No time now to explain," Richard replied, before taking hold of her arm. "All right, let's get out of here before we encounter any more of those hell spawn."

They ran back to Cordelia's room. The door was no longer locked. The sheet Jack had used as a makeshift barrier at the window had fallen off, and a couple of feet of snow had drifted into the room.

"Same plan as before," Richard told Annabel, and she nodded.

They bolted toward the window.

118

For Richard, it was almost as if time stood still. There he was, running for his very life, away from things he never believed existed just moments before, and yet, despite all those dangers, he was thinking of Amy.

He was thinking about how very much he had loved her. And how much he missed her. And how he would never love any woman ever again the way he had loved Amy, no matter how long he lived.

He had failed to save Amy. How he had tried. He had never accepted her diagnosis. Richard had taken his wife to see specialist after specialist. He'd investigated every new drug, every alternative treatment. But still Amy had died. Still she'd left him alone.

He'd saved Annabel, however. Richard felt confident that was true.

As he positioned her by the window so she could jump out onto the front porch roof, he realized something.

He hadn't saved Annabel. She had saved herself.

He had seen how she'd bashed that creature against

the wall. Annabel had survived this house of horrors. Her escape was entirely due to her. Richard was just driving the getaway car.

Annabel could survive anything.

Just like Amy. Richard hadn't failed her, because there was nothing to fail: Amy had been entirely in control the whole time. It was Richard who'd used terms like "beating this." Amy had always said, "I will face whatever I need to face with grace and purpose." And she had, right up until the end. Before she had fallen into her coma, she had looked up at Richard from her hospital bed, told him she loved him, and said she looked forward to the time they would meet again.

How very much he had loved Amy.

"Richard!" Annabel suddenly screamed, looking back from the window. "Look out!"

He only had a momentary flash of the gray-haired woman—Cindy—coming into the room behind him with a knife. He never had time to reach for his gun or feel the knife pierce his heart.

He was already with Amy.

119

"Noo!" Annabel shouted, leaping down from the window to shove Cindy off Richard's fallen body. "Noooo!"

Cindy pulled back, hissing like an affronted swan. Annabel knelt down beside Richard's body.

"Don't die," she begged. "Don't leave me alone. . . . I can't get out of here without you. I can't, I can't, I can't. . . ."

Her tears dripped onto Richard's face. But his glassy eyes stared up at her. He was dead. This time, he wasn't coming back.

Annabel felt herself falling. She was tumbling back into her black hole, unable to move, unable to think. Once more, it was the only way she could handle the terrible things happening outside her. She shut down. She was like a turtle pulling into its shell, only her shell was soft and vulnerable, and would not protect her.

"You stay inside there, you bad little girl," Daddy Ron's voice shouted through the closet door. "You stay in there in the dark because you're bad. Very bad."

"I'm not bad," Annabel replied, in a very small voice.

"Don't argue with me, you little bitch. You are bad!"

"No, I'm not!" Annabel suddenly shrieked, and she lashed out, kicking the closet door down with her feet.

She looked up. Cindy stood a few feet away from her, watching her with wild eyes.

I can't shut down, Annabel thought. I shut down and I die.

And if I'm going to die, she reasoned, *I'll die fighting to live.*

She turned and started to climb up onto the windowsill.

But Cindy leapt onto her back. Annabel tried to throw her off, but Cindy was so terribly strong. Her arms encircled Annabel in a vise grip, threatening to choke off her air. Annabel did the only thing she could do. She fell backwards, toppling down from the window with Cindy underneath her. It momentarily knocked the wind out of Cindy and the arms that had held Annabel so tightly suddenly opened.

Annabel jumped free and lunged for Richard's gun.

But Cindy was too fast for her. She nudged the gun away, out of Annabel's grip. Then she grabbed hold of Annabel's wrist, wrestling her down to the floor.

"Jack!" Annabel screamed.

He might help her. He might at least call Cindy off her. "Jack!"

Cindy lifted the knife over her head, its point aimed at Annabel's chest.

Annabel looked up into the madwoman's face. She was a little girl once, a happy child, until coming to this place. Even in that moment, Annabel felt pity for her.

Suddenly there came a shot.

And Cindy's face, so tensed with rage just a moment before, suddenly relaxed. A look of peace filled her eyes just before her body slumped over to the right, the knife she'd been holding in her hand clattering to the floor.

120

Annabel looked in the direction of the doorway into the eyes of her savior.

Jack stood there, holding Richard's first gun in his hand. The gun was smoking.

"I had to do it," he said sadly. "I couldn't let her kill you, baby cakes."

"Oh, Jack . . ." Annabel stood up, trembling terribly.

Jack approached his dead sister. "I mean, she couldn't go on this way. Like I said, if she kept escaping from the attic to slash our guests, we'd never be successful."

He knelt down beside Cindy's body. He had shot her clean through the chest. The blood that now seeped through her clothes, turning her blue dress purple, was her own.

"She was such a sweet little girl," Jack said, stroking her hair. "She used to have a real nice singing voice. She loved to dance. We used to watch *Sesame Street* together."

In the midst of everything—after all the horrors and all the abuse Jack had done to her—Annabel felt sorry for him. They had loved each other once. It had been a long time ago, but they had loved each other. Back then, Jack had been kind and good. Whatever demonic forces controlled this house, they had taken Jack's mind and warped it.

"Jack," Annabel said, stooping down beside her husband, "come with me. Let's get out of this house together. We'll go out through the window and ride back into town. I'll explain that you only shot Cindy to save me. No one will blame you for anything here. They'll come, they'll see what this house is, and they'll understand . . . they'll understand none of it was your fault."

Her husband snapped his face up to look at her. "Oh, but that's impossible," he said quickly. "The house won't let us leave, Annabel."

She studied his eyes. She didn't know what he meant.

But then she looked around and his meaning became unmistakably clear.

The room was filled with little men.

Once again they were coming up through the floorboards and stepping out of sliding panels from the walls. There were dozens of them. The house was infested with them, like cockroaches or termites. Three of them even sat in the window, blocking the way if Annabel suddenly tried to make an escape.

"No," Annabel said. "Please, no . . ."

They were coming closer. Slowly, steadily, their little feet moved, closing in on Annabel and Jack.

The little men were muttering among themselves.

"It's Cindy," Annabel realized. "They're angry about Cindy."

"She was their friend," Jack said, standing up now, facing them.

"Shoot them, Jack!" Annabel shouted.

"No," Jack said. "They're going to make me rich."

"No, they're not, Jack! They're going to put you down the fireplace!"

Too late he lifted the gun in their direction. Five or six of the creatures crawled up Jack's body, snatching the gun out of his hand and tossing it out the window. Then a dozen more covered him, knocking him to his knees. They were under him, trying to lift him and carry him away.

Annabel screamed in horror.

"No!" Jack cried. "I'm your friend! I will take care of you!"

The little demons ignored his words.

"She's the one!" Jack shrieked, managing to point over at Annabel. "She's the one who wants to destroy you! She'll destroy the house!"

His eyes met Annabel's.

She had just offered him a chance at salvation. He was offering the demons her life for his.

Annabel knew in that instant it wasn't the house that had warped Jack. He'd already been that way the day they arrived at this place. And probably for some time before that.

"Take her!" Jack was screaming. "Take Annabel instead!"

All at once, the little men stopped moving. They looked at each other. Then they set Jack down on the floor and turned their terrible blue eyes at Annabel.

"No!" she screamed.

The creatures marched toward her.

121

Annabel backed up against the wall in a vain attempt to get away from the little men. But the creatures were dropping down from the ceiling now, and crawling up her legs.

Annabel tried to fight them off, but it was useless. There were too many.

They had her. Their little pincers sunk into her flesh and held her tightly. They knocked her off her feet and scrambled under her back, hoisting her off the floor and carrying her across the room.

Annabel screamed.

Jack had vanished. He had condemned her to death, and would do nothing to save her.

Annabel's only hope was the gun—the one that Cindy had knocked from her hands and sent sliding across the floor. Annabel could see it as the creatures carried her past. She might be able to grab it—

She stretched out her arm when they drew close to the gun, which was sitting undisturbed in the middle of the floor. The little men seemed to have no interest in it. Their tiny fingers—claws—would not have been able to pull the trigger. Annabel had to grab it. She had to shoot them as Richard had, and she would take such delight in watching them explode into filthy protoplasm.

Her fingers touched metal. Yes! She closed her fingers around the barrel of the gun—

But the creatures were moving her too quickly. Annabel was unable to grab hold of the weapon. It slipped past her hand as she was carried past.

"Noo!" Annabel cried in frustration.

There was no more hope. She would die. She would be stuffed into a small, enclosed space and she would be eaten alive by dozens of Tommy Trickies.

Her mind shut down as she was carried out of the room, through the corridor, and down the stairs.

A series of images passed through her brain in those last few moments.

A picture of her father. Her real father. Colonel Malcolm Wish, in his beige-and-white camouflage from the Gulf War.

If you had only lived, Daddy, if you had only lived . . .

Her mother, her weary face at the end of the long day, her fear of Daddy Ron evident in the way her eyes flickered at the slightest sound. . . .

Jack, on their wedding day . . .

A party in New York, laughter, lights, music, the smell of cocaine in her nose . . .

The stultifying air of the hospital, the sense of being trapped, the sound of people crying down the hall . . .

Neville's face.

Chad's.

Richard's.

You can survive anything.

Had Richard said that to her?

Suddenly, Annabel opened her eyes. She was being carried through the parlor now. At any moment, the creatures were going to force her headfirst down the chimney. There were others, she knew, waiting inside to pull her down.

"No," she said quietly.

She thrashed her head from side to side. She spotted Jack across the room, watching from a dark corner, his eyes emotionless.

"No," Annabel said more loudly.

Such strength the house had given Jack, and Cindy, too.

But not as much as it's given me, Annabel thought.

"Get off of me, you filthy bastards!" she screamed, and in one powerful move, she shook the things off her, sending several of them flying.

The surprise on their little faces was beautiful to see.

They tried scrambling back at her, but Annabel managed to stand up, crushing one of the things under her bare foot as she did so, hearing its loathsome neck snap. The little men began making chittering sounds like monkeys. A number of them kept lunging at her, their pincers clawing into her legs, but others were backing away from her, not sure what to make of this suddenly powerful creature who had the ability to resist them.

"You only think you're real," she spat at them. "Mother told me you're not."

She shook the last of them off her legs.

"Grab her!" Jack shouted. "Grab her now or she'll get away."

The sound of Jack's voice drew their attention away from Annabel. A moment passed as all the little men turned to look at Jack.

Then, instantaneously, as if some psychic command had passed among them, they all started running toward him.

"Get away from me!" Jack cried. "It's her you want! Take her!"

But they overran him, knocking him to the floor.

Jack screamed.

122

Annabel watched as the creatures lifted Jack and carried him across the floor toward the fireplace. He swung his arms and tried to kick his feet, crying hysterically.

"Annabel!" he called to her. "Help me, baby cakes!"

But that wasn't going to happen.

Instead, Annabel turned and walked out of the parlor at the moment Jack's head was pushed down into the fireplace. Heading into the kitchen, she could hear Jack's muffled scream as the creatures devoured him.

She knew what she had to do.

The first thing was practical. Annabel found the boots she had kicked off, one in the pantry and the other in the kitchen. She replaced them on her feet and tied them as tightly as possible. She worked deliberately, but also quickly. She had very little time. Whether the creatures would come back for her, she didn't know. Perhaps she had proven herself to them, and they would leave her alone now. But they might be back for another round.

Still, if they did try, Annabel felt confident that she

could beat them off again. But frankly, she didn't want to have to bother.

Her boots on her feet, she walked over to the stove and grabbed the box of kitchen matches that were kept there.

Zeke had had the right idea.

Those little men weren't real. Tommy Tricky had been used to torment her, manipulate her, frighten her, exploit her. But he hadn't been real.

Her mother told her he wasn't.

And Annabel intended to make sure it stayed that way.

She walked back into the parlor, clutching the box of matches in her hand.

The little creatures were dancing around, celebrating Jack's death. The house had been fed. They were pleased.

Not for long.

Zeke had sprinkled gasoline all over the floor the rugs—the drapes. Annabel could smell it.

She struck a match against the side of the box.

A little flame sparked into life.

The creature nearest to her turned his face up to the match. Its flame reflected in his demonic little eyes.

"Good-bye, Tommy," Annabel told the creature, and dropped the match to the floor. The rug under the little man burst into flame, taking the terrified creature with it. Its face melted like wax in the conflagration.

Instantly, the parlor was ablaze, the room Annabel had thought she would modernize, make pretty, turn into a home. The drapes caught. The sofa was obliterated. As Annabel turned to leave, she caught a glimpse of flames hopping like rabbits up the stairs. The little men were screaming.

Walking out into the kitchen, Annabel kept striking more matches and dropping them to the floor. Little explosions followed in her wake.

She threw a lighted match into the pantry and listened to the roar. She placed a match on the center of the gas-soaked kitchen table, which burst into flames. Soon the whole room was an inferno. Annabel could hear the fire consuming the walls around her and ripping through the ceiling above her. But best of all, she could hear the high-pitched screams of the little men as the flames consumed their unholy blue flesh.

Calmly, she walked out the back door.

Making her way across the path that Zeke had dug for her, Annabel noticed that the snow had stopped and that breaks of blue were appearing in the sky. By the time she had crunched across the yard to Richard's snowmobile, the house behind her was burning out of control, sending a giant plume of black smoke rising above the trees.

Annabel mounted the snowmobile. She unzipped her coat pocket and removed the keys. Inserting the larger of the two keys into the ignition, she turned it to the ON position.

The snowmobile didn't start.

Was she going to be able to drive this thing?

Of course, she was.

She figured she could do anything now.

Instinctively, she pulled a cord in front of her and pushed the handlebars up, and the motor beneath her hummed into life.

Annabel sailed off across the snow.